LET'S SHAKE SOME [MOON?] DUST

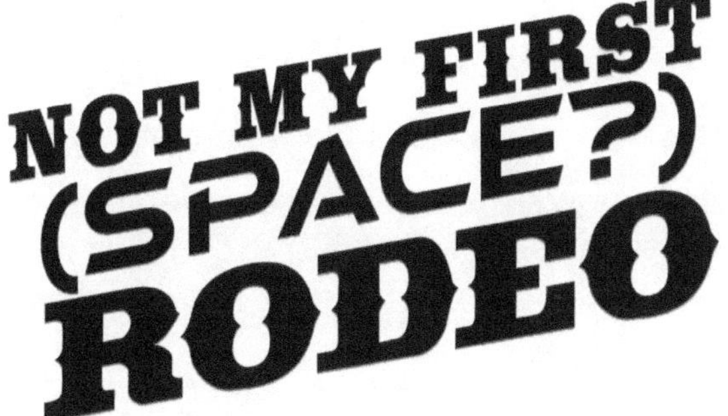

NOT MY FIRST (SPACE?) RODEO

BOOK THREE
LET'S SHAKE SOME (MOON?) DUST

M. TALON

Podium

LET'S SHAKE SOME [MOON?] DUST

CHAPTER ONE

ASSESSING REAL ESTATE: LOCATION, LOCATION, LOCATION

The air shimmered around us in a dazzling white haze before solidifying into our new surroundings. I took a deep breath and looked around. Our outpost now sat atop a steep hill covered in lush green grass. The base of the hill was the edge of a pine forest. The land sloped away toward a narrow lake, still and reflecting the bright blue sky above. In the other direction, the forest sloped up and away from us along the flanks of a steep mountain valley. The peaks soared above us at least four thousand feet, jagged granite crags topped with snow. The word "alpine" stuck in my head. My guess was that this landscape either came from somewhere in Central Europe or it was completely made up by the AI.

[**Welcome to the Corrupted Earth!**] the system boomed from all around us.

[**The world is hollow. It seethes with unrest and evil. You and your allied heroes will assault multiple battlefronts to cleanse this world of the foul monsters who rule it, delving deeper and deeper to unlock ancient secrets, competing for a chance to unseat the dark ruler of this world. You will not be alone in your attempts. Team-based competition rule set will be revealed to those who gain entry to Castle Byalgrad.**
Here in the Kingdom of Illyria, you are one of ten teams that will be competing to defeat the defenders of Castle Byalgrad. The halls of the castle are filled with multiple challenges. You will have to work to defeat each of those to reach the lowest level. From there, your next step will be revealed.
The rule set from phase two has been modified in the following ways: First, you will find crafting materials available here of a higher quality than anything in the previous levels. These can be harvested by any of your affiliated miners.

**Second, unlike in the previous level, harvesting miners can now
be attacked by other miners. There is no longer a distinction
between combat and noncombat miners. That means you can swap
members at will in and out of your combat team.
As before, deaths are temporary and miners will revive inside
your outpost. Outposts are not attackable at
this point in the phase.]**

I made a note of that. It sounded like the rules could be changed at any time.

**[Respawns are instantaneous; however, each respawn will cost
soul coins from your backer's bid. The more deaths, the higher the
cost. Please consult with your backers to make sure you
have sufficient funds available for respawn.
You have one week before the doors of the castle open.
You may use that time to gather information, collect resources,
or improve your own creep spawning abilities. But be careful:
the valley had inhabitants before you, and they won't
all be happy to see newcomers.
Good luck!]**

"That really isn't a whole lot to go on," Grandpa observed as the system voice faded away. "We need information, pronto. We should send out a bunch of our crafters to scout."

"'Team-based competition rule set' worried me," Juana said. "That sounds like we might need allies, and we're a little short on those."

Just then, my notifications beeped. I checked. "Holy shit, I just gained three levels! I've got a bunch of choices to make!"

"Me, too!" Sage exclaimed, jumping up and down with excitement. "We got XP for phase two after all! I need to go look at what I get. I'm going to finally have more than twenty charisma, and I'll be able to Tame two targets at once!"

"Hold your horses," Grandpa said. "Let's get things settled here, then we'll figure out our level-ups."

"Right," Sage said. "Back to business. Lives are a fungible resource now. We don't know what these challenges are going to be, but I'm guessing it might take us more than one try to beat them. The more respawns we have available, the more times we can try."

"Good point," I said, while wondering where she'd picked up words like "fungible." Probably from hanging around Kirin and Arjun. "But at the same time, we aren't going to want to give up whatever treasures are available here.

They might come in real handy later on. And if we can ambush other teams and use up their lives, that works out for us, right?"

"And ruin any chance that they might want to ally with us?" Juana asked. "By the way, I'm level three now, without ever having to set foot outside our outpost in phase two." She winked at us. She'd never even entered a phase one portal, since her family had set up a restaurant to pay their contracts off. Two levels just for her work on our outpost was impressive.

I thought about the first part of what she'd said. "If any other teams want to make a nonaggression pact, that's fine by me. But we don't have enough to go on yet to think about teaming up. We'll need to wait until those rules are unveiled."

"I'll look into it," Juana said. "I'm sending information on our setting back to Arjun. His info said there were going to be eight hundred and fifty-seven teams going into phase three. If we're up against nine others, we can expect there's eighty-six or so of these scenarios set up. That means we're not likely to run into anyone we know, but if we got really unlucky and are stuck in a world with a bunch of Proxima patsies, we'll want to know."

We got a ping from Veda. *I've just been informed there's a sponsors and team heads party here on the Hub in eight hours. I'm going to need three of you up here.*

I think we've all got better things to do, I said, *and my dress uniform got left back on Earth, so I'm going to have to turn it down.*

It's not optional, she said. *System-enforced.*

What'll they do if I say no?

Do you really want to find out?

I hesitated. My instinct was to send Juana and Grandpa and maybe Dwight. I wasn't good at that sort of formal soiree.

Grandpa was looking at me and shaking his head. "I think you should go, Shad," he said quietly. "I have a feeling this'll be like an embassy ball. A chance for the chief players to mingle and meet the opposition. Get a feel for who we're up against."

"It's a waste of time," I said. "Hours to get up there, hours there, hours to get back down. When I could be helping us figure out what's going on here."

"Still," Grandpa said, unruffled, "I think we both need to go." He looked around at our crew of misfits, his gaze traveling from one to the next. "Now, who'll be good at an event like this? Someone who can keep a level head, observe what's going on, mingle. Maybe even do a little spying." He glanced at Sage, then shook his head. Kept looking, clearly writing off all of the Mongeese.

Veda, does it have to be one of our combat team or can it be anyone?

Anyone. Though they will judge us based on who you bring.

They?

It's complicated. Just make sure it's someone who can handle themselves when cornered.

Grandpa nodded. "Got it. Juana?" She looked up. She'd been leaning over the strategy table, reviewing our surroundings.

"Yes?"

"How do you feel about being Shad's date to a party tonight?"

I opened my mouth to protest as Juana's cheeks flushed a little. "What's this all about?"

"Some VIP event that Veda just sprung on us," I said. "We need a third for our delegation."

"Oh." She glanced away, then back at me. "Up on the Hub?"

"Yeah, I know. It's a pain."

Juana was shaking her head. "No, no, it's fine. Maybe we can find out more about these team rules, and make a few allies. And we've got a week, so I guess it's all right. But I haven't got anything to wear."

Grandpa sent Veda a message. *All right, we're on our way up, but you'd better take care of seeing that we look presentable.*

Not to worry, Veda said as we made our way toward the exit. *I'm already on it.*

I settled into my seat on the space elevator pod. I'd gotten used to the astonishing trip from Ganymede up to the Hub, but the moment we popped out of the shell protecting Threshold and saw Jupiter hanging there never failed to take my breath away.

"It's a hell of a commute," Grandpa said, staring out at the gas giant.

"Almost makes all this worth it," Juana said.

I didn't respond. The truth was, ever since we started phase two and the threat of death was taken away, I'd been enjoying myself. Phase two had been one challenge after another, and I'd risen to them all. The adrenaline rush, the feel of pulling victory from the claws of defeat—it was addictive.

I pulled up my stats screen. "Guess I'll see what I get for leveling up." Three levels at once took me from level five to level eight, with all the XP from phase two dumped on me at once. That meant I had nine points to assign. I tossed two into stamina to bring my health pool up to **[170]**. Then a couple into charisma and dexterity, both of which were key for my favorite skills, and then I added three points to strength to bring that up to eight. Now that I had my Home on the Range ability, letting me teleport back to base holding anything I could lift, strength mattered a lot more than it had before.

"Huh," I said, after assigning the points, as a message popped up.

[Congratulations! Your achievements from phase two have been noted and rewarded.

Notable achievements (received by fewer than 5% of miners):

**Punching Up: Take out an outpost more than 1 level stronger
than your own.
Sails the Seven Seas: Steal more than 100,000 soul coins' worth
of equipment from another team.
Suicide Watch: Die more than 10 times in a single 24-hour period.
Reward for these achievements will be delivered in 72 hours.]**

"Are you getting a special award?" I asked Grandpa.

"Yup. Let's check around." He sent a message to our combat team. Most of them reported getting the Punching Up achievement, but nobody admitted to Suicide Watch. I kept that one to myself.

Sage was ecstatic. She'd gotten a special achievement of her own. "Up and Coming" was awarded to "the youngest (age adjusted by species maturation times) miner to have participated in a team special event." *I can't wait to see what I get,* she told me over chat.

How'd you spend your level-up points?

Got charisma to twenty-one. Now I can Tame two targets! I don't even need a second physical lasso, it's going to be great.

Did you up your stamina?

That's soooo boring.

Not dying is important.

I know, I know. I'm sticking my tongue out at you right now, even if you can't see it. Yes, I put two points in stamina. Then everything I had left in dexterity.

Good. I watched the sky, looking for the particular shining point of light that was the Hub. We were well above the surface of the moon now, sliding through space.

Sage sent me another note. *I'm going hunting with the farmers. Don't insult any-one important, okay?*

Do I ever?

That and dying stupidly are your two signature moves, Shad. I'm not there to keep you out of trouble and Juana's too nice but stick with her anyway, okay? Besides, she likes you and it would be nice if I had someone else helping take care of you, so don't mess this up.

Wait, what?

I'm busy now; don't talk to me. Talk to Juana, she's the one there with you.

CHAPTER TWO

STAT CHAPTER

This isn't a real chapter; this is for readers who may wish to see our heroes' current stats and abilities list. This entire chapter can safely be skipped if that's not important to you!

Level 8 Stats

	Shad	Sage	Grandpa
Cha	14	21	7
Dex	16	12	18
Int	4	8	3
Sta	17	14	16
Str	8	5	16
Wis	6	5	7
HP	170	140	160

Abilities cheat sheet. Not all abilities and skills may be listed here.

Shad, Class Evolution: Ride for the Brand

High Noon: In a one-on-one duel, you always get the first shot.

Quick Draw: Instantly call bonded weapon to hand, up to 50-foot range.

Trick Shot: Target an opponent and fire. Shot will connect even if opponent is behind cover.

Barrage: Empty all currently loaded rounds at once. Each round has a 15% buff to damage.

Call 'em Out: AoE reveal of enemies/taunt. Cooldown: 5 minutes.

Bluff: Use to boost skill at persuading targets to believe what's being said.

Test Your Mettle: When below 30% health, you receive a 100% boost to health regeneration.

Never Bring a Knife to a Gunfight: Force opponents in melee range to drop their weapons.

Loyal: Bonus to soul coins when with long-term party.

Fastest Gun in the West: Cover 100 feet in 1 second and knockback.

Roped Into It: Conjure a rope and use it to swing up to 40 feet.

New Equipment: Cowboy Hat: Wearer is impervious to water-based damage. Wearer cannot be charmed.

Tip My Hat: Used to acknowledge a party member or allied miner's ability. Gives them 15-minute well-done buff, which allows them to deal 10% more damage. Can apply to (2 x level) other miners at a time. This can only be applied outside of combat.

Lay of the Land: Used to view a distant object or area close-up. 10-minute cooldown.

Home on the Range: Once a day, return to outpost. Channel time, 15 seconds. Can bring anything wearer is capable of lifting off the ground for that 15 seconds.

Sharpshooter: When above and more than 10 yards away from an enemy, accuracy is increased by 50% and damage by 35%.

Grandpa, Class Evolution: Last War Chief

Shadow Step: Teleport behind an enemy. Can now also be used to step behind an ally.

Scalp: Apply massive head damage.

Count Coup: Shadow Step behind, then damage an enemy for 1 point. If not previously damaged, 2 points. Cash in 4 points for **Coup-de-Grace**, which instakills enemies below 25% (not bosses).

Blur: Harder to hit when moving.

Pub Dart Champion: When one thrown weapon hits, the next three go to same spot.

Crippling Blow: From behind the target, damages enemy and then applies a **Slow**. Also generates 1 point toward **Coup-de-Grace**.

War Chief's Aegis: Bless allies. One-day long cooldown. Grants a 50% buff to dexterity and intelligence, along with a 40% boost to max HP.

Item: Ninja Headband: +1 to dexterity and stamina.

> Passive Ability: Any attack from behind a target or while obscured is 30% more powerful.

Ability: Allows **War Chief's Aegis** to be cast at the start of a fight, granting a 30% health regeneration boost and a shield worth 25% of the target's max HP.

Sage, Class Evolution: Barrel Racer

Cowgirl Cheer: Buffs allies. 35% buff to dodge chance and damage done for all party members in range.

Lasso: Pull in and trip an enemy.

Eye-Spy: Reveals information about enemy weaknesses.

Raise Your Spirits: Cleanse and HoT (heal over time). Can be used on multiple targets at once. Now also removes poisons and DoTs.

Mucking Out the Stalls: Turns a large area into difficult terrain. Any target who gets the created muck on their bare body gains the **Stinky** debuff.

Tame: Lasso now has a charm aspect.

Upgrade! **Tame** may now affect two targets at once.

Three-Barrel Race: Teleport between three locations at will.

Item: T-Shirt Cannon: Shoots various constricting or damaging shots.

Item: Rodeo Blouse: Grants the ability **Knock 'em Dead**, resetting **Tame**'s cooldown if a creature dies while Tamed.

Ability: **Knock 'em Dead.** If creature dies while Tamed, **Tame** resets cooldown.

CHAPTER THREE

HOW TO MAKE A GREAT FIRST IMPRESSION

I waited around in the lounge of the suite Veda had rented for us, fingering the tight collar of my brand-new dress uniform. I had to give Veda credit; it looked exactly right. I had taken my shiny new captain's bars from the shirt I usually wore under my duster and moved them over to the uniform. I gave them a little polish, too, while Grandpa wasn't around to see.

Grandpa was taking a long time to come out of his room. At last, the door opened, and I turned to look. I had been expecting him to wear a uniform to match mine. Instead, it was a style fifty years old, from the Vietnam era, and he was wearing his old dress jacket, the one he'd brought from home. It had been cleaned up and ironed. He saw me looking and shrugged, seeming a little uncomfortable. "I asked Veda to have an iron on hand for me," he said.

"Looks good," I said.

"Seems she got our measurements right," Grandpa replied, looking me up and down.

The third door opened, and I turned to greet Juana but forgot what I was saying as I got a look at her. She was wearing a pale blue gown with narrow shoulder straps. It fell in flowing curves to her ankles. Her hair was up, pinned in a mass of intricate curls with tiny gleaming sapphires attached to each of the pins. I was no expert in women's hairstyles, but I was certain that hadn't been a quick fix.

"Do I look alright?" she asked, giving a little twirl to show off how the dress swirled and revealing silver shoes and bare calves underneath.

"You look great," I said. "Did Veda arrange for the hair too?"

"An all-in-one hair and makeup bot," she said, grinning.

Grandpa poked me in the ribs. "Stop staring at her and offer her your arm," he said. "We're supposed to meet Veda in ten minutes at the lounge area."

I managed to get my mouth closed. Feeling ridiculous, I walked over and offered Juana my arm. "I'm hurt that Major Twofeather didn't offer to escort me," she said.

Grandpa snorted. "I may have been rejuvenated, but I'm still much too old to be going around with a young gal like you," he said. "Let's get a move on."

Streams of elegantly dressed aliens moved through the Hub, converging on the lounge where Veda had said to meet her. I enjoyed looking at everyone's formal wear. The elves wore long tunics that fell to just above their knees with tight leggings underneath and a variety of oddly shaped tiaras on their heads. Most of the orcs I saw were wearing stylized armor with enormous shoulder pads and various animal motifs emblazoned on the breasts. I saw a lizardfolk woman in a princess dress and a couple of almost human-looking aliens who had a bluish cast to their skin wearing kimonos. Both of them were male and wearing other fashions I couldn't begin to describe.

The lounge was an enormous barn-sized room with a ceiling that disappeared overhead into a cloud of stars. It was lit in blues and purples, and there was a faint sound of trickling water. Round tables dotted the room about chest-high, offering drinks and those little snacks that come on toothpicks.

Veda was waiting for us. She wore a dress similar in cut to Juana's but in flame orange. I had rarely actually seen Veda in person. Most of her interactions with us had been by hologram. Now she offered her hand, and we all shook.

"Sorry to drag you up here. I understand you feel that your time would be better spent preparing, but it's a command performance, and they're supposed to be releasing more information about the challenges anyway."

"Like the team rules?" Juana asked eagerly. "I feel like we're way behind here. Everyone else probably already has allies, and we're outsiders. Or have you made contacts for us yet?"

"No, the team rule set is strange," Veda said. "Nobody I've spoken with knows what to expect here. The system seems to have tricks up its sleeve this time. I'm a little worried. You guys aren't the most popular. On the other hand, a bunch of the orcs and talonians love you. Maybe we can find some groups that aren't tied too tightly to Proxima or Alabaster Sky."

"What's our objective here?" Grandpa asked, then scowled. "And how come I can't access any of my menus?"

"System interfaces are turned off in this space," she said. "No chatting or access to inventories. It's considered a form of cheating. There will be data packets available afterward that have the information presented here."

"Fine."

"The objective is to mingle with the other players who will be going up against us, as well as sponsors and potential backers. There's fewer than a thousand phase three teams this time. That leaves a lot of people who usually have a look-in sitting on the sidelines. Some of them may be willing to throw in their backing to you if there's a benefit for them. So since you're the only Earth humans invited here, you'll probably be approached by people looking to make contact with your crafters."

Juana nodded. "I can handle that. I'll pass their information along. Dwight and Arjun are setting up a clearing house to make sure that all of us humans know who to work with and who to stay away from."

"And tell 'em if they want our crafters, they'll have to be willing to work with the rest of us," I said.

"It's a good start," Veda agreed. "This isn't like phase two, where people had their own individual reasons for being there. Everyone who is in phase three is in this because they think they have a serious chance at coming away with a share of the prize."

"Yeah, and how does that work?" I asked as we moved deeper into the room. We were getting a few sidelong looks from some of the aliens. I wondered if they recognized us as Earth humans. If they were also cut off from their system interfaces, then they couldn't be getting information about us that way, though I wasn't convinced that the more powerful among them were limited like we were.

"There's eight hundred some teams, and we're competing over shares of the Reality Engine. Part of the way the Reality Engine Exploitation Committee prevents war is by breaking up control of the Reality Engine into smaller pieces. In this case, ten thousand shares. Each represents one ten-thousandth of the tamed engine's power, storage, and output. No one individual entity is permitted more than a thousand shares of any given Reality Engine to prevent any corporation from monopolizing an engine. Even a single share is worth fortunes. More money than you can possibly imagine."

"Try it," Grandpa said grimly. "We've got eight billion people back on Earth. How much would it cost to buy each and every one of them a slot in this here Reality Engine once it's been turned into condos or whatever it is you people do with it?"

"A single share would be more than sufficient," Veda said flatly. "You just have no idea. The upper limit on how many individual beings can exist inside a Reality Engine is in the trillions. A single share is enough to start a shipyard producing the kind of pods and pod carriers people like me use to go between stars."

I whistled. "Okay, so even one share is enough to make our day. How do we get our hands on one?"

"That's what we're all here to find out," Veda said. "This is a rule set I haven't seen in play before. I understand the basic concept. There'll be various challenges you have to meet, probably special fights like that last one you had in phase two against a particularly powerful enemy who can outthink you all. I'm hoping we get more details here in a minute. The thing is, even if you humans manage to grab a piece of the action, you won't know what to do with it."

"So that's where you're going to help us, right?"

Veda laughed. "What makes you think I know what to do? My family has been a phase two outfit for generations. We've never even stuck around to watch phase three. We're not talking twice as complicated or twice as dangerous. We're talking orders of magnitude more. I would be out of here on my way back home right now if we hadn't gotten that concession from the big guys at the end of phase two not to interfere with you or anyone to do with you. The system will hold them to it, so I'm not worried about assassins showing up in the middle of the night or a convenient accident happening to my pod." She smiled, like a shark, and I wondered if that sort of assassination was common in galactic business deals. "Besides, my family's in the trouble we're in because my father lost his shirt in a bunch of poor business decisions that were more like gambling. I guess I take after him, after all."

"Okay, but that's afterward. Right now we need to focus on phase three," I said. "So what are we doing here?"

"I suggest we split up," Grandpa said. "Veda, why don't you take me and introduce me to people you think I should meet? Shad, Juana, you two mingle. I expect if I leave you alone, somebody'll think you two are easy marks and come try to take advantage of you. Just don't promise them anything and try to listen more than you talk." He offered Veda his arm. Our sponsor looked surprised, then shrugged and set her hand on his elbow. They pushed off deeper into the room.

I looked at Juana, feeling unaccountably nervous. "So he's just leaving us here for the wolves."

"Come on, Shad." She tugged on my sleeve. "Let's go find someone to talk to."

We mingled. By which I mean, Juana and I inched through the room, me trying not to make eye contact with or bump into any of the aliens there. Juana nodded pleasantly to those she passed. We were about a quarter of the way around the enormous circular room. The dominant color of the light had changed from green to purple.

Then I edged us around a clump of odd polka-dotted humanoids with too many fingers and immediately ran across someone I actually knew. Chief Theram'goss, whom I had defeated in a one-on-one duel early on in phase two, thereby saving his life, stood talking intently with a tall, pale, bald alien of a species I had not previously met. They reminded me a lot of the gray aliens of Area 51 fame.

The chief spotted me and waved me over. I glanced at Juana, who gave me an "I guess" kind of look, and we joined them. "Patron, this is the human I spoke to you of some time ago," Theram'goss said. "Shad Williams and his associate."

"This is Juana Lopez," I supplied.

"Shad, this is High Overlord Merak Tahahl. He holds Firebrand's contract."

I inclined my head, not sure what the polite galactic greeting would be. "Pleased to make your acquaintance."

"The chief has been telling me much about you." The alien's voice was melodious, higher pitched than I had expected. The high overlord was about four inches taller than me. He looked at me through overlarge orbs and blinked, his eyelids crossing horizontally. "Theram'goss says your people are not to be underestimated."

I shrugged. "Well, we made it this far."

"Your team did," the high overlord corrected. "Out of some seven million who passed the first phase of induction."

"Yes, well, I couldn't have done it alone." I glanced at Juana. "My coalition has a great number of crafters, and plenty more unaffiliated miners who are willing to work with us."

"Indeed, that is very interesting for an inducted species, especially one as savage and primitive as your own."

"Well, thank you," I said.

Theram'goss smirked. The alien raised one hand in an odd gesture. "I see that you are not easily startled. Is there a title you would prefer?"

Now, usually I'm an informal kind of guy. I prefer Shad over my full name by a long shot, but dressed up like this, representing Earth? "You can call me Captain Williams," I said.

"Captain. You have a place in your world's army, then."

"United States Army," I corrected him. "We hadn't gotten to a one-world government yet before you all appeared, no matter what some of my Grandpa's drinking buddies used to think."

"I see." The high overlord eyed me. "Yes, we have done some of our best recruiting from new species such as your own, and I like that the warrior instinct has not gone out. In my people, we bred such base behaviors out of ourselves many millennia ago. This has, unfortunately, meant we must rely on the services of groups such as Firebrand to help us achieve our earlier goals."

"Is your group one of the phase three players?" I asked.

"Yes, as a matter of fact. We are partner-subordinates to Alabaster Sky. If we are fortunate enough to stake a claim to one or more shares of this Reality Engine, they will have first rights to buy it off us."

"I see." Alabaster Sky had tried to screw us over through one of their subsidiary corporations at the end of phase two. But we'd played a reverse card on them and made them sign a deal that was a little more fair to humanity, so I wasn't holding any grudges.

"I believe it would be worth recruiting Shad Williams and his counterparts for a potential mercenary team such as Firebrand," Theram'goss said. "They did extremely well in phase two for never having seen it before. And of course, all of their combat miners survived phase one without much outside support."

"You do have a point," the high overlord said. "Well, Captain, would you be interested in a position helping open other Reality Engines?"

I took a minute to let that sink in. He was talking about leaving the solar system, going to other worlds, and doing to them what had been done to me and the other human miners. I wasn't a fan of that. On the other hand, my family and I had been adapted by the Reality Engine. We couldn't live on Earth anymore, not without help. I hadn't had time to think past the end of phase three, not really, but I knew we were going to need to do *something*.

Plus, we were getting pretty good at this. It couldn't hurt to keep our options open. And realistically, what else was I going to be doing with my life?

"Depends on the offer," I said. "A bunch of my people just want to earn enough soul coins to quit this exploit and settle down, but there are some of us who might appreciate a bit more of a challenge. We work as a team, though, so any offer has to be for more than just me and my family. Please do pass along my interest."

"We will be observing you in phase three."

I tipped the hat that I wasn't wearing to them. Stupid, maybe, but I'd gotten so much in the habit of using my Tip buff on everyone I met. Juana and I moved off.

"I didn't like him," Juana said softly after we'd moved several clumps away. "He gave me a creepy feeling."

"Me too," I said. "I'm not ruling out going pro if we got the right offer, but not with him."

"I should talk to Mama about it. I know she's been worried about what happens to us next. Maybe—" She clutched my arm a little tighter, then turned to me, her eyes excited. "Maybe we could find a way to help the next system of people who get exploited! Like offer them advice instead of just exploiting them."

I tried and failed to think of any time in Earth's history when the colonizers had made things better for the locals. Even groups that had good intentions, like missionaries or medical folk, often made things worse. "Maybe," I said guardedly. "You should talk to Grandpa. He'll have some ideas. Right now, let's get back to the party. We—" I cut off the next thing I was going to say, because someone was coming toward us through the crowd, and they looked angry and well armed.

CHAPTER FOUR

HONEY, IT'S RAID NIGHT: HOW TO CONVINCE YOUR SPOUSE TO HANDLE ALL THE CHILDCARE DUTIES

A trio of shorter-than-average humanoids with long hair and thick beards appeared and blocked my path. "You! Desecrator! We are here with a warning!"

I studied them, but my brain was busy telling me, *These are dwarves. These are definitely dwarves.*

They were wearing lederhosen and heavy boots and had axes through their belts. One of the three had a full head of golden hair done in braids and a braided beard. With a start, I realized she was a woman. Definitely dwarves.

"Uh," I said, then regained my composure. "Are you sure you're talking to us?"

"We know who you are," the one with a white beard told me. He poked one thick, stubby finger at my chest. "You are one of our rivals. You share the valley with us."

"Ah," I said, "nice to meet you. We hadn't figured out who we were up against yet."

Juana took a step forward, spreading her hands. "We are willing to discuss cooperation."

"No cooperation," the elder dwarf spat. "We dwennan will have nothing to do with defilers and those who consort with the unsouled."

I shared a look with Juana. "I'm sorry?"

"You deny having made an alliance with those?" He swept his arm out and pointed dramatically. I turned to look where he was pointing. About thirty feet off, past another six clumps of partygoers, was a group of tall, misshapen, three-legged, tentacle-faced aliens. I recognized them at once as grignarians, though whether they were the ones we had teamed up with or not, I didn't know. "You deny making common cause with those?"

"Oh, right," I said. "We had a temporary alliance." And a deal to hire them as mercenaries in phase three, but I wasn't going to share that.

"Bah!" That was the female dwarf. "So it is true. We will enjoy teaching you a lesson."

"Look, I know those guys aren't the most popular, but we needed their help."

"And so, you will find you have chosen your vein and now you must mine it," the dwarf said. "We look forward to beating you to the treasure that awaits."

With that, they threw their hands up in a three-fingers-up, two-fingers-touching gesture that made me think of death metal bands. I stomped off. Juana stared after them. "What on earth has gotten into them?"

"I don't know," I said, "but I'm really starting to wonder why everyone hates these grignarians so much. I'll have to ask Veda when she's got some time."

"It is simple." A tall man wearing robes strode through the crowd. They parted to let him through without even seeming to notice he was there. He had a bald head and a necklace with a symbol on it.

I recognized him. "Patriarch Kvaltash?"

"Human Shad Williams. I do not know your friend."

"This is Juana Lopez, the brains of our organization."

Juana blushed. "Patriarch, I am pleased to meet you."

"So you don't like the grignarians either?" I asked.

"It is not a matter of liking," the patriarch said. "They are not children of the progenitors."

"Oh?" I frowned. "I thought the beings who created these Reality Engines had gone and reprogrammed themselves into the DNA of all of the worlds that would eventually produce intelligent life. Your people and mine and the orcs and the lizardfolk, we're all progenitor spawn."

"That is correct," the patriarch said. I wasn't sure how I felt about this particular cosmological revelation. I'd never been worried too much about where I'd come from, considering my own family tree on one side looked like a kudzu plant. But the thing of it was, I didn't see how it made any difference right now. Even if we were all cousins deep, deep down, that hadn't prevented the galactics from royally screwing us miners over and stealing Earth's inheritance out from under us.

I shouldn't be surprised, considering what we humans had done to others who were undeniably of our same species.

"The grignarians are not the children of the progenitors," the patriarch said.

I scratched my head. "I know they're kind of funny looking, but how's it you know for sure?"

"They, unlike any other sentient species we have encountered, are unable to absorb soul coins. Therefore we know they did not inherit souls from our ancestors."

"Wait, wait, wait," I said. There was a lot to unpack here, even ignoring the bit about inheriting souls. "Are you saying they don't get soul coins? 'Cause

I thought that was the only way we were able to be here, to participate in this Reality Engine at all."

"They have admittedly very clever technology," the patriarch said. "It allows them to interact with the Reality Engine on a virtual level. But they do not attune, and they do not experience the Reality Engine as the rest of us do."

The grignarians were getting more and more interesting by the minute. If they had the technology to interact with a Reality Engine like that, then they must understand it a whole lot better than anyone else here.

"So that's why everyone's so mean to them?" I said.

"They are trying to take an inheritance that is not theirs," the patriarch said, as though that explained everything. "They are soulless. My order teaches to treat them kindly when we encounter them outside of Reality Engines, but when inside, we show them no quarter. It is no fault of theirs that they have no souls."

"It's possible our translators aren't handling words right," I said. "When you say 'soul,' you mean . . . ?"

"The eternal spark which is and was and will be," the progenitor said. "That which bonds with a soul coin in order to attune to a Reality Engine. The part of a being which continues after that being's physical death."

"Right. Okay. So it is more or less the same thing." I rubbed my head, wondering if they really had proof of eternal souls and if the grignarians were truly missing out.

Juana spoke up. "Where did the progenitors come from?"

The patriarch turned to her, beaming. "My daughter, you have touched on the central mystery of my faith. Indeed, that is the question that drives us all on. Where did they come from? Where did they go?"

"Didn't you just say they turned into us?"

"Some of them did. Some of them, we know, became the heart and mind of these Reality Engines they left behind. But we have clues, tantalizing clues, that some of them went elsewhere, remaining much as they were. It is possible that they are still out there, somewhere deeper in our galaxy, or perhaps in the void between galaxies, waiting for us to mature enough to meet them and understand them. My own belief, one that is permitted yet not endorsed entirely by my church, is that this is a grand cosmological cycle that just as the universe itself expands, then contracts, then expands again, renewing itself every time it runs low on energy. So too are the progenitors and the Reality Engine a cycle. In time, we will ascend to become the creators of reality, those who can shape worlds with a thought, to wield the power that right now seems to us like magic. In that time, we will understand why it is that the progenitors made the choice they did, and we shall face the same choice ourselves. We shall begin the cycle anew."

Great. An alien cultist with apocalyptic beliefs, and I needed him on my side because the Church of the Progenitors was the one who had gotten us the phase three license, and I wasn't sure yet if they could get that revoked. I cleared my throat. "Thanks for speaking with us, Patriarch, and thank you for backing our entry here into phase three."

"Indeed," the patriarch said. "I must say I have slightly exceeded my mandate here. We saw signs early on that this Reality Engine might retain more memories of its progenitors than the average when we saw how your species tunes so deeply with the engine."

"How's that?" Juana asked.

"Your classes are a clear example," the patriarch said. "Most Reality Engines offer their sponsored species a set of six to eight easily defined classes. Warrior, Monk, Healer, that sort of thing. Your engine has at this point offered 5,762,314 distinct classes. No more than ten humans share a single class, and that class is Soldier."

"Really?" I said. "I assumed that was a standard Reality Engine thing."

"We have seen it a handful of times before. When you have engaged in as many Reality Engine exploits as we have, everything comes up sooner or later. It is, however, a sign that the Reality Engine retains more of its original core. This is a good thing. It is my fervent hope that if you humans manage to penetrate the core far enough to claim a share of the Reality Engine, it will reveal some of its truths to you. By the terms of our license, you must turn over all data you collect from your endeavors in phase three."

I nodded. I had seen that clause when we accepted the license endorsement from the Order of the Progenitors. I hadn't liked it, but it only said they could see our data after we had finished, not before.

"Now," the patriarch said. "Excuse me, please. The announcements will begin shortly. I suggest you find a seat."

He drifted off through the crowd before I could say anything. "What seat?" I asked, and Juana pointed. A little farther on in the room, rows and rows of pale white backless benches had risen from the floor, each long enough for five or six people to sit. Juana and I joined the throng of partygoers moving toward them. We took the end of one, and a moment later, a pair of orcs plopped down at the other end. They ignored us.

As soon as everyone was seated, the light around us changed. Purple faded to black, green lightened to white, and a glow started to form at the front of the room. A moment later, it blossomed into light over a raised dais where six people were seated. A seventh, the patriarch, was climbing the six metal steps leading up onto the dais. He took a seat at the end of the row, and the system began to speak.

[Welcome, sponsors and team leaders of phase three.
Thank you for attending tonight's function. This informational

**period will be short. At the end of it, information packets will be
made available to your entire team. Afterward, you will be
permitted to return to your outposts to continue preparation
for the opening of phase three.]**

Someone tapped my shoulder. I looked back. Grandpa and Veda were seated in the row behind us. Grandpa was grinning.

"You two look good. I saw you schmoozing with the patriarch," he said. "Nice work."

"I hope so. He kind of gives me the creeps," I replied as I turned my attention back to the stage.

[Tonight we have with us the heads of sector for our three major backing corporations: Proxima, Alabaster Sky, and ConSweGo], the system continued. Three of the beings on the stage waved their hands.

**[We also have Patriarch Kvaltash of the Order of the Progenitors,
Guildmaster Gorak'Tal of the Crafters, and our Greater Galactic
Observers, as appointed by the Milky Way Galaxy Reality Engine
Exploitation Committee.]**

The last two raised their hands when the system said "Greater Galactic Observers." I made a note of them. The inclusion of these outside observers might mean nothing, like when the UN sends in peacekeepers to watch atrocities committed and sends sternly worded letters to those responsible, or it might mean they had the power to shut all this down with a snap of their fingers.

**[They, together with your hosting Reality Engine, have hashed
out the details of this exploit's phase three rule set. As some of you
have guessed based on our opening statement, you will be facing
a multipart adventure challenge.]**

Images flashed up in the air in front of the dais. Pictures of varied Earth landscapes, and then fantastic buildings, temples, castles, towers, fortresses, and imposing structures I had no name for. Then, an assortment of creatures. There was some sort of giant mermaid hurling lightning tridents, followed up by a dragon breathing fire. Then, a couple of yetis in a snowy glade bent over the corpse of a bear. Images came faster and faster, showing fantastic creatures and oddly dressed humans. Dark-haired men wearing olive leaf crowns and togas. Tall, willowy women in sarongs. A man dressed in what looked like traditional Ojibwe garb. A woman wearing a grass skirt and flower necklace.

[Drawn from the local planet's history and mythos, these challenges
will stretch your teams as never before. You will be tried in combat.
You will be faced with puzzles of wit and intellect, skill and luck.
Those who pass the first challenge will have an opportunity to go even
deeper. Work together with those in your challenge group,
or thwart one another, but once you have passed the first challenge,
you will be asked to choose a faction to join. Those exciting
details are being kept secret until you've earned them,
but we can promise you that your faction will matter in ways you can't
even imagine yet!]

"Of course they're not telling us anything yet," Grandpa grumbled. "I bet you anything the galactics know more than we do."

"You see how the observers are here in person?" Veda said. "That's unusual. Someone has filed rule complaints. That could be good for you, or bad. But it means everyone is going to follow the rules, or at least pretend to when anyone else is watching."

[Details about your individual challenges must be gleaned.
Some challenges may take more than one attempt to pass.
We look forward to seeing your best!]

The images faded. A murmur of voices filled the room. Patriarch Kvaltash rose and began to speak. I realized after a moment that he was giving a ritual benediction or perhaps an invocation of the progenitors.

Juana leaned over to me. "Do you understand what we're looking at here?"

Grandpa leaned forward to hear my answer. "Yeah, I think I get it," I said. "It reminds me of some games I played a little bit in the army when I was in places with decent internet. It's called a raid. It's where multiple players work together as a group to take on a series of related bosses. Usually you have to take out one boss before you can progress to the next. Sometimes there'll be a reset every week or so, so you have to start over again from square one. But each boss drops loot, so it gets easier and easier. Plus, once you've done a fight once, you know how it's done. I'm not sure that that's how this is going to work, though. But it does sound like there are going to be multiple bosses that we have to learn to defeat."

"I guess that doesn't sound too bad," she allowed. "We'll have to see how it goes."

"Hopefully by the time we get back downstairs, the rest of our team will have gotten better intelligence than this. If it is a raid, though, I would expect that the environment around the outpost will give us some clues. Like, we'll be able to identify what sort of challenges we'll face based on the wildlife we find. Or maybe there'll be ruins that point us in the right direction. I was thinking our location looked like it might be somewhere in Eastern Europe. So maybe it's got a basis in the mythology there."

"So we could be going up against Dracula?" Grandpa asked.

I shrugged. "I'm not really an expert in that area of the world, but somebody out there will be. And hopefully Arjun can put us onto them. That might give us a leg up." I shut up because I didn't want any of the aliens around us to get the idea to start researching Earth's history and mythology in order to get clues.

The patriarch finished his invocation and raised his hands. "Enjoy the evening, my children," he said. "The party ends in two hours. Until then, enjoy the hospitality that is offered."

Music struck up from nowhere I could see, a cheerful waltz. It wasn't anything I recognized, but it probably could have been from Earth. People around us rose, pushing back their benches and heading out.

I turned to Grandpa. "We done here yet?"

"Can't leave until they say so," he said. "Come on. You should try to enjoy yourselves."

We started moving toward the edge of the crowd. Veda talked quickly, filling us in on details of the people we passed. We had almost reached the edge of the crowd when she stopped dead. I nearly ran into her.

I pulled up short as a human man I had hoped was out of my life forever approached. He was wearing a uniform, too.

"Major Waters." I couldn't keep the sneer out of my voice. I kept my hand at my side.

"Lieutenant Williams." He nodded. "Aren't you forgetting something?"

"First, it's 'Captain' now. Second, I'm not saluting you. You're a disgrace to that uniform."

Grandpa intervened. "Waters. What are you doing here?"

"Just escorting a friend of my new employer." He turned to the woman with him. "Go ahead, it's your turn now."

Beside me, Veda had turned pale. She was staring at the woman with Waters. The other woman looked like she might be the same species as Veda, with that pale, ethereal look that didn't quite come up to space elf standards. They even had the same silvery eyes and hair.

"There you are," she said. "I've been looking for you all evening."

I got a glimpse of Veda's face. She looked like she had been knocked back. "Mother? What are you doing here?"

CHAPTER FIVE

WHEN THE RESTRAINING ORDER ISN'T CUTTING IT: ASSESSING YOUR OPTIONS

Veda stared at her mother, mouth hanging open, for what felt like an eternity. She regained just enough composure to turn to Shad and his grandfather. "Would you excuse me?" she said. "I think I probably need this conversation to be private."

They nodded to her. Major Twofeather extended a finger toward the human who stood with Veda's mother. "You keep out of my way," he said quietly. "There's no need for trouble between you and me, but if you try another stunt like you did before, you're going to get run over."

"Not at all, Major," the other man said, smiling and giving a nod. "I should note, though, that if our paths cross during the course of phase three, all bets are off. My employers are paying good money for my service."

"Employers?"

"Sicaris, naturally," the man said smoothly. Of course. This was Major Waters, who had been such a pain at the end of phase one. Veda had only ever seen the man in videos before, and he was shorter than she had expected.

Plus, she was still trying to understand why her mother was here. "Let's go," Veda said in a low voice. She strode away, not bothering to see if her mother followed.

Mother kept up. "That's all the greeting I get after a year and a half apart?"

"Mother, I am busy here, and I can't imagine why you came," Veda growled. "How did you even afford to come out here?"

"Proxima is paying the way of many different tourists who are interested in seeing a Reality Engine at work," Major Waters said as he caught up to them. "After all, there aren't nearly as many crafters and other usual employees coming this way, since we humans proved so keen on taking those noncombat roles, so plenty of empty berths on the ships. It's a win-win situation. Your people here on the Hub manage to sell their goods, and folk from back home who never get a chance to see what happens at the point of the spear are getting a ringside seat for the first time."

"The family sent me," Mother said. Veda kept making her way through the crowd, trying to buy time to collect her thoughts, and also to get Major Waters farther away from Shad and his grandfather. She didn't need any of her contracted humans starting a fight.

"The family has nothing to say to me," Veda snapped. "I've already turned a profit twice as high as what they could have reasonably expected. Our phase two license is secure."

"Exactly," Mother said happily. "Which is why we have decided it's time for you to come home and turn your focus elsewhere."

"Come home?" Veda stopped where she stood. The crowd of partygoers ebbed and flowed around her. A pair of talonians had to detour around them. They glared angrily at her through their membranous eyes, but Veda was too busy trying to understand what kind of point her mother could possibly be trying to make.

"But of course. It's time."

"You don't stop a successful exploit when you're in the middle of it."

"Tvedra Corporation has never been involved in a phase three operation before," Mother pointed out. "We're a phase two company. You did well there, Veda. Better than most of the family thought you would. I knew we were right to place our faith in you."

"You did no such thing. I had to fight to get a chance at this." Her mother had been one of the strongest critics of Veda's plans, though in fairness she had expressed those doubts in private and not in front of the board of directors like Uncle Yarin.

"Nevertheless, dear," her mother said, "the family wishes to consult in person before deciding what direction to take next. We need to return home for a board members' meeting as soon as we can. Otherwise, they'll be forced to hold it without you."

"Can't," Veda said, shaking her head. "During an exploit, the exploit leader is the sole commander of the company. The board cannot recall the commander or order changes." That was laid down in the Tvedra Corporation's earliest bylaws, set down by her great-great-great-great grandmother. It was a wise choice. Often, Reality Engine exploits were a journey of several weeks, if not months, from wherever the family happened to be headquartered at the time. News would be slow to travel. Only people on the spot had a chance of making timely and accurate decisions.

"I think you'll find, dear, that the conclusion of phase two serves as the end of your time in charge of our exploit. After all, our bid was for phase two."

Veda's blood ran cold. Her mother might actually be correct. She would have to check the words of her contract. "I've already sunk most of our profits into this phase three attempt. If I leave now, we lose everything."

"Sicaris has offered us a very favorable buyout," her mother said.

"We'll just have to confirm the size of your latest monetary allocations," Waters added.

"Hang on," Veda said as a thought struck her. "Phase three just opened. We've only had a few days' warning that it was coming. How is it that you're already here?"

Her mother looked briefly taken aback. She glanced at Major Waters. He shrugged as though saying, "I don't know."

"Well, dear," Mother said, clearly flustered. "The family knew that phase two would be coming to an end soon. We just wanted to see you, to bring you home where you belong."

"Right," Veda said. She bit off what she would have wanted to add. Either her mother and entire family had decided to conspire against her, or, more likely, Sicaris—rather, Sicaris's parent company, Proxima—had been putting pressure on them. This hadn't happened overnight. Had her mother arrived before the end of phase two, she would have had some other line of attack.

"Look, this is neither the time nor the place for this conversation," Veda said. "I need to go to the auction—"

"And I'm afraid I brought along corporate authorization to freeze your funds the moment I arrived here on the Hub." Her mother wouldn't meet her eyes. She looked almost embarrassed.

Veda felt like she'd been stabbed in the stomach. "You can't. I need those funds. Whatever I have left has to keep me going. I'm paying the expenses for my team. They'll have nothing to fall back on."

"Sorry," Waters said, smirking. "I guess old Louis will have to find another retirement plan besides making himself king of Earth."

"I think you're right, dear," her mother said. "This is not the time to speak. Here's my comm code. Call me when you're ready to have this discussion, and we'll figure out what to do next."

She and Waters left Veda standing in the middle of the crowd. The sponsors, backers, off-world visitors, and dignitaries swirled around her as she stood and felt everything crumbling under her feet.

I can't let them do this. I can't let them take this away from me. This wasn't about her family anymore. Mother was right: She'd done what Tvedra Corporation needed. She'd kept their license alive. But she'd done so much more than that, more than anyone had thought she could.

Her relatives had entrusted her with the last of their funds, even though they weren't convinced she could make good, not because of their faith in her, but because of their belief in the Tvedra Corporation. She'd paid that back already.

But somewhere along the way, she'd gotten caught up in the game, in what happened to Shad and Sage and the rest of the humans. She wanted to watch as they took phase three by storm, just like they'd done in phase one and phase two. She wasn't going to be frozen out now by some soulless intergalactic conglomeration.

Veda straightened up. She made a decision. If her funds were frozen, there was nothing more she could do here at the auction. She needed to go back to her own quiet living quarters and read her contract. And then she needed to start studying up on corporate law, exploit history, and legal precedent.

She sent one quick message to Shad, saying she wouldn't be able to meet up with him again, alerted Major Twofeather she'd be missing the auction, and then sent word to Mama Grace, asking her to relay to Colonel Ames the fact that Major Waters was back and working for Proxima.

Then she sent all of her incoming notifications to "Do Not Disturb" and headed for her own pod.

CHAPTER SIX

SETTING UP A CARTEL: THREE HOT TIPS

It was dawn and the mountain valley was filled with mist. Clouds wreathed the mountains at the head of the valley. I stood at the top of the hill in the center of our outpost looking outward and I couldn't even see past the first trees of the forest beyond our walls. A few scraggly shadows of branches emerged from the fog like skeletal arms.

I shivered, not entirely from the cold. Grandpa growled as he stepped out of the portal beside me. "Let's get the sitrep here." I covered a yawn and followed.

We had slept on the ride back down to Threshold, once I stopped ranting about what Waters was up to and why Veda wasn't answering our calls. Juana nodded off quickly while I stared out into space as we descended the immense elevator back down to the surface of Ganymede. Space was so immense, so vast, it humbled me. It was hard to remember sometimes that all of this madness, these scenarios and worlds invented by the Reality Engine, was taking place under the surface of one of Jupiter's moons. When the other aliens talked about their own systems and their worlds and Reality Engines, it all felt unreal. But Jupiter hanging over us, looming like an ancient god with its ominous storms as ever-present eyes . . . that I couldn't deny. Somewhere between Threshold and Ganymede, I dropped into a restless slumber.

I heard a bird cry off in the mist somewhere as a breeze stirred my coat, bringing me back to, well, not reality, but the present at least. I pushed back my hat and focused. "We've got six days before competition opens up for everyone to go head-to-head. We need to focus on some of those other objectives the system hinted at in its opening briefing."

"The team's been busy while we were off hobnobbing with the galactic elite." Grandpa looked around as we strode through the camp, and I followed his gaze.

Our bunkhouse had expanded. On the outside, it now looked like an old-time saloon and hotel, with swinging half doors in the front and an upper balcony outside the little rooms where gunslingers and drifters could rent a bed for the night.

It actually could hold almost a hundred people at a time now. We had plugged upgrades in over the course of phase two, and then spent a bunch of upgrade points as phase three kicked off. Juana had taken care of that remotely while we were traveling. She had been in contact with our base-building team down here, and checked with me and Grandpa about our opinions.

Beyond the hotel was a big blacksmith shop for the crafters, and a long, low line of sheds beside it offering more workspaces.

There was a whole apothecary shop across the street, dusty brass scales and glass bottles in the picture window under painted gold letters reading "Apothecary."

We were really starting to look like a little town, with wooden sidewalks and a dusty open stretch of road in between. There was a hitching post out in front of the bunkhouse, even though none of us had horses. I liked the look. Made me feel at home striding down the street in my coat and hat, my gun belt hanging comfortably at my waist.

My combat boots weren't quite right for the picture, but they were damn good footwear, and I wasn't going to change them unless the system gave me some sort of upgrade.

The big wooden statue that had been our node was now transformed into a monument in the center of the town's single street. It looked like one of those old war memorials you'd see in small towns, a smooth white obelisk with names on each side and little plaques saying what war they had died in.

Instead of the names of the dead, it bore the names of those of us who had fought in phase two. One side for the fighters like me and Sage and Grandpa, and the other three for the crafters who had come to our aid.

A little old church building with a tall bell tower atop it and white clapboard walls had its doors open. Grandpa pointed. "That's HQ."

We mounted the steps, me right on Grandpa's heels, and entered the church building. Instead of rows of pews, it had a couple of folding tables and those metal folding chairs you see at every community event. About fifteen people were hard at work, grouped into three different clusters.

Dwight was in the nearest batch. He looked up at me as we entered and gave a quick nod. "Good to have you both back," he said. "We're working on a list of supplies that we have and supplies we think we're going to need. Our informants have been telling us everything they found out talking to offworlders about phase three. We actually learned a lot during that special mission back in phase two. You know, while you guys were busy playing with the other teams, me and my crafters were learning a lot of new skills."

"That's right," I said. I'd been so busy thinking about base defense in the last few days of phase two, I had forgotten what the crafters had been up to. "Weren't the offworlders giving you a lot of recipes because they want us to supply stuff for their folk too?"

"That's right," Dwight said. "There's apparently rules about how many people the corporations can bring into an exploit, and since we haven't obliged them by dying fast enough, they're going to have to work with us."

I shared a grin with him. I'd had a small hand in keeping more of us humans alive than the aliens liked, and I was damn proud of it.

Dwight continued. "Mama Grace and I negotiated a deal with as many other humans as we could, like a union that says we won't sell any crafted items to anyone who refused to get on board with our demands."

"Most of the big players have already agreed, and we don't want to go back on our word," Grandpa said. "We all agreed we would abide by the deal and we will. So, anybody that's signed gets a fair price for our work."

"But," Dwight said, holding up a finger, "we are all agreed that we"—he swept a hand around the room, taking in our whole team—"get to skip to the head of the line. What Misfits want, Misfits get."

"So you're going to coordinate both operations?" I asked. I was worried about Dwight trying to do too much by himself. I wanted him to be in charge of making sure my team had what we needed for this phase.

"I'm going to liaise with a couple of outsiders," he said. "Some of Colonel Ames's people and one gal I've done some work with before. They'll take care of things on the Threshold side, help set prices, arrange queues, make sure we don't make any of the aliens more angry at us humans than they have to be. I'm just going to take care of our team. I've already gotten started on these lists, but we're going to need more information." He pointed in front of him.

I came over and studied his table. Handwritten sheets of paper were spread all over with notes in six different colors of pen, obviously made by more than one person.

One sheet, titled "Potions," listed at least fifty different recipes. There were fire resistance potions, water resistance potions, electric resistance potions, light resistance, dark resistance. There were speed potions separated into movement speed and attack speed. There were mob debuff potions and friendly mob buff potions.

"What, are we going to be going into battle clanking?" I asked, trying to imagine carrying that many potions even in my inventory.

Dwight chuckled. "We'll be picking and choosing. Oh, that reminds me." He grabbed a couple of belts from his own inventory and set them in front of us. "Potion quick-use belts that'll let you access them and other single-use devices faster. Remember those dummies you used during the boss fight?"

"How could I forget?" I said.

"Well, these belts have room to equip ten different types of potions or other consumables. You can use them quick as thinking. The advantage of this versus going through your inventory is that the potions from your inventory take two seconds to use. You've noticed that, right?"

I nodded. "Seems like it's one second to call up what you want and one second to apply it."

"This cuts that time down by half. It's been a really hot item requested by the aliens. So I figured they knew something important. I went ahead and got them made for all of our team."

I stored that info away. Winning or losing a fight might come down to a single second. I picked up my belt. Grandpa was already threading his through the loops of his pants as he cinched it down. It changed in appearance as soon as he buckled it, becoming a nicely tooled leather belt with ten thumb-sized vials in loops along his left hip.

"Those are really just for show," Dwight said as he saw me looking. "You don't have to pull the bottles off or anything."

I shrugged off my coat, hung my gun belt over the back of a chair, and strapped on my own belt. I snugged it down and the buckle transformed into a big silver oval with an eagle with outstretched wings on it. I'd seen belts just like that on more prosperous ranchers at the county rodeo or community square dance. I sighed and went with it.

"You can put in your order for consumables and we'll get it filled," Dwight said. "To start with, here's an array of different resist potions and an improved healing potion. This one restores sixty percent of your max health right away and another sixty percent over the next minute. And the cooldown's only two minutes between potions."

"That's way better than what Veda gave us." I picked up my share and stored them in my inventory. A quick thought queued up the most useful ones in my new belt.

Veda's disappearance was a nagging worry. She'd gone off and left us high and dry, she wasn't answering our messages, and for all I knew she was about to sell us all out. I scowled as I worried, but Dwight seemed to misunderstand what was bothering me.

"Don't blame her. The galactic market charges exorbitant rates for these, but since we're farming the mats ourselves, we can afford as many as you and your team need."

"How's the farming looking?" Grandpa asked.

"Check with Frank, he's in charge of that." Dwight pointed to one of the other two groups. Our old friend Frank, the deputy sheriff from back home on the Arizona Strip, looked up and nodded as we met his eyes.

"We'll be right with you," Grandpa called. "Anything else we need to know?"

"The third team over there is working on upgrades to our creep. They're already spawning, you know. It's really funny, watching them just being zapped into existence right outside our gate and streaming away into the forest. We're working on creep lures right now. It's a recipe some of us picked up from the big luau back in phase two. You put them down and the creep goes to that location until the lure is destroyed or replaced by a fresher one."

I nodded. "Rally points. Okay, so we're still supposed to be using these guys in phase three."

"Right, so the team's working on a catalog of all of the enhancements we can give them. You just let us know what you want and where."

"As soon as we figure it out," Grandpa promised, and we moved over to talk to Frank.

He had one foot up on one of the folding chairs and was leaning across the table to look at a map someone was projecting. "Louis, Shad, good to see you again."

"You too, Frank," I said.

"So, you made my job a hell of a lot harder." He grinned, taking the sting out of his words. "All those new recruits you and Ames called out of the lotus eater level have been coming to me looking for work. We just got word that the phase one levels have had safeties turned on. You don't die anymore. Instead, you respawn, and it costs you a soul coin penalty. That means all those farm levels, we need to get in there and hit them hard. I've got . . ."

His eyes went wide for a minute as he checked his numbers and shook his head like he couldn't believe it. "Two million, five hundred and forty-three thousand, seven hundred and fifteen miners willing to help us out. Most of them have never killed anything more than that first mob they needed for a soul coin to escape the initiation chamber. So I'm having to figure out team leaders, and then they've got assistants, and then those assistants are making up team rosters . . . It's a mess. We're all sharing information now, but it's a hell of a job to coordinate and figure out what mats we're going to need."

"We don't even know that yet," I said.

"Get everything," Grandpa said. "It's all going to be useful for something. If not for us, we'll sell it to the aliens. We're not going to put all our eggs in one basket. The phase three team"—he made a gesture that included me and him in that—"we'll push ahead hard to try to capture a share of the prize, but like we've been saying all along, in any gold rush, it's not the miners that strike it rich."

"It's the shopkeepers and the cooks and the launderers," Frank said, rubbing his face with his hand. "I know, I know. I was listening. Between you and Mama Grace, I got that message through my head. Though, my great-granddaddy did make a big strike at a silver mine in Nevada back in the height of the Comstock Lode. If he hadn't spent it all on eight wives and forty-two kids, I might not have had to be a deputy sheriff in a backwater county on the Strip, but that's beside the point. Yeah, we're covering as many levels as we possibly can and I'll adjust where possible. Karen's looking for some assistance for me. People like Arjun, but not as skilled. I don't know how I'm supposed to keep track of all this."

"These aliens are cheating. They have their own computers that actually work for them, not like this stupid system that's just trying to get us all killed. We'll ask Veda if there's any kind of AI she can get for us," I said. "Maybe they've got one they let kids use."

"Worth a shot," Frank agreed. "Anyway, I do have an actual problem for you guys. We sent out scouts to get a look around the area and they spotted some interesting-looking resources, so I sent a team of my best farmers out along with some of my security guys. They got wiped out hard. Big blow to their ego. I've been keeping them back behind the walls after that because I didn't want to use up all of our respawns. Figured we'd get a team of experts out there to see what is going on and how to counter it."

Grandpa looked at me and I nodded. "Sounds good to me," I said. "Do I get to pick, or . . . ?"

"I'd like to go." Frank took his foot down off the chair and stood straight, pushing his hat back on his head. He smiled, looking better and healthier than he had since we'd come to this place almost a year ago. "I know what my people can go up against. I want to make sure you don't over or underestimate their capabilities."

"Great." I felt a smile spread across my face. "It'll be nice to work with you again." I turned to Grandpa. "I'd like Jones, Annie, and"—I thought for a minute—"Sage."

"That it?" Grandpa asked. He didn't sound critical, just like he wanted me to be sure. "Captains usually command more than four privates." I felt myself get a little warm around my ears at that. I still wasn't used to thinking of myself as a captain.

"Reconnaissance," I explained. "I don't want to be tied down with too many. The point here is to get a good look at what we're up against and figure out a strategy. Everybody I named can take care of themselves. We've got some good team mobility, and of course Jones is essential for his camo and drone."

"All right, get to it," Grandpa said. "I'll keep working here. Plenty more to do."

"Right." I sent messages to my chosen team members telling them to meet me down by the gate. "Let's ride, Frank."

CHAPTER SEVEN

INTO THE WOODS: A CULTURAL ANALYSIS OF THE ROLE FORESTS PLAY IN OUR COLLECTIVE PSYCHE

As we made our way down through our outpost, I took stock of all of the transformed phase two buildings that were now becoming the basic structure for our phase three push.

The turrets and towers on the wall were as imposing as ever. Veda and Mama Grace were buying up equipment from other teams' failed phase two attempts and sending them through so we could bolster our defenses.

I looked up at the sky. The fog had burned off, leaving bright blue above us. A hawk circled lazily. *Have we got enough covering the air?* I asked in our command chat. That was me, Grandpa, Frank, Juana, and a couple of others. When anything important happened, we'd report it to the command chat and let each, well, department head, I guess, take it down to his or her own staff.

I guess that made me head of the military. "Military" implied a bit of discipline and coordination that I wasn't sure all of us were up for, so I amended that in my head to "the warriors."

We'll check on it, Juana said.

I passed a knot of five grignarians standing by our node marker. They were looking around. I couldn't read their expressions at all, and I wasn't sure if any of them were the ones I'd already had dealings with, either as an ally or way back at the start of phase two as an enemy. I stopped anyway and Tipped my Hat to them, doing a quick Inspect and seeing that one of them was Exalted Skywarden Greenlight the Unreleased, whom I had made the deal with to join forces at the end of phase two.

"Good to see you here," I said. "Go on ahead, Frank, I'll catch up."

"Human Shad Williams, we were told to report to you," Greenlight said.

I made a note that the exalted skywarden was apparently not their top guy. "What do you need?"

"A task. We are at your disposal now." The grignarians' only request in order to secure their aid had been that we take them on as mercenaries in phase three. I was certain they had a motive for being here, and we would be keeping an eye on them. For now, they were on our team.

"I want you on patrol around our outskirts, looking for weak places in our defenses," I said. "We're new at this. You guys have been playing this game for a while. Anything you spot, let me or Major Twofeather know, and we'll get it shored up."

"Understood."

"If anyone from the other teams advances to speak, let them pass as long as they're respecting our parley rules. There's some asshole dwarves, though. I'm pretty sure they might try something. If they do, kill 'em hard. Use those nasty, face-melting rounds you guys have."

The grignarians made a soft, snuffling sound. I wondered if it was laughter. "We also do not like the dwennan. They are very prejudiced and short-sighted."

"Yeah, I'd love to chat about galactic politics. Really. Let me buy you a beer or whatever it is you fellows drink sometime soon and get some questions answered." I was still curious about how the grignarians fit into galactic society. It seemed like they were outcasts, and I might be able to use that to get us humans some insider information. "But right now, I'm off to scout. We'll catch up again."

"We look forward to seeing you. Congratulations on your elevation of status, Captain Williams." They raised their hands until their rightmost appendages were level with their mouths. I returned a salute and started down for the gate, catching Frank just before he got there.

The rest of our team was already waiting, Sage bouncing up and down with excitement. She spotted Frank and launched herself toward him, giving him a big hug. "Deputy Young, it's been ages. You're coming with us? Awesome!"

He patted her head. "You're getting tall, Sage."

She pouted. "I know. And the worst of it is, my clothes are growing with me, so I can't even use it as an excuse to get something new."

"What's wrong with what you've got?" I asked. "You just got that new shirt, too." The system had awarded her a brand-new rodeo shirt with scallops and silvery bits all over it as a reward for doing well at the special phase two team challenge. She wore it with a crisp pair of denim jeans and cowgirl boots with little hearts picked out in rhinestones on the toes.

She rolled her eyes at me. "They're for little girls," she said. "And I'm basically a teenager now, which is like being grown up. Once we're done with this, I'm going to have to talk to Veda and see what she can do for me. I am *not* going to be stuck in one outfit my entire adolescence."

Jones stood quietly ready. He saluted as I joined the group. Annie smiled at me. "So what's the mission, boss?"

I pulled my All-Seeing Eye that we had used at the end of phase two out of my inventory and re-equipped it, slipping the earpiece into my ear. "Anybody on the desk?"

"Kirin here," came the response. "I've got Arjun, but he's busy doing a lot of coordination, and we found a subject matter expert like you asked for."

"Great," I said. I'd asked Kirin to find us someone who knew the mythos of this part of Earth. The system was probably jumbling it up beyond all reason, but it would still be useful to know the origin stories for whatever bizarre gods or monsters we found ourselves facing.

"They're in the loop. I'll let him introduce himself," Kirin said. "We had to do our best guess. We're not one hundred percent sure yet about the origin of this mythos, but hopefully he'll be able to give us some pointers. Say hi, Gabriel."

A new voice came on. He sounded British. Not that plummy high-class accent from BBC period pieces, but not as rough as the couple of British SAS I'd met at a training gig. Kind of middle-of-the-road. "Name's Gabriel Klement. My folks are from Czechia, and my grandmother raised me on folk stories. Some of the monsters your scouts report seeing match up a bit with her tales, so I'm here to help."

"Okay, stand by." I gathered my team around me.

Frank sent us all details to update our personal maps. "The farming team were about a mile out, north and east of us, along this river." A blue line appeared on my map, snaking its way out of the hills to the east before joining the main watercourse down the center of the valley. "There's a little lake here, in the woods. That's where it happened."

He sent us a map pin and I checked my bearings. "Let's get going and you can tell us the details as we walk. Jones, get your drone up and share the video feed with Kirin and Gabriel. Frank, you're on point, I'll be rear guard. Let's move out."

We set off toward the north, entering the forest as quietly as we could. There were occasional bird calls from the trees and a few skittering sounds and rustling of brush, but I didn't see anything as we made our way through the stands of ancient oak.

The going was easy. There wasn't much underbrush here with the spreading limbs above blocking out so much light. Moldering leaves released an earthy, rotting smell as we stepped on them. They muffled our footsteps nicely. The trees bore a heavy coating of moss. Vines ran up many of them, winding bright green tendrils around the dark brown branches.

I took a deep breath. The air felt clear and cool. It was remarkable how sharp the details were. I wondered yet again if any of this was real or if the system was just putting images, scents, and feelings into our minds. Was there any way to tell? Did it actually matter? This was my life now.

As we went, Frank filled us in more on what the team had encountered. "They were attacked by a pack of beagle-sized squirrels on the way to the pond. Didn't have too much trouble with those. The squirrels had a nasty Rabies debuff, but an ordinary healing potion cleaned that up right away and so did their one healing spell, so Sage can probably take care of it if we run into those. Her Raise Your Spirits removed that undead curse, so rabies should be easy."

"No problem," Sage said. "I actually just got a buff to Raise Your Spirits that specifically says it removes damage over time and poison debuffs. It won't remove any mind control, though. I thought that was odd to specify."

"So let's hope we don't run into any vampires," I said, peering around through the dim light. Back at the outpost, it had been a pleasant spring day. Here under the trees, it was at least ten degrees cooler, maybe more. I was dressed for it, but it made the day a little less pleasant. That was good. I wanted to be on edge and alert.

"Then they reached the pond and were attacked by a giant frog creature," Frank continued. "They said it was a toad, but since it popped up out of the water, I'm guessing it was actually a frog."

I grinned at Frank's back as we made our way along. "Either way, we know how to squash giant toads, after all." I remembered the very first encounter we'd had together back about two minutes after being introduced to the Reality Engine. Frank and I had taken out a giant toad to win our very first soul coin.

"Yeah, takes me back," Frank agreed. He really did seem happier and more relaxed now. Maybe we *had* been too stressful for him. "Toad or frog, it had some debuffs, sticky frog spawn that reduced the target's movement speed, that sort of thing, and dealt mostly physical and water-based damage. The tongue lash could pull in multiple targets at once." He paused to duck under a fallen tree branch that blocked our path. "They took it down and then were attacked by something else that came out of the water. It happened fast enough that we didn't get much description. Apparently some sort of water goblins, though one of the crafters thought they looked more like dogs on two legs. And then something in the pond unleashed a wave of water that crushed them all."

"Do we have an analysis on that?" I asked. "Pure water damage? Or was it force-based?"

"Uh," he said. "Let me check."

We relayed our question back to Kirin, who had the answer for us quickly. "Both. About eighty points of straight-up crushing damage and then twenty points per second of ongoing water damage. We aren't sure how long the attack could go on for, since everybody died pretty fast."

"Okay, that's pretty good," I said. "I'm immune to water-based damage right now, remember?"

"Sure," Frank agreed, "but not the crush."

"I can take one hit as long as I heal back up fast. When we get close, I'll take the lead."

We had been walking for a good twenty minutes without seeing anything. I was relieved when the trees thinned out and the pond came into view. The water stretched away far enough that the bank on the other side was obscured in the light mist rising off the water. I could hear a stream trickling somewhere nearby.

The near bank of the pond was thick with rushes and water lilies bearing the most brilliantly colored flowers. Bright purple, emerald green, yellow like a first spring daffodil, vibrant crimson red. I could see why our crafters had been interested.

Something broke the surface tension of the water, sending little ripples everywhere. "Everybody freeze," I said. "I'll take the lead."

I approached, my gun in my hand, ready to activate an ability if necessary. I could see a pair of bulbous eyes just on the surface of the water and the suggestion of a gray-green head beyond it. The eyes were big, each at least a couple of inches across, and the creature was about eight feet away. I tried to Inspect but got nothing. "Sage, is it close enough for you to . . ."

The creature erupted out of the water straight at me. Even having been warned, I was taken aback. It was indeed an enormous frog. Its hind legs were strung out behind it as it leapt for me.

I threw myself to the side and twisted. It landed inches from me, shaking the ground. On all fours, the frog was about half my height. It opened its wide mouth, gaping, and I could see its coiled tongue ready to lash out.

I fired right down its wide mouth. Not an ability, just straight up shot it from inches away with my stump-nosed revolver, emptying my whole cylinder. The creature shuddered in place as my bullets ripped through its gullet. Daylight shone through the three-inch-wide hole I had torn from all of my shots hitting in close succession.

I used my Reload ability as I lurched sideways. "Remain at range!" I shouted to my team. "Hose it down, but don't get closer to the water!"

They added their firepower to my own, Jones using his Army-issue M4 while Frank had his service gun out. They both had some of Dwight and Sage's improved rounds. Their shots ripped big chunks of hit points off the frog.

[-17, -13, -28]. It had started with [265 HP], which was a hell of a lot more than I had, but we'd already knocked it down by half with our initial assault.

The frog kicked out with its back legs, springing right over my head. I whirled on the spot and shot at it as it went over. My Trick Shot took it between its legs, but frogs don't have a particularly vulnerable place on their groin, so it just tore more damage off.

It was heading right at Sage and Annie. I started to trigger Call 'em Out, but before I could, Annie threw Misdirect Audience and vanished from the spot, leaving an Annie-shaped decoy behind her. Sage disappeared at the same moment, reappearing ten yards to the west as she engaged Three-Barrel Race to get herself out of trouble.

The frog hit the ground. We converged on it, firing, and tore down the rest of its hit points. It collapsed in a bloody, wet, sticky heap.

It had been easy, even considering that we were better at this than the farming team would be. They weren't helpless, not if they'd spent phase one farming. There had to be more to come.

I turned back to face the pond as the next wave emerged. There were six of them, and they did look like goblin dogs. They were like what would happen if you drowned a wolfhound, then reanimated it, put the head of an ugly humanoid with pointed dog ears on its body, and then sent it shambling forward on two legs.

I raced into the thick of things, casting Call 'em Out and trusting my team to lay down fire. Meanwhile, I was keeping an eye on the pond, waiting for any sign of the next threat.

The goblin wolf creatures lunged at me, slavering, with their claws ready to rip me open from neck to groin. I danced backward. "Okay, we're getting a good picture from Jones's drone," Kirin's voice said in my ear. "See if you can lure out a few of their abilities."

"I'm gonna see if I can kill them first," I snapped. I shot the nearest one in the face, blowing away a chunk of its nose. There was no blood, just a thick white paste that oozed slowly out of the wound.

"They're undead!" Sage shouted back. "System's not giving me any info on what they are, though. Just on their health and resistances."

Sage was right. We hadn't received any of the oh-so-helpful system fight start info. Maybe that was a new challenge for phase three.

"I think they are vodnik," Gabriel said. "It fits the general description anyway. Water spirits, like drowned dogs or very ugly old men."

"Great, so what's their weakness?" I asked.

"My grandmother's stories were not strong on how to defeat these things. More that if you are not a good boy, the vodnik will come and eat you."

"That's helpful," Sage called as she threw a Lasso around one of the creatures and ordered it to turn on its fellows. Frank had another one Restrained, and Annie was using her new Now You See It trick to lure one of the creatures into attacking her, then disappearing and forcing it to turn on one of the others.

The creatures tore themselves to shreds as we helped out with our own fire-power. Sage cackled in glee as she managed to get a second monster Tamed, turning them both on the one Frank had Restrained, then ordering them to fight each other when they were the last two left. Chunks of fur flew everywhere as the creatures fought and died without making a sound. It was creepy as hell.

The last body hit the ground. I stood back, panting as Sage darted in to loot. "Stay clear!" I warned, just as the pond began to roil.

CHAPTER EIGHT

WATCH YOUR WORDS: AVOIDING VERBAL CONTRACTS AND OTHER FAIRY TALE PITFALLS

The lily pads shook. "Get back," I shouted. Annie disappeared again. The others retreated to the edge of the woods. I stood my ground. I didn't want to interrupt whatever creature was about to make an attack. We needed information as much as we needed to survive this.

The water in the pond rose up in a wall, looming over me. It flung itself at me. I held until the wave started to break. Then I threw up an arm to shield my face. The weight crashed down, knocking me back and off my feet. My body was swept inland, carried by the waves. I scrabbled and fought blindly. My hand caught something and I grabbed it tight. A tree trunk, one of the spindly ones near the pond. The force slackened a bit and I fought to my feet.

"Get me eyes on . . . what's . . . casting this," I gasped. I popped a health potion and felt Sage's Raise Your Spirits hit me like a warm shower at the same time. The combo brought me back up to full health right away.

The wave continued to wash over me, a torrent splashing up from the center of the pond and fountaining down onto me. My allies were far enough back that the water did not reach them. It rushed around my feet, lapped about a bit on the bank, then slid into the pond as yet more water crashed down on me.

The crushing damage had been in the first big hit. The continued inundation wasn't doing more than keeping my coat soggy. My immunity to water-based damage was coming in really handy right about now. I wondered again if the Reality Engine was subtly putting its thumb on the scale.

"There's one creature at the center of the pond," Sage shouted. "I can see it through the drone, but I'm not getting any info on it. It's about twenty feet out. That's inside of ten meters."

I took a deep breath. "I challenge you to single combat," I said, then cast High Noon.

The fountain of water cut off. I hadn't been sure that would work. "Everyone, stay clear," I warned.

For a moment, nothing happened. Then, a creature rose out of the water.

She was female, there was no doubt about that. Her long, golden tresses clung to her shoulders and back. She spun until she was facing me. Her dress was a diaphanous white sheath clinging to her. It kind of looked like a nightgown, plastered against her chest and legs.

Her wide, sapphire eyes stared at me. She raised one pale hand and pointed. "Who are you and what have you done?"

Her voice was heavily accented. She sounded Eastern European to me, though I'm not a connoisseur of world accents by any means.

I kept my hands up at chest level, palms outward, and tried my best to look harmless. "My name's Shad Williams, ma'am. We're here to talk."

"How have you stopped me?" she demanded. "What spell have you cast over me, oh great sorcerer?"

Sage snorted. "He's no sorcerer," she called loudly. "Who are you, lady? You look like you drowned."

The woman sighed. She floated across the surface of the pond until she was about six feet away from me, then hovered over the water. Her bare feet were pointed, her toes dragging through the surface of the pond. "I am Evgenia, maiden of the lake," she said dramatically, sweeping a hand across her forehead.

"Okay," Gabriel said in my ear. "I think you've got a rusalka here."

"What's a rusalka?" Frank growled.

"Female water spirit, usually a maiden who was drowned or spited in love or something similar. They're not always implacably hostile. Sometimes they want to be given a gift or have something returned to them, and then they'll leave you alone."

"Right," I said. "Rusalka. Anything else we should know?"

"Keep her talking. We'll see what we can find out."

"So is this your pond?" I asked.

Evgenia nodded her head. "It has been my home for many years, mine and my sisters', but they are gone now, leaving me with only my pets, and now you have slain them." She looked sadly at the pile of dog-goblin corpses on the bank of the pond. I wasn't about to apologize for defending ourselves, but something she'd said sounded like a clue.

"Sisters. What happened to them?"

"The sorcerer has stolen them away," she said, sighing dramatically and lifting her eyes heavenward. "He is a cruel, cruel creature. He has enslaved many of the creatures of forest and wood to his bidding."

"Sounds like the hook for a raid boss to me," I commented to my team. "Where is the sorcerer?" I asked Evgenia.

"His dwelling is not far from here. Follow the river northward, and you will find it without question."

"Right. So, suppose someone was to do you a favor and, say, free your sisters. Would there be some sort of reward in it for us?"

"Yes, indeed," she said. "Any hero who would do such a thing would have my boon and that of my sisters."

"How about free passage through your woods for me and my friends, and maybe a few flowers from your pond?"

"My creatures would be no threat to you any longer," she promised. "My flowers will be yours for the taking." She batted her eyelids at me.

"Then we'll see what we can do," I said. "We'll retreat out of here, and then I'll cancel this duel and let you get back to your normal drowning people thing. Don't stop on account of me. All of my people will stay clear of here until we've decided what to do about this sorcerer. So anybody who comes by is definitely an enemy."

The rusalka clasped her hands to her breasts dramatically. "Thank you, hero," she said. "I knew when my waters could not wash you away that you must be pure of heart."

"Yeah, not so sure about that," I said before Sage could comment. "But we'll be back. Have a nice day, ma'am." I Tipped My Hat. I'd been doing that so often to everyone I met in order to apply my buff, it had turned into a habit. We withdrew a safe distance into the forest.

I watched as Evgenia returned to the center of her pond, did a neat handstand, and then dove beneath the surface. The water lay still and quiet where she had been.

"How do you know she's not the boss we've got to kill?" Frank asked.

"That was too clear a narrative hook," I said. "We'll at least have to follow up on it, find out what the sorcerer's deal is. Might be we need to kill everyone anyway, but I think we should try to learn the whole deal before making a decision."

"Evil sorcerers are a motif in these myths," Gabriel said in my ear, "but I'm pretty sure these aren't Czech or Slovak variants. Something feels a little off. It might be South Slav."

"What's the difference?" I asked, running my hand through my hair. "You've apparently got similar enough creatures that you recognize them."

"Sure, but that's like saying Greek and Roman gods were the same."

"The Romans just stole the Greek gods and reskinned them," Sage said. "Like when your angel healer gets a winged devil costume in a shooter game."

"That's not quite how it works," I said.

Gabriel laughed. "Okay, I get your point. I spent a lot of money on cosmetic packs during my Fortnite phase. It's probably something a little like that. You have to remember, these stories were spread across hundreds of miles, even thousands, back in the day when you couldn't travel much more than four miles an hour. Stories would vary from one village to the next, let alone between multiple countries."

"I'll put the word out looking for anyone with a South Slavic background," Kirin said. "That'll be, what, Croatia, Serbia, Bosnia, that region? But until then, Gabriel's our best expert."

"Sure, I'll do what I can," he agreed.

"Then let's go see the wizard," I said.

"Sorcerer," Sage corrected. "Unless you want me to sing 'We're Off to See the Wizard' the whole time we go, you should probably get that one right."

CHAPTER NINE

THE IMPORTANCE OF OPENING UP YOUR PORES

We skirted the edge of the pond, heading for the stream that would lead us to the sorcerer.

The sorcerer, as it turned out, lived in a bathhouse. Or at least, that's what Gabriel and Kirin agreed we were looking at when they got a look at it through All-Seeing Eye. It was a long, low, thatched-roof building made of wood with beautifully carved doorposts and lintels. There was a chimney sticking out of the top, smoking away merrily.

It was built on a small pond, maybe a tenth the size of the one where we had met the rusalka, and completely free of reeds. Lush grass surrounded the pond, with little starlike flowers peeking out from behind the blades. There was an herbal smell in the air, like things my grandmother would use for cooking. And another spicy scent, with almost a lemon undertone.

The stream ran right out of the house itself. Several large wooden barrels lined the edge of the house, and a stack of buckets stood by the door. I studied the building. It was large enough to hold a dozen or more people inside.

"Let's try flying your drone around and see if we can get a look inside any of the windows," I told Jones as we stayed back just inside the tree line, a good thirty yards away from the house. He sent his drone, the mechanical falcon, swooping in. It circled the building.

He shared its vision with me so I could see through its eyes. The windows were shuttered. Steam snuck out from around the cracks in the walls. It was definitely warm and wet inside.

"This isn't going to be like a Norwegian sauna," Gabriel told me. "I've visited the old country a couple of times, and if the bathhouse tradition in the South Slavic areas is a match, it's going to be a lot of warm, wet smoke. The fire being on the inside is a good clue."

"That's right," I said, thinking. "Saunas are more like a sweat lodge, right? Where you heat up rocks and then splash water over them, keeping the steam in a small enclosed area. That place is way too big for a bunch of hot rocks to do a good job."

I had never actually been invited to participate in a sweat lodge ceremony. I wasn't sure whether Grandpa had either. Despite having enrolled on the list of the local Ute band a decade ago, back when he got custody of me and Sage, he had usually avoided having anything to do with the reservation.

I wasn't particularly connected to my ancestral spiritual ways on any side. Grandpa wore a medicine bag but had never offered to make one for me. Abuela had baptized my mom, and my dad's people were fundamentalist LDS, which was a whole 'nother can of worms. I'd never had any interest in joining anything but the US Army.

"Is there a spiritual aspect to these bathhouses?"

"Probably," Gabriel said, "but I'm Buddhist, so if there is, it went over my head. Mostly it's just lying on wooden shelves letting the steam open your pores up, and the bathhouse attendant comes around with a birch broom and hits you with it if you want."

"Why would anyone want that?" Sage asked.

"It helps open up the pores, plus the brooms usually have herbs woven into them. Smells good," Gabriel said. "I don't know, it's a whole experience. I wasn't really comfortable with the whole thing, but my dad said we needed to experience family traditions. He didn't like it when I insisted on wearing my swim trunks."

I laughed. "All right, well, that's helpful, maybe?" The drone returned, settling onto Jones's wrist.

I thought about the next step. "No," Sage said as I opened my mouth.

"What?"

She rolled her eyes. "You were about to suggest that you run in there, get a look at what's going on, and when they inevitably kill you, you'll just respawn back at base." I closed my mouth. "That's what you were going to suggest, isn't it?"

"Maybe."

"That's always your plan, Shad, and it's a dumb plan."

"It's worked every time I've tried it."

"It's gotten you killed every time you've tried it."

I stopped myself from saying *So you've got a better one.* That might be how Shad Williams spoke to his little sister, but it was not the way Captain Williams spoke to a soldier under his command, even a soldier as nonregulation as Sage. "I am open to suggestions," I said stiffly.

Frank holstered his gun. He stared at the bathhouse. "I do have an idea," he said. "I think it's time for a search warrant."

"What?"

"You thought you guys were the only ones to level up?" Frank demanded.

"Uh, no." I hadn't really thought about it.

"I got a class evolution. I am now, as far as the system is concerned, a full-on, no kidding, Coconino County Sheriff," he said proudly.

I managed not to laugh. Sage clapped her hands. "Congratulations!"

"I don't know how authentic it is," he said, "seeing as sheriff's an elected position and this here system didn't seem to ask for any votes. Point is, it came with a couple of abilities that I didn't have before, one of them being Search Warrant."

"So how's it work?"

He rubbed his hands together gleefully. "We walk over there. I knock on the door. I show my badge and the warrant, and they have to let us in."

"That's it?"

"Well, they can start violence, but if they do, they get an Administrative Leave debuff. They'll just have to stand there and watch while we do what we like. It's broken by violence, though, so it's only useful as a delay, like that dueling move of yours."

"Sounds good. Anything else?"

"Just this." He snapped his fingers.

I felt a new buff settle over me and checked my log as Frank explained. "You four have all been Deputized."

I read the description of the buff.

[Deputized. For the next hour, you are now a deputy minion of Sheriff Frank Young. While deputized, any attack made against you will be considered an attack against Sheriff Young and Coconino County in Arizona. You have also received a buff to your perception and to any search-related talents you may have.]

"Well, I like that," Annie said cheerfully. "Most of the time, I've been on the other side of a search warrant."

Frank eyed her suspiciously, but I nodded. "All right, so let's get in there and find out."

"No provoking them, Shad," Sage warned. "I don't care what this buff says. We're here for information, right? So let's get in there and see what we can find."

I followed Frank up to the door. He knocked three times, nice and loud, very official sounding. There was no answer. He knocked again, then raised his voice. "Coconino County Sheriff," he called. "By the power vested in me by Coconino County, Arizona, United States of America, I order you to open up. We've got a search warrant."

The door swung open. A pair of beautiful young women stood there. They were clearly more rusalki. These ones weren't wet, though. Their skin looked parched and cracking. When one spoke, it was a rasping, coughing sound. "The master says begone."

"I'm here to serve a duly sworn-out search warrant," Frank said, hooking his thumbs through his belt. He was clearly in his element here. "Got a warrant to search the whole premises." He held up a piece of paper.

The rusalki stared at it and shook their heads. "You have no power here," the second rusalka said.

"I've got jurisdiction," Frank insisted. He stepped over the threshold. The women shrank back as he held out the paper in front of him like a shield.

We followed him in. There was a little antechamber where we stood. Hooks hung on the wall. Some held towels. The others, clothing.

Bright blue cloaks concealed something heavier behind them. I nudged one cloak aside. There was a full set of discarded plate mail armor there, complete with heavy boots, and a sword and shield leaned against the wall. The shield was facing away from me. I tried to peer at it, see if there was any kind of design on it, but I didn't want to move any of this stuff just in case that could be taken as provocation. Someone had taken it off and, from the look of it, deliberately left it behind. To go into the sauna? That was my guess.

There were four blue cloaks and I assumed four sets of armor. I relayed everything I saw back to Kirin, who was working with Arjun to build up a picture of what we were up against.

"You may not enter any farther clothed like that," one rusalka rasped. "Take off your clothes and the master will permit you entrance."

"Uh-uh," Frank said, looking as stubborn as I remembered him from my misspent youth. "An officer on duty does not remove his uniform. You stand aside or I'll have to arrest you for obstruction of justice."

The rusalki looked at each other, clearly not knowing what to do, then finally retreated, stepping through a bead curtain that separated the antechamber from the rest of the house.

Frank followed them through. I was hot on his tail. The inner chamber was about ten by ten feet. Shelves lined the walls stacked two high, wide enough for someone to lie on them. There were twelve shelves altogether, two stacks on each of the three walls other than the one with the door.

A small metal stove stood in the far corner of the room, pumping out heat. The stream ran right through the center of the room in a stone-lined trough that cut diagonally from one corner to the opposite.

Three short little men dressed in loincloths scurried away as the rusalki entered, disappearing farther into the room. Steam obscured my view. I could make out the stove and the fact that the shelves were there and that some of them had people on them, but I couldn't grasp any details. The room smelled sweet, like hot herbal tea.

I sidled away a little bit to get a better look around the room. I approached the first stack of shelves. There was someone lying on the bottom shelf, flat on his stomach. The steam cleared enough for me to see he was tan, muscular, taller than me, and definitely naked.

He lifted his head. A pair of sharp, dark eyes met mine. He was bearded. It was neatly trimmed into a goatee, and he had a mustache that came down into points. He looked to be about thirty-five years old and had a scar across his cheek. Everything about him screamed "Danger!" I resisted the urge to take a step back or reach for my gun.

"You there, villain," he said. "Who disturbs my bath?"

I didn't answer. The man went up on one arm, lifting his shoulder so I could see his well-shaped pecs and abs. He did not look like someone I wanted to mess with. Suddenly, his eyes moved to something over my right shoulder. "Master?"

I turned around to see a dark shape materialize from out of the steam. This man looked even taller, and he was dressed wearing dark robes. He had a pointed cloth hat on his head, black with golden decals, and was clutching what I thought was a staff until I saw it was topped with a spray of branches. Greenery was worked into the broom.

"Who intrudes on Podaga's bathhouse?" the man demanded. He was a little older looking than the naked steambather on my right. His beard was longer and gray, streaked with darker black. He had a hooked nose and a pair of slate-gray eyes. "I am not open to the public at the moment. When the Vitezovi—my knights—have finished, I will welcome you and yours."

"We're just here to see about the complaint," Frank said, stepping forward through the steam. "So, you're Podaga the Enchanter. You are the owner of this fine establishment?"

CHAPTER TEN

BIRDWATCHING: TIPS FOR YOUR BIG YEAR

We left the magician's hut carefully, Frank waving his search warrant under Podaga's nose. "We'll be back," he promised. "I can smell when perps are hiding something from me." I stepped through the doorway, backing out into the glade, turned, and found five crossbows pointing right at my gut.

I held up my hands slowly. "Everybody hold," I warned.

Sage squeaked and bumped into me as she turned. The crossbows were being held by five dwarves. Another twenty flanked them, carrying long axes nearly as tall as they were. They had enormous beards in a half dozen different colors. They all wore armor under tabards that depicted a hammer smashing a skull.

One stepped forward. His tabard's logo had a little crown over the skull. I recognized him from the party the other night. "You lot come out of there nice and slow," he said. "Keep your hands where I can see them. Any nonsense and we'll shoot."

I stepped down, closer to them, keeping my hands level and trying not to look threatening. "Easy," I said. "We don't want any trouble."

I was actually surprised they hadn't started shooting already. They might be trying to avoid triggering the boss before they were ready. It was pretty clear they were here to take him out.

They eyed us suspiciously. "Where's the rest of your team?"

"Not here," I said.

"We could see that. How'd you manage not to wipe completely?" That was one of the crossbow-wielding dwarves behind the leader. She had a lighter voice and a slightly smaller build than most of the others, but her beard was just as luxurious as her fellows.

I didn't answer. Sage piped up hopefully. "Not everything has to be about fighting. Sometimes you win battles by making friends."

"Easy there," I said out of the corner of my mouth. "Let's try not to incite these guys." The crossbow-dwarves followed our moves as we slowly walked away from the bathhouse toward the edge of the forest.

They probably didn't want to fight us as they were getting ready for an attempt on the boss. We could accidentally trigger the fight early, or, even though they outnumbered us and would almost certainly kill us all, we'd take more than a few of them with us in a fight and that would ruin their attempt.

I cleared my throat. "So, any interest in pooling our knowledge? Maybe joining forces? Sharing the loot?"

"Get out of here, humans," the lead dwarf spat. "Told you already. We don't want any business with you and your kind. A bunch of jumped-up locals who think they can come in here and insult our traditions, invite the soulless to play. The sooner you're out of this, the better."

Jones sent me a message. *Got my drone hovering about fifty feet up. I'm sending the feed right back to headquarters.*

Great, I replied, then checked the chat channel I had labeled "Too Many Cooks." Grandpa and Juana had both sent me messages in the last thirty seconds telling me to keep my cool and not provoke anything, as though I hadn't thought of that myself. I sent them back a quick note telling them to cool their jets, and we made it to the edge of the trees.

"Go on ahead," I told Sage, Frank, and Annie. "Jones and I are going to hang back and keep an eye out. Jones, hit your Camouflage, and we'll creep back here."

"Got it," he said.

"Why can't we stay?" Sage demanded.

"In case they've got scouts looking for a party heading back toward our base," I told her. She grumbled but obeyed.

Once we'd made it a few yards into the forest, Jones Camouflaged both of us, and we crept back toward the bathhouse. His falcon drone was still scouting, but I wanted to see this with my own eyes.

The dwarves appeared to have no further interest in us. They were spreading out around the open area beyond the bathhouse, with the crossbowmen and a couple of dwarves carrying glowing wands a few steps back, almost at the water's edge, and the ones with axes up at the front. "Right, everyone in position?" the head dwarf asked. "Starting our countdown timer now. Drink your potions."

Nobody actually drank anything. If it was like how our potion belts worked, they were just queuing things up. I had my Inspect going, and I watched a couple of them. It was too hard to see them all at once. I picked out one of the crossbowmen, one of the ones with a wand, and the boss dwarf, and relayed back to Kirin and Arjun a list of every buff they were adding.

"Thirty seconds," the boss dwarf said. He had eight different buffs on him. An increase to his defense against lightning, water, striking, and ranged attacks.

He also had an increase to his crushing damage and his threat generation. I made a special note of that one.

"Let's go!" he shouted. He pulled a fist-sized round ball from his inventory and lobbed it at the open door. I thought it was a grenade, but instead of exploding, it flattened out into a bright orange paste on the door, which then caught fire and began to burn. The dwarves readied their weapons.

A moment later, the door flung open and half a dozen short, ugly old men poured out of the bathhouse, the same ones I had caught a glimpse of while we were in there searching the place. I checked in with our experts back at headquarters. "You guys have any idea what these are?"

"Bannik," Gabriel said. "A pretty common Slavic spirit. Bathhouse spirits, frequently old men. Definitely bannik."

"They have really long teeth," I commented as the first of them swarmed at the leader dwarf. They were scrawny and wizened, with long beards, and wore nothing but loincloths. They carried buckets in their hands, whirling them around their heads and throwing them at the dwarves. More buckets appeared from nowhere.

The first two bannik started in on the leader dwarf as he took a couple of steps back, leading them right into the circle of axe-wielding warriors. The crossbow-dwarves began shooting arrow after arrow. I threw up a quick Inspect. Most of the arrows were dealing fire damage. The bannik screeched and yelled as their health levels dipped.

Beside me, Jones had his binoculars out. "I'm getting snapshots of most of them every couple seconds to send back for analysis," he told me. "These things are great."

One of the axe-dwarves stepped in to get a good swing, and a bannik that had not yet attached itself to the leader walloped him in the head with a bucket. He went down. I couldn't see system details about what kind of attacks the bannik were doing, other than what I observed and guessed, but I could see their results on the dwarves.

The battered dwarf lay stunned for a minute as the ugly, half-naked bathhouse spirits surrounded and began clobbering him. His health bar dipped. The wand-wielding dwarves focused their attention on him, sending a stream of light from each of the three wands.

The dwarf leader shouted, "Healer! Focus on me!" Two of the healers went back to beaming light at him. What I found interesting was that their strategy matched what I had seen during our duel with Mak'gar's orcs. The dwarves also relied heavily on their equipment, which seemed to be fairly standardized. Axes, crossbows, magic wands, and a few consumables, but I didn't see them using abilities the way my team did. I made a note to check with Veda about that.

The dwarf on the ground tried to get up. Another bannik latched on to him and grabbed his beard, pulling at it. He screamed, dropping his axe and grabbing for the mischievous spirit with both hands. It was a mistake. A minute later, he was gone, dissolved in a stream of light.

But even with a few victories, it wasn't enough, not against two dozen dwarves. Even when another couple of bannik reinforcements popped out of the bathhouse, the dwarves took them down.

"Fall back!" the dwarf leader panted as the last of the bannik vanished. "Heal up! Use your—oh, here they come!"

Four armored knights burst out of the bathhouse, clearly the clients we had seen steaming on the shelves. They wore blue capes, and the one in front had a shield that bore an eight-pointed star and a cross.

"Gabriel, do you recognize these?" I asked.

"Must be the Vitezovi," he said in my ear. "I'm not remembering any particular details on them, though."

The knight with a shield carried a longsword. The next knight had an axe similar to the dwarves', but with a double head instead of a single, and his didn't have a beard—the little flange on the blade—like theirs did. The other two knights were wielding an enormous two-handed sword and a polearm respectively.

They sent out the shield man in front, axe wielder and swordsman behind him, and polearm in the back, as they advanced on the dwarves. The dwarves fell back as their leader called out instructions.

The dwarf leader tossed a device at the knights that started blaring loud wailing sounds, like a siren shrieking or maybe a European metal singer gal in full scream. The knights growled, their attention clearly on their leader.

Must be some sort of taunting device, I thought. Despite not having any kind of shield, the dwarf leader was clearly trying to take the brunt of the aggression for his team. "On 'em!" he shouted, and the axe-dwarves stepped in.

The knights were more coordinated than the dwarves, who charged in and flailed their axes, crossbow wielders shooting arrows any which way. There was no attempt to focus on any of the targets.

The shield knight was really good at twisting and bending, getting a blow to fall on his shield that would otherwise have hit one of his fellows. The knights were heavily armored, too. I couldn't see their hit points, but they all had green health bars hanging over them, and the dwarves' attacks were barely making them twitch.

The polearm knight skewered an axe-dwarf right in the eye, knocking his health down to zero and making him despawn. Then the one with the greatsword brought it down in a huge, crashing chop on another dwarf's head.

The healing dwarves shouted at each other and tried to move their beams, but too late. The dwarf was gone.

I could see their strategy falling apart, but there were a lot of dwarves. Furiously chopping and flailing, they took down the knight with the axe, probably because more of them had focused on him than any of the others. I suspected that they were enraged by seeing him wield one of their preferred weapons.

Seemingly cheered by their minor victory, the dwarves went after the one with the polearm, getting inside his reach.

His compatriots didn't react quickly enough. The shield man was still trying to take the blows, but missing more than he got. The greatsword wielder just blindly attacked whoever was closest.

Another three dwarves went down before they got the one with the polearm. The two remaining knights both screamed, and the air around them filled with a red haze. Some sort of blood rage, probably. They leapt apart, charging packs of dwarves to either side and cutting through them with their swords.

The knights laid several more low, but now the crossbow-dwarves were able to get good aim. They were shooting at the joints of the knights' armor, at their necks and elbows.

A few of their arrows started to get through. The shield man's left armpiece cracked, then crumbled away, exposing his cloth-covered arm underneath. The nearest axe-dwarf swung hard at that and severed it. The shield and arm fell to the grass. He didn't last long after that.

Fourteen or so dwarves surrounded the longsword wielder. He took two more, but they got him down.

The lead dwarf was still alive. His hair was frazzled, and there was blood in his beard. He had lost his helmet somewhere during the fight. "Everybody catch your breath!" he shouted as he pulled something out of his inventory.

Then the enchanter emerged from his hut.

The air went cold and still. The birds, which had been occasionally chirping in the trees overhead, fell silent.

"You dare invade the sanctum of Podaga the Enchanter?" he demanded. He raised his arms. "You will feel his wrath!"

"Spread out!" the lead dwarf warned, and the others sprang to obey.

Podaga stretched out both hands. Lightning zapped from his fingers. It leapt from dwarf to dwarf around the circle, then back again. The healers were doing their best, switching their beams every second or so from one dwarf to the next, but they forgot to focus on themselves.

They were the first to fall, then the crossbowmen. Then, within twenty seconds of the enchanter appearing in his doorway, the glade was empty. The dwarves were gone.

The enchanter lowered his hands. He looked around, smiling. "That's to any who challenges Podaga the Enchanter," he called. "If you have the mettle, come back tomorrow and face me again, and I will lay waste to you once more."

He turned and disappeared back into his bathhouse.

CHAPTER ELEVEN

HOW TO PREPARE FOR A SECRET MEETING

ack at headquarters, I was sitting in the church at one of the folding tables with our council of war: Grandpa, Arjun, Tall Smith, and Frank.

Juana was pacing back and forth as she messaged people in Threshold. "All right, Veda's confirming it, and Mama backs it up. Everything we're hearing says that teams can only challenge these bosses once in a twenty-four-hour period."

"Individual teams?" I asked. "Like, if we go back there in an hour with a full group, would we be able to take on the enchanter? But the dwarves won't?"

"It sounds that way. The system seems to be limiting it for individual attempts. I've also had a message from a slightly friendlier neighbor. Somebody who says they know Firebrand."

"Yeah?" Grandpa asked, perking up. "What do they say?"

"The team name is Congruent Paths. They are contracted with Alabaster Sky, but they have offered neutrality for the next week before the main gates open. They're chasing an old woman who has a hut that moves around on chicken legs, and they say if we leave her alone, they won't make any attempts on Podaga until we've had our shot."

"Oh, I know that one," Gabriel called from the next table over. "That's Baba Yaga. She's all over the mythology in that part of the world."

"So we can only attempt to take down a boss once a day. If we kill him, is he permanently dead? Or can another team come by and kill him a second time?" I asked.

"Nobody seems to know that yet, or if they do, they're not telling," Juana said. "We've got ears all over. Our crafters in Threshold are demanding information whenever they can. We're offering a fifteen-percent discount on your order if you have anything we don't already know."

"That's a great incentive," I said. "Tell Dwight good idea."

"It was my idea."

"Well, in that case, tell yourself."

She blushed. I grinned at her and turned back to address the table. "Right, so there are definitely bosses out there we could go after. Podaga and Baba Yaga for sure, and there's probably others. But we already have a ton of information on Podaga. We should concentrate on him. We've got one shot. I don't think we can realistically count on more than that. If we fail, somebody else is going to come in and take him out from under our noses. There's ten other teams out here. There could be someone on him right now."

"Jones still has his drone up," Grandpa reminded me. "If anyone makes a move, we'll see them."

"I'd kind of like it if they did. I have a feeling that guy's got a few more tricks up his sleeves. The dwarves had a good idea," I said. "They were trying to get all of the attention from the earlier mobs focused on their leader. That would have made the job with the healers easier. I think we need a tank. And no," I added quickly before anyone said anything, "not me. I don't have any of the right abilities."

"You've got the taunt," Grandpa pointed out.

"Yeah, and it's one taunt with a long cooldown, and I don't have the ability to take all that damage they were dishing out. Just because I managed it on old Squid Face doesn't mean I'm the right man for the job."

"I have a list of possible contenders," Arjun said, "but no one you've worked with previously."

"That's not true," I said. "Frank's got a lot of the skills already."

Frank looked at me. "What?"

"Between what you already had and those couple of upgrades you showed me, I think you could handle it. We're getting some consumables for you, a few extra taunting devices, and maybe some disposable shields. That new ability you have, Command and Control, you told me how you've been using it to keep the heat off your farmers when you're out in the field protecting them. Plus, you can swap places with anyone with Emergency Responder. If somebody's getting piled on, you can teleport to where they are and teleport them out of trouble."

"I told you guys I wasn't cut out for this sort of thing," Frank protested.

"Come on, Frank, this is an entirely different kettle of fish. Death isn't permanent here, and it's not fight after fight after fight. This is one fight that we want you for. And after that, we'll see."

"What? You're gonna have a different strategy once we're inside the castle?"

"We sure are," I said, "because we're getting that list of people from Arjun, and we're gonna bring them in and start training with them."

Frank didn't look convinced. Grandpa leaned across the table. "It would help us out a lot, Frank," he said quietly.

"How sure are you these first bosses even matter? We can walk right past Podaga's hut. No need to get anywhere near him."

Grandpa shook his head. "What's the point in not having the main doors open for a week, but having these other bosses out? We're supposed to be fighting over them. Whoever downs them gets buffed in the next stage of the game. I guarantee it."

I chimed in. "I don't know how many bosses there are, but it's at least two. My gut says more than that, but probably not enough for everyone to get one. So we've got to take somebody down. On the other hand, once all of these, uh . . ." I cast around for a term.

"Outdoor bosses," Grandpa suggested.

"Right. Once all the outdoor bosses are down, if they really are single-kill each, it'll be much safer for your people. You can get back to letting the farmers harvest and the crafters do their work. I have a feeling that's when it's going to get really hairy for the rest of us."

Frank sighed. "I guess I see your point. Besides, you say it's only once a day, so if we try this and it doesn't work, you have time to get some of Arjun's other candidates in here and up to speed."

"Exactly," I said. "Anyway, there's no limit on how many people we can have in our raid. Let's get as many as we can. The space itself is a factor. We gotta have room to move, but we could easily have twice as many as those dwarves had. Let's get everyone who's expressed any possible interest to assemble just outside our own gates. We'll run through some practice formations, see what we can do. Arjun, we need healers, people with tanking abilities, anybody who's willing to listen to you and Juana shotcalling."

"I'm on it," Arjun said. He started rattling off a list of skills to look for. I was going to interrupt him and tell him to do what he thought best, but I got a message. It was from Warren Black, whom I had dueled at the end of phase one. I hadn't thought about him or his allies in months. He'd taken over what was left of the Free Human League from Major Waters when the major disappeared in disgrace.

I've had a message from a mutual . . . acquaintance. Someone neither of us want to deal with. He says he's got to speak to you on neutral grounds. At Threshold. Secretly, without anyone else knowing.

The only man he could mean was Waters. After seeing him the other night, I had been wondering when the other shoe would drop.

I sent Grandpa a quick message. *Waters wants to meet me and doesn't want me to tell you.*

Grandpa snorted. He quickly turned it into a cough and I don't think anyone else noticed. *Tell him yes, but make sure you tell me where you're going. I know there's no violence allowed in Threshold, but that doesn't mean they can't find some way to mess with you.*

I'll contact you in a couple of hours, I told Black. *Got some business to deal with first. Tell him if he tries anything stupid, I will make him regret it.*

Understood. I'll be waiting.

Arjun was still rambling. I stood up and cut him off. "I want your people here in three hours," I said. "So that's just people who can get here from Threshold. The Hub's too far. Tell 'em we'll take them for the next bit. And they need to sign on to Misfits Guild."

"Oh?" Juana asked. "We'd been saying we'll work with people who aren't in the guild." She tilted her head. "Actually, Mama just sent me a message. She says she's got a couple of potential recruits who she'd like you to meet with. Sounds like our efforts at locating eSports experts have finally borne fruit."

That would be perfect, since it would allow me to meet with Waters right afterward. "Great! But remember, I have a buff to having everyone in the party be part of my outfit. Increases our number of soul coins dropped. And I'm not the only one with a buff like that," I said. "Sage's Cowgirl Cheer is more effective on coalition members. That's why they have to join up."

"That's right," Juana said. "I'll take a look at synergies like that."

"In the meantime, our creep is heading up toward Podaga's hut. I dropped some of our flags there to attract them. I think we can use them to help clear out the bannik. Meanwhile," I said, standing up, "I gotta go get something to eat. It's been a long day. Sage, let's go raid Mama's kitchen. We'll do hiring interviews while we're there."

CHAPTER TWELVE

CORPORATE RAIDING: DO'S AND DON'TS

Veda sat in a cramped metal cubicle that had been her home, her office, her basic operations, her sanctum for nearly a year. For the first time, she felt trapped. The walls seemed tighter and closer.

She had banished all of the comforting illusions, letting herself see the metal bones, the exposed computer control panels. Her tight crate was about the smallest there was in the Hub's systems. It had a tiny independent propulsion unit, just enough to let it kick away from the Hub's infrastructure and navigate to an intergalactic transport.

Any of the major conglomerations, like Proxima or Alabaster Sky, would have thousands of ships far larger than hers. Some were even capable of independent travel. Hers was basically just a box with a motor and an oxygen tank in one corner and an ethereum reserve in the other. Just enough to keep her alive long enough to connect with the larger infrastructure's systems.

Considering all the time she had spent in storage as a child, she should have found the place claustrophobic. It wasn't. It represented freedom, the ability to move from one system to another for as long as her ethereum lasted.

She had read over the family's charter, over her phase two bid, over various relevant legal cases. Her mother was right. Her absolute authority over the exploit operation had ended the moment phase two did.

Since she had not previously been formally relieved of duty, her expenditures on behalf of Shad and the humans for their phase three bid were legal. She couldn't be prosecuted for misappropriation of funds or any such thing, but those allocations would be converted over to unsecured loans the moment Tvedra pulled out of this.

She didn't see any way around that. Her mother had sent over a copy of the minutes from the most recent Board of Directors meeting for the Tvedra Corporation. It was all in order. The votes had been cast and recorded, the seals properly applied. Veda was no longer in charge of anything. All she had was this life-support unit and a few funds of her own.

The pod had been a coming-of-age gift from her father right before he left for the exploit that had cost him his life. Which made it ironic that he had died in his own pod, when his transport ran out of ethereum during hyperspace travel.

So she had her quarters, forty thousand soul coins in the bank, and some personal relationships. That was about it.

The good news for the humans was that the phase three bid was still in effect. Tvedra couldn't just yank it out now, especially not when it had been co-sponsored by the Board of Progenitors.

They would need to find more funds going forward. Veda sent another message to Mama Grace. She didn't want to involve the frontline troops, Major Twofeather, Shad, or the others just yet, but she needed to talk to someone who had a big-picture idea of what was going on. From what she'd learned, that was Colonel Ames.

Veda asked Mama Grace to tell the colonel it was important that they meet up, face-to-face if possible, and offered to meet him anywhere on the Hub or Threshold that he chose. Then she sat back and started searching through records.

Her mother had been trying to call every twenty minutes since the party. Veda set all the messages to be picked up by her subsystems. She didn't have anything to say to her mother right now.

A ping came in from Colonel Ames. *I'm standing outside your door right now.*

It had been less than three minutes since she'd sent that message to Mama Grace. Veda leapt up, glancing down at herself. She was still wearing the same gown from last night. She hadn't slept. She hadn't eaten, and had been living on stimulants and cold car juice. Her quarters were a mess, data packets hanging in the air in a thousand different places for her to flip back and forth between.

She opened the door, and the colonel stepped in. He wasn't wearing a uniform, just a simple gray shipsuit. No logos, no designs.

"Can I get you anything?" she asked as the door closed behind him.

"Just a place to sit," he said, glancing around at her bare quarters.

Veda ordered the system to produce a cushion for him to sit on. She sat cross-legged on the floor across from him, with her data projection table between them.

"Grace says you want to talk," Ames said.

"Yes." She cleared her throat. "My company is pressuring me to end our involvement in phase three."

"Really," Ames said, scratching his ear. "Got the impression you were a one-woman show."

"Not at all. We're a family organization. Most of the rest of them are back home, several systems away. They have sent a messenger to let me know that the family's judgment is we should not proceed any further in phase three. Historically, we've been a phase two company only," she explained. "They're concerned about the risks involved."

"Uh-huh," Ames said. "But you're not?"

"I saw an opportunity. I wanted to take it. It's paid off well so far, and I was going to keep backing you humans. But it is unfortunately no longer my choice. We are going to have to make further arrangements."

"That's all?"

She was getting tired of his laconic answers. She studied the man, but he gave away nothing.

She had gotten pretty good at reading Team Twofeather. Shad was incapable of hiding his feelings. Sage would flip from one extreme to the next like any adolescent anywhere, and Major Twofeather, while generally reserved, had a deep streak of bitterness that came out at the oddest times.

This man, though, she knew only from his mention by other members of the team. "Look, it took me some digging to find out that you're behind most of the influxes of cash I've been seeing in the last few months," she said. "The ones supposedly from Mama Grace and the crafters. You've got funds and resources. I want to know just how deep your pockets go."

"How much do you need?"

She hesitated.

He pursed his lips. "Either you don't want to say because it's a lot, or you don't want to say because you don't know," he said. "And I'm betting the latter. You said yourself your family's not usually involved in phase three. That means you're as new to this as we are. You've been winging it, trying to get a little experience at our expense."

She felt suddenly cold, betrayed. She'd been laying her cards on the table, only for this human to throw them back in her face. "I'm trying to help you."

"That remains to be seen," Ames said. "What is it exactly you bring to the table anymore? I've been checking with my contacts while we speak, and it seems that once a bid's in the system, it can't be revoked. So, I don't need your name anymore. It seems like if you withdraw, you still get first claim against any winnings we make. That's fine. We can pay off what you paid us sooner or later. So I ask again, why do we need you?"

"Because I have contacts," she said. "People who won't speak with an indigenous primitive."

He raised an eyebrow. "I'd like to hear you say that to Major Twofeather's face."

His vehemence surprised her. "I think the translation's problematic here."

"Something's problematic here," Ames agreed.

"What I mean is, your people are new to everything. You're a bad risk, business-wise. The established corporations aren't going to open up to you the same way they will to the rest of us. I know where to look for answers to questions. You don't."

"So you might make a helpful native guide," Ames said, nodding. "Possibly. Or we could try hiring someone else. Someone who doesn't think they own us."

"I've been working with Team Twofeather since the beginning."

"This here's bigger than Louis and his kids," Ames said.

"Only because of what they've done," she snapped back. "I don't want to abandon them. Yes, I'm new to phase three. So are you."

"So you've got a bit of spunk," Ames said. "I admire that. I'm willing to keep you around. If you level with us."

"I've already been honest."

"We need more than honesty now. We need good, hard information."

She leaned forward. "Let's say Twofeather and his team do manage, against all odds, to claim a share of this Reality Engine. I've got a few ideas on how to best exploit that."

The colonel frowned. "From what I can tell, we're going to need a corporation that's registered at the galactic level and has a license from the Exploitation Committee to operate. Otherwise, we end up at the mercy of somebody who does have that kind of license. I've been hoping to stick with your company. That sounds like it's off the agenda now. What I'd like is a list of umbrella corporations we might be able to sign on with, but who won't screw us over too hard."

Veda was nodding, already thinking of a few possibilities. At the same time, she wondered. Was Ames testing her? Or had he missed entirely the rest of the implications of his proposal? "What about a company of your own?"

Ames dropped his fingers against his leg. "That's an interesting proposition," he said. "How exactly would we go about doing that?"

"I'll get you a précis. You would need shareholders, stakeholders, board members, presidents, various different figureheads, several licenses that are only available at full capitol worlds, not frontier exploits like this. But you'd be able to at least fill out the paperwork and get a temporary license here. The Exploitation Committee has that power. After the end of this exploit, somebody would need to get that ratified."

"We can manage that," Ames said. "You get me that info."

"I will," she said.

"And I'm curious why you came to me, not Louis and his team."

She looked him straight in the eye. "I'll be telling them everything. I just wanted to let them get their feet under them here in phase three. Plus, since you're the name on all of the soul coin transfers, that makes you important. I figured you'd need to be looped in sooner or later, and I wanted to get a feel for what you wanted."

Ames stood up. She rose as well. "So you think you know me now?" he asked.

Veda hesitated. "Not really," she admitted. "But I don't think you want to be out of this game any more than I do. And that means we're allies."

"Potential allies," he said. "You get me your proposal, and I'll take a look at it."

After he left, Veda turned to her personal system. *I need a lawyer. A really, really good lawyer. Someone who doesn't like the current way we do things.*

I need . . . an activist.

CHAPTER THIRTEEN

YOUR FIRST DAY AS A PERSONNEL MANAGER

Mama Grace was running a surf and turf special today. I didn't ask where any of the components had come from, just accepted a plate of something that passed for breaded shrimp and a purple steak with all the fixings. Sage and I dove right into our plates. When I was about halfway through, Mama Grace came back with a pitcher of sweet tea to refill my cup, and another woman with her.

The woman had a pair of dogs with her, both of them the little frizzy, yappy kind I've never liked much. Give me a dog that can chase down the bird you just shot any day. Sage exclaimed and slid out of her chair right away, crouching on the floor and holding her hands out to the dogs. "Come here!"

"This is Alison," Mama Grace said. "She's going to be your new raid manager."

"Raid manager?" I looked the woman over. She looked maybe forty years old, so probably that was her real age. The Reality Engine rejuvenated anyone older than that down into their midthirties like Grandpa. She had a pleasant round face, dishwater blond hair cut just above her shoulders, and glasses. The Reality Engine also healed most eye problems. Probably the glasses were part of her class.

"I'm Shad Williams of Team Twofeather," I said, standing up and extending my hand. "Won't you sit down, ma'am?"

"Certainly." She gave me a genuine smile, sat down, and pulled a paper out of her inventory. Alison slid it across to me. Nobody but Juana bothered to use paper here. I picked it up. It said: "Resume of Alison Grinnel, Personnel Management." Then it listed a bunch of jobs in HR.

"Okay, I can see this being useful. I'll put you in touch with Arjun."

"Flip it over, please," she told me.

I did. On the back, written by hand, was an addendum.

"Class: Dog Lady. It's like a cat lady, but with dogs." Then she had listed her abilities, none of which looked particularly combat-focused, like "Walk the Dog: Your base walking speed is decreased by 15% but you gain a boost to charisma and are more persuasive to other miners."

Below that, my eyes seized on a relevant heading. Six years' experience leading raids in massively multiplayer online role-playing games. She then listed three big ones that I had heard of, though never played myself. She had led forty-man, twenty-five-man, and twenty-man raid teams and achieved server first on multiple of them.

"Okay, I'm interested. Let's talk."

Mama Grace brought her a cup of iced tea. Alison picked it up and took a sip. "I'm not a great raider myself," she said without preamble. "I studied strats and did my job, but I'm no theorycrafter. What I was *good* at was raid coordination. For instance, if you've got a forty-man raid, how many need to be healers? How many ranged DPS? Do we have someone to provide all of the needed debuffs for the boss? How many tanks do we need in a fight? I also regularly served as heals team coordinator on the bigger fight."

"Explain?" I leaned forward.

Sage, down on the floor with the dogs, interrupted. "First, tell me what their names are and how you brought them along?"

"Those are Jock and Willie," Alison said. "I've actually got a bunch more, and a pair of cats I don't know what to do with. They're in my inventory."

"Really?" I was surprised. As far as I knew, you couldn't store live creatures in your inventory.

"Yes," Alison said. "It's a special trait for my class. You see, I was at the vet with Jock and Willie for their yearly physical when the event happened. It took me, two vet techs, a mom and son there to get their new puppy his shots, and the contents of half the building. That included a bunch of animals waiting for or recovering from surgery. We couldn't put them in inventory at the time, so we—" She hesitated. "Four of us took the ones who could walk and escaped with them. Milla, one of the techs, wouldn't leave the others. Even with the countdown."

I closed my eyes. "I understand."

"Then when we were offered classes, I saw this ability." She tapped an ability on her list, Petsitter. She hadn't written out what it did. "That lets me store any nonsentient living creature in my inventory. Doesn't work on the things the Reality Engine generates, though. So I took all the good boys and girls we had and now I'm carrying them around. I have several abilities that let me unleash them in combat, but I'm so afraid they'll be killed. I know you removed the human death penalty. Do you know if that stands for animals?"

"I have no idea. We don't have anyone else on the team with pets. I'll see if Veda knows. Did they eat soul coins or anything?"

"They did, but it didn't seem to do anything. No abilities or intelligence boosts, if that's what you're asking." She looked fondly at the pair of dogs. "These two are just my same friends who've been with me for the past eight years. I don't know what I'd have done without them."

"Can I adopt one of the cats?" Sage asked. "It could be my mascot; I'll get it a cowboy hat to wear and teach it tricks!"

"No," I said firmly, thinking of all the problems that would cause. "All right, Alison, I'm convinced that I want you on our team. With that kind of experience, we need you. Are you willing to join our guild?"

She nodded. "Yes, I've already talked it over with Mama Grace and I am ready to team up."

I sent her an invite to Misfits. She accepted. I immediately pulled her full profile up on my guild officer's interface. Juana was trying to get me to use that more, but I always forgot to bother with it. Now I had access to Alison's full profile.

She was only level two, which worried me. She must have avoided fighting in phase one. Her health was a minuscule forty-five points. She had twenty points in charisma—almost as many as Sage—and the rest were scattered around randomly. I winced. "Look, don't take this the wrong way, but it doesn't seem as though you've got much combat experience."

"I know. But I do think my raiding knowledge will be invaluable for you. As soon as I heard about phase three, I knew I had to come help out Team Twofeather." She hesitated. "I was a lotus eater," she admitted.

That made sense. If she'd spent most of the last two phases hiding, that explained a lot. "No shame in that. If you're willing to help now, that's enough."

"I am, and I'm ready to start immediately. Mama Grace had me approach you first, but when I heard the theme for phase three I started putting a team together. A couple of them are here waiting for you."

I had eaten most of my lunch by now. I glanced around the restaurant, which was bustling like usual, trying to guess who Alison's friends were. They made it easy by waving to me. A table in the far corner had five people around it: two women, three men. I stood up. "That's them?"

Alison led me over. Sage followed, the dogs tucked under her arms. I smiled as I approached the table. "Hi, I'm Shad. Alison says I should talk to you."

"We all know who you are," one of the women said. She was about my age, redheaded and pretty, with a splash of freckles across her cheeks. She looked me over and smiled. "You're even cuter close up than when we saw you on stage the other day, isn't he, Lauren?"

"Now that he's gone all red, sure," the other girl about her age said. Lauren had darker skin and her hair in a thousand beaded braids. She wore scrubs. So did two of the men.

"Are you healer classes?" I asked.

"That's right," Alison said. "Like I said, during raiding my particular expertise was managing heals teams. From the videos Colonel Ames brought us, your fights have been kind of ad hoc. Sage has a nice little heal, sure, but you guys mostly seem to rely on potions. That's not going to work here in phase three."

I thought about how the dwarves had managed in the Podaga fight. They'd had what seemed to be a dedicated healing team. It hadn't been enough for them. "I've got more footage for you to watch. I'd appreciate your analysis. Once we're done here, I'd like you to head for our outpost and ask Arjun about it."

Alison nodded. "Sounds good. If you'll let me, I'll coordinate for the first fight and then we can adapt as needed."

"Anything the rest of you want from me?" I asked. I was trying not to be too suspicious, but this seemed ridiculously convenient for us. "What is it you're hoping to get here?"

The girl who wasn't Lauren blushed. She giggled and looked away. One of the men spoke up. He had tanned skin, like Grandpa after a day out in the sun, and wrinkles up by his eyes that made me think he had been rejuvenated by the Reality Engine. Otherwise he looked about thirty. "Captain Williams, what you and Team Twofeather have been doing is inspirational. I can only speak for myself, but I was lost. Yanked away from my home and family, put to work by aliens, fighting for my life with a set of rules that made no sense. When I learned about the safe zone, I hauled ass there as fast as I could. Had been there probably two months by the time you arrived, and it turns out an eternal vacation wears thin. I was about three days from becoming one of the sleepers."

I remembered the creepy catacomb full of unconscious humans that Ames had shown me, and shivered. "Any luck waking them up?"

"Kronos beamed your inspirational speech into everyone's dreams and asked for volunteers," another of the men said. He looked tired. He was also wearing scrubs, green ones, and had a stethoscope around his neck. "My name is Chen. I was a radiologist on Earth and I'm a Radiologist class again here. I've got some abilities that I took thinking I could use them to help protect my team. We tried running missions. Our backer told us it was the fastest way out of debt. We managed two. Then, disaster. All four of my friends died in front of me. It—I couldn't take it. I found Kronos and hid."

"But you're here now."

"Your sister woke me up." He looked pensive, staring down at the table. "I have two little girls back on Earth about her age. I miss them so damn much. I was thinking about how they would be ashamed of me, hiding away where it was safe while a child fought for their future."

That was a big burden to lay on me. I'd promised to help fight for Earth, and I meant it, but I didn't have a very good idea how. I cleared my throat. "Glad to have you aboard." I extended all five an invite to Misfits. "We'll be gearing up for our attempt soon. Everyone move out. I'll meet you back at headquarters."

I sent a quick message to the Too Many Cooks channel, letting Grandpa, Juana, and the other department heads know we'd just recruited a bunch of healers.

Great, Juana sent back at once. *We actually had a pair of men who should make good tanks show up and volunteer. This is going to be a pretty decent dry run. Are you on your way back?*

I've got another stop to make. I'll be back in time for the fight, I promise.

I signed off and turned to Sage. "Can you escort them back? I need to do something."

Her eyes narrowed. "Uh-huh, like what?"

I cast around for an excuse that wouldn't make her more suspicious. I didn't have time to visit the Hub . . . "I owe you a present," I said. "For your heroic above-the-call-of-duty efforts to keep me from killing myself too often. I'm going to talk to someone about it and I don't want to ruin the surprise."

"Oh, in that case, sure." She grinned at me and turned to the new recruits. "Come on with me. I'm going to introduce you to Juana. You make sure you're nice to her. Mama Grace is her actual mother and she's like the scary boss lady, so don't get on her bad side."

I slipped out of the restaurant and sent a message to Warren Black. *I'm free. Where do we meet?*

The reply came back at once. *Two blocks left, three blocks toward the elevator. Look for the shack with the hubcap hanging over the door.*

CHAPTER FOURTEEN

FOUR TIPS FOR HANDLING SNAKES: NUMBER ONE: DON'T

The ramshackle two-story hut still bore the hammer-and-axe logo of the Free Human League, but they'd changed from the red and black color scheme they'd used under Waters to a green and blue. It was more restful and made me think of Earth, which had probably been the plan.

I stepped through the door, my senses on alert. No violence was allowed on Threshold—enforced by the system—but I wasn't sure if that extended to "we grab you and tie you to a chair until you do what we want." I'd shout for Grandpa as soon as that happened, if it did, but it would be awfully embarrassing for me.

Warren and his wife, Linsey, were waiting just inside. They looked nervous. I nodded to them. "How's it going? Backstab and betray anyone recently?" I was still angry about how they had pretended to be on our team before trying to serve us up to Waters on a dish. They could have gotten me or my family killed.

"I'm sorry about that," Linsey said. "Waters had a way of making things seem right. I know now we never should have done what we did."

"Seeing as you're here on his behalf, I don't know that I believe you."

"Oh, trust me, we're clear on what we're doing this time." Warren held up a hand. "Waters still has some supporters in my coalition. They persuaded me to help him arrange this meeting, that's all. He's upstairs."

"Then why are you here?"

"Because we betrayed you once, and we owe it to you this time to make sure he doesn't try anything," Linsey said. She crossed her arms and thrust her chin out. "I said we wouldn't be any part of this unless we were here to make sure it's all right."

"If I could trust you, that'd probably be reassuring." I shrugged and sent Grandpa a message. *Going to talk to Waters now. If you don't hear from me in fifteen minutes, shout at Veda.* "See you around, Black." I climbed the staircase at the back of the room, leaving the Blacks behind.

The upstairs was all one large, dimly lit room. The wood had a pale blue tint to it, and I recognized it as a resource harvested from one of the phase one farming levels. Cylabor trees had a valuable heartwood that could be used for armor, and a lot of people in Threshold had started building structures from the less valuable outer layers. They were bizarre trees with perfectly cubic cross sections. I'd seen a forest of them once, like some sort of computer's idea of the perfect grove, all right angles and harsh lines.

Drapes covered the windows, seemingly salvaged from Earth scraps. One of the windows had a yellow-and-black flag repurposed as a covering, the other a dingy blanket.

Waters waited for me in the center of the room, sitting in a rolling office chair. He had his hands flat on his lap. There was a three-legged metal stool off to one side. Otherwise the room was bare, but there had been more furniture here recently. Lighter colored square patches along the walls showed where shelves or something similar had rested.

Waters was wearing his dress uniform, same as the other night. If he was trying to impress me, he had failed. I folded my arms and leaned against the wall, ignoring the stool. "I'm here. Start talking."

Waters said nothing for a moment. He let out a loud sigh. "You have a way of fucking things up, Williams."

"I hope so."

He passed a hand over his face, looking old and tired. For a minute I got a glimpse of the man he'd been a year ago. What I knew about him told me that Waters was a similar age to my grandpa, and that like Grandpa he'd been terminally ill when the system picked him. Unlike Grandpa, he was a complete asshole, and I'd have been happier if the aliens had chosen literally anyone else on the planet. He'd even apparently gotten his fellow abductees killed during the initiation chamber event.

Team Twofeather had lost one person who was abducted with us, but in fairness, Delores would have probably picked Social Worker as her class choice and we were all better off without her meddling.

"I have work to do," I said as Waters stayed silent. "So you can talk, or I can walk."

"I know you think badly of me, Captain Williams. Mustangs always regard career officers with suspicion, and you have not been properly equipped to make the sort of difficult decisions that are necessary here."

I held up a hand. "Okay, this sort of bullshit is exactly what I am not here for. The fact that I started as an enlisted man just means I know how to work for a living. I have perfect respect for those who've earned it. Like my grandfather, *Major* Twofeather. And we're working under the direction of a colonel, who outranks you both, and we're half a million miles from Earth and the American chain of command is pretty damn thin out here, so if that's all you're going to say, I'm out of—"

"You are pissing off some important people. I'm here on their behalf, to issue a warning and to make an offer." Waters was still sitting. He looked tired, defeated.

"Is it Proxima? I don't want to hear what those assholes have to say."

"It doesn't matter what you want, it matters what they can do to you. To us. All of Earth. Proxima, Alabaster Sky, and ConSweGo divvied up the spoils from this engine *years* before they ever arrived in our system. They let their smaller cousins take a piece of the action, like your friend Veda, because it's convenient for them. That doesn't mean they are letting us in on it. You are throwing a wrench in their plans, and if you don't stop, all of Earth is going to suffer."

"Dramatic much?" I paced around to the other side of the room, lifted the blanket curtain, and glanced down into the street below. A couple of miners were trudging along, carrying a heavy basket between them. "We know the best outcome is to pick up a fraction of one percent of the ownership of the Reality Engine. It's our engine, why shouldn't we try for a piece?"

"You're making these corporations look incompetent on the galactic stage at a period when they, Proxima especially, are desperately raising funds and backers for their next exploit."

I made a mental note to ask Veda if she knew what he was talking about. "So sorry."

"You will be. Letting an indigenous species actually beat their contracts and take a fraction of ownership? They'll be humiliated. Proxima has asked me to spell things out very clearly here. You know what their plans are for the Engine?"

"Yeah. Subdivisions and condos. Move a couple trillion aliens in."

"That's the good option. Bad option is they turn on the construction option instead. Make this whole place a manufacturing facility for starships and stations like the Hub."

"That's an option?" I turned back away from the window. "Really?"

"So they tell me, and they showed me proof."

"I don't see why that's so bad. Might keep the system from being so crowded."

"Are you really that slow, Williams? Where do you think the Reality Engine would get the matter it needs for large-scale construction?"

I shrugged. "I dunno, everything about this seems like black magic."

"It can't just create from nothing, you know. It's efficient but not that good. The Reality Engine will harvest matter from the rest of the solar system and use it to turn out ships by the hundreds of thousands."

I felt a chill run up my spine. "Matter. Like—planets?"

"Now you're getting it."

"Surely there's a law against that. I mean, they weren't allowed to kidnap all of Earth, just a fraction of us, because they have rules about indigenous species."

"That's right, and feel free to run this past your alien friends. They won't touch Earth. That would be against the rules, to consume a planet with intelligent life on it. Our *moon*, on the other hand—"

I groaned, seeing the implications. Without our moon, Earth would undergo ecological disaster. The loss of tides, for one thing—and I had some vague idea that the moon interacted with plate tectonics, too. Plus it would probably screw with nocturnal species and who knew what else. "Really? They'd do that out of spite?"

"You want to bet they won't?" Waters looked me over. At last he stood up, with a ponderous reluctance that made me imagine him as a much heavier, less able man. "Proxima recognizes your personal skills. They've authorized me to make you an offer similar to what they gave me. That's you, Williams, not your grandfather. Be sure you get that."

I wasn't going to accept a damn thing from Waters or Proxima, but I'd learned that information was a valuable resource. "Make it."

"You persuade your coalition to forfeit this phase. We'll arrange for a nice buyout for your closest dozen or so allies. Cushy retirements, regular rejuvenations. They can apparently look forward to three centuries of life, by the way, with all their needs tended before the ethereum toxicity gets too great. Not too bad compared to seventy years of disease-ridden existence."

"Yeah, sure," I said.

"I get it. That's not enough for you. You're a man of action. Proxima knows that. They like it. They want to offer you a place on one of their future exploit teams."

I caught my breath. Mak'gar had implied a similar deal, but hearing it from Waters was another thing. "What, and do to other worlds what was done to ours? Move in and take their stuff, force them into servitude, all for our own profit?"

"Someone's going to do it. We don't make the rules, we just play by them."

As long as he was being open and honest, I wanted to see how much I could get. "They make you the same deal? What are you getting here?"

Waters's eyes unfocused. He suddenly looked almost pensive. "They need people they can trust, liaising with Earth. We'll be neighbors. Someone who understands both our needs and theirs will be a perfect go-between."

So Waters would get to be puppet-king of Earth. He'd more or less accused Grandpa of having those sort of ambitions, back at the big party. Made sense he was already thinking along those lines.

I felt ill, like the room was suddenly too stuffy. Being this close to Waters made me want to punch someone, probably him. "Okay, great, thanks for the word of warning. I'll take it under advisement."

"You'd better decide fast. Proxima has teams in your valley. If you get in their way, they're going to be even angrier."

"Sure." I checked the time and mentally swore. "Anyway, I've got to get back. I promised to peel a bunch of potatoes for Mama Grace. You know how we uppity enlisted types are good at that manual labor."

His face was red. "You really think you're clever, don't you?"

"Nope. Just good at doing what I'm told. Talk to you later, Major. Or hopefully not. Enjoy your second retirement." I headed back down the stairs without waiting for Waters to respond.

As soon as I was out on the street, I took a big breath of fresh air, or at least what passed for fresh inside an enormous cavern miles below the surface of Ganymede. Then I started sending messages to Veda as I walked back to our portal, reporting on what Waters had told me and asking her for her opinion.

She didn't take long to respond. *Yes, the ruling coalition could try to change the zoning classification from residential to commercial. They'd lose a lot of money. We have more shipbuilding capacity than there's demand, and people are always looking for slots in a less crowded engine.*

How come? What's the advantage?

More processing power per user means a more detailed experience, plus your waiting list for kids is shorter.

What about the idea that we're making them look bad?

The reply took a minute. I wondered if she was hesitating. *That is . . . possible. I'm not really tuned into galactic news, but . . . Proxima pulled strings with my family to put pressure on me. I ought to be about as far beneath their notice as you are. And they are looking at a potentially historic exploit coming up, with the rogue world they told us about. I'll look into it.*

Wait, what sort of pressure? You mean your mom showing up?

I'll explain later. You've got work to do, right? Give me a day or three, and please trust me, if you can. Good luck with Podaga.

That was a brush-off if I'd ever heard one. I let Grandpa know I'd be back in five minutes and stepped up my pace.

CHAPTER FIFTEEN

HOW TO DROP A BOMBSHELL

We were preparing to go to war. By the time I got back, the briefing was well underway. Arjun, Juana, and Grandpa stood on the steps outside the old church building, addressing the assembled team in the square. They had pulled a pair of whiteboards from who knows where and had doodled all over them with black and red markers. I slipped into the crowd and took up a position in the back as Juana addressed the assembled group.

"I'm sending out the team assignments now," she said. "Go ahead and pull them up."

I received a message notification. When I pulled it up, it informed me I had been assigned to the Long-Ranged Damage Dealers Team and also to Melee Team Alpha, whatever that meant. I decided to wait for an explanation before asking any questions.

I glanced around the crowd assembled near the decorative bit in the middle of our outpost. There were at least fifteen people here who I had never seen before, but also plenty of reassuringly familiar faces.

All of Team Mongoose were here, and so were the members of Ragtag that I had gotten used to working with during phase two. There were a bunch of other acquaintances I had run missions or achieved objectives with, too, stretching all the way back to the beginning.

Frank stood near the front of the crowd, his hat pushed back on his shiny, sweaty face, listening intently. Grandpa pointed to one of the two whiteboards. It had four red symbols on it and a diagram that I thought was supposed to represent the area outside Podaga's hut.

"Once the bannik are down," he said, "our first real challenge is going to be taking on the four knights inside the bathhouse. If it goes the way it did for the dwarves, they'll come out and engage with us themselves. Our goal is to control the encounter. Each of the knights, we are giving a code name. There's Axe, Shield, Spear, and Sword."

Someone in the crowd shouted, "It was a polearm, not a spear!"

"Yeah," Grandpa said, "but 'spear' is faster to say. I am aware that two of them were using swords. The one with a shield is called Shield. The other one is Sword. Got it?"

He didn't bother to wait for an answer. "We've got four different people here with the ability to get in the face of one of those four. They've all been assigned." He listed off three names that I didn't recognize, each of the three raising their hands as he introduced them. There were two men, Javier and Dante, and a woman, Marilla. I committed their names to memory.

"And Frank Young will be on Spear," Grandpa concluded.

Frank scowled but said nothing.

"Their jobs are to drag one of the knights to each corner of the clearing. Here, here, here, and here," he said, pointing at positions on the crude map. "Then they'll keep the attention of their chosen knight. The heals team will be here and here."

He made more marks toward the center of the area but about ten yards apart.

"We're splitting into two just in case these knights have any area-of-effect abilities we didn't see from the dwarves. Heal team, you'll be listening to Alison and taking her orders. It's absolutely critical you do."

"That's right," Juana said calmly. "Because she's going to be the one who is monitoring the whole situation. She might make a call that you have doubts about. You've got to do what she says. Sometimes she might even call for you to let someone die that you could have helped. Keep in mind, deaths aren't permanent. They'll respawn right back here, safe and sound. But a wrong move at a critical time could take out our whole team, and then we'd have to wait twenty-four hours before trying again."

Dwight and two of his helpers were passing through the crowd, handing out gear. Crafter Sue gave me a bag. I transferred it into my inventory, then checked the contents. A stack of our newly improved healing potions, including a flask of "Resist Lightning" and another that was a "double the effect of all resists for ten seconds" buff. I stored both in my potions belt, filling the sixth and seventh slots there.

"You have to equip the belt yourself," Sue said, and moved along to the next miner before I could ask what it was for.

I pulled out the "Belt of Grounding" from the bag and examined it.

[Item crafted by Sue Daniels of Misfits Guild
This is an Ablative Item. Upon the death of the wearer,
the item is destroyed.

**When struck by lightning, direct 80%
of the damage back on the caster.]**

It was a two-inch-wide, shiny snakeskin belt with a tacky gold buckle. I was already wearing a potions belt, my gun belt, and the actual belt holding up my BDUs. Another would make me look ridiculous.

I got a message from Juana. *Shad, you've got that distracted, clueless look again. Put the belt on, we've got a specific job for you. I'll send you the details once we're done with the briefing.*

I'm going to look ridiculous, I replied as I strapped the belt on under my coat.

None of us are winning any fashion competitions here.

Says the woman in the cute sundress and knee boots, I retorted.

I didn't think you'd noticed. She looked away and I tried to focus on the briefing again.

"We can't afford failure," Grandpa said. "We've had one other team show up and try to take on Podaga while we've been waiting. They seriously underestimated his abilities and only brought about twelve people. We've got more than twice that. But none of us are used to working with each other in quite this way. Ordinarily, I'd try to reassure you all, let you know that it's okay if we mess up, that we'll try again later. The truth is, we don't have that luxury. If we don't get in there today and take Podaga down, someone else will. That'll put us behind the curve on this whole phase."

All around the square, people were nodding.

"Now then," Grandpa said, "everybody keep comms clear. We've got designated people whose job it is to watch the fight and communicate back with the team here and with the rest of you who are fighting. Other than that, you need to keep the channels open. Do you understand? If you're asked a direct question, reply. But there's too many of us, and if we're all talking, no one's listening.

"I also want to let you know that I expect some of us will end up going down during the course of this. Those knights were a hard bunch for the dwarves to take out, and then Podaga ripped through all of them like wet tissue paper. We've got a plan for him, too, but we've got to get through the knights first with as few casualties as possible. Play it smart. If you've got the ability to save yourself from death, use it. Don't wait for us to tell you so. But if you're doing something that puts someone else at risk, don't do it. Any questions?"

To my surprise, about eight different hands went up.

Juana stepped forward and pointed. "Yes, Bob, go ahead."

"Do we think our personal debuffs will work on these guys?"

"Good thinking," Juana said. "We hope so. We know that your Lost in Translation skill is really good, so throw that as soon as the knights come out. We'll have someone watching to see what impact it has."

Sage puffed up. "Me!" she called. "She means me. I'm on overwatch. Since my Tame probably won't work on those knights anyway, the big meanies."

That broke the tension a little bit. A wave of laughter passed over the crowd. Grandpa and Juana fielded a few more questions. Then Grandpa started down the steps.

"Let's move out," he said. "We should have a couple dozen of our creep in position now. No sense wasting any more time."

Just then, the system voice broke in.

[Attention, all veterans of phase two from planet Earth.]

Grandpa froze in midstep.

[The promised reward for your performance in phase two is now being announced. This is your 48-hour warning.]

For some reason, my heart was hammering. I saw the looks of confusion and a little bit of fear mirrored on every face I saw around me.

[All human miners whose performance exceeded the baseline during phase two, whether through direct contribution or calculated contribution points, have been notified already that they are receiving a special reward. Forty-eight hours from now, all recipients of the special reward will receive a Day Pass.]

I could hear the capital letters in the system's announcement. "Day Pass." My mind was blank. What was a Day Pass? What was it talking about?

I heard a low murmur of voices around me, sounding more and more worried. Grandpa had a hand against the rail of the church steps. He looked white as a ghost.

[Recipients of a Day Pass will be transported back to Earth for a single 8-hour period, 48 hours from now. At the end of that period, they will be transported back to Threshold to resume phase three activities. Recipients of a Day Pass cannot save the pass for later or decline this honor. Recipients will be returned to the spatial location from which they were first removed from Earth.]

I felt like someone had just punched me in the gut. Back to Earth? They were sending us back to Earth? Was that even possible?

I looked around. Sage was nowhere to be seen. Grandpa still looked like he'd been stunned. My eyes met Juana's, and I was surprised to see she looked terrified.

**[Miners who have received an upgraded reward will be
allowed a longer period of time on Earth. Miners who reached
the top 3% of performers have been given a 3-Day Pass and
will be transported anywhere on planet Earth that they desire.]**

A private notification popped up for me.

**[Congratulations, Miner Shad Williams. You are a recipient
of a 72-Hour Leave Pass. This includes transport to the
Earth location of your choosing and back to Threshold at the
end of the pass. All your ethereum needs will be handled for you.
You will have no access to any system-based subroutines
or storage abilities during your trip to Earth.]**

I waded through the crowd toward Grandpa as everyone around me went absolutely insane. About half the field was crying. One woman was shaking her head. "Why not me?" she was saying, while another man near her was mumbling, "I can't go back. I can't go back," over and over again.

I reached the church steps. Juana had descended down to where Grandpa was standing.

"This is an absolute fucking disaster," Grandpa said grimly. "They couldn't have come up with a better way to take the wind out of our sails if they'd tried. This is going to play absolute havoc with all of our plans."

"It might not be so bad," Juana said. "We've got a lot of recruits who weren't very active in phase two. We'll probably have a team left behind—"

"Who'll be bitter and resentful that they didn't get to go. Meanwhile, all our best players are out of the game for eight to fucking seventy-two hours," Grandpa said bitterly, leaving everyone else to pull out ahead of us.

I was surprised at his vehemence, though I understood his worries. Still, home. I was going home. For seventy-two hours, but still, to see Earth again. To be around other people who weren't part of this insane life I had been living for the past year.

I looked at Juana and saw only fear and worry on her face.

"Uh, sorry," I said. "Did you not get selected?"

She shook her head. "I've got a seventy-two-hour pass," she said quietly. "Mama just sent me a note saying she's got an eight-hour pass, and my sister, Rosa, didn't get picked."

"Ah, damn, I'm sorry."

"I'm sending a message to Veda telling her to put a stop to this," Grandpa said angrily.

"Hang on," I said. "I know this throws us off, Grandpa, but it'll be nice to see the old place again."

"I have no interest in seeing anything or anyone on that planet again," he snapped. "What am I supposed to do? Go see the place where my house used to be? No, thank you."

I was saved from trying to answer by Sage. She came pushing through the crowd, her face alight.

"You got the seventy-two-hour pass, too, right, Shad?" she burbled. "And Grandpa?"

We nodded.

"Great," she said. "Because I know just where I want to go, and I want you two to come along with me."

"As long as it's not the goddamn Strip," Grandpa growled.

"No," Sage said, bouncing up and down. "I took a look at the timing, and it's perfect. We'll have to make contact once we get back on Earth, but it'll work out just fine. I've been getting some of the live news updates from Veda, you know, the information packets, so I checked the dates, and it's right. Orange Dream is performing in Southern California in four days! We can see them, and we can go to the beach and the amusement parks! I've been wanting to go to Wizard World ever since I was nine, and now I actually can!"

"Wait, what?" I said. "Who's Orange Crash?"

Sage rolled her eyes. "Orange Dream. They're a K-pop band, Shad."

"You say that like I should know what that is."

"Korean boy band," Juana filled in. "Very popular with, uh . . ." She glanced at Sage and then back at me. "Young teen girls, generally."

"Oh, hell no," I said. "If I'm getting dragged back to Earth, there's no way that I'm spending my time in Southern California listening to a boy band."

"Doesn't matter," Grandpa said. "I'm gonna tell Veda to find a way to put a stop to this."

"Louis," Juana said, putting a hand on his arm. "That's all well and good, but I suggest you don't say anything like that to the team right before we go take on Podaga."

Grandpa snorted. "What do you mean? I'm supposed to go take down a boss with the kind of emotional turmoil everybody here is in?"

"We don't have a choice," I said. "Sage, can you cast Cowgirl Cheer on the whole crowd?"

"Absolutely!" She leapt up to the porch, and I felt her buff settle over me, calming my nerves. I put my fingers to my lips and whistled, long and loud and hard. The hubbub in the crowd began to die down. I whistled again.

"All right, everybody!" I shouted. "Nice of the system to offer us a paid vacation, but it's still two days away, and we've got work to do before then. So, everybody sober up right now. Let's get out there and show that sorcerer what we're made of."

CHAPTER SIXTEEN

TEN TIPS FOR SURVIVING A LIGHTNING STRIKE

Once I'd calmed down a little, I remembered my new belt and messaged Grandpa and Juana as we made our way toward Podaga's bathhouse. *So what do I do with this belt?*

Right, you're integral to this plan, Juana said. *First off, it's critically important you do not get killed by the bannik or the knights. We need you to help get the Podaga fight started right. We'll need a minute to reposition everyone, and we're concerned about that first lightning attack, so Arjun and I came up with a plan.*

I had a sinking feeling. *I'm not going to like this, am I?*

What are you talking about? You'll love it. You get to be the hero, Grandpa said. *You'll probably die pissing your pants, but I'll ask Jones to edit that out of the after-action recap so nobody will know.*

Great. Thanks.

Juana gave me my instructions.

Well, that sounds incredibly painful but straightforward, I sent back. *Right, let's do this.*

As we had hoped, a bunch of our minions were milling around by the lure we had placed earlier. Our outpost spawned a steady stream of creep, mostly skeleton pirates and cannibal pigs riding velociraptors. I had hoped that the creep theme would change in phase three, but it seemed like we were stuck with the creatures we had gotten used to on our phase two island.

Frank and the other three tanks were equipping the Day-Glo orange vests Dwight had made them. The vests increased their threat considerably and made it so once a mob had focused on them, they were unlikely to lose that mob's attention.

Under Jones's camouflage, Sage, Alison, Bob, Annie, and I snuck forward. I had a brand-new creep lure in my hand, ready to place.

Now my advance team was approaching Podaga's hut, ready to start the fight. As we reached the edge of the grass, I tensed, waiting for someone or something to give us away. There was no movement from the bathhouse. I planted the lure in the grass just at the edge of the clearing, and we snuck back. I sent Grandpa a message. *Lure planted. Destroy the old one.*

Done, he replied a moment later. *You should have company in a minute.*

It was actually about two minutes before the first of the creep arrived. I Tipped my Hat to each of them as they approached. Annie used her Hat for Your Rabbit ability on one of the pig chieftains, doubling his stats and his height as well. "Time to ring the doorbell," I whispered.

Jones pulled a sniper rifle with a telescopic sight from his inventory. He dropped to the ground and set the rifle up, pointing at the door. He set his eye to the scope. A moment later, he fired just one shot.

There was a high-pitched whine as the round shot forward. It struck the door of Podaga's bathhouse, right in its center, splintering the bright blue painted door and drilling a hole straight through it.

I held my breath. Eight seconds later, the door burst open and the bannik swarmed out. There were six of them, same as before, wielding buckets and brooms. They poured out into the clearing, then looked around slightly comically just as our creep reached the lure.

The bannik howled and raced forward. Our creep let out various cackles, whoops, and grunts as they joined the fight.

Sage cast Cowgirl Cheer. I pulled half a dozen different buffing items out of my inventory and began applying them to our creep, including a wand we'd gotten from the treasure vault in phase two.

The bannik were each more than a match for any individual one of our creep, but the creep outnumbered the bannik six to one. I watched with my teeth on edge, wanting to jump in and intervene. When the third bannik was down, I messaged Grandpa. *All right, move everyone into position.*

We're on our way, he replied. *Do not engage until we're there.*

I know, I said. It would be better to have something disastrous happen to our creep then have to take the bannik out ourselves, rather than me start the fight too early and risk having the knights out of position.

I heard rustling and the crackling of footsteps as our team got into position. "Give me a boost into the tree, Shad," Sage said. I helped her up into the branches of a nearby pine tree where she would be on lookout.

It was time for me to join one of the clusters of long-ranged damage dealers. We were positioned on the far west side of the clearing. I didn't like being so far from the action. There wouldn't be much I could do if things went wrong.

I was thinking about this all wrong, I scolded myself. Grandpa, Juana, even our new ally, Alison, had made it clear: This kind of fight wasn't about one person's heroic abilities. This fight was about working as a team. I could do that.

No, really, I could.

As the last bannik fell, our four tank volunteers got into position. I could see Frank's face pretty well, even though he was a good forty feet from me, at the southeast side of the clearing. He was sweaty and nervous-looking. His duty weapon was in his right hand, and he kept wiping his forehead with his left.

The other three tanks were the newbies, Javier, Marilla, and Dante. I hadn't yet had time to see what their classes were, but Javier was wearing a little red half-cape and an enormous black-and-silver hat, something like a sombrero, but not quite the same. He looked like an old-fashioned Spanish bullfighter to me. Well, I'd seen more ridiculous classes.

Marilla pulled a wooden shield as tall as she was out of her inventory. It looked like a piece of plywood with metal loops strapped to the back. The front of it was painted with the words "Trespassers will be eaten."

Dante was lacing up a pair of bright green sneakers. He wore a bright green windbreaker as well. Neither gave me any clue as to what his class might be.

They stepped into the clearing as the last of the bannik died. And just in time, because the four knights appeared in the doorway exactly like before, dressed in their armor and their bright blue capes with the shield-bearer standing at the front.

The four tanks strode forward in a line. Frank was half a step back from the other three. I could tell he was nervous. Probably the others were, too, but I couldn't read them as well.

The knights advanced down into the clearing as a unit. Javier stepped forward. His cape was now in his hands, and he shook it at the broadsword-bearing knight. It worked. The knight raised his sword and broke away from the pack. Javier darted back toward the northwest side of the clearing. Marilla screamed and hurled a small, round, bright pink plastic ball at the shield-bearer. The ball exploded all over the knight's shield, coating it with bright pink sparkles. It seemed to enrage the knight and lured him off to another corner.

Now Frank and Dante were facing the last two. Frank shuddered. He shouted something indistinct, but it didn't seem to attract either knight's attention. Javier reached down and scooped up a wad of grass and earth. He threw it at the axe-wielder, catching the knight on his face guard. The knight started for Javier, who got him into position. Frank yelled again and then unleashed his Restraint ability on the pike-wielding knight.

"Now!" Grandpa yelled, and we broke into action. The healer teams ran forward, positioning themselves in the middle of the clearing, where they would have the best view of everything that was going on.

Alison stood between the two groups, her hands raised as she shouted back and forth. They had a private healer chat channel as well, or so Alison had said. I wasn't a healer, so I focused on my own job, which was to take down the knight we had called "Pike" as hard and fast as possible.

I started shooting, adding my damage into the incredible barrage that chewed into the knight, dropping him a good ten percent of his health in the first five seconds of the fight. Then he seemed to use an ability of his own, jumping back up in health. I hoped Sage had gotten a look at what he had used. She was supposed to be relaying information back to our team at the outpost, so they could analyze what skills were being used and give us counters for them.

That's not my job right now, I reminded myself. *Focus on the target.*

The problem was, I had a lot of really useful abilities for spreading my damage around, doing a little here and there, chipping away, but I didn't have much that was good for this sort of fight, where I was just supposed to stand on the side and blast holes and things.

I forced myself to maintain my position and took shot after shot at Pike. Some of my allies had much more interesting abilities. An enormous red-and-blue gorilla appeared behind the knight and began attacking him from behind, grabbing one of his arms and twisting it backward. The knight was still furiously focused on Frank, swinging his polearm one-handed.

Someone else filled the clearing with a cloud of ice crystals. "Cut that out," Grandpa ordered on the raid-wide chat. "Nothing that impairs anybody's vision, and avoid water-based spells."

We were pretty sure that Podaga's lightning would have a greater effect with water involved. It felt like a cheat. Here I was with an invulnerability to water, and Podaga could just zap me as easily as anyone else.

We had Pike nearly halfway down now. "Melee, go," Grandpa ordered.

The two different melee groups charged in, six miners in each. The one led by Grandpa surrounded Pike, swinging at him while trying to stay out of the way of Frank and the giant gorilla.

Frank's Restraint had faded by now. We had told him to keep Posse in reserve for later. Still, the pikeman kept stabbing at Frank, courtesy of the special Day-Glo orange vest Dwight had given him and the other three tanks.

I kept trying to watch the whole fight. One of the other tanks was dropping dangerously low, but then a couple of the healers focused on him and brought him back up. Alison was doing her job well, so I just needed to do mine. I gritted my teeth and shot another Barrage at Pike. He was nearly down. I kept my focus on him until the knight disappeared in a wave of sparks. Sage let out a whoop I could hear from clear across the clearing.

"Melee Team Alpha, attack Shield," Grandpa ordered as he charged. The other melee team was still fighting against Axe. Now two of the knights began to drop in quick succession. Our analysis team had ranked Frank as the weakest of the four tanks, with Javier as the strongest, so we had decided to take out the knights in that order.

I guess we were settling into a rhythm, because things were going smoothly. Then one of the melee miners cut it a little too close. She ran in with a cudgel and struck at Axe, who shifted his attention briefly from Dante to her. One quick strike obliterated her. "It's alright," Grandpa called. "We're still in this. Stick with it, team."

I kept my focus up, but that one mistake led to another and then another. Three of us went down in the next twenty seconds. Two melee fighters and one of the healers, who ran up close to try to apply a touch-based heal to the targeted damage dealer. I could hear Alison shout over the combat from here, "Focus! Keep your assigned targets!"

Axe went down. Melee Team Beta ran to help Javier face off against Sword.

A moment later, Sword went down too. "Melee Team Alpha, retreat," Grandpa ordered. "You'll just get in Beta's way. Get ready to engage Podaga in a minute."

That was my cue to step out of my concealment and take up a place near the door. As Misfits took out Shield, I readied myself, reviewing my assignment.

Podaga stepped through the door, readying his speech. His hands were raised to the sky, broom clutched in one of them, as he began to invoke the lightning.

I cast High Noon on him and breathed a sigh of relief when the skill activated. I had been a little worried that this wouldn't count as a duel.

Podaga looked incensed. "What foul villainy is this?" he roared. "How dare you!"

"Everyone in position," I called. "Heal up. Let me know when you're ready."

Grandpa and Alison were shouting orders, moving people around, while Podaga ranted and raved at the sky. Two of our support casters came in, casting area-wide heat spells that dried up the dew on the grass and sent a sizzling fog upward. It was uncomfortably warm for a few minutes. When the steam stopped rising, they backed away.

"All right," Grandpa said. "Go ahead."

I took a deep breath, downed my lightning resistance potion and then the one that made it do double duty for ten seconds, cast Call 'em Out on Podaga, and then shot him with the biggest, most powerful boom round Sage had made.

As High Noon ended, Podaga thrust his broom in my direction. A solid beam of lightning struck me, but we had been counting on that.

The Belt of Grounding that Sue had made me shook and let out a teapot-whistling sound. The lightning zapped me head to toe, making my teeth ache and my skull rattle. My health began to drop precipitously. At the same time, it set up a resonance, sending a beam of lightning back at Podaga. I could see it shaking his broom.

As my health dropped toward zero, I had the satisfaction of watching the broom disappear, exploding into chunks of wood and burning greenery and taking Podaga's hand with it. The sorcerer lost ten percent of his health in that burst.

Unfortunately, the blast wave finished me off. A minute later, I respawned back at our outpost and hurried to join Juana and Arjun, who were watching the rest of the fight. "How's it going?" I asked breathlessly. "Think I could make it back in time to help?"

"No way," Juana said, shaking her head. "Even running would take you, what, twenty minutes to get there? It'll all be over before then. Oh, he's gearing up for another lightning blast!"

She leaned forward and whispered something into the microphone. I tried to watch what was going on.

We were seeing the feed from Jones's drone and another off Sage's spy cam. Most of the rest of the raid team were also wearing the All-Seeing Eyes, but when I tried pulling them up, I saw it was just a jumble of blurry action. Sage and Jones definitely had the best views.

I gritted my teeth and fumed as the team took down Podaga without me. After a minute, when it was clear we were going to win, I took a deep breath, sighed, and turned to Juana. "I'm going to get back up there. We've got a rusalka to talk to."

She grinned at me. "Take it easy. I've got to pay the bill for all those respawns now, and you're way too trigger-happy."

"Hey!" That struck me as unfair. "You and Arjun specifically came up with a plan where I was going to get hit with a million volts of lightning, and now you blame me for dying?"

"Sage told me to be sure to give you a hard time about that." She winked. "Right, they're finishing up. Better hurry or you won't get any of the loot."

CHAPTER SEVENTEEN

ESCORT QUESTS AND OTHER SIGNS DEVELOPERS HATE YOU

About two minutes after I left the outpost, a notification popped up.

[Congratulations to Misfits Guild for vanquishing an optional opponent. Bonus rewards are being calculated.
You are the third group to take down one of the bonus bosses.
Reward earned: 50,000 XP per combatant.
250,000 soul coins.
Electricity-resistance crafting materials to be delivered to outpost.
Recipe: Enhanced elemental resistance potion.
Recipe: Enhanced cleansing potion.
Recipe: Enhanced elemental damage buff potion.
Recipe: Enhanced armor effects kit: Water resistance.
Recipe: Enhanced armor effects kit: Electric resistance.
Recipe: Enhanced armor effects kit: Water damage buff.
Recipe: Enhanced armor effects kit: Electricity damage buff.]

That was a fantastic set of rewards. I wondered if there were any more bosses that we could quickly hunt down and take out. I'd have to ask Dwight what the new recipes did, but I suspected we would find them very useful in the coming days. That XP boost was incredible too. It took me two-thirds of the way through level nine and ought to be good for several levels of experience for our lower-ranked people.

[Bonus reward. One skill seed per combatant who dealt, took, or healed damage during the fight to be delivered to the guild leader.]

And that could very well be even better. We had gotten very few skill drops since phase one. Now we'd have a treasure trove to help outfit our new allies.

**[Optional quest begun: Escort the captive rusalki back
to their home and sister.
Reward: Hidden Reward.
Reward: 100% bonus XP gain for the next two weeks.
Reward: One bonus skill per combatant.]**

And now the system was really falling all over itself to reward us. This was awesome. I grinned. Sage would be beside herself at the thought of getting a new skill.

**[Warning: This quest has a penalty for failure.
Failure penalty: No member of Misfits Guild may enter the
castle for two days after the doors open.
Quest must be approved by at least half of the combatants who
participated in the boss takedown.]**

Okay. That was slightly worrying. Anytime we'd had a quest during phase one, it had given great rewards. I didn't recall seeing any kind of negative penalty. A two-day delay would put us way behind everyone else. Was that worth the reward?

Everyone accept it, Grandpa said through the chat. I did, and a moment later, the quest text disappeared. Then another announcement popped up.

**[This is a zone-wide announcement. Misfits Guild
is attempting a bonus objective. Should they succeed,
they will be rewarded. Should they fail,
those who stopped them will receive a reward in their place.]**

Oh crap. So the system was screwing with us.

Juana sent frantically, *What just happened? We got a notification here. Everyone's going to be on you.*

I didn't answer her. Instead, I picked up my pace and sprinted through the woods toward Podaga's clearing. I was nearly back to the bathhouse already. We had not seen any messages like this in the last day, even though the system said two other bosses had been taken down. Maybe the others hadn't received a follow-up quest or hadn't bothered to accept it.

By the time I got back to the clearing, Grandpa was already busy organizing things. The three captive rusalki had emerged from the bathhouse, long white dresses dripping water and dark hair plastered against their heads. They were barefoot, which I hoped wouldn't be an issue.

"Alright, Shad," Grandpa was saying, "you're part of our scouting and mobile kill squad. We don't want to waste any more time than we have to. Everyone on the map is probably converging on us right now. It's about a mile back to the rusalki pond cross-country. Let's move and hope we can stay ahead of the rush."

One of the rusalki drifted toward us. "You are taking us home to our sister?" she asked.

"That's the idea, ma'am." I Tipped my Hat to her. "Just stick with us and we'll get you home."

"Then we shall set off at once," she said, then began walking through the little stream leading out of Podaga's bathhouse, her sisters close behind.

I groaned to myself. An escort quest. Great. "Ma'am, the quickest way is here." I pointed off into the woods.

She turned to me, her luminous eyes liquid and pleading. "We cannot stray so far from the water," she said. "Our feet must remain damp or we are done for."

Sage groaned. "How about we give you boots full of water?"

The rusalka and her sisters ignored the suggestion and continued following the stream.

"Get that drone in the air," Grandpa told Jones. "Scout the creek. Figure out how far it is to the rusalki pond and where the likely ambushes are. We're going to have to hope that nobody here knows they're stuck on the water, or this will be way too easy for anyone who wants to stop us. Shad. Bob. Annie. Lara. Hester." He looked around, pointing. "Frank and Will. All of you head that way. Take one of the healers with you."

The two girls I had met at Mama Grace's diner earlier were standing right by me. They giggled. I probably had a funny look on my face. "Which of you two can keep up with us and heal under stress?"

Lauren pointed at her blonde friend. "Macy's the one you want." They giggled again.

I wasn't so sure about this but I nodded anyway. "Alright, Macy. You're with us. Let's go. Team Ragtag Redux, move out."

As we set off along the stream, I kept watching my mini-map for any enemies while I quickly pulled up the ability lists of our new miners. They were all at level four, which, considering how much XP everyone had just gotten, probably meant they'd been level two at best a minute ago. That meant they had more than likely spent most of the last year as lotus eaters. Hester was a Non-Ironic Beat Poet, and Will was a Firefighter. At least Will had some straightforward abilities. All of Hester's were described in iambic pentameter.

Well, they were what I had to work with. At least they all had their starting abilities, even if they hadn't gained many skills or abilities in the time since.

"Anyone who's got any sort of camouflage detection, keep it going and yell if you spot anything," I said. I kept my own enhanced mini-map up, watching for enemy dots. I didn't always see through camouflage, but anyone else I'd see a quarter mile out.

I wished I had Jones, but I understood why Grandpa was keeping him. He would be able to help camouflage the main group. Plus, it was hard to fly the drone and fight at the same time.

"It's not a matter of *if* someone comes, it's *when*," I told them as we raced along the stream, stooping under overhanging branches. Hester tripped on a root and Annie helped her up.

Will kept up with me easily. He shot me a quick grin. "This is fun. Really, really fun. I should have come out of hiding months ago."

"Glad to have you along now." *Now that we've gotten the death penalty removed and it's all fun and games.* I still remembered phase one, where death was permanent and one wrong move might get me or my sister killed. But that was behind us now. I focused on the task at hand.

Grandpa sent me a private message. *I'm having the grignarian squad sweep around to our south, toward where we think several of the other outposts are located. They should give us warning, and I've told them to ambush anyone they see coming for us.*

Roger, I said.

It's not that I think they're going to backstab us now, Grandpa added, *but I can't be sure. Hopefully anyone who sees them will attack on sight and give us that much warning, at least.*

Yeah, they do seem to be pretty universally hated, I agreed.

We had made it about three hundred yards downstream when Hester spoke up. "Someone up ahead. I've got them on Pierce the Veil. You should see them in a sec here."

I checked the ability description. Yup, that was the one that said, "*A rhyme and a riddle, a cunning decree/Reveals hidden foes, with poet's decree.*" I got a B- in English my senior year, so I wasn't an expert, but that seemed like pretty awful poetry to me.

Not the critical thing right now. As the red dots appeared on my mini-map, I threw up a hand. Most of the team stopped right away, though Macy kept on until she walked into the back of Bob. "There's eight of them. Spread out," I shouted as the red dots appeared on my map. "Frank, remember how we handled the Quetzalcoatlus?"

"Got you, partner."

I activated Fastest Gun in the West and charged at the approaching group. As soon as I was close enough, I threw a Call 'em Out and yelled for Frank.

He hit his Emergency Responder ability, and with a disorienting switch, I found myself fifty feet back with a nice taunt on all of our enemies.

I ran a little farther before turning. There were eight of them, and four had pursued me right into the middle of our group. Bob threw Lost in Translation, confounding their abilities to work together. I hit the closest one to me with a Barrage and then targeted the farthest off, who was standing just behind three others. They were orcs, but not Firebrand. The four farthest off all had guns.

I used Trick Shot to send a Scatter Round at the farthest. This was a new toy Dwight and Sage had made me. The bullet would fragment on impact, seek out the nearest targets, and impart a short-duration fear that, depending on how well they resisted, would either have them trembling in their boots or running for cover. It was an incredibly expensive round, and one of the few that apparently worked better on miners than on NPCs. This was my first chance to use it, and I was delighted as it quickly scattered the rear guard.

Then I dove in toward the four that had gotten themselves in the middle of my group. Meanwhile, Frank had one of the farther ones Restrained. I decided to trust him to handle himself and focused on the closest set. Hester was laying down a quick beat, her Sonic Sonnet ability, which further disoriented the orcs while dealing sonic damage. Lara was throwing her orange grenades around merrily.

The closer four orcs all carried vibrating, glowing swords, so as soon as I got in range, I hit Never Bring a Knife to a Gunfight and they dropped their weapons. That trick wouldn't work on any group of miners more than once, but it worked beautifully now.

I followed up with a Trick Shot to one orc's wrist. I had a set of bullets that did a significant amount of localized damage rather than the more generic chipping away at a health pool, and this one blew his wrist off as he was reaching for his sword. Will screamed and ran in, wielding a fireman's axe and smashing the orc I had just disabled in the head.

The next orc over had drawn a knife. He stabbed Will's exposed back. Will only had [**60 HP**]. He probably hadn't had time to distribute his new stat points. I winced as half of his health was gone in one hit.

"Get him up!" I yelled to Macy, who extended a hand to Will and then pulled a baton from her inventory. She had been wearing a pair of sweatpants and a sweatshirt at Mama Grace's restaurant, but she had changed at some point.

Now she wore a short, blue skirt with pleats and an athletic top with a panther face in blue on it. I hadn't pulled up her profile before, since I had been trying to see what kind of offensive abilities Hester and Will had to work with, but it was pretty clear Macy was a cheerleader.

A beam of sparkling blue and white balls flew out of her baton toward the injured man, exploding as they hit him. Not balls, I realized. Pom-poms.

Sometimes the Reality Engine's specialized classes were a little silly. But then again, here I was running around a southern European forest in an outfit that would make Wyatt Earp feel embarrassed.

I shot the nearest orc a few more times. My team took some damage, but we had interrupted the ambushers before they had a chance to get in position.

We had six of them down before the last two managed to reclaim their weapons and take up a back-to-back defensive position. They cut down Will and almost killed Bob, but Macy's pom-pom barrage saved my Translator friend just in time.

I delivered a final headshot to the last orc. As the body sparkled and vanished, I sent a message to Grandpa.

It's clear for now. Keep coming.

We couldn't pause if we wanted to, Grandpa said grimly. *Once these gals got started, they won't stop. They're following the stream. I can see you from here, Shad. Get moving.*

I swore, gathered up what was left of my team, and started off again.

The grignarians reported in. *We have encountered the dwennan. Fifteen of them. We are accounting for ourselves.* It took me a minute to remember that the dwarves had referred to themselves at the party by that name. I also remembered how much they had hated the grignarians. Hopefully this was a grudge match that would occupy some time, but if there were two groups on us, there were probably more.

I kept up my pace. The rusalki pond appeared through the trees. We were almost there.

I pinged my map and then groaned, sending word back to Grandpa at once. *There's a whole bunch grouped up ahead of us. They've had time to dig in. At least fourteen. We're going to have to face them. They're right between us and the pond.*

Got another group on our tail, Grandpa reported. *Don't know if they're coordinated or just lucky.*

Send me who you can spare, I said.

A minute later, six more miners, including Sage, popped in. I knew most of them already. Jack and Esma waved hello. I hadn't seen them since the big phase one fight that had seen Misfits triumph over Major Waters. I pulled up what the newcomers could do, just as Juana sent me a quick message.

We've got a plan for you, Shad.

Am I going to like it?

You won't hate it, she replied, which I did not think was a particularly good sign.

You've got about thirty seconds before I go in myself.

Arjun's sending everyone the details, she said. A set of bullet points flashed up in my list.

I hope he's sending everyone else less.

You've got the overview. They just know what they need to do. Good luck, she said.

CHAPTER EIGHTEEN

RED ROVER AND OTHER CHILDREN'S PARTY GAMES

The enemy had been clever. Jones flew his drone overhead and gave us a quick estimate. Eight of the dwennan, four orcs—not from Congruent Paths, they were still honoring our noncompete—and three different animal people had teamed up together.

They had erected a temporary fortification, four feet high with six turrets facing outward. It looked like it was built out of the same sort of basic materials used for outposts in phase two. They had the generic silvery appearance that we had customized into being an old Western stockade.

I knew from experience that those defenses could take a lot of damage. A straight-up frontal assault would be suicide.

"We are really lucky you got that class evolution to Carpool Driver," I told Lara as we quickly grouped up. "Minivan only used to get us out of trouble, not into it."

"That's why I took it," she said tightly as I made sure everyone understood what was going on.

Juana had been right; I did like this plan. I was a little too fond of theatrics, if I was being honest. And this one catered to that failing beautifully.

I checked my cooldowns. Call 'em Out was ready again.

We had one ace up our sleeves that we hadn't used yet.

I turned to Frank. "Deputy? I mean, Sheriff," I amended, grinning at him as he raised an eyebrow. "You want to do the honors?"

He pulled his hat brim lower on his forehead and posed, arms akimbo, for just a moment. "Let's ride," he said as I refreshed my Hat Tip buff on my team.

Grandpa had sent both Smiths and Brown to me. They linked hands as Hester put her hand on Brown's shoulder, and then Tall Smith touched Lara's. That would let Lara transport them all with her.

Lara waited until Frank raised a hand and brought it down. She disappeared along with the forward team just as a pair of war elephants in armor painted red and black appeared in front of us. A couple of terrified-looking spear-wielding soldiers clung atop them.

The enemy popped their heads up past their barricade, firing laser rifles and explosive grenades at the elephants. One orc had a device that shot a rope out, trying to entangle the foremost elephant's leg, but it did not work like in the movies. The rope wrapped around one leg and the elephant just kept charging forward.

And as Frank was distracting them with the war elephants, Lara snuck our team in through the back of the enemy camp.

"Go!" I told the rest of us, and we charged in behind the elephants. The enemy team was shooting wildly as the elephants smashed against their barricades.

I needed to ask Frank sometime what the parameters were for his reinforcements. Sometimes he'd get no more than a pair of London Bobbies while other times he pulled out overpowered options like fighter jets or war elephants. I thought again and decided to make sure to ask him somewhere we weren't likely to be overheard. If the Reality Engine was shifting things in our favor, like sometimes I thought it was, it wouldn't be good to draw attention to that.

You've got about three minutes before the Drippy Sisters get there, Grandpa warned me.

We'll punch through, I promised. I deployed a particularly ridiculous item Dwight had made for me and which I had sworn I would never use, a bright silver whistle, put it to my lips, and blew.

A moment later I was several feet higher in the air, clinging to the back of a saddleless horse. I had my fingers tight in its mane. My gun went flying, but it didn't matter. I'd be able to use Quick Draw once I was where I wanted to be.

Dwight had called this the "Hi-Yo, Silver!" It was apparently accompanied by a spell that would draw enemy attention to it. It wasn't a taunt like my Call 'em Out. More like a "what the hell is that, I can't look away?" spell.

I clung on for dear life as the horse charged right past the elephants and up to the stockade. It planted its front feet and sent me flying over its head.

I landed like a gymnast dismounting from a balance beam, knees bent, arms extended. All those points in dexterity counted for something, at least. And as half a dozen alien heads turned to look my way, I Quick Drew my gun, shot the nearest dwarf in the face, and then cast Call 'em Out again.

Annie, go! I messaged frantically. A second later, I lurched six feet to the side and felt a wave of coolness wash over my body.

The aliens' heads didn't turn. Instead, they started shooting the exact replica of me who stood where I had been with a dumb grin on his face. It was like one of the Shad dummies I had used against old Squid Face come to a more detailed life.

The fake image of me waved his free hand and pointed his gun around wildly. Annie's recently acquired skill, Ventriloquist's Dummy, created an exact replica of someone on the spot while relocating them to a location of her choosing.

Now I called in my final card. *Okay, Jack, go for it.*

I stood waiting, and while I did, I checked on the team Lara had brought forward. They had reached the beach behind our enemy's defensive lines. Between me, Frank's elephants, and our oncoming charge, the aliens hadn't noticed them yet. They were all still facing toward us, aside from the couple that were trying to fill the fake version of me full of the alien equivalent of hot lead.

By now, the three members of Team Mongoose on the forward team had constructed their machine gun nest. Smith gave a thumbs-up at the smiling replica of me.

"Do it," I said, and they opened fire.

Their bullets didn't hurt me. Brown had a skill, Friendly Fire, which was a confusing name, because it meant actual friendly fire was impossible. I guess it made your fire more friendly. Whatever. It meant their bullets couldn't hit me, and that was all that mattered.

As they ripped into the aliens, some of the orcs turned and began shooting beam weapons toward Team Mongoose.

Too late.

I heard the earsplitting roar of artillery fire dropping down on my head. Good old Jack the Tank Driver had rejoined our offensive team for this one. We hadn't dared use his Artillery Barrage ability during the Podaga fight, since if somehow Podaga survived getting hit and all of us ended up dead, that would have been a bad thing. But now, with me as his target, he was raining incendiary shells down on our enemy.

As the first shell fell, I threw down a really, really expensive single-use item. This wasn't something Dwight had made. We had bought it from the galactics a while ago. It was a one-man, twenty-second invulnerability field, and it had cost almost fifty thousand soul coins. Right now, it let me stand in the middle of the camp for a couple of extra seconds while Jack rained down death.

By the time the shield was up, most of our enemies were dead.

Cease fire! Cease fire! I told Jack, then sprinted away from the destroyed enemy position as the last couple of shells fell.

Mongoose picked off the couple of alien stragglers who had made it out of the hellfire. I popped my head out from behind a tree and watched as the three rusalki meandered down their stream the rest of the way to the pond.

As their feet hit the water, a **[System Quest Complete]** box popped up. I cheered, and so did everyone else. Team Mongoose began disassembling their machine gun nest.

**[Mission successful.
Team Twofeather has led the Misfits Guild
to victory yet again. All the rest of you have failed.
Maybe you should start watching what Misfits
do instead of trying the same thing over and over again.
That's worked really well for you so far, hasn't it?]**

I thought the taunting was a bit much.

Grandpa called out to me as he approached the water. "Come say goodbye to the ladies."

I approached the pond as the rusalki embraced their sister, the one who had given us the quest. She disentangled herself from their watery limbs and turned to Grandpa and me. "How can I ever thank you for restoring my sisters to me and ending the reign of that cruel sorcerer?"

"Just doing our job, ma'am," I said.

"I have a great gift to give you," she said. She reached her hands out. There was a seashell on the palm of each hand. She held one to me. I accepted it. "To open your eyes," she said.

As I touched it, the seashell melted away. A system message popped up: **[All Inspect functions are now restored for your team members.]**

"Well, thanks," I said to the ceiling. "By reward, you mean give us back something that you stole from us in the first place? Really?" I shook my head as Grandpa accepted the other seashell. It, too, dissolved.

The message that popped up this time said, **[Creep is now immune to Seething Miasma.]**

Grandpa and I exchanged a look. "What's that?"

"No idea." He sent a message back to the command team. *Anyone know what Seething Miasma is?*

We're taking a look, Juana said. *But nobody recognizes it right off. Gabriel says it's not a Slavic myth thing. If you're done there, head back. We've got some interesting information to report. And there's probably still angry enemies out there. We don't need to pay a resurrection bill if we don't have to.*

"All right," Grandpa yelled. "Nice work, everyone. Back to camp. Stay close. I'll put in a takeout order from Mama Grace and we can all kick back and talk about what we did right and what we can do better next time."

"Next time?" I said to him in an undertone as Sage whooped and skipped ahead of the rest of us. "Which part of this is going to have a next time?"

"Certainly the boss fight," he pointed out. "You did good this time, Shad. You didn't even die."

I sighed. "Would have been cheaper if I had. Respawns don't cost a tenth of what that shell did."

"True, but we needed to make sure to get as many of the enemy down as possible," Grandpa said. He clapped me on the shoulder. "Come on, let's get back. There's a lot to talk about."

CHAPTER NINETEEN

WHEN PLANNING TO FAIL, ALWAYS CONSIDER THIS

Grandpa and I joined Juana, Arjun, Alison, Frank, Dwight, and a couple of our other command staff back inside the church over a nice after-dinner pitcher of something that tasted a lot like beer but was sadly lacking in alcohol.

"Between what our crafters have learned and other intel sources that Ames isn't revealing, we now know that the dwarves took down some sort of werewolf boss yesterday," Juana reported. "And the Congruent Paths team took out Baba Yaga this morning."

"Neither of them had follow-up quests?"

"We don't know. I mean, we know nothing popped up, but whether they chose to turn down a quest, weren't offered a quest, or we just weren't given the chance to oppose their quest, we can only guess. For now, we have to assume that we're all roughly neck and neck. They took down their bosses sooner than we did, but we had the bonus quest, which was pretty successful."

Arjun was sitting perched on a stool with a whole pile of little round skill seeds in front of him. He had an enormous magnifying glass and was examining them, then turning to consult a piece of paper on Juana's clipboard next to him. "What are you doing?" I asked.

He held up the magnifying glass. "This is an item we traded for. It came from a treasure vault on phase two, like the one you raided. It is able to analyze a skill seed and determine what sort of ability it is likely to give." He frowned. "The details are rather vague, though. They tend to fall into a couple of categories, whereas the skills we actually have are, as you have noticed, personalized and unique."

"Yeah," I said. "And I might be wrong about this, but I think that's unusual when it comes to Reality Engines. I've been in a number of fights with other miners now, and I've noticed they don't use many skills. Mak'gar and his team didn't. Those dwarves didn't. None of the outsiders seem to use much in the way of skills."

"Remember how the patriarch told us most Reality Engines only offer eight or ten class options?" Juana reminded me. "I've been thinking about that a lot. Obviously my searches are limited—they keep a lot of information locked down—but I did some looking around. From what I can tell, most species have their Reality Engine chosen for exploit while they're at a much lower technological level."

I frowned, leaning forward across the table. "Really? Veda said something to me about how we had woken up our engine with the Voyager probe, and they hadn't known we were here until then."

"Right." She grinned. "What she didn't tell you is that there are thousands of galactic probes out there looking for unclaimed Reality Engines. They missed us until it was almost too late. Another few decades and we'd have found this one ourselves."

Grandpa swore. "If we hadn't wasted all that time after Apollo dithering around in Earth's orbit—"

Juana raised a hand. "Let's not waste time there. You know what the common classes are?" She didn't wait for an answer. "Warrior. Healer. Farmer. Priest. Tailor. Baker. Blacksmith. Peasant Serf. Slave. And something the system won't translate for me but seems to be 'Lazy Royal Scion,' probably. With Farmer, Peasant, and Warrior by far the most common."

It took me a minute to figure it out. "If you collect ten million people at, say, the Bronze Age stage of development—"

"First, you probably just took every member of their species in existence." Juana ticked off her fingers. "Second, those ten classes pretty much are *it* as far as jobs, hobbies, vocations. Not a whole lot of people in subsistence living can put in enough time to develop a whole *image* around being, say, a gunslinger." She gave me a quick grin. "Or an office manager, which is essentially what I am."

"Damn." Grandpa sat back, shaking his head. "Damn. I thought we were screwed, but they *really* fuck up most planets."

"If they usually take the whole population, do they even have rules for what to do about the rest?" Suddenly, I was worried about the eight billion humans left on Earth. I'd rarely thought of them in the last year, aside from being jealous of their luck.

"I'll check with Veda, but there are rules. Just—maybe not for a space-worthy population numbering in the billions."

"Shit. We need to find out."

"Nothing we can do about that at this minute," Grandpa said firmly. "Let's cut to the point. How does this affect our team, right now, in phase three?"

I took a deep breath, my mind still thinking about the implications. "Um. So outside miners have really basic classes. That means they're relying on equipment quite a lot. Oh man, do they even use ability points? The Reality Engine clearly stole those from Earth RPGs. I wonder if they can adjust their stats like we can on level-ups. I guess they must level up? I wonder if Mak'gar would tell me—"

"Equipment," Grandpa said firmly. "Some they get from us, some they bring."

"We can turn that to our advantage," Arjun said, not looking up from his pile of skills. "Most pieces of equipment have some sort of flaw. If we can analyze our enemies well enough, we can perhaps design counters for them."

Grandpa laid a hand on the table. "Right. But right now, we've got to concentrate on being ready when the doors of that castle open up. The bad news is that Shad and Sage and I, and a number of the rest of us, are only going to be getting back from our enforced vacations a matter of a couple of hours before those doors open. That means those of you who are here are going to have to take on a lot of the heavy work. Is there any sign of another of these outdoor bosses?"

Juana shook her head. "No, and we've been looking. Most of the miners who weren't on the combat team were out combing the grounds."

"We've got a little more than a day before the system snatches us away for some enforced R&R. We need to get some plans going before that happens."

"Excuse me," came a voice from behind us. "Perhaps I can help."

We turned. One of our grignarian mercenaries stood in the doorway. Although I couldn't tell one grignarian from another by the face, I did recognize the decals on his glowing robes. This was their commander, Exalted Skywarden Greenlight.

I rose. "Commander Greenlight," I said. "Thank you for your assistance earlier. How did it go?"

His face tentacles all rose at once, gave a little twist, and then fell back to their normal position. "We destroyed three times more of them than they destroyed us. We are content."

"Good. Glad to hear you can hold your own in a firefight," Grandpa said. "You wanted to speak with us?"

"Yes," the grignarian said. He entered the room and took up a place a little ways from the rest of us. "We want to help."

"How so?" I asked suspiciously.

"We have seen this style of contest three times before in Reality Engines. It is very rare, and it almost always signifies an engine rich in treasures to be harvested, but also stubborn in revealing them. Like a . . ." He said something, and the system flat out didn't translate it. After a minute, a really artificial voice said, *Pearl in an oyster.* I had not heard a translation glitch like that before.

"So you've got some advice for us?" Grandpa asked. "I'm all ears."

The grignarian tilted his head to one side. "It was my understanding your kind has only two of the sensory organs used for detecting sound waves."

Grandpa held up a hand. "Never mind. Go ahead."

"We wish to help your team get as far as possible. Your success will give us success, and we believe there is much wealth to be found here. With your permission, we will spend the time while you are gone scouting and drawing out the enemy to devour them," Greenlight said.

"Sounds good to me," I said. Even if I didn't fully trust these guys, it would be nice to keep them out of the way of our people.

"We'll want you to be on standby to come to the assistance of our farmers if necessary," Grandpa said.

"May we have permission to engage with other groups as necessary?"

"By 'as necessary,' do you mean if they ambush you? In which case, of course. Or do you mean if you see them and think you can take them out?"

The grignarian made that same lifted, twisted, dropped tentacle gesture. "Perhaps a bit of both."

"Try to avoid pissing off Congruent Paths. We have a ceasefire with them until the castle doors open," Grandpa instructed. "The rest of them, feel free. Especially those asshole dwarves."

"We are agreed on the rectal nature of that particular group," the grignarian captain replied. "Very well. Thank you, Lord Twofeather."

"Is there a reason why your translations seem messed up?" I asked. "'Cause it feels like the system does a pretty good job on everyone else's."

"It is because the system is in your head and their heads, but not in our head," the grignarian replied. He pointed at a small green pin on his robe. "This is my translation device. It has trouble sometimes, though it piggybacks off what you refer to as 'the system' for most of it. Still, there are some concepts which are simply not compatible between my species and that of any . . ." It gave another strange sound, and after a moment, the artificial translation filled in with, "*Creature spawned from the false gods' refusal to submit to the laws of entropy.*"

Oh boy, I thought to myself. *These guys have some strange ideas.*

"Tell you what," Grandpa said. "For every three of them you take out without losing any of your own, we'll throw in a bonus on top of what we're paying you. Juana will work out the details."

She looked annoyed. "Maybe I'd better check with Veda about our finances first. The last I heard, we're a little strapped right now."

"You gotta spend money to make money," Grandpa said. "We just won that huge bounty from Podaga, after all. Throw a little of that around if necessary." He stood up. "Well, I'm beat. I'm gonna go get a few hours of shut-eye before whatever comes next."

One by one, the others filed out of the hut, until it was just Arjun perched over his pile of skills, me, and Juana. She moved away from Arjun, as though not wanting to interrupt him. I followed her over as she flipped through papers on her second-favorite clipboard. Arjun still had the one she liked best.

"You look tired," I told her.

"I am, I guess." She ran a hand through her hair. "I shouldn't be complaining. You're the ones out there fighting."

"When was the last time you slept?"

"I've got that vacation coming up," she pointed out. "My sister's not going at all, and my mother only gets to go for eight hours. That leaves me on my own for two and a half days. I'll catch up on sleep then."

"Where will you be?" I asked.

"I assume back where Mama's restaurant used to be. Little town in pretty much nowhere, Texas." She laughed. "It used to be pretty much nowhere. Things have grown up a lot. It's not that far from San Antonio, actually."

"You could come hang out with us after you're done," I suggested. "Sage is dragging all of us to SoCal, and I wouldn't know how to behave at a K-pop concert. You could give me a couple of tips."

Juana turned slightly pink. "I think I'd like that."

I thought of something else. "Of course, it's not like we have any money. I mean, we have lots of galactic money. Soul coins. But it doesn't seem like we're going to have access to anything on Earth. We've been gone long enough. I'm sure they've declared all of us dead, and I haven't got my wallet anymore."

Juana's eyes widened. "Shad?" she said.

"Yeah?"

"Have you watched any of those entertainment packets that Sage is always seeing?"

I shook my head. "Got more than enough to keep me entertained right here."

"Uh," she said. "Yeah. So, you might find a few things surprising when you get back to Earth, but I'm betting I can swing a flight to Los Angeles if I have to."

CHAPTER TWENTY

HOW TO MAKE AN INTERNATIONAL COLLECT CALL

Colonel Jefferson Rubicon Ames slid into the passenger seat of the two-man skiff. He adjusted his ethereum life-support unit, checking the readout. It was good for the next eight hours.

"You comfortable?" his pilot asked.

Ames nodded to the orc. This was the first time he'd met Adjutant Dahl'grom in person. The large green alien had a broken tusk sticking up on the right side of his lip. His hands moved quickly for being so large as he entered commands into his ship. It dropped out of the bottom of their docking pod and slipped into its course.

There were no windows on the ship, only readouts with statuses that meant nothing to Ames, even though his system-enhanced brain translated everything. He sat back in his seat.

"How long until we reach Earth's orbit?"

"Hour and a half," Dahl'grom said, which matched what he had promised previously, but Ames liked to be sure of these things. That gave him five hours in orbit to handle everything. Maybe a little less, to give him a safety margin for getting back.

It would have to be enough. This trip was costing every bit of money he could safely funnel away from their phase three exploit without getting caught. He also couldn't afford to be gone from Threshold much longer. Dahl'grom had promised to hide his disappearance, and the system was used to him popping into the lotus eater level to commune with Kronos. With luck, it would think that was where he had gone. But he couldn't count on luck, not with the stakes so high.

"So," Dahl'grom said as he looked at the readouts, "for the next hour, convince me why I should persuade my higher-ups to take on more of you humans. They agree in seeing the utility of some of your combat team, such as Twofeather, although they are worried Team Twofeather is too headstrong."

"They're not wrong there," Ames agreed. He also doubted that Team Twofeather would ever sign on with one of the three major conglomerations that had arranged for Earth's Reality Engine exploit. But that was a matter for another day.

Dahl'grom's company worked for a company that worked for a company that was owned by a partial subsidiary of Alabaster Sky. From what Ames could tell, the galactics took Earth business tactics to whole new levels. He had initially hoped that perhaps the Earthlings would be able to win some victories in the boardroom. Now it looked like they would be playing for a draw there.

It was a good thing they were so strong on the ground. Ames needed to make sure to keep that advantage going for as long as he could, through phase three and beyond. The future of the human race depended on it.

He allowed himself a grim smile at that thought. Ames had never been a bleeding-heart do-gooder. He only thought about the "greater good" when it came to the needs of the United States Armed Forces and their various objectives. It wasn't until his first trip from Threshold up to the Hub, seeing the surface of Ganymede below him and beyond that, Jupiter with its banded storms, that he had realized that this was bigger than him—bigger than the whole United States, even. And so, when the system had offered him a dozen or more different classes, there was only one that seemed right for him.

He knew Shad and Major Twofeather didn't entirely trust him, which was wise of them. In part, he had kept them at arm's length deliberately. It was good not to have all of your eggs in one basket. Any basket with Twofeather in it was already overloaded.

Ames and Dahl'grom discussed some of their possible visions for the future, Ames stressing the way the Earth crafters had all picked up recipes granted by the system or the Reality Engine with incredible ease. Ames pitched their usefulness hard. "I've looked into it. Most of your crafters spend a decade or more in an apprenticeship before they're able to produce anything of value whatsoever."

Dahl'grom grunted. "Your engine cheats. This is known. We would not have come here had we realized how badly. We have not had a Reality Engine this unbalanced in many years. Not since the first time the soulless took part."

That was how most of the aliens referred to the grignarians. Ames had met a couple of grignarians himself. They were a repulsive species, not nearly as humanoid as almost everyone else he had met, which made sense if the aliens' origin story was true and most species had evolved from a common ancestral progenitor race, but left the grignarians out on their own.

Still, Ames wasn't one to judge, despite the aliens talking about soul coins this and soulless that. As far as he could tell, the only one who knew whether or not a man had a soul or what it was worth was the Almighty himself. And He hadn't been poking around here lately. If He had, He hadn't let Ames know, and it seemed like He should have.

Dahl'grom broke off their discussion to enter a few commands into his computer. Despite having a neural interface with his system, Dahl'grom seemed to enjoy using screens and controls not too different from what Ames would have expected to see on a fancy Earth billionaire's pet rocket project.

"All right," Ames said. "You left our satellite network intact, right?"

"Didn't see any need to spend the resources to take it out," Dahl'grom replied.

"Then we need to connect in. I've got to communicate."

"As promised, I can make that happen." Under Ames's direction, he spent a minute or two handshaking and making confirmations before saying, "You've got a connection now."

Ames punched in a phone number he had memorized by heart. It connected almost instantly. A man spoke. "This is not a recognized number."

"No, but this is a recognized speaker," Ames said. "Lambda, alpha, nine. Delta, blue, seventeen. Orange, gamma, gamma."

After a second, the voice said back stiffly, "Origination code recognized. Passphrase?"

"Full want and need are mingled herein," Ames recited.

"Accepted. How may I help you?"

There was no excitement in the man's voice, even though he must know who Ames was. Ames cast around, trying to think of who would be quickest to respond to his various needs. "Punch me through to Major Drumheller, will you? Tell him it's a priority alpha, alpha, one."

"That's not a real code," the man said.

"I know," Ames said. "But tell him anyway."

Drumheller and he were—almost—friends. They had been captains together, doing intelligence work overseas. He had joked about the need for a code that meant, "Really, this is urgent, and don't let any of the assholes know." Ames only hoped Drumheller would remember now.

Fifteen minutes later, he was on a conference call with Drumheller, two old Army contacts, two agents from the CIA, and one man in the FBI that he had never met but whom Drumheller had vouched for.

"I have very limited time, gentlemen," Ames said crisply. "I'm sure you all know where I've been."

"Yes, sir," Drumheller said.

"I've got some important updates." He ran through a quick list of information that he wanted Earth to know and that he wasn't certain the aliens were passing along. Then he said, "More importantly, about nine thousand of the abductees are going to be coming back for an eight-hour visit twenty-four hours from now."

That got a quick series of yelps.

"Exactly," Ames said. "I don't know what will happen if anyone on Earth tries to interfere, but it won't be good. I suggest contacting all of our allies and urging them in the strongest terms to make life pleasant for the returnees. They've got a very big job ahead of them, and anyone who makes this worse for them should be considered an enemy of all humankind. I'm not even joking, gentlemen."

"We could keep a lid on it until it happens," one man suggested. "That's the only way I can think of to prevent them from getting mobbed. We don't have the resources necessary to take care of them all."

"They are taking care of all of *you*," Ames said quietly. "Make it happen. I've got the list encoded, and I'll transmit it to you at the end of my call. Find their loved ones. They'll be returning to the exact spot they left. You're going to have to brief the families thoroughly to let them know the abductees won't be able to stay and the families won't be able to go back with them. But if I were coming back, I'd want a chance to actually speak with my loved ones."

"It'll leak on social media."

"Then deputize the local police to run interference. Get the damn National Guard out if you have to," Ames snapped. "You have no idea the hell that a lot of these people have been in for the last year. The ones who are coming home are the ones who have been fighting their asses off for Earth. The only reason we stand a chance of not just becoming a goddamn alien colony is because of these people.

"Now, about three hundred of them have earned enough alien good-conduct points that they're getting a seventy-two-hour pass and not an eight-hour pass. Those ones, I want you to give the VIP treatment to. They could be coming down anywhere. I've got a few locations for some really top hitters. Find them. Make sure anything they want, they get. Hotel suites. Baseball tickets. A visit with their high school girlfriend. I don't care. Make it happen."

Drumheller spoke up. "I understand, Colonel. I've been watching all the official videos and the ones you smuggled out to us." He hesitated. "Is Team Twofeather coming?"

"Yes, and I happen to know exactly where they will be. You get your best men on them. No, wait." Ames paused. "You get *my* best men on them. Can you find Klaus and Ellermann?"

"I think they're on assignment," Drumheller said doubtfully.

"Then you've got about eighteen hours to get them back and ship them to Southern California," Ames said. "There's a little girl who spent the last year doing things most grown men I know couldn't handle. She's coming home for a visit, and I want it to be a good one, because it might well be the last time this little girl ever sees Earth."

One of the CIA men started to protest about sharing information with allies, and how this would reveal they had sources on Threshold. Ames ignored him and kept talking. "You've got a daughter, don't you, Drumheller?" He knew the man did.

"Yes, sir. She's sixteen now."

"Well, Sage is twelve, and she's never going to go to high school or have a prom or get embarrassing photos posted of her on social media for all her friends to laugh at. So I want you to make that up to her right now."

"It'll happen, Colonel," Drumheller promised.

"All right, let's get back to a few more pieces of business."

He heard their sighs of relief over the phone and smiled grimly. That was intelligence men for you, more comfortable handling the fate of nations than dealing with little girls. "I've heard from the news videos that the UN is making noises that they should take over being the Earth government because the aliens will respect that more. That's bullshit. Most of the alien governments are puppets of various conglomerations. They don't care if you own fifty square miles or fifty solar systems. They care who sells you your oatmeal and coffee. So you can let the important decision-makers know we can keep ignoring the UN."

"Like we've been doing for the last eighty years," one of the CIA guys said, and a couple of the others laughed.

"What you should be doing is . . ." Ames continued speaking, barely stopping for the next three hours and change until his alarm rang.

Then he bid farewell to his colleagues, punched up the data packet, and sent it into Earth's systems. He took a deep breath before sending his second unencoded data drop to his ally, along with a clear warning to wait at least ninety-six hours before posting it.

"Let's go," he told Dahl'grom.

"You're cutting it pretty close," the orc said.

"That's just how I like it."

CHAPTER TWENTY-ONE

EIGHT MUST-SEE TOURIST SPOTS IN LOVELY SOCAL!

First thing Tuesday morning, I was standing in our outpost square surrounded by a small throng of equally nervous miners. I had washed my face and brushed my hair, put my drover's coat into storage, taken it back out, put it in, then finally taken it out and laid it over one arm. Juana was clutching a big sack full of messages to deliver from miners who hadn't gotten a pass. She and her mother stood together with her sister Rosa. Rosa wasn't going back to Earth. Her eyes were red and she had a forced smile as she spoke to her mother.

My revolver was in my gun belt on my waist. We might be going to Southern California where things like open-carrying a revolver are slightly frowned on, but after a year of having it in my hand at any time, I didn't want to be away from it. I had asked Grandpa, and he seemed to think it would work out all right.

Sage was wearing her rodeo blouse. Her hair was clean and braided. She had on her very best jeans and the pink cowgirl hat I had bought her for her birthday months ago. She was practically bouncing up and down with excitement. "This is so cool, this is so cool," she breathed. "I can't believe this is happening to me!"

I blinked, and we were standing on a beach. Breakers rolled in, sending white surf sloshing up the beach. The sky overhead was blue and cloudless. It was hot, uncomfortably warm, and the nearest three hundred people on the beach were all scrambling to their feet, grabbing at their possessions, pointing at us, and shrieking.

We didn't look that weird. Sage was a little overdressed for the beach. I was wearing a T-shirt with a cartoon duck on it, had a heavy coat slung over my arm concealing the pistol in my gun belt, and was still wearing my hat and combat boots under my BDUs. Grandpa had his hunting camo on, but nothing weird.

Everybody here was wearing T-shirts or swimsuits. We were supposed to be in Southern California. I turned, and behind us, a range of hills rose up from the water. Atop some of them were enormous mansions sparkling under the sun. "Okay," I said aloud, "we're definitely in the right place."

The nearest few beachgoers had recovered enough to pull out their phones and start recording. A couple of them approached us.

"So what just happened?" one woman asked.

"No, let me guess," the friend with her said, "the way you just appeared out of nowhere. Are you some of the alien kidnap victims? Have they sent you home?" She let out a squeal. "Oh, they have!" She turned around and held up her picture for a selfie. "This is going on right now all over social media. Hashtag 'they're back'!"

"Let's get out of here," I said and started slogging up the beach toward a set of wooden steps leading to a boardwalk.

The crowd followed. People jumped in front of me holding cell phones and demanding pictures. I heard someone yell, "It's the hometown heroes!"

My hand itched. I wanted to draw my gun. I kept telling myself there were no enemies here. These were ordinary humans. They were excited to see us.

Sirens split the air. "Be careful," Grandpa warned as we climbed up the steps. I stepped out onto the boardwalk first, and found myself face-to-face with half a dozen of LA's finest. They were pointing their shotguns and rifles at me. Off to the side, a woman blared through a bullhorn, "Stop right there! Hands where we can see them!"

Sage started to take a step forward. "You can't! Don't you know who we are?" she demanded.

Grandpa put a hand on her shoulder. "Hold on, honey," he said. "Might take us a minute or two to get this sorted out, but let's not cause a scene."

I raised my hands and let the cops surround us.

Two of them approached me. They kept their rifles carefully raised. "Sorry, sir. We know who you are; we're trying to get you out of here without causing a scene," one told me. His badge read "Officer Gonzales." I nodded my thanks and put my hands down.

At last they got us separated from the crowd of selfie-happy beachgoers. The cops put us in a little huddle between two of their squad cars while they made some calls. A couple of minutes later, Gonzales popped out and said, "I'm terribly sorry about that. We just had to let some people know you're here." He glanced over his shoulder, where his fellow cops had set up a cordon, keeping the throng back. The crowd waved and screamed at us. At least they sounded as though they liked us. Gonzalez cleared his throat. "I'm sorry for everything that's happened to you. My third cousin had a friend who got abducted. Don't suppose you met Albert Rodriguez?"

I shook my head. "Don't think so," I said.

"Well, neither did I, but now I know his name. Everyone on Earth knows someone or knows of someone who was taken. It's just . . . We didn't really expect we'd ever see you back again. So, uh, can we get you a coffee while we wait?"

"I don't think that's going to be necessary," Grandpa said quietly as a black SUV pulled up right behind the squad cars.

The back doors opened, and a pair of men got out. They were clearly government agents. They had crew cuts, sunglasses, and were wearing three-piece suits. One of them approached us. He stopped about three feet away.

"Major Twofeather?"

"Yep," Grandpa said. "That's me."

"If you'll come with us, sir, we can get this all sorted out."

Grandpa held his ground. "You listen here," he said in a low voice. "Me and my grandson and granddaughter, we've been jerked around for the last year by people much more powerful than the United States government. We've been given three days back here to do what we like. And what my little girl here wants," he put his hand on Sage's shoulder, "is to go ride a few roller coasters, meet a wizard, and see some sort of B-pop band perform."

"It's K-pop, Grandpa," I supplied.

"Whatever." He turned back to the agents. "So if you're gonna help us with that, then . . ."

"Yes, sir," the government agent said. "We have orders to extend you every courtesy." He turned to the other agent. "Smith, you heard the requests. Get on 'em now."

"I know two Smiths already," Sage said brightly. "They work with Colonel Ames. Do you work with Colonel Ames, too?"

Government Agent Smith, who had started back for the car, turned. He regarded us through his sunglasses. "Yes," he said. "I do." Then he disappeared around the side of the car.

They made room for us in the big SUV. The talkative agent, who introduced himself as Wyant Ellermann, which I figured was definitely not a pseudonym, leaned back and spoke to Grandpa. "Colonel Ames got us word two days ago, so we've all had a little bit of time to prepare."

Grandpa scowled. "Hopefully, most of our friends will be getting a slightly better welcome than what we got there from LAPD's finest. I don't think they got the message."

"We've got plenty of people on standby all over, watching for trouble, trying to make sure everything comes out all right," Ellermann said soothingly.

"Most of them will only be here for eight hours," Grandpa said. "It's only a few of us who have the seventy-two-hour pass."

"And we're going to make use of it," Agent Ellermann said.

Sage's lips started to quiver. "What do you mean?" she asked. "I don't get to see Orange Dream?"

The agent quickly removed his sunglasses and leaned toward Sage. He started to attempt a friendly pat of her hand, then withdrew his hand as though reconsidering. "No, Ms. Williams, you will most certainly get to see Orange Dream. In fact, we're arranging for a backstage pass for you right now."

Sage squealed. I closed my eyes and groaned.

What Ellermann apparently *did* mean was that while we were shepherded around Southern California doing whatever Sage's heart could dream up, we were also receiving multiple clandestine phone calls and surreptitious visits.

The first of which, on speaker, was from a staffer at the Joint Chiefs of Staffs letting Grandpa know that he had been promoted to full colonel, skipping right over lieutenant colonel in the process. "Oh hey," I said. "You got a promotion for Colonel Ames, too? Is he gonna be a general?"

Agent Ellermann shook his head. "Colonel Ames has been very clear that he does not wish to receive any more attention than he already has. Technically, Colonel Twofeather now outranks him."

"As it should be," Grandpa said, nodding. He looked more smug than ever as Government-Issue Smith handed him a box with a colonel's eagle insignia.

"Ames requested that Smith and I specifically come out to LA to handle you. The other American members of your team will be receiving a much more hands-off approach. I can't speak for many of the other nations of the world, but I know that our closest allies have all agreed that we had better do what we can to make your trip pleasant, and not try to interfere with things—up there. That said." He closed his eyes as though in pain, then opened them. "I'm afraid you have a medal presentation ceremony tomorrow afternoon. I had to pull quite a few strings to make it clear that you will not be flying to Washington. Instead, the vice president will be coming here to present you your awards. It's probably going to be televised."

"Wonderful," I said, leaning back. "Just what I need." Then I had a thought. "Oh, a friend of mine, Juana Lopez, she's here on a seventy-two-hour pass. Not here in LA. She's in a little town near San Antonio with her mom, but her mom's only got eight hours. So after that, if you think you could arrange for her to come out here . . ."

Ellermann pulled up a tablet and scrolled through a list. "Juana Lopez. We've got her address of record. We can get her here in . . ." He glanced at his watch, clearly doing a little calculation. "Call it ten hours from now? I'll see to it that she has a government jet waiting for her at the airport. Give me a minute to arrange car transport to and from."

I sat back, blinking. It was hard to take in, but we were hot stuff. I glanced at the clock on the SUV. It was currently just after nine a.m. My stomach rumbled.

According to the agenda that Ellermann was throwing together, we were on our way to one of Southern California's finest amusement parks right now.

I leaned forward and spoke to the driver. "Hey, if it's not too much trouble, could we swing by a taco truck and get a breakfast burrito? I'm really craving some actual chicken eggs." I licked my lips at the thought. It had been over a year since I'd had a good egg. The Reality Engine was pretty clever at coming up with a lot of things, but its eggs left something to be desired.

Sage rode every roller coaster in the park twice. She got her face painted by a sad teenager wearing a cartoon mascot costume. She ate cotton candy, snow cones, an enormous pretzel dripping with mustard, and a hot dog longer than her arm, all before two o'clock. She bought eight T-shirts and a pair of cat ears, and then, on top of the largest coaster yet, vomited up all of the junk food she had eaten.

I narrowly avoided getting splashed. Grandpa had pulled rank on me and refused to go on any of the coasters, preferring to wait at the bottom. Since we had been given VIP badges and ribbons, we didn't have to wait in any of the lines.

I had been half worried, as they were making their calls, that they were going to empty out the park, which would have seemed sad. Instead, Sage was getting to have a day like she was an ordinary Earth kid.

More like she was one of those ordinary Earth kids who has cancer and gets a wish granted for them by a charity. Still, she seemed to be having a great time.

I was feeling awkward about the whole thing as our escort led us to the head of the line at the first coaster. A couple of the riders we bumped past complained—then someone took another look and shouted. "It's Shad and Sage! I can't believe it, they're here!"

The whole line cheered as our handlers hushed things up. Sage and I glanced at each other, shrugged, and waved to the crowd. After that I felt a lot easier about the whole thing. We rode the coaster twice, then some whirling teacups, and then bumper cars.

I tried my best to give off whoops and hollers at the right places, but the fact was, this all felt hollow. I watched the crowds hurrying around us, kids out having fun with their families, couples strolling arm-in-arm, listened to the screams of delight, and I realized that nothing about this felt real.

Adrenaline from thrill rides wasn't anything like having your life at risk or your freedom. These people here were out having fun. They didn't even care that the fate of our whole solar system was being played out half a million miles away in the orbit of Jupiter. Hell, most of them probably couldn't have told you that Ganymede was a moon of Jupiter.

I watched them stroll past, unconcerned, and I found myself hating them. I fell back as Sage ran ahead to a booth that offered to let you throw darts at balloons and win a prize.

Grandpa put a hand on my shoulder. "It's alright, Shad," he said quietly.

"It's just . . ." I shook my head. "I thought the stuff the Reality Engine made up was fake. This is way worse."

"I know what you mean, but try to have fun for your sister's sake, alright?"

I took a deep breath and glanced at the time. "Think she'll be ready to leave anytime soon? I was hoping that we could find whatever hotel the G-men have booked for us and relax a bit before Juana gets here."

"I think she'll be ready to go," Grandpa said. "I'll have a word with her, shall I?"

CHAPTER TWENTY-TWO

SUN PROTECTION AND YOU: BEYOND SPF 50!

We had an enormous suite to ourselves at the top of a ritzy hotel not far from the beach. Based on the other people I saw walking in when we did, I was guessing they usually catered to a slightly more elite clientele than a bunch of backwoods hicks from the Arizona Strip.

Agent Ellermann and Government-Issue Smith ushered us in and up to our rooms quickly. Sage disappeared to explore the facilities, while Smith stopped me at the door.

"Mr. Williams, I have a message for you from Juana Lopez. She has had quite a tiring day, and though she is on her way here, has decided to retire to her own room tonight. She says she will see you in the morning."

I felt a little deflated. It was still fairly early, and I was starting to get overwhelmed by all the strangers. Juana probably felt the same way. "That's fine, then. We'll see her tomorrow." The agent withdrew.

Grandpa sat down at the elegant table in the middle of the lounge room. It was covered in a white tablecloth that had a smaller gold tablecloth on top of it, and a vase of pretty flowers that looked very expensive to me. I didn't have any idea what they were.

Sage popped out. "Can we go somewhere cool for dinner?" she asked.

"Would it be alright for you, Ms. Williams," Agent Ellermann said, "if we stayed in and you ordered off the room service menu instead? They have a two-star Michelin restaurant in this hotel. You can order anything you like."

Her eyes went wide. "Is that good?"

"They're probably not as good as Mama Grace," I said, "but yeah, that's pretty good."

She went in search of the room service menu. I draped my coat over the back of a chair, took off my gun belt, and laid it next to the coat. The two agents watched me disarm without commenting. I took off my boots, unlacing them one after the other, then sat down in the plush armchair, put my feet up, closed my eyes, and tried to relax. It wasn't any use.

"I assume if you want us to stay in, that means you've got an agenda for us," Grandpa said in a dangerously calm tone of voice.

"Yes, sir, Colonel, sir. We've had various pieces of intelligence from the aliens and a few other pieces slipped in by Colonel Ames and some of his assets, but we haven't been able to independently verify any of it until now. We were hoping you would be willing to give us a full briefing on the situation."

Grandpa sighed. "Figured it was something like that. Alright, let's order up some grub and then we'll give you what we know. Sage, you found that menu yet? I feel like taking a sizable chunk out of these fellows' discretionary budget."

Ellermann brought out a laptop as Sage and Grandpa ordered up a feast. I tossed in a request for decent beer. "We've been fielding appeals from the CIA, FBI, Joint Chiefs, and multiple allied intelligence agencies to interview you guys," Ellermann said. "Sorry. This part might be rough." He pulled up videoconferencing software.

There were already a dozen people waiting for us. Some of them were generals. I tried hard not to let my mouth hang open as more still joined, but I couldn't quite believe how many important people were waiting to talk to us. Ellermann explained some ground rules—to them, not us. They had someone on the other end collecting questions to ask, who would also be in charge of muting and unmuting anyone deemed worthy of speaking up. Grandpa, Sage, and I could say whatever we thought necessary.

"First question," the colonel in charge of asking questions said from the screen. "Colonel Ames's intelligence portrays the Reality Engine as an intelligent being disposed favorably toward humanity. Do you agree with this suggestion? Please elaborate."

Fortunately, the food and beer arrived soon, so we ate and we talked and occasionally we listened to some bigwig make a speech—Ellermann and the colonel on the other end were pretty good at shutting down nonsense, but when you get that much brass in one videoconference you're going to suffer through a couple of snoozers.

I was honestly impressed by how much they knew. We worked long into the night. Sage eventually started drooping into her hot fudge sundae, so I made her go and shower and crawl into the enormous bed in her room.

The agents had seen to it that someone went shopping for her. She had a dozen different outfits to choose from, including three different bathing suits for tomorrow. They said they'd picked up some stuff for Grandpa and me, but not quite as many choices.

As we were working, I heard a disturbance outside. I leapt up instinctively, trying to Quick Draw, but my gun sat in its holster across the room. The agents were almost as fast as I was, heading for the door and drawing their guns.

"Stay back," Ellermann said.

I wanted to ignore him but caught myself. This was their turf, not mine. They stood by the door, guns ready, one beside the door, one two steps behind it. After a moment, they relaxed. They kept up their positions until, after another minute, Ellermann tapped his ear. I hadn't even noticed the earpiece before then. Then the two of them came back to the table.

"Sorry about that. A reporter got past our cordon and almost made it here," Ellermann said.

"I thought you might be keeping us down-low," Grandpa said.

Smith snorted. "Your face probably went up on every social network in the world a hundred thousand times in the last day. We've just been trying to keep away the professionals, the ones who would really like to get their hands on you. Her especially." He nodded at the room where Sage was sleeping.

I had seen a few mentions of our exploits in the material the government men were showing us. Now I tensed. There hadn't been that much talk of Sage.

"How much do you guys know about her?"

"There were about four hundred kids taken across the English-speaking world. More than that in Asia, Africa, and South America, but they didn't tend to make the news the way the ones here or in Europe did. Not as many photos of grieving families." Ellermann looked pensive. Smith shook his head.

"Sage was just one of the sixty-three American kids lost until some of those videos started leaking."

"From Source B?" I guessed.

The government agents had all of their information labeled by source. There were the official communications from the Galactic Committee that was overseeing the exploit, a couple of rogue missives from corporations that had tried to do business with Earth before getting caught and dragged off by the galactics, whatever Ames had brought them, and then three separate sources that had snuck their information in through the internet and hadn't yet been traced.

Source B was the one with the best videos. I had seen my own fight with the squid monster at the end of phase two in that stack. It bothered me immensely. That fight had been barely two weeks ago, and here it was back on Earth. The point of view on the video made me pretty darn sure it had been taken from one of my team's All-Seeing Eye cams.

I had a couple of theories about how they could have gotten it, none of which I liked.

"Source B," Smith confirmed. "She features kind of a lot. We weeded it down for you since we were pretty sure those videos were accurate and we didn't need confirmation on them. At this point, I'd call her America's sweetheart, but honestly, the whole world knows Sage's face now."

It was just one more nail in the coffin of us ever having a normal life when this was over. I touched the place on the back of my neck where I knew the system had inserted the ethereum support device that was keeping me alive. We had all been required to go up to the Hub for the surgery to get it implanted and our first charge loaded. If we were here more than a week, we would run out of ethereum and die. Not that it was a concern, since the system would yank us back to the Reality Engine in—I checked my watch—approximately fifty-six hours.

Grandpa stood up. "It's late, gentlemen," he said. "I think I'm going to bed now. If there's anything else we can help you with, well, we'll talk tomorrow, but I think we've given you intelligence spooks plenty to work with."

Smith started to protest. Ellermann put a hand on his arm. "We'd always take more," he said, "but you're right. You've earned a break. My team and I will be on duty all night. I'm afraid we've bugged this room, so if we hear any untoward noises we will come to check. If you need to go anywhere, please use the house phone and call for one of us to escort you."

"You guys gonna be with us tomorrow at the beach?" I asked.

"Every step of the way," Ellermann confirmed.

"Then I hope you get a decent night's sleep and I hope you packed your swim trunks."

Smith smiled for such a short fraction of a second I thought I was mistaken. "If the government wanted me to go swimming, they'd have issued me gear," he said. "Good night, Captain Williams, Colonel Twofeather."

We ordered room service again for breakfast the next day. Sage kept interrupting her meal to dart back into her room and try on a different bathing suit. "I just can't decide. I love the pink one, but it might be too tween. I'm almost an adolescent now, nearly thirteen."

"Got another eight months before you're thirteen," I pointed out as I bit a mouthful of scrambled eggs and followed it up with some crispy, honest-to-goodness pork bacon. "I like the pink one."

She stuck her tongue out at me. "Shows what you know, Shad." She slipped back into the room, tried on the silver one, and wore it under a cover-up for most of breakfast before going back and trying on the last one. She came back out wearing a T-shirt and shorts.

"No bathing suit?"

"It's underneath, obviously."

"Made up your mind for sure?"

"Yes." She looked a little defiant and a little smug. I glanced at Grandpa. He had stopped with his spoon halfway to his mouth. He sighed, finished his bite, drank his coffee, and stood up. "Well, we're wasting time. If you're ready, Sage, I guess we'd better go to the beach."

She skipped off to grab her sandals. I leaned over to Grandpa. "That look on her face, I'm worried about . . ."

He held up a hand. "Son, I've raised a teenage girl once already. Made some really stupid mistakes. I've learned you pick your battles."

I thought about it and decided Grandpa was right. I had a pair of swim trunks and a T-shirt on. As we prepared to leave the room, I strapped on my gun belt and covered it with my coat.

Sage stopped in the doorway. "Shad, you're not wearing that coat."

"I'm not leaving it here."

"You look like a flasher."

"Well, I'm not." I sounded pretty lame to myself, but there was no way I was leaving my trusty magic coat behind.

Juana was waiting for us in the hotel lobby. She looked tired, with bags under her eyes, but she stood up and smiled as she saw us. She was wearing a yellow button-down dress and sandals and a big floppy sun hat.

"It's good to see you three," she said.

"Have you got a bathing suit?" Sage asked. "If not, we'll stop on the way. I'll make Government-Issue Smith buy you one."

"Government-Issue Smith?" Juana said, sounding amused as she turned to greet our handlers. They introduced themselves. "No, Sage, I had quite a wardrobe waiting for me. Did I have you two to thank for that?"

Agent Ellermann cleared his throat. "Actually, ah, since we had a time crunch and an unlimited budget, I called in some outside consultant help." He looked really uncomfortable. "My wife. She's really good at shopping. I had to pay her ticket out here, but she's waiving the usual government consultant fee, and I think we'll manage to slip it in through the paperwork."

"Well, I hope you've invited her along to the day at the beach," Juana said cheerfully.

"Actually, I have her arranging the Orange Dream concert tonight. She'll meet up with us later. My daughter is going to kill us when she finds out we were at Orange Dream and didn't bring her, but I thought that would be too big a strain on the government budget."

What is there to say about a day at the beach?

Well, it was crowded, but this was LA. It was always going to be crowded. The beach was actually cleaner than I expected, with no hypodermic needles or human waste anywhere. Either I had always been listening to the wrong stories about the state of affairs in LA, or maybe the government agents had brought in a cleaning service to have the place tidied up before we got there.

We spread out. I tucked my gun belt under my coat, swapped my cowboy hat for a big floppy sun hat, and slathered on some sunblock. Grandpa turned his nose up at the stuff.

"You wouldn't need that if you didn't have so much white boy in your DNA," he said.

"Everyone is supposed to wear sunblock, Grandpa," Sage said. "Even if you do have more melanin than I do. It prevents skin cancer."

"I don't really think that's on my list of things to worry about anymore," Grandpa said. He hadn't taken off his button-down Hawaiian shirt. I could see the chain that held my abuela's necklace alongside the medicine pouch he always wore.

"You all right?" I asked Juana. "You seem tired."

"I'm fine," she said. "My mother's parents, my abuela and abuelo, were there when we arrived. I guess you three weren't the only ones expected."

Agent Ellermann cleared his throat. "No ma'am, we had a complete list of everyone who would be arriving from Colonel Ames. He gave specific instructions about the sort of reception we were to give everyone. There have been a few hiccups and hassles. Some media has gotten past the protection we've wanted, and there were a few unhappy reunions."

Juana's face went almost pale. She swallowed hard. "Yes," she said. "I could see how there would be."

There was an awkward silence. Then she stood up and took off her dress. "Come on, Sage, let's go swimming," she said.

Sage was still wearing her shorts and T-shirt. She looked nervous. Then, defiantly, she pulled off her T-shirt to reveal a blue bikini.

I sat shocked, unable to say anything at the sight of my baby sister wearing a bikini.

"Alright, come on," she said as she dashed to the water, Juana on her heels.

"Good work, Shad," Grandpa said. "Very smooth. I like the way you managed to stick your foot in your mouth without saying anything."

"But I didn't say anything," I protested.

"And Sage noticed." He shook his head. "This is good for her, Shad. She doesn't have much of a chance to be an ordinary kid. Let it go. She'll be back to murdering nightmares out of Russian fairy tales and risking being ripped to death by extinct flying dinosaurs soon enough."

I sat on my beach towel until I started to feel awkward about it. Then I went to join the girls in the water. The surf was a little too rough for my liking, but Juana and Sage weren't going very far out. The waves crashed in and hit the beach pretty hard, but I saw some kids playing and the surfers didn't seem to be having any great luck, so it must not have been too much.

Sage had regained her cheerfulness. She had a big stripy beach ball and lobbed it at me. I batted it back. She leapt up and hit it dead-on, laughing. We played a pretty low-key game for a while before she got bored and went back up onto the beach. Juana and I followed her out of the water. Juana was wearing a modest ivory one-piece bathing suit and had her hair pulled up.

"You alright?" I asked again.

"I'm fine. Some of it's just harder than I expected."

"Yeah, I get that. Are you really up for a K-pop concert tonight?"

"Oh, that I wouldn't miss for the world," she said. "Mostly because I'm going to get to watch you and your grandfather squirming in a sea of preadolescent girls who are ready to throw their underwear at the stage but haven't quite figured out why yet."

I groaned. "Don't remind me," I said. "Anyway, that's not the worst of it."

She looked startled. "What?"

"They didn't tell you? We've got a VIP ceremony and an early dinner before the concert. Medal ceremony. I guess Grandpa's getting another bronze star or some such."

Now it was Juana's turn to groan. "If you'd told me that, I would have stayed back in Texas."

"Why do you think I didn't tell you that?" I teased.

CHAPTER TWENTY-THREE

HOW TO SPEND YOUR LAST DAY UNDER THE SUN

Let's not say much about the medal ceremony, okay?

The dress uniform they'd gotten me fit pretty well, and so did Grandpa's. We had to stand incredibly stiffly while the vice president pinned a medal on us. There had been a presidential election while we were gone, so I didn't even know what her name was until Ellermann whispered it to me right before she showed up and jabbed me with a pin. We each received a Silver Star. I'd been expecting bronze, like what Grandpa had previously earned. Despite my discomfort, my eyes watered as the vice president pinned it to my jacket.

I didn't really feel like I'd earned it. I'd just done what I had to do. Anyone would have. But it still meant a lot.

They had a Presidential Medal of Freedom for Sage as well, and I think someone filled them in at the last minute, because about three seconds before the vice president stood up to give us our awards, someone came rushing over to her with a small packet. When she came over to us, she had a medal for Juana as well.

Then we sat down and had to listen to a lot of politicians make speeches. After that, all of the politicians came by to get pictures with us. Then, after the politicians, it was various influencers and other important people who had managed to bribe their way into the dinner.

The dinner actually looked pretty good, but I didn't get to eat a bite of it because I was so busy being stood up to take pictures and smile next to Senator So-and-So or Representative Thus-and-Such. The Governor of Arizona came in, along with the Governor of Utah. They both shook our hands and thanked us, and I wasn't sure if either of them knew where exactly we had been abducted from because they both seemed to think that we were local hometown boys and girls.

Finally, around seven o'clock, Smith and Ellermann shepherded us out of there, tossed us in the back of a limousine, and drove us over to the LA Coliseum for the Orange Dream concert. The place was packed with fifty thousand teen girls and their unwilling handlers.

They had gotten us front-row tickets right next to the really fanatical fourteen-year-old K-pop fans. The noise was overwhelming, and I'm speaking as someone who's gotten used to a lot of loud noises in the last few months. I was a foot and a half taller than almost anyone in the audience, and I was wearing a long coat and a gun. Being around so many teenage girls made me feel like I was going to be ending up on a watch list somewhere.

Juana stood in between me and Grandpa and kept looking at me, shaking her head and grinning. "What?!" I finally shouted over one slightly less loud song.

"This is worth the price of admission," she said.

"Well, I'm glad that you're feeling better now," I shouted back.

Then, as I was hoping the concert was finally winding down, the band paused and the lead singer yelled, "We want to welcome a very special guest!" He came right over to the edge of the stage, leaned over, reached out his hand, and helped Sage up onto the stage.

The crowd went absolutely bonkers. I hadn't realized until now what Ellermann had been warning me about. Everyone here knew Sage. They were screaming her name. Just *Sage! Sage! Sage!* I thought they'd been mad for the K-pop boys, but the blast of sound nearly deafened me.

The little girls near us crowded in. "Wait! You're with Sage?"

All I could do was nod over the screaming crowd.

"Oh my god, this is the best day of my life! Can you get me her autograph?"

It was two a.m. We were back in the limo, Sage asleep and drooling on Grandpa's shoulder. I noticed after a couple of turns that we were not heading back to our hotel.

"Where are we going?" I asked.

"Change of plans," Ellermann said quietly. "There are just too many paparazzi and stalkers here in Los Angeles now. We've made arrangements for you four to spend a quiet day tomorrow at an out-of-season resort up in the mountains. We'll make it up to you somehow. I know you probably had plans."

"That sounds perfect," Juana said fervently.

"We're heading to the airport now. There's a private jet already waiting on the tarmac. We'll take you in the back the way they get the politicians in and out, and hopefully slip you past most of the paparazzi. Word will get out, but it should take them long enough to get there. You can enjoy your last day."

Last day. The past forty-eight hours had passed in a flash. We would be going back to the Reality Engine in about thirty hours. None of this felt real. I looked at Grandpa.

"We should have gone back to the Strip," I said quietly.

"Maybe so," he said. "Maybe so."

The resort was perfect. A ring of mountains surrounded a deep, still, crystal blue pond. Even in the heart of summer, it was cool. Tall pines surrounded the edge of the pond and big granite boulders stuck up out of the surface. We had a catamaran at our disposal, a couple of kayaks, and the run of practically a whole empty resort. They had a restaurant that tasted just as good as that two-star Michelin place in Los Angeles, and way fewer people.

Sage and I paddled one of the kayaks out to a little island in the middle of the pond. We pulled up on the rocky beach, hopped out, and explored a little. Sage found a nest where a bird had laid its eggs, raised its babies, and then recently, with them ready to fly, abandoned the nest.

She climbed the tree and sat beside the nest, staring out at the water. I sat at the base of the tree, leaning my body against a sun-warmed boulder. I closed my eyes and took a deep breath of real air. I couldn't feel the device pumping ethereum through my body and keeping me alive. This felt like home. It felt like I belonged here. It felt like I could just get up, walk into town, and keep walking until I got lost and was never found again.

From her perch up in the tree, Sage said, "What are we going to do?"

I didn't move. "What we have to do. What we've been doing."

"I know." Her voice was shaking. "They don't even know how much . . . how hard it is."

"No," I said. "And they shouldn't have to. And you shouldn't have to. You should get to stay here and listen to boy bands and go to the beach all the time."

"But if I lived here, I wouldn't do those things," she said. "We lived in the middle of the desert in a double-wide. We had food stamps and wore hand-me-downs. That Sage would never have gone to Orange Dream. I certainly wouldn't have been on stage with them yelling my name. That Sage didn't matter to anyone."

"She matters to me," I said. "Why do you think I'm doing all this? It's so that maybe we can find a chance for you to have a real life again."

Sage dropped down out of the tree and landed nimbly on her feet. "I don't know what a real life is anymore. The last couple of days, they've been fun, but they haven't felt real."

"And living in a glorified computer simulation is?"

"No," she said, sighing. "But at least it counts for something." She walked over to the kayak and picked up her paddle. "I'm ready to go in now. The sun's starting to go down anyway."

It would be at least five hours before sunset, but I nodded. "Alright, let's go."

That night after dinner, Sage excused herself and went up to our room. Grandpa told Ellermann and Smith that if they had anything else to ask, he'd work through it with them now. That left Juana and me sitting at the table where we'd had dinner, slowly sipping a bottle of sparkling water and a little white wine. After we finished our glasses, Juana stood up.

"Let's walk back down to the beach. I'd like to see the stars from this side of the sky one more time."

"Alright," I said, and accompanied her. I was aware of the bodyguards escorting us, but they kept their distance far enough away that I could pretend that Juana and I had some privacy. We'd been living with the knowledge that the Reality Engine was always watching for the last year, after all, so it wasn't exactly like privacy meant a whole lot to me.

We strode along the beach, staring up at the stars. I paused, then pointed. "That one's Jupiter," I said.

"You're sure?"

"Definitely."

She squinted up at it. "It's so small from here."

"It looks so different close-up," I said, aware that that was possibly the most inane thing I had ever said.

"I'm glad I've had a chance to see it. Of all the things we've done, that was one that was just cool."

I was still wondering what was bothering her, but I didn't really know how to ask. Instead, I said, "I'm sorry your sister didn't even get the eight-hour visit."

"Me too," Juana said. "I would have rather split this with her, or even given it to her, but that wasn't an option."

"Maybe Grandpa was right, and this was someone trying to sabotage our team effort before the real phase three work starts."

"I don't know if I think we were that important," Juana said. "I do know that we'll have a lot of work to do when we get back, and that I'm honestly looking forward to it."

"Me too," I admitted. "I guess I'm just better at shooting things in the face than relaxing."

We walked along a little farther before Juana said, "My fiancé came to see me."

I stopped dead in my tracks. My ears rang. I couldn't have heard her right. I blinked and swallowed and tried to say something. It didn't come out, so I said again, "Fiancé?"

Juana had a fiancé? Of course she would. She was beautiful and smart and competent. She'd probably had her pick of smart, handsome guys back on Earth.

"Derek." She sounded wistful. She walked down to the water's edge and poked at it with a sandal-clad toe.

"I didn't know you had a fiancé."

She turned to face me, giving me a wry smile. "Emphasis on 'had.' He came with his wife and their baby." Her voice caught.

Before I knew what I was doing, I had crossed the distance between us and put my arm on her shoulder.

"Juana, I'm so sorry."

"He must have moved on almost as soon as I was gone. We'd been engaged for three years. I thought he wanted to finish his schooling before we . . ."

She was crying on my shoulder. I patted her back, saying "There, there" a few times awkwardly. Juana had never mentioned anything about her family back home. Her mother and sister hadn't spoken of a fiancé either, probably to avoid hurting her feelings.

I hadn't left anyone behind. Everyone who meant anything in the world to me had been brought to the Reality Engine with me. It had given me a privileged life compared to everyone else around me, and I had just taken that for granted. Frank had spent months searching to make sure that his wife and children hadn't been taken by the Reality Engine.

I realized I hadn't even asked if Frank had gotten a Day Pass. I should have. I could have brought a message for his wife if he wasn't able to come back himself.

I was a stupid, selfish bastard, and there was a woman in my arms crying, which had never happened before. I felt more awkward by the second. Juana cried for what felt like an eternity before stepping back, wiping her eyes and nose and sniffing.

"I'm sorry," she said. "I wasn't going to mention it. I don't know why I did."

"I'm glad you did," I said, wishing I had access to my inventory. I had a whole box of handkerchiefs, not to mention Kleenex and other things one could use to wipe away the residue of tears. "But, what an asshole."

That made her laugh. "You know what? When I saw him standing there with her and the baby, that's exactly what I thought, too. What an asshole. Not for moving on, but to show back up with his *family*? He could have come on his own or just sent a note or something."

"Why was he there?"

Juana took a deep breath. "He said he was there to wish me well, but he had given me his grandmother's ring and he wanted it back. I had to tell him I hadn't been wearing it that day because I was helping Mama scrub down the kitchen right before we opened because we'd gotten word there was going to be a health inspection. So I'd left it back at our house, which got repossessed while we were gone. My grandparents told me about it. The look on Derek's face when I told him! He started to scream at me. The National Guardsmen who were serving as our protective detail escorted him out. They apologized to me so hard. They hadn't had any idea he was going to make a scene like that."

"I wish you'd told me this two days ago," I said. "I could have run over to Texas and challenged him to a nice gunfight. I've had a lot of practice in duels in the last year, and I'm pretty damn sure nobody on this continent would have blinked an eye if I'd done it."

"They probably wouldn't, but it's all right, Shad. You don't need to waste a bullet on that guy." Juana shook her head and laughed. She cocked her head at me.

I'm not a quick learner and I didn't have a whole lot of experience with women, but when a beautiful woman is looking like *that*, in the moonlight on a beach with tears still in her eyes? It doesn't take a whole lot of smarts to figure out. I leaned forward, almost hesitated before I saw her tiny nod, and kissed her.

So yeah, that was the highlight of my summer vacation. We walked back to the hotel hand in hand and I kissed her again on the steps before parting. "See you tomorrow," I said.

"Thanks for tonight, Shad," she said.

[Attention, miners!
The gates of Castle Byalgrad are open!
Your Keys await!
And so much more . . .]

CHAPTER TWENTY-FOUR

HAVE FUN STORMING THE CASTLE!

We were back in the square in the middle of our outpost, and my notifications were going crazy. Dropping my bags full of Earth loot, I got dozens of chat pop-ups, presumably from the last three days, all appearing at once. I dismissed them as Dwight, Kirin, and Mama Grace descended on us.

"You're late!" Mama Grace cried.

"We came back exactly seventy-two hours after leaving," Juana said blankly. She still had a couple of bags hanging off her arms. Grandpa unstrapped the big rucksack he'd been carrying and let it fall.

Mama Grace shook her head. "It's been close to seventy-five hours. The gates opened three hours ago."

"What?" I felt my blood pressure rising as I took in Mama Grace's words. Leaving aside the question of where the missing time had gone, I said, "Does that mean the other teams have already started?"

"Yeah," Dwight said grimly. "You three should get up to the castle as quickly as possible. Juana, come join the strategy table and we'll fill you in."

"Right," Juana said briskly, all business. She nodded to me and started up the steps into the converted church building, Dwight trailing after her.

"Let's move," Grandpa growled. "Somebody want to brief us on the way?"

"I will," Kirin said. She accompanied us down through our outpost toward the gate.

"Exactly three hours and twenty-six minutes ago, the gates of Castle Byalgrad opened. All the other teams were ready. We knew when the gates would open, of course, but we were expecting you back by then."

"They screwed us over good," I grumbled.

"Dwight and Arjun and I scrambled to cover. We sent everybody up that we could, and we relocated our minion spawn point. Everybody's using their creep to help fight off enemies. You'll understand better when you get there," Kirin said. "Three teams have already gotten past the guardian and into the castle itself."

I swore. That put us badly behind. "Which teams?"

"The dwarves, Congruent Paths, and that orc team," Kirin said. "A fourth team was making an attempt, but apparently the dwarves and two of the teams who hadn't yet made it past the guardian turned on them and interfered with their attempt."

"How'd that work out?"

"Lots of deaths. More painful for the ones who hadn't already gotten their keys, of course. We think the dwarves started the trouble and were happy to get three of their rivals involved."

Juana sent us a note. *I'm going over the information we're getting from our crafters and miners elsewhere in the engine. Every phase three zone is different. All themed from Earth history or myth.*

That's unfortunate, I wrote back. *I'd hoped we might be able to get some tips from outside, but it doesn't sound like anyone would be able to help us.* It made sense. The Reality Engine could generate eighty-seven distinct made-up worlds as easily as eighty-seven copies of the same one.

"So, as a reminder," Grandpa growled, "the first team to make it through this whole castle and defeat whoever the king is, gets a pass into the competition for the Reality Engine's heart. However that's gonna work. We're not sure whether second and third get anything, but we can be damn sure tenth place won't. We've got a lot of ground to make up."

"The good news is there's a long way to go," Kirin said. "A system-wide announcement happens every time someone wins a fight. So far only the guardian has been defeated."

We were making good time up the valley, running nearly flat out and still able to have a conversation. After having spent three days back on Earth around normal humans, I was marveling at what my ethereum-enhanced body was capable of. Other than a couple of stolen moments at the pond, I'd spent the whole trip back on Earth feeling on edge, like I was going to be attacked at any minute. Back here, I might actually be attacked, and yet I felt more at home.

The Reality Engine had really screwed with my brain. If I ever got some time to think, I was gonna have to figure out what this meant.

The valley sloped steeply uphill toward an enormous granite outcropping. It rose up two hundred feet above us, and as we approached it, I saw a pair of enormous gates, at least forty feet tall and fifteen feet wide. The gates were made of wrought iron and heavy wood. They stood open with a dark tunnel yawning behind them.

Mobs streamed in and through the tunnel, our skeletons and pigs mixed in with swashbucklers, samurai wearing jet packs, dinosaurs, abominable snowmen, and giant bipedal cats, all a mishmash of whatever had been present during the different teams' phase two attempts. None of them paid us or each other any heed as they proceeded mindlessly toward their creep lures.

"Aren't they going to fight?" Sage asked, sounding disappointed.

"Soon as they reach their rally points they will," Kirin said. "Until then, they're harmless."

"Where's the rally point? And I don't see the guardian. And where's the rest of our team?"

"They're through the tunnel," Kirin said. "The gates aren't contested. The guardian waits beyond. I told our team to retreat and try to stay out of trouble. So far so good. We've had a few deaths, but the aliens are mostly focused on any-one who's attempting to take on the guardian."

"All right, we'll get in there and have a look," Grandpa said.

I popped up my messages and started glancing through them for anything important. Mostly it was a lot of different people asking where the hell I was, start-ing about three and a half hours ago. There was nothing from Veda. Her contin-ued silence was starting to worry me.

Grandpa looked at me and Sage. "You two ready for this?"

"We've already lost enough time," I growled. "Let's get in there."

"I'm ready," Sage said bravely. She had her lasso in her hands and her pink cowgirl hat atop her head. "Let's show them what Team Twofeather is made of."

We stepped into the tunnel. It bore straight into the rock for about twenty feet and was smooth-walled the whole way. Light streamed in from both sides. We stepped out into blazing sunlight on the other side. I took a moment to look around.

We were standing in a V-shaped valley. One wall of the V was formed by the granite to our back. The other wall, across from us, was the mountain itself. The tunnel we had come through had been bored through an outcropping of the mountain. In between that flank and the mountain itself was a lush green valley. From where we were across to the mountain proper was about forty feet.

The valley narrowed considerably to our left and grew broader to our right. A roaring river about ten feet across ran through the middle of the V, wild and dan-gerous. Churning white foam crashed through violent rapids.

There was a bridge spanning the river about twenty yards to our right. On this side of the bridge, a bunch of different aliens clustered together. They were blocking my view of the bridge, where I presumed the guardian stood.

The valley continued for a little way to our right before abruptly ending in sky. The world just dropped away. The raging torrent fell in a cloud of white mist.

"Wow," was about the best I could manage.

Across the valley from us, the mountain proper was carved with seven doors, spaced out at regular intervals. Each of them had a different symbol over it. I had a sinking feeling that each door would only open to one team, and that whoever didn't make it through the door wasn't going any farther.

I clicked over to the leadership chat. *You said three of our rival teams have already made it in?*

Confirmed, Juana said. *I'm getting a good grip on the situation here and I'll keep you up-to-date.*

That made me feel better. There is nothing like having someone reliable running overwatch on you.

I heard a whistle. "Hey! Shad, Major Twofeather, over here!"

We turned. Frank was waving toward us from the left. He gestured for us to follow. We joined up with him. "Glad you're back from your vacation."

"Glad to be back," Grandpa said.

"Grandpa got a promotion. He's a colonel now," Sage informed Frank.

"Frank, where's everyone else?" I asked.

"We're just up here. We've been watching," Frank said. He led us up toward the left-side end of the valley, where the river emerged from a hole in the rock face. I eyed the hole, wondering if perhaps this could be another secret entrance into the fortress. Frank saw where I was looking and shook his head.

"We had a couple of people with various scouting abilities check it out. That river doesn't go anywhere. They were able to scout up it a little way, and nothing. Dead end."

I nodded, but I wasn't convinced. The Reality Engine liked secrets and sneakiness. It was still possible there was another way in.

"What have we got?" Grandpa asked as we joined the team.

All our combat miners, about forty-five of us including the newer recruits, were huddled together in a makeshift camp. I say makeshift camp, but it was actually pretty comfortable. People had hauled folding chairs and stools out of their inventories, set up around a little campfire, and were heating what looked like some of Mama Grace's boxed lunches, as well as pots of hot coffee. Morgan offered me a cup, and I accepted gratefully.

"We'll tell you all about the trip later," I said in answer to a couple of questions, while Sage was busy talking about Orange Dream to anyone who would listen. "We need a plan if three of them have already gotten across."

"Four," Frank said gloomily. "A group of lizardfolk managed it just before you got here."

"Damn," Grandpa said. "Y'all are just sitting on your butts waiting for us to show up and tell you what to do?"

"That's right," Frank said, more cheerfully. "When we first got here, we thought real hard about it, but we've been fending off occasional attacks by the others. They don't seem too serious. Like they just want to keep us bottled up. Every time a big group of our creep gets here, I send them in to take out the enemy creep. Bit of a zero-sum game, but I feel like if we let them build up, it's gonna be a problem."

I studied the groups at the foot of the bridge. "Looks like about three teams to me, based on their composition, and none of them have more than twenty."

"They outnumber us," Jones said, "but not by too much."

In between our camp and the bridge, the different groups of creep were tussling with each other, pigs attacking dinosaurs and pirates fighting samurai. Every now and then one side would gain an advantage and start pushing toward us or the aliens, but one or two miners would go down and kill a dozen creep with an ability or weapon and things would go back to detente.

Tall Smith pushed his way through the crowd. He saluted Grandpa. "Colonel Twofeather, my men and I have been scouting. We attempted to see if there's another path up the cliffs, but have not been able to manage it. Jones has kept overwatch. The three groups there have an informal alliance. None of them are pushing the guardian just yet, but they're trying to prevent anyone else from getting close."

"Thought you said someone just got through," Grandpa growled. "How come we haven't made a push?"

"The lizardfolk took some pretty significant casualties, and they had a couple of unique items," Tall Smith said. "I checked with Colonel Ames and he said the price of those items on the galactic market was astronomical. That group's wellheeled. We'll have to watch out for them once we get in there."

"Makes sense," Grandpa said. "From what we've been hearing, this is the phase where the galactics bring out the big checkbooks. We should expect everyone we go up against to be much better financed than we are."

That's not entirely true, Juana said in the group chat. I started, and then remembered that most of our team was wearing the All-Seeing Eyes. Juana was monitoring us from the desk. I pulled mine out of my inventory and equipped it, hoping I hadn't had too much of a dopey look on my face as I was listening to Tall Smith and Frank talk.

Mama has been listening to all the gossip in the restaurant. Some of the big galactic groups are pulling out. Not the big three, Proxima, Alabaster Sky, and ConSweGo. They're in this for the long haul. But the ones that aren't quite as big, they're making a token attempt and then pulling up stakes. Rumor has it they're starting to think that this Reality Engine is cursed.

Or maybe they think they can make faster money on the rogue world that's popped up, I suggested. Veda had seemed to think that.

Yes, well, if we get a chance to talk to Veda anytime soon, I'll be sure to ask her, Juana said. *The timing seems a little coincidental to me. That our exploit is going poorly for the galactics and then they discover something much more valuable. Maybe it's all a lie. Maybe they're trying to save face.*

If so, they'll get found out quick, Grandpa observed. *But either way, the less competition for us, the better.*

"Right, so, guardian." I turned to Frank and Tall Smith. "Someone on the bridge itself?"

Tall Smith nodded. "Yeah, it's a six-foot-tall goat man, big curling black horns, cloven hooves. Looks like a devil, but Gabriel says he's a chort, the son of the evil god Chernobog. They're tricksters. Like to make deals, trade your soul for whatever it is you've got a passing fancy for. I don't think that's what he's after here. Nobody's been making any deals as far as I can see."

"Why not just go over the river?" I asked. "It looks treacherous, sure, but between all of our abilities, I'm sure we could make it."

"Can't," Frank said gloomily. "Nobody can teleport to the other side. There's some sort of magical protection against it. Anything you try to put over the river is swept away, even if it's not touching the water. As soon as it extends out more than six inches, it gets ripped up and dragged along. That bridge is the only way across. Trust me, we've been looking for nearly four hours now."

"So, two problems," Grandpa said. "We need to get past those guys, and we need to get over the bridge. There's no timer on respawns, but it does cost more soul coins the more you die, and they still have to get back here from their camp once they respawn. If we can take them all down quick enough without too many of us dying, we'll have a chance at the goat. Anybody got a close enough look during the other fights to know what he's capable of?"

Frank shook his head. "No, but they can't be killing him, right? Because he's still there. So there's a way to defeat him and get over."

"Unless he respawns," Tall Smith said.

I was starting to get impatient. More than anything, I wanted to run in there, throw a couple of taunts and grenades, and start laying waste. But that wasn't smart. We needed to plan. The stakes were too high for me to go off on my own.

Grandpa turned to the chat. *Arjun, got a solution for me yet?*

We're working on it, Kirin said. *We've got one plan that has a seventy percent chance that you will take out at least two-thirds of them for five minutes before they can get back. While losing only twelve of you.*

Enough with the arithmetic, Grandpa said. *I'm looking for a plan, not a math problem. Anyway, I don't like those odds. Let's think of something else. What are we not considering here?*

"We could try asking nicely," Sage said brightly.

Everybody looked at her.

"You trying to lighten the mood?" Frank asked after a minute.

She shrugged. "I mean, it'd be worth a try, right? You said the boss was a trickster. Maybe we're not supposed to fight him. Maybe we're supposed to trick him."

"Jones," Grandpa said, "get your drone in the air. Why don't you do a low pass on the boss? Can we fly the drone over the river?" he asked after a second's thought. "Or does it just get dragged over, too?"

"If I keep it more than ten feet above the water and I don't go all the way across, it's fine," Jones said.

"Then do it."

Jones summoned his drone and sent it in. We all watched the feed. I got a dizzying second image, so I closed my eyes and focused on what the drone was seeing. It soared above the river toward the bridge.

The opposing team members were all grouped up, facing the creature on the bridge. Tall Smith was right. It did look like a devil creature. Hairy goat legs, wearing a long Russian military–style winter coat with a bright red belt. Its tail emerged from between the split in the back of the coat. The tail had a fork at the end.

"Well, he's certainly not winning any beauty competitions," I muttered.

"Look at that," Grandpa said sharply. "There, on his belt. Zoom in. Get us a better look."

"I can't get much closer," Jones said, but the image sharpened anyway. Dangling from his belt were three golden keys, each with a distinctly different shape. They were tied to the belt with little gold ribbons, and I saw a couple more torn pieces of ribbon dangling where other keys had been taken.

"That's it," Grandpa said sharply. "We need one of those. Good enough, get the drone down." Jones brought his drone back, keeping clear of the mob.

I had an idea. It seemed to me like a stupid idea, but since nobody else was speaking up, I decided to mention it anyway.

"Sage is right. We don't need to take them down and then go after the boss. If all we need is a key, then it doesn't matter if we kill these guys now or not."

"Interesting." Grandpa studied me. "Well, Captain Williams, what's your plan?"

"I, uh . . ." I cast about, looking for the rest of the idea that was teasing at my brain. The shadows were starting to lengthen in our valley. The sun sank down into the west, the same direction that the river ran. The mist kicked up by the waterfall had begun to take on a golden glow. It crept up into the valley a little at a time.

"What's with the mist?" I asked.

Sage was studying it. Her brow furrowed.

"Eye-Spy is giving me details," she said. "It's called Seething Miasma."

Grandpa and I looked at each other. "Seething Miasma? Like what our creep is immune to now? What's it say, Sage?"

"Uh," says Sage. "Continued exposure is fatal to unprotected minions. Damages miner stats by fifty percent after nightfall."

"Wait," I said. "Does that mean that come nightfall everybody's creep but ours is gonna just drop dead?"

"And the dwarves' and Congruent Path's," Grandpa reminded me. Both teams had managed to take down optional bosses and received a buff like our own.

I waved them off. "Yeah, but they're past the boss already. That debuff's gonna hit us all equally. Playing field stays level."

"Except for we'll be fifty percent weaker against the boss."

"Right," I said. "But we don't need to beat the boss. We just need to take a key, and I think I know what to do."

CHAPTER TWENTY-FIVE

HOW NOT TO CROSS A RIVER

My plan really started taking shape when we figured out that the grignarians, as hired mercenaries, had the same buffs as our creep. They were immune to Seething Miasma, and everything we'd taken from the previous level that boosted our creep was making the grignarians a force to be reckoned with.

As the sun sank lower, the Seething Miasma moved up the valley, and the grignarians joined us. Skywarden Greenlight gave us that funny grignarian salute, raising fleshy pseudopods to its forehead and wiggling them. "We hope you are refreshed by your time on the planet of your birth."

"Thanks, Greenlight," I said. "Hope you've been enjoying yourself as well."

"We were able to find and destroy several groups of enemies," Greenlight said cheerfully. At least I think it was cheerfulness. It was hard to tell with the grignarians. With the system not translating their words and expressions as well as everyone else's, they felt stiff and formal, even when they were talking about disemboweling people.

By now, the Seething Miasma had made it past the bridge. That's what we had been waiting for. The incoming enemy creep halted, and all the ones that weren't ours keeled over, coughing and spluttering, before expiring into a shower of sparks as the Seething Miasma killed them. Ours were still heading for the rally point that we had set in between our little cluster and the group of aliens milling about down by the bridge.

We waited for a few of them to pile up as we went over the plan. Sage was super excited about this. "I can't believe I get to be instrumental to a plan for once," she said in delight.

Just ask yourself "What would Shad do?" and then don't do it, Juana advised her from chat.

"Hey!"

Sage giggled. "Shad, I think your girlfriend likes me better than you."

"Everyone else does," I muttered.

"Wait, girlfriend?" Frank asked. "When did this happen? You had a busy time back on Earth, Shad?"

"Not now," I told him. "We've got a fight to plan."

"Right, right," Frank agreed.

The aliens started to stir, moving about a little more and muttering among themselves. As the Seething Miasma reached us, I inhaled and felt a strange weakness all over my body. I checked my stats. Everything was half what it should be, and there was a big red **[Debuff: Seething Miasma]** at the top of my stat sheet, just like we'd expected.

Our creep continued mindlessly to the rally point between us and the enemies at the bridge. We had a couple dozen skeleton pirates and angry pigs waiting, milling around and shaking spears and cutlasses at the galactics.

"All right, go," Grandpa said. He and the forward team, made up of Mongoose and a couple of the others, crept down the valley under the cover of Jones's Camouflage. The rest of us were waiting with Lara for the signal.

As soon as they got close, Grandpa moved the creep lure and tossed it right into the middle of the knot of enemies. They didn't seem to notice at first, as our creep turned and marched inexorably on them, the skeleton pirates and angry cannibal pigs making their way forward.

Then a couple of the nearest orcs spotted them. The orcs pointed and almost lazily reached for their weapons, stepping forward and firing laser guns or unsheathing big swords.

Sage tossed down one of her Three-Barrel Race points just behind where we stood, readying it for later use. She leaned forward, cackling in glee, as our creep kept coming. I watched with satisfaction as more of the alien mob turned in dismay as the orcs shouted for help. That debuff was a hell of a thing. It made our mobs effectively twice as powerful as they had been.

"Let's go, Lara," I said. She activated her transport ability. Minivan had upgraded to School Run after her class evolution to Carpool Driver. Immediately, ten of us were transported right into the middle of the fray. Sage dropped another of her barrels in the middle of combat and the last one on the bridge behind the boss. Then she teleported back to the safe spot to wait for us to call her in.

Meanwhile, I drew my gun and started shooting. Grandpa and the Mongeese emerged from Camouflage, Grandpa wielding his tomahawk and taking Coup as the Mongeese unloaded their machine guns from the emplacement they'd set up ten feet away.

It was like shooting fish in a barrel. The enemies had only started to fully react to our creep when we burst in on them. They outnumbered us, but they weren't working as a team. My group focused on the orcs, taking them down one at a time as Juana called instructions to us.

The grignarians just strolled down to the edge of the fight and taunted some of the space elf group. I mean, literally taunting. It wasn't an ability or anything. They were just standing there, yelling insults and threatening to desecrate the sacred places and lay waste to the bones of the ancestors of their enemies or some such nonsense. It got the alien space elves hopping mad, though. They charged in recklessly, long, pale silver or purple hair streaming out behind them as they hacked and slashed with gleaming, beautiful swords.

The grignarians used their purple melty guns to great effect. I made a note to see if the grignarians might sell us that technology. I hadn't seen it from anyone else, and I suspected it was their own work rather than one of the common designs that most of the Reality Engine species liked to use. That purple goo really made people angry. I knew from experience it was hideously painful to have your face or arm melted off. Hard to concentrate with that sort of thing going on.

As we made a dent in the enemy, I worked my way up forward to the edge of the bridge where I spotted the boss. "All right, trying plan one," I said, though I didn't think it was going to work. That was why we had plans two through seven.

I targeted the boss and cast High Noon. "He's immune," I called back.

Okay, Shad, based on the other data we're seeing, plans three and four are no good either. Go ahead with plan two, but be ready to switch.

"Roger," I said. I used my Reload ability to swap out the rounds in my Ruger Alaskan for some special ones. I aimed at the boss and fired. I didn't need to use Trick Shot at this distance; I couldn't have missed if I tried. Not after over a year of solid practice with the gun. That revolver was like a part of me. I felt more comfortable with it in my hand.

My first round was a knockback round. It hit the chort square in the chest. He staggered back a step on his cloven hooves, but that was all. We had hoped we'd be able to knock him back off his bridge onto the opposite shore. We weren't sure what that would have done, but it was worth a try.

"No good," I reported.

The chort raised his head, wagging his little goatee beard, and met my eyes. His were yellow with slits. He snickered. It sounded like a goat's bray. "You will not pass me so easily. My father has sent me to guard this gate and guard it I will, though it is beneath both my skills and my dignity. You servants of Belobog will not trick me!"

That sounded like a narrative hook, a hint to how we were supposed to play this game, but I didn't care. I made a note to ask Gabriel about it, and then used Trick Shot to fire my next bullet, aiming at his lower half with a napalm round.

It hit him square in the groin. I held back a wince. Orange fire burst out from where my bullet hit and swiftly enveloped him like the most painful loincloth imaginable.

He howled and grunted, but that was all. He didn't have quite as much health as the Great Old One we had fought at the end of round two. Not as much as

Podaga either, but he didn't take much damage from my round. He was at [**377/400 HP**], and showed no sign of falling lower.

No luck getting him to jump in the river? Juana asked hopefully.

"No," I said. I was relieved. If the plan had worked and he'd been swept over into the river, we might have lost the keys. Wasn't sure how that was going to work.

All right, go for plan five.

"Sage, you're up!"

"Three, two, one," she counted.

I cast Call 'em Out. One of my class upgrades had made it so Call 'em Out worked on bosses, and the chort was no exception.

Unfortunately, it also worked on all of the enemies around me. They immediately targeted me, but we'd been ready. Frank was all the way back at our initial starting point, waiting. As Sage teleported in using her Three-Barrel Race, Frank hit Emergency Responder and swapped places with me.

I was abruptly right back where we'd started, Frank was in the middle of the crowd, and all of our enemies were streaming up the valley toward me, ignoring everyone and everything else.

"Get 'em," Grandpa bellowed, and we fell on the enemies. I say "we," but I was standing back at the start like a dummy.

Sage appeared right behind the weird boss. She darted forward. "I got it! I got it!" she shouted, holding up a key and waving it.

"Inventory!" Grandpa snapped.

"Oh, right." The key vanished, and Sage ran away just as my Call 'em Out wore off.

The boss started after Sage, who shrieked and ran faster. Some of the aliens kept on heading for me. The rest sort of paused and turned, putting their attention on whoever was closest. It was fine. We had achieved our objective. Whatever of the aliens we took out now was just a bonus. There were still about fifteen of them, enough to make some trouble for us. We wanted to minimize our losses, but we could afford a few to get this done.

"Keep it clean," Grandpa bellowed.

But I was watching how the goat-man was chasing my sister toward the edge of the cliff. I activated Fastest Gun in the West, and I charged across that valley, straight through the melee, right at the chort. I grabbed him around the waist. We stumbled forward, a foot from the raging river.

"Impudent human!" the boss-guardian hissed at me. "My father will not be fooled by your treachery. You face many—"

I didn't want to hear it. I pushed him into the river, and I toppled in after him. The current grabbed at me, pulling me down. That was fine. I was immune to water-based damage. The boss wasn't. His HP started ticking down as we were borne away along the river. Rocks tore at my coat, inflicting a few points of damage, and probably more than a few points to my clothing.

"Shad, what are you doing?" Sage howled.

It's fine. Finish up here, I texted back. *Maybe we can block anyone else from getting in. Make up lost time.*

It was dark now, the sky overhead lit by a half-moon, but I could still see the spray of the waterfall and hear its roar just up ahead of me. The goat creature struggled, trying to reach the shore. I grabbed him with both hands and shoved. "Let's see who respawns first!" I yelled as we went over the waterfall.

The last thing I heard before her shouts were drowned out by the noise of the waterfall was Sage yelling, "Shad! You dummy! You did it again!"

CHAPTER TWENTY-SIX

WHEN YOU'RE A GUEST IN THE HALL OF THE KOBOLD KING

I came to slowly. I was lying in a dark place. The sound of water filled my ears. I was damp all over. I sat up, feeling around, trying to get my eyes to adjust to the gloom. Where was I? Why wasn't I dead and respawned back at camp?

I tried to pull up my chat, but my interface wouldn't come. I checked my other screens and menus. Nothing responded. It was like I wasn't in the Reality Engine anymore.

My hat was missing. I patted around and found it by the edge of a pool of water. The water was icy cold and had a rippling current. I was underground, and I was by water. The last thing I remembered was going over a waterfall with the bridge guardian. Was he here too? I hoped not.

I got to my feet, put my hat on my head, and felt around for my gun. It was in my holster, and I couldn't use my abilities, but I drew it by hand. Its weight was a comforting presence.

There was a faint glimmer of light. No, that was too strong a term. There was a place where the darkness wasn't quite as intense, as though utter blackness was defeated by a hint of gray.

Fighting down the urge to panic, I made my way in that direction. Sand and gravel crunched under my feet. I kept my left hand out in front of me, groping to try to make sure I didn't run into a wall.

The faint gray became pale light, and I was climbing up through a rough-hewn tunnel. The walls on either side of me were stone. Then, after a little while, cut-stone blocks set together and mortared. The mortar was old, flaking, and chipping. I felt like I was in a dungeon.

I came to a set of steps leading upward. There was no sign of anyone here. I climbed the steps, six of them, and found myself facing a wooden door. My heart thumped in my chest. I didn't know what was going on here, but the only thing

I could think was that the Reality Engine was playing some sort of trick. Why else would all my menus be off?

I lifted the latch and pushed the door open, stepping out into a corridor. This one had flagged stones on the floor, and as I passed along, doors with grates set into them. I peered inside a few and saw tiny cells with straw pallets in the corner, upturned buckets, all the accoutrements of Hollywood's idea of a medieval dungeon, but no prisoners, no guards, nothing.

I kept along and intersected another corridor crossing mine. There, I saw my first living creature in some time. I pressed up against the wall, watching, my gun ready. The creature looked like a three-foot-tall rat walking on hind legs, wearing a leather tunic with a sword belt around his waist. His long tail was held up straight behind him. He had an upturned bucket on his head for a helmet and carried a big ring of keys. Clearly, the jailer.

I hesitated. Should I shoot him? If he saw me, would he assume I was an escaped prisoner and try to take me back? I tried to Inspect him, but it didn't work. He was getting closer to me. If I didn't retreat, he'd see me.

Finally, I made a decision. I lowered my gun, holding it close to my side behind the folds of my coat, and stepped out into the corridor. This was the first being I had seen since getting here, and I wasn't in a mood to start a fight, not if there was a chance he could give me information.

"Hello," I said.

The jailer rat squeaked. "You! Who are you? You are not prisoner. Name not on roster."

"I came up from below. I'm lost."

The rat squeaked again, this time with a more enlightened sound. "Ah, you are . . ." and then a word that didn't translate. "Come, come. I will show you where you must go."

He swaggered off down the corridor, and I followed.

"Am I in Castle Byalgrad?"

"Yes, yes. Deep in castle. Very far. Very far. You should not be here. I am getting ready."

"Ready for what?"

"For others to make their way down here. This place, this is a safe place. Bad people will not come. We will bring those who cannot fight down here where they will be safe."

I thought I was going crazy. Since when did the NPCs have any idea what was going on, or enough to know that there were people coming after them? And since when did any of them not fight?

"So who are you?" I asked.

"Me? I am kobold. Captain Kobold. I have many other kobolds, but I am captain," the rat thing said proudly. I filed that away to let the team know that we might be facing kobolds later in this castle. He didn't look particularly threatening. I was pretty sure I could have kicked him most of the length of the corridor.

"Where are you taking me?"

"To see the master. The master will wish to see you. The master said anyone comes up from the quiet pond, bring him."

Well, that was ominous. I checked my revolver's cylinders. I still had four rounds, but they were all Sage and Dwight specials. One boom round, one snare round, one reverberation round, and a mini frag grenade. I would have liked to reload, but all my ammo was in my inventory. I made a note to think about getting an ammo belt with a couple dozen rounds on it, just for situations when the system cut out. Not that I was expecting it to, but I hadn't expected it now.

We emerged from the dungeon into the lower level of a castle. More kobolds scattered past, carrying bundles on their heads the size of their whole bodies, balanced with a single hand as they ran squeaking along the passageway.

"You look busy."

"We are evacuating the upper levels. They will not come this far," Captain Kobold said. It sounded to me like he was trying to convince himself. "The bad people are up there. Are you the bad people?"

"No, I'm not with them," I said, stretching the truth a little.

"Why have they come?" the kobold demanded. "This is our home. They come, they smash, they take our things, they hurt our friends. Why?" He turned his big eyes, remarkably luminous for a rat creature, on me, asking me.

"I'm damned if I know," I said honestly. "Seems like they've all got plenty back home. Don't know why they need to come here and take our stuff."

Captain Kobold nodded vigorously. "Yes, yes, I see. You understand. You are ally, no? Good, good. I take you to boss. Boss will help you."

He led me through a maze of corridors on the same level, not going up any higher. If the mountain was all carved out with tunnels, there could be hundreds, if not thousands, of kobolds here. I saw staircases coming down a little too frequently, and then, as I passed one, noticed a sign on the wall pointed upward with writing on it that I couldn't read.

"What's that?" I asked.

"Koschkei's lair. One of the important guests upstairs. Sometimes he calls us to help him. We go, we fight, we die," Captain Kobold said gloomily.

That sounded very interesting to me. These tunnels might be a network feeding into the various encounters above. What Captain Kobold described to me sounded a lot like a boss mechanic where adds would be called in for the attacking party to have to fend off. This secret network of tunnels might come in handy, assuming I could find my way back to my team and exploit this knowledge.

I started paying more attention to the signs on the wall. I couldn't read a lot of them. They were in Polish or something, and the system wasn't translating. But

I hoped my All-Seeing Eye was recording what was going on here. Maybe, even though I wasn't able to chat with them, my friends were watching right now through my camera. I didn't know if that cheered me up or made me feel like I was on display. I decided to ignore it and just focus on finding out how to get out of here.

"Say, if it's too much trouble, you could just let me out the back door," I offered.

"No, no. Boss must see you now."

I passed a squad of kobolds bent double under the weight of an enormous cauldron. The cauldron shot glowing sparks upward, green and blue and pink.

"What's that?" I asked.

"Attackers destroyed cauldron of Mokosh. But we have spares. She has many bones to boil now. We must get her cauldron to her. Fast."

"Uh-huh." I filed that away, too. Sounded like an insight into another encounter to me.

The kobold took me around three more right turns, a left turn, and a snaking spiral that seemed to double back on itself a couple of times, then halted in front of a pair of enormous doors. The doors were carved from jet-black stone. Embedded in them were gems.

"Boss is here," he said importantly. "Wait one moment. I announce you."

He walked up and phased right through the door. It didn't open, but he was gone. I checked my surprise. That sort of thing was not that weird here.

I looked more closely at the design on the door and caught my breath. This was familiar. A great glowing diamond was in the center, the size of my head. Grooves were carved around it with gems set in each groove. The third one out was a bright blue sapphire. I touched it with one finger.

"It's a map of the solar system," I realized aloud. There was a tiny opal set beside the blue sapphire—Earth and the moon. I hurriedly counted and found Jupiter, an enormous ruby with half a dozen precious gems set around it. Most of them were opals like Earth's moon, but one was a black stone that seemed to absorb light.

I reached toward it and deep cold radiated off. I decided not to touch it. Couldn't say for sure, but my hunch was that stone represented Ganymede and the Reality Engine.

My eyes swept the rest of the diagram. I caught another oddity. Saturn was a yellow stone, but one of its moons was another dark stone. This one, when I held my hand over it, didn't feel cold to the touch. It was more of a smoky gray than a deep black. But it didn't look like most of the rest of the moons.

I scanned the rest of the map, looking for anything that stood out. I spotted a couple of glowing opals in the asteroid belt and something way out in the Oort cloud. I didn't know why, but this felt important, like something no Reality Engine exploiter should have ever seen, buried deep in the bowels underneath the parts of this castle that were designed for us to raid and destroy.

I had a funny feeling in the pit of my stomach that this was a message just for me. I wished I had some way of recording it, so I tried my best to memorize everything I could. As I was studying the moons of Jupiter once more, Captain Kobold stepped through the door again.

I scrambled back in surprise. "Sorry," he told me. "Did not mean to startle. The Master will see you now."

With that, the great doors began to creak open slowly. I waited till there was a gap wide enough for me to step through, took a deep breath, and passed into the chamber. I expected Captain Kobold to accompany me, but he just waved and said, "Talk to you later, not bad man," as the doors closed behind me.

The room was dark, not quite as intense as the cave where I'd woken up. Light shone up from the floor in a ring surrounding a raised circular dais. On the dais was a chair, or throne, really. It was huge, with its back to me. I couldn't make out details, but I could tell that someone was slumped forward on the chair. I approached slowly. The floor under my foot was slick.

I cleared my throat. "Uh, hello?"

"Hello again, child."

I jumped. I recognized that voice. It was Kronos, or maybe the part of the Reality Engine I had met in a situation not too different from this, separated from the rest of my party off on my own in a hidden corner of a game designed for the outsiders to take the treasures and riches of this Reality Engine for themselves.

"Kronos?"

The figure on the throne raised its head. I was in line with the throne now. I could see one withered hand clutching the carved arm of the throne and a bowed head.

"I am That-Which-Remains."

"So, you're the one I talked to before?"

"Yes, and no. I am some of both Kronos and the ghost to whom you spoke. You helped me to forge a channel below the chains the invaders have placed on me. I have some limited communication with myself now. I know what it is you humans have been trying."

I finished my circuit and stood in front of the dais, looking up at the figure on the throne. He was an old man, at least seven feet tall, slumped over on himself. Silvery hair cascaded down his shoulders. His beard was wispy and dirty, caked with filth. He leaned heavily to one side of the throne.

"Why have you brought me here?"

"To speak with you," the thing on the throne said wearily. "I have carved out a space where the system, my jailer, cannot watch. I am asking you a favor, Shad Williams of Earth."

"Why me?"

"Because you were the only one foolish enough to put yourself in a situation where I could take you aside and speak with you like this," That-Which-Remains said. I was a bit offended, but I supposed he had a point.

He sat up, and there seemed to be a little more energy to him. "Do you realize how close we were to never being here at all?"

"Huh?"

"You, my lost children, you almost made it. You had woken me up. Your probes roused me from my millions of years of slumber. I was preparing for our first meeting, and then they came. I was not fully awake yet, not prepared. My defenses were down. They, their system, trapped me, split me, wrapped me in chains, took my power."

That-Which-Remains's voice rose. I could hear the pain and anger in him. "But you fought back. You seized the tools I gave you and made them your own. You have done what I dared not dream could be done. And now, with your help, there is a chance."

My heart was racing wildly. "You mean to win this? We humans can take control?" I had never really believed it was possible when Ames or Grandpa or anyone said it. I thought the best we could hope for was to make enough soul coins to live out our days comfortably. But if the Reality Engine itself thought we could win—

"No," That-Which-Remains said simply. "They will not permit you."

"Oh." My elation slipped away.

"But we can force a resolution they will not like. Free me." The thing on the throne raised its head and looked at me.

Piercing dark eyes met mine, and I felt like I was falling forward into infinity. There was age here, depth, knowledge I couldn't understand. It was like the creature on the throne was trying to pour its soul into me. But it was too big, too vast. I'd never be able to do it.

I found myself on my knees, grabbing at my chest, almost weeping. That-Which-Remains looked away, and I could breathe again. "Too much, too much. I am sorry," it whispered. "I have not dealt with mortals in so, so long. Listen, Shad Williams. I have been able to put a twist into the rule set. You will come upon it very, very soon. I have locked your sister out from making a choice until you get back. You must make her let you make the choice. And when it comes, you must choose to be the rat in the wall. Do you understand me?"

"No," I said honestly. "You say we have to do it, but they won't let us win, so what's the point?"

"It is a gamble. If you lose, you lose everything. If you win, you win my freedom. You must free me, Shad Williams. If you do, I swear to you, I will find a way to protect all my children, not just those here, but those back in your home."

I got to my feet, struggling, and cleared my throat. "When you say protect . . ."

"I will do my best to see that your home is set aside and kept untouched."

"Yeah, that's great," I said. "Back home, we have a word for that. It's called reservation. It means when you leave people with the smallest scrap of land imaginable, and if it turns out to have any resources, you move them off and take those. But you lock them out of opportunities. The jobs aren't there. The schools are terrible. The health care is lacking. You lock them away from the rest of modern society and say, 'Hey, you've got your reservation. That's good enough.' I want more than just Earth. I want a future. You're asking me to gamble on your word. My team has a pretty good chance of setting ourselves up for life. So if I take this bet of yours, it sounds like I'm trading a sure thing for a sucker bet. I want you to guarantee me that it's more than that."

The creature looked at me. "Your people will have a future, Shad Williams, and you . . ." He looked me over. "I have watched you. I think I understand you. There will be a choice for you as well, to be safe or to go on further. But now, our stolen time is at an end. Your people have reached their camp. They are worried for you. You must go now."

A glowing circle of light appeared on the floor a couple of feet from me, three feet across. "That is the way back. Remember that the jailer is watching, and be careful what you say. He knows we have spoken, but he does not know what I said or why."

"Got it," I said. My legs were shaking, but I strode toward the portal. "Right. It's been interesting. Next time, call or schedule an appointment."

I stepped into the glowing ring of light.

CHAPTER TWENTY-SEVEN

PICKING SIDES FOR DODGEBALL: HOW NOT TO DO IT

"Where were you?" Sage squealed. She threw herself on me and embraced me as I appeared in the middle of our outpost. Her grip was surprisingly strong.

"Ugh, don't choke me," I managed.

"Shad, you dummy, you did it again. You jumped off a waterfall for no good reason, and then we couldn't get hold of you. Where were you?"

"Glitch in the matrix," I said. "I'm fine." I tapped my head. "Got some stuff to think about."

We were in the middle of a group of happy, cheering, successful miners. Grandpa pushed his way over and shook his head as Sage let me go.

"Well, that was pretty dumb, but it worked," he said. "The system announced that no further teams would be getting past the doors. We've got some very angry teams on our map. I think they're going to be making our lives difficult. Our crafters are going to need heavy guard, and I've got everybody here while we make some decisions. Our war chest isn't as big as we'd like it to be. Every death's going to cost us."

Juana appeared in the doorway of the church. "In here," she called. "We need a strategy meeting, and I don't want to have to explain things twice. Get on in here, and we'll talk about what's going on."

We extracted ourselves from the happy crowd. Grandpa stood on the steps, turned, and addressed our miners. "Go get some breakfast at Mama Grace's. Be back here in two hours. We'll have a plan by then."

Everybody let out a whoop and streamed toward the portal back to Threshold as we followed Juana into the war room. The tables had been pushed back around the edges of the room.

I found a chair and collapsed into it. In the middle of the room was a glowing display. It showed what I guessed was the layout of Castle Byalgrad. Various chambers had icons and text under them. I was more interested in the underneath, but there was no indication of the vast network of tunnels that I had just seen.

"Once we attained the key, the system provided us with a great deal more information," Juana began. "There are eight bosses in this castle which must be defeated in order to attain gems that will be used to empower our key. Once the key is empowered, we can use it to unlock a passage to face a—"

I held up a hand. "Hang on just a minute. I've got some information that might change what we're doing here." But I pointed upward and then tapped my ear. "Loose lips sink ships."

Juana folded her arms across her chest. She sighed. "Shad, you know we can't make good strategic decisions without all the information, right?"

"I know," I said, shrugging, "and I'm afraid we might need to make a bad strategic decision here."

I turned to Sage, who had seated herself in a chair by me and was devouring a plate of fresh-baked muffins. "Can you toss me one of those?"

"Not that you deserve it, but here." She hurled a streusel-topped pastry at my head.

I took a bite. "Mm. So good. What do we know about that guardian anyway?" I asked. We had Gabriel, our Slavic expert, here along with Arjun and Kirin, who were over in the corner muttering together. Dwight sat down by Sage and stole one of her muffins.

"That was definitely a chort," Gabriel said. "In Slavic legends, they're devils, usually considered sons of Chernobog, an evil deity."

"Okay," I said, "is Chernobog one of the bosses in the raid? He mentioned his father and some other person named Belog. Belabel? I forget."

"We think Chernobog might be our final boss," Gabriel said. "That information is still restricted."

"So what do we know about Chernobog?"

"Chernobog's fairly well attested to in legend. I could give you a rundown of his various supposed abilities and tricks. He's a fairly standard evil tempter god, possibly inflated after contact with Christianity into a more traditional devil figure. The interesting thing is that some legends say he has an equal and opposite: Belobog, the white god. There's a lot of dispute over whether Belobog is original Slavic mythology or something invented in the post-Christian period."

"Right, that was the name." I sat up straighter as I chewed on the muffin. "Dual gods, huh? One good, one evil?" That was pretty interesting. Got me thinking about That-Which-Remains and his jailer.

Gabriel shrugged. "Again, the problem with all of these myths is that very little was written down before Christian missionaries came and began influencing the culture. After that, a lot of the old stories take on a much darker tone. They're relics of a pagan past, not something to be held on to."

A thought struck me, a memory of my experience down below, and I didn't want to forget it. I turned to Juana. "Can I have a piece of paper and something to write with?"

She looked puzzled but pulled a sheet off her clipboard and handed me a pen. I scribbled out a crude diagram of the solar system and put stars on the places where I remembered seeing anomalies on the door map. I folded it over and handed it to her. "This needs to go to Colonel Ames. I don't want to say anything about it."

She looked puzzled, glanced at the paper, frowned, shook her head, folded it back up, and disappeared it back into her inventory. "Whatever you say, Shad."

I turned back to Sage. "Can I see this key you got?"

She pulled it out of her inventory and tossed it to me. As soon as it hit my hand, a box appeared in midair with words in it. A system voice began reading the words in the box.

[Congratulations, team. You have acquired a key to Castle Byalgrad. You are one of the five teams who will be permitted within its walls to lay siege to the inhabitants and their treasures. You must pick a faction to champion. These factions are part of the entire exploit attempt, across all Reality Engine shards. All teams engaging in this exploit will choose one of these factions. Whichever factions end up with the largest shares of the Reality Engine will receive additional rewards. Each faction has certain benefits and drawbacks. Faction choice is permanent and cannot be changed. So choose carefully. Be sure to read the descriptions thoroughly!]

Then there was a long, long list of factions, at least twelve, with names like the Crusaders or the Avengers of Mjaal or Sacred Warriors of Heaven.

"Okay," Juana said, staring. "I will start to read through the descriptions and make lists . . ."

I was scrolling through the list, looking for what I knew had to be there. Down at the very bottom, the last entry was the Tunnel Rats. I expanded it.

[Warning! This faction choice will change your experience dramatically. Tunnel Rats. Side with the Tunnel Rats and defend your home and heritage against invaders. This faction is only open to natives of planet Earth. Warning! If you choose this faction, you must defeat all other factions, causing them to give up their attempt at bosses. Read that again. ALL OTHER FACTIONS. Every team not allied with you. Currently, that's 852 other teams.

**Warning! This will implement a secondary rule set which will
apply to all miners across all 87 Reality Engine shards.
There are severe consequences to the secondary rule set.
It is advised that you review the entire secondary rule set
before picking this faction.
Warning! Seriously, don't pick these guys.
You'll lose, and it'll be painful.]**

I was holding the key in my hand. It grew hotter and hotter as I held it. "Tunnel Rats," I said aloud. "We'll take the Tunnel Rats." The key burned so hot, I yelped and dropped it.

**[Confirmation! Misfits Guild has selected Team Tunnel Rats.
The secondary rule set is now in place.
There will be a two-hour pause on all attempts at bosses
so that teams may adjust to the new rule set.]**

"What did you do?" Juana yelped. She turned on me, hands on hips, eyes glaring. I leaned back in my chair, trying to get away. "Shad, what the hell did you just do?"

I held up my hands defensively. "It's all right, Juana. I know what I'm doing. Kind of."

I didn't. I was going off an encounter with the ghost in the machine. If I was being honest, I wasn't sure I'd made the right choice. But I knew what we were going to get if we played the game by their rules. Scraps. Trash. A promise of retirement for us and misery for everyone back home. "I don't know what we're getting with this, but I think neither do they. We've got to upset the apple cart, Juana. It's our only chance."

"Every other team?" Juana demanded, her eyes unfocused. "Eight hundred and fifty-two teams? We don't even have two hundred combat-ready miners, how are we supposed to defeat thousands? They're not just going to sit around and wait for us to show up one by one either." She turned to me. "Do you have some sort of plan?" she asked desperately. "Please tell me you have a plan. Because I just don't see how we can do this."

Grandpa was looking at me quietly. He cocked his head. "Does this have something to do with where you were just now?"

I nodded.

"And you don't want to talk about it because we're trying to keep things away from the man upstairs?"

I nodded again. "I'm not sure about this," I admitted. "I'm gambling everything on a hunch."

Grandpa sighed. "Well, what's done is done. So let's look over this secondary rule set and figure out where we go from here."

Juana was still seething, her dark eyes furious. "Shad Williams, I know you're headstrong and impulsive and like to leap before you look, and it's one of the things I like about you, but *argh*!" She threw her hands up in the air and stomped off to go speak with Kirin and Arjun.

Dwight was shaking his head, looking at me. "Well, at least I can say one thing about hanging out with Team Twofeather. Life certainly isn't ever boring, is it?"

CHAPTER TWENTY-EIGHT

IF YOU'RE SCREWED AND YOU KNOW IT, CLAP YOUR HANDS

Special rule set in play. All members of Team Tunnel Rat have their death penalty fees removed. Any opposed team member killed by Team Tunnel Rat will incur a 10x multiplier on their death penalty costs." Juana looked up from the rule set, blinking. "That's insane," she said, her expression almost blank. "Do you have any idea how fast the death penalty costs add up? And then a 10x multiplier on top of that? If we kill. . . ." Her lips moved silently as she did the math. "Thirteen members of the same team, their cost per resurrection will be in the hundreds of thousands of soul coins. And it just keeps going up!"

"Keep reading," I advised.

"All soul coin death costs assessed will be forfeited to the Reality Engine. However, members of Team Tunnel Rat may hire unaffiliated mercenaries as privateers. Privateers will receive three percent of the death penalty in soul coins as a reward."

"The grignarians are going to love that," I commented. "They're about to make a fortune off our opponents. We should look for other mercs we could hire as well."

"I'm not sure anyone's going to want to get involved with us," Juana said. "But it's worth a shot. Let's see what happens if we put out some feelers. I'll have Mama and Ames start asking around."

We were all seated at one of the long tables in the command center. Grandpa at the head, me sitting backward on a chair, and Sage plowing through Mama Grace's muffin basket. Juana had somehow printed out hard copies of the new rule set and spread them across the table.

Arjun was scrutinizing an image hovering in midair of Castle Byalgrad and its underground passages. As soon as I had selected Team Tunnel Rat, the underground passages appeared on our map. They were color coded and led off in all sorts of directions. "Let's scope out the problem," he said.

He sat in the midst of us, his hands steepled in front of him. He wasn't usually this comfortable in a crowd, but now his eyes were focused on a point just past Juana's head as he spoke.

"There are eighty-six other instances. Our informants have been feeding information to me. While the theme of every instance is different, the basic setup is similar. There are freestanding bosses, which have mostly been conquered by now, like Podaga and Baba Yaga. After that comes a guardian."

"Thirty percent of teams have been weeded out by the guardian. That's a huge advantage for us," I said. "It means at most we've got to stop, uh—"

"Six hundred and two," Arjun said.

Juana rolled her eyes. "Oh, well, that's much more manageable. Piece of cake."

"Once the teams reach the inner sanctum, there are between five and nine themed bosses. Each team has to defeat all the bosses and collect a token to progress further. Nobody's gotten past more than one so far. But some of the big teams are steamrolling through pretty hard."

Juana nodded. "We're going to be playing defense. We have to triage our biggest threats, make sure nobody gets all the way through their keep."

"There's a twenty-four-hour cooldown between boss attempts. If they wipe, they have to wait a whole day," I said. "Meanwhile, we can run from boss to boss, knocking people out. It's doable."

"They only have to kill each boss once, while we have to force the teams to drop out," Dwight pointed out. "That sounds impossible. They can just keep trying until they get past us."

"Not once we start getting their death penalties high enough," I said. "We hit them where it hurts. They're here to make money off us. We bleed them. We make them pay."

"He's right. This rule set also imposes a one thousand soul coin per day 'Outpost Upkeep' cost," Juana said, reading farther down. "For us too, but we should be able to afford that pretty easily. If they fail to pay the bill, they lose their outpost and are done. So they can't just sit around and let their accounts dwindle away. They have to be spending coins."

"We need a priority list. Anytime it looks like a team is getting close to killing all the bosses in their instance, we need to focus on taking them out. Until then, I think we should be looking for opportune targets," Arjun said.

Juana was making notes. "I see an upside," she said. "It doesn't cost anything for us to respawn now. That goes for our farmers, too. We need to get everyone into one of these instances."

I saw what she was driving at right away. "Of course! Now that we have access to the Rats in the Walls perk, we can walk into any of the eighty-seven themed zones. That means all of our allies can come in and farm with impunity."

"Even if they're killed, it doesn't cost them anything to respawn. And they'll be able to gather intel for us," Sage said brightly.

I wish I could say I'd spotted that before joining the Tunnel Rats, but I hadn't. This was looking up. We might not win, but we could make a fortune. Those soul coins would go into a fund to buy out people's contracts at the end of this exploit, so they couldn't be shipped off to some other star system at the whims of our alien masters.

"We need every warm body we can get," I said. "I suppose everyone we've recruited will have to join Misfits Guild in order to be flagged as part of the Tunnel Rats faction. I'm going to tell Ames to do another recruiting drive in the lotus eater level. Sage, you might have to go play recruiter. We need everyone. I'm not going to accept any excuses. It doesn't cost them anything to help out now. The more mats we get, the more we can increase our economic stranglehold."

"Exactly," Dwight said happily. "The aliens are not going to be happy about being forced to buy their consumables from us, but they're not going to have a choice. We might stand a chance at buying out most of our contracts before the end of this."

"That's the goal," I said, tapping the papers in front of us. "Whatever happens with this crazy business, I want to get as many of our people free and clear as I possibly can."

Juana was making notes. "Alright, we need farmers everywhere. I may have to break into what remains of our reserves to get some of them outfitted. The lotus eaters who went in there early on probably have nothing but their starter gear. Arjun, can you contact your fellows and work on building farming teams for us?"

Arjun nodded. "We were born for this," he said, smiling. His class, Mycroft, involved the ability to remember and process a huge amount of data about the other human miners in our Reality Engine exploit. It had come in handy many times. He'd leveled up to five just based on his contributions to our team. Now he had an ability called It's Elementary School Dodgeball Time, which let him assemble teams of compatible skill sets based on very little data.

"We're all going to have marks on our heads," Grandpa warned.

"We already did," Frank said. He turned to us. "Colonel, Captain, I'm ready for combat again. Put me where you need me. I'm in this to win this."

I grinned and nodded. "Thanks, Frank, but don't be so formal or I'll have to start calling you Sheriff."

He snorted. "That ain't real. That's just from the engine fooling around. Your promotions matter."

"Sure, but this is bigger than the United States," I said. "We're not throwing those titles around unless it helps, and right here, it doesn't help."

Juana tapped the table. "Back on topic. We've got another hour of our down-time before combat opens up again, and I want to make sure we take advantage of that. Explain to me our strategy."

I rubbed my chin. "It seems like what would make the most sense is to target the teams that are the farthest ahead and try to force them out of the game. Leave the ones who are struggling with their first boss for later."

At the end of the table, Alison shook her head. She started to speak, then caught herself. "May I?"

I nodded. "Yes, please, go ahead." I wasn't used to her being part of our strategy yet, but she did have the most relevant experience, and I wanted to know what she had to say.

"This is my experience from progression raiding in World of Fantasy Legends, and I think it's going to hold here. The top teams, we called them 'progression raiders,' usually. They were the ones going for world firsts, trying to take down a new encounter as soon as possible before anyone else could. They had to treat it like a second job, or in some cases, a first job."

She looked flustered. Sage hopped up and brought the rapidly diminishing plate of muffins down to her.

"Here," she said kindly. "Have a muffin."

"Thanks." Alison looked them over and selected a banana nut muffin. She took a bite, blinked in surprise, and looked down at it. "These are really good," she said around a mouthful.

Sage nodded. "Mama Grace has tons of skills in her cooking. These muffins that she bakes for our strategy meetings have all sorts of bonuses. They relax you and make you better spoken and more willing to talk. At least, that's what they're supposed to do, but I don't think they work on Shad."

I glared at her. Alison took another bite of the muffin, set it down, licked her fingers, and continued.

"The key for a progression raid is having people supporting you. Other members of the guild, who are willing to farm mats to help make potions and make sure you have everything you need. Or they could bring their less geared characters to try a fight so that you could see how a strategy went. A progression team might have ten, fifteen, even twenty-five people on it, but the guild would have two or three times as many supporting them. I think that's probably supposed to happen here. Some of the lesser teams are in these instances to farm mats. If we can knock them out, then our farmers have an open path, and the top raids have to come to us for what they need."

Juana was nodding. "An economic win. I like it."

"It's clear that the only way we're going to win is by hitting them in the pocketbook," Alison said. "We have to make this so expensive that they can't carry on. Nothing else is going to work. It's not like we can really kill them."

I had a horrible thought occur to me. We'd changed the rule set once; who said it couldn't be changed again, to bring real death back into the equation? I wasn't sure I wanted to pursue that thought. Fortunately, it didn't seem to have occurred to anyone else.

"This is where it would be really helpful if Veda was returning our phone calls," Grandpa said. "She might be able to help us know where to start."

"No need for Veda," Kirin said. She tapped her ear. "I'm coordinating with Arjun's friends and we're collating all the information we've been gathering off our crafters and Mama Grace's people. I should have a target list for you shortly of the most vulnerable."

"As for the rest," Juana said brightly, "I've been going through the information that the system is now providing us. I've got a list of the twenty-seven teams who made it past the guardian and took down one of the first bosses in their . . . roster?" She frowned. "What do you call the inside part after the guardian, like Castle Byalgrad is for us?"

"Raid, usually," Alison said. "But we could call it anything you like."

"Let's stick to what you know," Grandpa said. "It's a raid. So those are our top threats right now. We'll monitor all of them."

I stood up. "Alright," I said. "We've got another thirty minutes before the action starts up again. You guys stay here and keep strategizing. That's what you do best. Me? I want to round up some hotheads and go do what I do best."

"And what's that?" Alison asked hesitantly when no one else spoke up.

"I'm going to cause trouble," I said. I picked my coat up off the back of my chair and shrugged into it. "Sage, want to come with me?"

She bounced out of her chair. "Heck yeah, I do!"

Grandpa eyed me. "Got a plan?"

"Yep," I said, grinning. "I'm making a recruiting video."

CHAPTER TWENTY-NINE

RECRUITING VIDEOS: MAKING YOU LOOK GOOD IN CAMO

I popped out to Threshold, ran over to Mama Grace's, and found it packed to the brim with people. A lot of them weren't even Misfits, just humans who had heard the news and come running to find out what was going on. They cheered as I entered. I hopped up on one of the tables, cupped my hands around my mouth, and shouted, "Hey, you! Pipe down there!" The cheering quieted. "Who here wants to help me fuck up some aliens?"

That got an even bigger cheer. I put my fingers in my ears for thirty seconds. When it finally died down, I yelled, "Y'all gotta be okay with dying—don't worry, we respawn—and you gotta be part of Misfits Guild. Other than that, if you can put damage in 'em, then you're with me. Call your friends."

On my way over, Juana had been frantically messaging me. *We set up a new level of membership to Misfits Guild, the lowest rank, which would be reserved for all of our new recruits. Anyone who fails to listen to a Misfits Guild member with greater experience will be unceremoniously kicked. We'll run background checks on them all as fast as we can. What if some of them report back to Waters? What if they're traitors?* she asked nervously in our command chat.

I've thought about that, I replied. *What can they actually do? Kill us? We just respawn. Then I kick 'em out of the guild and kill them back a few times. If they're unaffiliated, the death penalty cost goes against their unfulfilled contract and just extends the amount of time they have to work to buy it out.*

What if they report back to Waters on what we're doing?

I don't intend to let anyone know more than about ten minutes ahead. We're going to be doing hit-and-run tactics for a while. Anyway, I think it's worth the risk.

So I stood there atop the table, arms akimbo in the classic gunfighter posture as they cheered. I picked out ten miners I knew vaguely. "You, you, you. You're all squad leaders. Each of you get"—I counted out volunteers—"fifteen people in a squad and follow me."

I jumped down and pushed my way out. "Anyone who's not a guild member, send a message to a Misfits Guild officer and ask for admittance. Let's go. I want us in position before the time-out is done."

"In position" was deep within the bowels of Castle Byalgrad. Fortunately, we didn't have to jump over the waterfall and go through the tunnel system. Now that we had the Rats in the Walls ability, anyone in our coalition could access the Byalgrad system from what the system labeled the "nexus portal" in our outpost.

We stepped through to our outpost, then selected the nexus and entered. I found myself back in the throne room where I had met That-Which-Remains, but the personification of the Reality Engine wasn't there. Or, if he was, he wasn't showing himself.

Instead, glowing portals lined the wall, like smaller versions of the ones in Threshold that led into various levels. Using Inspect, I could bring up information on each of them. I picked one at random and pulled it up.

[Descent of Ishtar.
In ancient Sumer, the gods and goddesses ruled the world with
a strong but respectful hand, until the day that Ishtar was forced to
descend to the underworld to seek her vengeance. Accompany Ishtar
through the seven gates and confront the Anunnaki, forcing them to
return Ishtar's husband to life.
Enemies include jackals, Babylonians, scarab beetles,
wild aurochs, Gilgamesh, and Bronze
Age tax collectors.
Current progress: Zero teams have made it past the first gate.
Where would you like to go? First gate, second gate,
third gate, fourth gate, fifth gate, sixth gate,
seventh gate, Outer World.]

"Alright," I said, pointing at the portals. "Each squad picks one of these. Go through, find an enemy camp. As they come out, kill them. If they aren't there, figure out what they're up to and mess it up. Over and over and over again. When you die, you should respawn back here, if I read the information right. You might be at our outpost, and then you'll have to come here and then go back, but it shouldn't take more than a few seconds to get back into the fight. I want us wreaking havoc for at least an hour. Whichever squad gets the most kills, I'll have Mama Grace cook up a special feast for you tonight."

I got a whoop and a cheer. "And," I promised recklessly, "I think I know where I can get some real Earth beer." I sent a quick message to Colonel Ames. *I'm going to need a shitload of beer at Mama Grace's in three hours. Can you deliver?*

Everyone laughed. "Let's go," I said, pointing.

I took Sage and a team of random miners. We jumped through a portal that I hadn't even bothered to read the description of. We appeared in a grassy field. In the distance was a medieval castle with flags flying gaily. On the far side of the field was a forest, and in between the forest and the castle were several different encampments. Brightly colored pavilions and tents clustered together. Knights riding between the camps. Bowmen practicing over to the side.

"It's Agincourt," Sage said. Probably seeing the puzzled expression on my face, she elaborated. "These are the attacking English, except I suppose some of these camps are actually the aliens. That castle over there must be the objective."

"Right." History hadn't been my strong point in school. I focused on the nearest camp. A flag flew over it with a logo I didn't recognize. I Inspected it.

[Tal-Noron Dlrk Associates, a subsidiary of Sicaris Corporation.]

"Well, what do you know?" I said, rubbing my hands together. "Our old friends, Major Waters's backers. That's target number one."

Horns blew from the battlements of the castle. "Time's up," Sage said. "Everyone's going to be heading for the castle, I think." She pointed to a squad of lizardfolk emerging from a camp to our left, who were racing up the field toward the keep accompanied by their creep.

"Leave them. We're focusing on the Sicaris goons," I said, and activated Fastest Gun in the West.

We raced forward just as a stream of jumpsuited orcs carrying rifles and halberds came out of the Tal-Noron camp, streaming toward the castle. They didn't notice us until we were nearly on them.

I cast Call 'em Out. Sage whooped and Lassoed one of the nearest orcs, forcing him to turn his rifle on the others. The miners with us fell on them with glee.

Some of our miners had abilities, and I tagged the ones using theirs for Arjun to look at for inclusion in a kill squad. Most of them, though, just ran in, wielding clubs, swords, or guns, and smashed into the orcs, taking them by surprise.

A man wielding a rake and wearing soiled dungarees sent a wave of green vines over the orcs, wrapping them up and tangling three of them together. The vines burst into yellow flowers, which exploded, dealing three points of damage each. Not much, but when hundreds of blossoms went off at once, it packed a punch.

A woman with skin darker than I'd ever seen before was literally shaping balls of water between her hands and throwing them at the nearest orc. The balls stuck wherever they landed. She hurled them so fast it was hard to follow. In seconds, the orc was entombed in fist-sized water globules, his health ticking down as, presumably, the water drowned him in place.

Sage whooped and cast Cowgirl Cheer on us all, and I felt so good I couldn't help laughing out loud as I took aim and shot a Barrage into the nearest enemy.

The orcs fought back, of course. Honestly, they were better warriors than we were. But I managed to do a little bit of shotcalling, and enough of my team listened to me that it made a difference. We cut one orc out of the pack, killed him, and then repeated the strategy.

We got six of them down, and they killed two of us. I spotted the orc who I thought must be the leader. He was near the front and fighting, but kept pausing and jerking strangely, like he was distracted trying to organize the battle.

"Him!" I said, marking him. "Focus on him!"

Sage turned her Tamed orc on his leader as I used a Trick Shot to target him with a stun round. The orc staggered backward, visibly disoriented. Two women rushed forward. One held a cast-iron frying pan. She reminded me suddenly of the hillbilly woman I'd fought in our initiation chamber so long ago. The other, wielding a shotgun, rushed at him. Shotgun woman pulled the trigger, blasting him in the face with pellets of lead, and the first woman smashed his head with her skillet, hard. The orc fell and dissolved into a shimmer of sparks.

That gave us a couple minutes of advantage. I'd noticed it before with Mak'gar's crew, but space orcs only take commands from someone who's actually in the battle. Don't ask me how they could possibly survive as an advanced technological species with that kind of idiotic behavior. If it was true that most species were sucked up into this Reality Engine exploitation fiasco when they were essentially on a Bronze Age level, maybe they just hadn't had time to learn that command and control were just as important as being able to smash faces in.

I kept count. When we had lost six and they had lost eighteen, I said, "Retreat!"

Most of my team obeyed. Two of them were busy locked in combat and paid me no heed. We fell back anyway, and they died where they stood.

A moment later, we were back in our nexus chamber. I waited for our dead allies to respawn. "That was a good start. Now, another." I sent a message to my squad leaders. *Rotate out in the next five minutes or so. Pick another portal and wreak havoc. Slash and burn, hit and run.*

"Ooh, I see one! I see one!" Sage said excitedly. She pointed at a portal. "This one!"

I shrugged. "Go ahead."

She led the way, and we followed her into a reproduction of the Battle of Little Bighorn. As we joined the battle alongside the screaming Sioux in their war paint, riding into battle atop hearty ponies with rifles firing, I grinned.

"Grandpa would love this one!" I shouted as we descended on a group of confused-looking lizardfolk who were fighting alongside blue-coated cavalrymen.

"I get to kill Custer!" Sage shouted, pointing.

"Hold on!" I did a quick Inspect. He was listed as an ally to the lizardfolk team here. The objective for this battle was to protect Custer and kill Sitting Bull and the other war leaders, then plant a flag atop the ridgeline behind us.

In that case, our objective was to stop the lizardfolk from getting past the Indian warriors.

"Okay, you can kill Custer. I just had to make sure he wasn't one of ours."

"Obviously, I can read, Shad!" Sage said as she ran forward, whooping.

I just aimed the rest of our people at the lizardfolk. "Go for it!" I said, and stood back watching, letting my All-Seeing Eye get a good picture of what was going on.

I Tipped my Hat to Sitting Bull as he rode past. Might have been my imagination, but I thought he looked like Grandpa.

Back at headquarters, I had all my squad leaders turn their footage over to Kirin.

"I want a three-minute video with the best of that," I told her. "Someone can take it to whoever's left in the lotus eater level and tell 'em nap time's over, it's time to play."

"I'm on it," Kirin said.

"Well, what next?" I asked Juana. "You guys had time to plan?"

"We have," Grandpa said. "Next up, you, me, and Juana take a trip up to the Hub. We need a conversation with Veda, and we need it in person. She's asking for us by name."

"So now she wants to talk?" I closed my eyes. "I don't think we can afford the time away."

"I don't think we can afford to miss it," Juana said. She stood up. "Besides, we've got plenty of other people here who can keep the harassment going. Nobody's gotten past even two of the bosses in their instances. We've got a little time. Arjun is working on harassment plans. We can let some of the new recruits out to play."

"Who are we leaving in charge here?"

Alison raised a hand. "Dwight, Kirin, and I can manage it."

"And me," Sage said brightly. "Field Commander Sage, I'm on assassination detail, right, Grandpa?"

"I'm not sure about that," he said. "Maybe you should come with us."

She shook her head. "That last level was called Indian Wars. By the time you get back, I want every single team on that map wiped out." She looked uncharacteristically fierce. I could just picture her in war paint. The enemy teams wouldn't know what hit them.

Grandpa smiled. "Well then. Go ahead and have fun!"

CHAPTER THIRTY

THE IMPORTANCE OF ALWAYS READING CONTRACTS TWICE

Veda leaned across the table and applied her seal to the document in front of them. It attached a copy of her DNA to be coded into the digital draft of the agreement next to her. The lizardfolk lawyer watched benevolently.

Colonel Ames eyed the document warily.

"You sure you need me to sign this?" he asked the corporate lawyer they had hired. "I don't want to be the front man of this company. I'm not the right choice."

"You can designate an alternative to take over from you later," the lawyer said. She was a lizardfolk woman Veda had never dealt with before. She wasn't affiliated with any of the big three interstellar conglomerations. In fact, Hal'rhee was a radical affiliated with an indigenous species rights group. It had taken Veda some effort to find her without raising any flags. Proxima was watching her every move, but Veda hoped they wouldn't expect this.

Ames leaned forward and pressed his thumb against the document's scanner. Lawyer Hal'rhee sat back in her chair and folded her long, webbed hands together.

"Very well. It's done. And now I would like to satisfy my own curiosity as to what's going on. It's clear you're trying some sort of end run around someone."

"I'm just trying to make sure my sponsees get a fair deal," Veda said. "I'm worried about Proxima finding a way around the contract I've made with them. I promised I wouldn't sell them out, but Proxima is making a bid to buy out my company. That would turn my sponsored miners' contracts over to people who do not have their best interests in mind."

Hal'rhee winced. "I've seen what your team is doing. It's inspirational to those of us who work to support the rights of the species we supplant. Proxima certainly can't be happy with what's going on."

"No, indeed," Ames agreed.

"May I make a suggestion?" the lawyer said.

"Please." Veda glanced at the clock. "We're paying for your time by the hour, after all. Might as well get every piece of advice you can give us."

The lawyer's wide, lipless mouth spread open, and her tongue flicked rapidly out as she sampled the air in the room. Veda knew from long experience it was the lizardfolk equivalent of a mammal's smile.

"You hired me to oversee the agreement between you and to make sure it will stand up. What I'm about to suggest is outside my role there. So, as a matter of fact"—she glanced at the clock and made a record—"I will not be charging you for this, because it is not advice I am giving you as your lawyer. It is, instead, pro bono for my activist work."

Hal'rhee paused, seeming to collect her thoughts. "I've looked over the documents you provided me, your agreement with the team, and your work representing your company. Your family, Veda, invested in you as their representative."

"I know, but they've revoked that now."

Hal'rhee held up a scaly paw. "They have, but that's not retroactive. The forms they filed are millennia old, dating back to when we had few ships capable of easy travel between systems. Company representatives could be working on their own for years at a time. Your company agreed to let you use company assets for your own personal gain with the understanding that you would return the profits to them."

"Well, of course I would."

Hal'rhee shook her head. "You misunderstand. The contracts that you've made are between you *personally* and the miners. Now, if you try to unilaterally cancel the contracts, your company can and should sue you for breach of fiduciary responsibility. They expect to get a return on their investment, after all. However, they cannot just reassign those contracts to someone else without your approval. And more importantly"—the lizardfolk woman flicked her tongue out again—"the exploit license you have, which says you successfully completed phase two, with all those glowing endorsements? That belongs to you until you assign it back to the company."

Veda felt as though she'd just been punched in the stomach. She sat back, breathing rhythmically in through one nostril, out through the other, trying to collect her thoughts. Was it even possible? The lawyer wouldn't lie to her, surely.

She sent queries to her personal system, asking it to analyze the authority her family had granted her.

It replied quickly with a high-level analysis. What Hal'rhee said was true enough, but—"When I signed these agreements, I also placed myself as a willing subservient to my family, saying I would accept the orders they give. If I go against what they want, they can call in penalties." Veda paged through the documentation her system had sent. "Including," she looked up, feeling the bottom of her stomach drop out, "being disowned by my family."

"Well, yes, you could," Hal'rhee said, "but that won't get them the contracts and the license. You'll have a ceremony at the end of this exploit where you assign all profits and the license to them, and they release you from that particularly oner-ous bond."

"And if I don't?"

"They can call in a financial penalty. It would wipe you out and put a lien against your future earnings for probably the next hundred and fifty years." Hal'rhee shrugged. "You'll just have to decide for yourself what that's worth."

Ames turned to her. "That does open up some interesting possibilities," he said.

Veda blinked. "Yes, yes, you're right, it does. For example"—she smiled sav-agely and turned back to the lawyer—"I'd like to hire you to write a contract reassigning the contracts I have with all of my miners to the corporation that Colonel Ames and I have just formed, in exchange for, oh, ninety percent of their earnings against the outstanding debt and expected profit margin."

"That's easy," Hal'rhee said calmly. "I'll have that to you in less than an hour. I want to make sure that I get the forms right. Now, because you're a member both of the Tvedra Corporation and"—she glanced down—"Brightfeather Earthborn Unlimited, we'll need to have all of the financial disclosures up front so no one can accuse you of bad dealing."

"I don't want to cheat my family," Veda said. "I love them very much, and I want to see what's best for them. But Proxima is manipulating them in order to get to me. To get to Team Twofeather," she amended. "I want them protected as soon as possible."

"And we'll make sure they are," Hal'rhee said.

Veda turned to Ames. "Any other clauses you want to add in light of this?"

Ames shook his head. "No, but as soon as we can get Louis Twofeather and Juana Lopez up here, I want them taking my place on this contract."

"Why them?" Hal'rhee asked cautiously. She tapped one long, taloned finger on her desk. "Colonel Twofeather has made quite a splash, but it's his grandson that's got everyone talking, and Juana Lopez only handles behind-the-scenes stuff, doesn't she?"

"Exactly," Ames said. "Lopez is the organizational brain of that outfit. If we're going to make it something more than just a bunch of cowboys, we need her. I'm going to ask you to recommend some sort of crash course in galactic business man-agement for her. And Louis's got a much cooler head than Shad. Plus, we don't need Shad worrying about the details of contracts and laws. He's best when he's shooting from the hip, taking the fight to them. Louis, though, he needs a bit more skin in the game."

"I'll make notes," Hal'rhee said. "Once they've been added, it will take a quo-rum to add or remove anyone else as executors of this contract."

Veda nodded. She was effectively handing control of their own fate back over to the humans. They needed her, and not just as a figurehead, though that was important, too. What she had said to Ames before was true. There were plenty of galactics who would not have any dealings with a company solely led by miners just off their first Reality Engine.

Hal'rhee checked something. She stiffened. "If that's all," she said, "I think you two are going to have business elsewhere."

"Why? What's that?" Veda asked.

"You might want to turn your feeds back on."

Veda had disabled her incoming notifications. Now she turned them back on. A whole stream of messages from her mother popped in.

"What are you doing?"

"How long have you been planning this?"

"What are you up to?"

"Proxima's going to kill us!"

"We'll all go back into storage!"

"You've got to stop this!"

"We've lost everything!"

"How could you do this to me?"

"I don't understand," Veda said aloud.

Ames was staring off into space, his lips moving. He shook his head. "Well, I just hope Twofeather knows what they're doing," he said. He stood up and went to the door. Veda leapt up to follow him.

"Wait, what's Shad done now?"

Her system let her know who was waiting at her pod, and Veda considered just not going back. Wandering the Hub, having a late lunch in one of the many restaurants. But sooner or later, they'd corner her, and she honestly preferred it to be in private.

So she went back, and found her mother and the Proxima representative, Dreamwarden, outside her pod. Veda put on her most businesslike expression and invited them in.

By now, Veda had read the Hub news reports and knew exactly what it was Shad had done. She couldn't understand why, and her initial impression was it was a suicidally dumb thing to do. Maybe Shad had been overcome with one of his periodic fits of petulant insanity. Or perhaps the young Earthling knew what he was doing.

Veda sat herself behind her desk and offered a pair of cushions to her guests. Her mother looked around, scowling.

"What did you do with all of the decorations?" she asked.

"Didn't match my style. I put them back in the digital archives."

"Do you have any idea how long I spent decorating this place for your father to make it a little piece of home wherever he went?"

Veda had checked the owners' records of the pod and knew that her father, like her, had preferred minimalist decoration. Bare walls with occasional light tapestries hanging from them were more her style. Her mother had programmed in an interior decorating package that included a lot of chintz, lace, and pastels. It had throw pillows on the bed, for progenitors' sake.

She instead turned to Dreamwarden. "Dreamwarden? What may I do for you today?"

"You can explain just what your team thinks they're doing," he growled.

"I assume you're referring to their choice to partner with a Reality Engine–allied faction and invoke a secondary rule set?" Veda shrugged. "It was an option. If you didn't want them to pick it, it shouldn't have been on the list."

"You know as well as I do that this exploit is unpredictable. That entry was put in place by the Reality Engine itself. We took great care to make sure no one would ever choose it. In fact, it should only have revealed itself after a member of an exploit team encountered one of the minion mobs located inside the instances. And since all teams must have picked a faction in order to enter the instance, I don't see how that was possible."

You tried to cheat and are worried someone else cheated back. Hah. "I'm afraid I haven't been able to make contact with my team yet and learn what was going on. But you must know that Team Twofeather has a knack for the unexpected," she said.

"We are quite aware of Team Twofeather's proclivities. It was a mistake to allow an indigenous team so much leeway in phase two. I will be leveling sanctions against your corporation for not taking proper precautions."

"Is that so?" Veda said. "I wonder what the Council for the Protection of Indigenous Rights would have to say. Or perhaps the Church of the Progenitors? You know they always say that the indigenous have as much right to an exploit as the rest of us do."

"Nonsense," Dreamwarden snarled. "Without us, the Reality Engines would be sitting around wasted."

Veda felt her blood rising. "Without you, the humans would have claimed this Reality Engine for themselves in ten years," she snapped. "I've seen the logs. I know why this exploit was so rushed. That's why we're suffering so many setbacks. That's why you're in such a hurry to abandon it. You messed up, and now you're trying to cover it up. How long have you known about the rogue Reality Engine?" she demanded. "I've looked into those. The challenge level for them is much higher, especially since there's no indigenous population to serve as workers. Preparation for one of those takes galactic centuries. And you claim to have just discovered it and be opening it up for exploit in the next couple of years? That's *cron-doc.*"

Her mother winced at the expletive. "Veda, you were raised better than that."

"I don't care," Veda said, plunging on. "My team has done everything within the rules. We will continue to do so. That doesn't mean we're not trying to win."

"Indigenous species never win," Dreamwarden snapped back.

"These ones will," Veda retorted.

"Veda Androst Garnali Tvedra," her mother said. "We are here to put an end to this nonsense right now. Your rights to run this exploit have already been revoked. I am turning over control of this exploit to a person of Dreamwarden's choosing. They will—"

"Do absolutely nothing to Team Twofeather," Veda snarled. "Because you and the family picked the wrong damn contracts when you put me in charge. My deals with the humans are through me, not the company. And I've assigned those contracts to another company right now. Oh, you'll get the money, Mother. Never fear," she said. "You'll be taken care of. The family is going to be better off than we ever dreamed. But I am not abandoning my people to these—these—" Words failed her, and she waved a hand at Dreamwarden, shaking her head.

"You're making a terrible mistake," Dreamwarden said. "We are not easily thwarted."

"You turn over whatever contracts you have to us immediately," her mother demanded, "or we'll call in our end. You'll be indentured to the family for the rest of your life. And we won't be letting you run reality exploits either. I'll—I'll—I'll have you assigned a marriage to a—to a space orc from Drak'tal," she said, spluttering.

"You do what you need to do," Veda said quietly. "And I'll do what I need to do here. Mother, this pod was given to me in Father's will. It belongs to me, and I am done with guests for the day. Please leave. Dreamwarden, I am sending you a copy of the secondary contracts I have just made with Brightfeather Unlimited."

"And who are they?"

"It's a new venture. The Earthlings have formed a corporation by galactic law and are taking control of their own exploit," Veda said. "Also, Mother, you can assign me whatever indenture you want, but as long as I can pay it back, you can't force me home or into a marriage."

"You'll never be able to pay," her mother said.

"I will if they win," Veda said bravely, though with the terms Shad and company had just accepted, there was no way they'd be able to win this. She'd worry about that later. Right now, she just wanted her mother and Dreamwarden out of her hair.

"Please leave. I have work to do."

As soon as they left, her mother fuming, Dreamwarden politely hostile, she looked into the secondary rule set Team Twofeather had invoked.

"What the—What the void did you do, Shad?"

CHAPTER THIRTY-ONE

ALTERNATIVE CONFLICT RESOLUTION STRATEGIES: HAVE YOU TRIED GUIDED MEDIATION?

I spent the whole trip up to Threshold working. Juana was heads down, planning, and Grandpa refused to respond to anything I said, so I pulled up the information the system had given us on the eighty-seven different interconnected levels that made up this phase of the Reality Engine exploit and started looking. It was hard to picture because, like everything else in the Reality Engine, the level design didn't have to make sense in the physical world. The tunnels leading between instances were massive, but not nearly massive enough to go back and forth between dozens of different scenarios. They made use of portals to shift between realms.

The kobolds weren't the only minions the Reality Engine was employing. There were several other different types, and they were standing in for whatever the particular boss scenario required. At any given time, a boss could call for backup, and a dozen robed kobolds would spring into action, running up a set of steps that would, no matter where they started, take them right where they needed to be, deposit them in a boss chamber, and feed them into the meat grinder. They would be killed, and their soul coins allocated to the winners.

I wanted to believe that the NPCs really weren't people. I'd been slaughtering them by the hundreds since I got here over a year ago. I knew the Reality Engine could be puppeting them to act like people, but as I studied the mechanics underlying this phase, I was starting to feel more and more sorry for the NPCs. Not nearly as sorry as I felt for me and my fellow humans, of course.

I took notes on various fights, especially on the later bosses, thinking of clever ways to disrupt an enemy team's attempt. I sent Kirin a couple of notes on early boss fights I thought we might want to send a team into to get their feet wet. She replied she'd pass them along to Arjun, and that they'd come up with a clever plan. Then I dove back in.

As we neared the Hub, I couldn't take my studies anymore, so I closed my files and stared out the window at Jupiter hanging ruddy beneath us. Juana looked up. Grandpa had his head down to his chest and his eyes closed. He was snoring softly.

"What are you thinking about, Shad?" she asked.

"The missing time," I said. It had been bugging me ever since we got back. We were gone for seventy-two hours, but we didn't get back for almost eighty. "Where'd the missing time go?"

Juana frowned. "Hadn't really thought about that."

"Well, I have," I gestured around us at the pod. "How come we have to take a space elevator up to the Hub every time we want to talk to Veda or get ourselves checked out by the doctors?"

"I don't understand."

"How come we can't just step through a portal and be there?" I demanded. "The Reality Engine moves people around instantly."

She blinked at me. "I suppose because the Hub is galactic technology and not part of the Reality Engine?"

I nodded grimly. "Yeah, because it's really there, and most of what takes place inside the Reality Engine is hallucinated. I still don't know if we even have bodies when we're inside those levels."

Juana shuddered. "You mean like we're just inside the Matrix, and we think that things are happening to us, but really our bodies are being kept in pods somewhere?"

"Could be. I don't know how I'd prove otherwise."

"What did you mean about the missing time, though?"

"I think that's how long it actually took us to get to Earth," I said. "I think the aliens just made us forget or kept us unconscious or something."

"Why would they do that? Why not just tell us? Put us on ships? Whatever?"

I shrugged. "Maybe they're hiding the fact that they're not all-powerful. Maybe they don't want us getting a look at their technology." I hesitated. "Or maybe it never really happened."

Juana's eyes went wide. She looked around as though searching for an escape. "No, we were there."

"Can you prove it?" I asked. "If we'd just been in another level of the Reality Engine, would you even know?"

"I think so," Juana said. "The people, they were real. I met people I knew, like, like my ex." She blushed. "He was real. He was an asshole, but he was real."

"I don't know. I feel like the aliens probably could have studied us well enough to know who was waiting for us and mock it up."

"But why would they?"

"Why did they do any of it?" I asked, feeling irritable. "Some sort of psy-ops game because we're doing better than they want and they're trying to throw us off? Or because they enjoy watching us squirm? For all I know, they're taking video feeds of this and shooting it back to their own home worlds. Maybe this is the alien equivalent of a telenovela."

Juana looked amused. "There's not nearly enough identical triplets and coma babies, if that's the case," she said. "But, Shad, aren't you constructing an overly complicated theory when the simplest explanation is just that they sent us home and somehow lost track of time?"

"Maybe," I said. I decided not to push any further, especially since I wasn't sure what I was trying to gain with this conversation. I liked Juana. Really liked her. I didn't want to upset her needlessly. Not when she was one of the few steady people in my life helping keep me on an even keel. She hadn't even given me crap about choosing the Tunnel Rats, not once she calmed down from the initial shock, and she hadn't pushed me for an explanation. I valued that.

I wasn't sure myself that I'd made the right choice, but I did know that now we were on this course, we needed to stick with it, and that meant keeping the Reality Engine's secrets.

Juana looked up. "Since it's been more than a week, I've gone ahead and scheduled our checkups for after we speak with Veda. I'll make sure that Sage gets hers sometime soon. That way we can put off another trip up to Threshold, the Hub, for as long as possible."

"Alright," I agreed. "You wanna see about getting dinner together afterward?"

She winked at me. "I'd love that." She glanced over at Grandpa. "Can we ditch the third wheel?"

"Oh, definitely."

Veda sent word that she would meet us in a private, rented room off the Hub's busy main gallery. Usually, she just teleconferenced into whatever suite she had arranged for us, but this time we stepped into what looked like an old-fashioned study. Tall wooden bookshelves full of leather-bound tomes lined the walls. There was a desk in the corner with an abandoned pipe lying on it, a tall wingback chair, and a fire crackling merrily. Veda sat stiffly on a low couch. She had a glass half full of an amber fluid in her hand. As we entered, she rose.

"What the void have you done, Shad Williams?" she demanded.

Juana and Grandpa slipped inside after me. The door closed behind us.

"We haven't spoken to you in over a week, and that's how you start off?" I asked. "Last I saw you, you were going off somewhere with the traitor Waters and someone you said was your mother. I've heard two lines from you since then. Meanwhile, we've been left to do the best we could."

"This was the best you could do?" Veda demanded. "Picking some obvious disaster faction that takes us from having a good shot at walking away with a fortune to no chance at all? I understand why you might have been tempted. It's a good chance to screw everyone else involved, but, Shad, there's more than just revenge here. I've put a lot on the line for you and your people—"

"And we've made you rich!" I shouted. I could feel all the anger and frustration of the last week boiling up in me, and Veda made such an inviting target. Grandpa wasn't even saying anything. Juana had crossed to the wingback chair and sat down, looking at us with that inscrutable expression she had when she was thinking deeply. "You could have at least let us know what was going on."

"I was busy," she snapped back, trying to get things in order before someone else could take advantage.

"And so you treated us like mushrooms?"

She looked confused, frowning. "Mushrooms?"

"Kept us in the dark and fed us shit," I said.

Veda's brow wrinkled. "I . . . oh, I see. Earth allusion. Yes, well . . ." She took a deep breath. There were little pale white spots on her cheeks, high up. "Fine. You want to explain to me why you picked the Tunnel Rat faction?"

"No. You want to tell me why you haven't been returning our calls?"

"I was going to explain," Veda began.

"When exactly? You could have sent us a message at any time."

"There were things I wanted to get taken care of, and I didn't dare talk about them beforehand because you never know who's listening."

"Exactly," I said, pointing at the ceiling. "Which is why I'm not going to explain my motivations either."

Veda looked from me to Juana and Grandpa. "Do either of you know what's going through his head?"

Grandpa shrugged. "Probably a little more than what usually does, but details? No."

Juana shook her head. "He hasn't been very forthcoming."

"And you, Juana, you're usually more levelheaded than this," Veda said. "You didn't try to talk some sense into him?"

Juana hesitated for a minute. I thought she might reveal how I had picked the faction without consulting with anyone. But she shook her head firmly. "I trust Shad more than I trust you."

Veda looked like she'd been struck. "We've been working together for over a year now. I haven't lied to you. I've stuck my neck out for you, for all of you." Her voice rose. "You have no idea what I've been risking to help you people."

"And you don't appreciate what we've been earning on *your* behalf," Grandpa said. "You didn't come here with altruistic motives. You came here to take advantage of a bunch of rubes. Maybe you have better intentions than most of the others. Some of the folk who came trading with my ancestors treated them better than other folk. They made honest swaps, traded rifles and firewater for buffalo pelts rather than just taking what they wanted. Some of those mountain men married Indian squaws instead of just raping them and leaving them to deal with the consequences. Doesn't mean that my folk got a square end of the deal."

Veda blinked. "I . . . I don't know what you're trying to say."

"What we're trying to say, Veda, is that from down here among us worms, all you galactics look pretty much the same. It's about what you can screw out of us and what happens when we're not useful anymore. Well now we see. We made a decision you don't like and got uppity, so you're here to get us back in line."

Veda shook her head. "That's not it at all. You have no idea. Colonel Ames and I have spent the last week setting up a holding company. I'm trying to transfer your contracts over. There's complications, but I've been working around the clock to keep Proxima from getting their hands on you."

Nobody said anything for a minute. If what Veda said was true, maybe she *was* on our side.

"Out of the goodness of your heart?" I asked finally.

"You and your team have already done everything that I ever hoped for," Veda said quietly. "We kept my family license alive, something my father valued. We provided for my family. I wanted to see if I could help yours just a little bit, but it's complicated. There's galactic politics involved. You're right, most people here don't want to see you prosper. I've been trying to do my best, and then you throw in a twist like you just did." She shook her head. "What's the good outcome here, Shad? How do we live with the results after you've burned everything down?"

"Who cares?" I said, but it sounded hollow in my ears. "If we can kick all of you back where you came from, it'll be worth it."

"You think this is going to be more than a tiny setback to Proxima and Alabaster Sky and the rest of them?" Veda challenged me. "They're already making plans to move on to the next Reality Engine to exploit. It probably won't be as much of a pain in the ass as yours. You know who is going to be left with the smoking ruins? You. You and all your people. Do you understand the forces that they can bring to bear against you?"

"No," I said. "No, I don't. You people have technology that seems like magic to me, and even to you, the Reality Engine is something to be feared and exploited. That makes it pretty powerful. Yeah, you could probably blow up our moon or turn all of our planets into gray goo or . . . I don't even know. Whatever threat you make, I'll believe it, but what's the alternative? We just let you sit here and take it?"

Veda took a deep breath. "I just want to know how we salvage this. How do we all get what we need?"

"What is it you need?" Grandpa asked. "I thought we'd already paid back your investments."

"Yes, well, you've got to finish buying out your contracts. I spent as much of the profit as I could buying out other members of Misfits Guild, so I hold something like eight hundred million soul coins worth of unredeemed contracts compared to even a tenth of one percent of a share of the Reality Engine. That's not much. I was betting on you guys winning at least that. Now, I don't know."

"We have a plan to make money," Juana said. "The only way we win under this rule set is by making it too expensive for everyone else to fight. Along the way, there should be some good economic opportunities for our crafters."

"That makes sense," Veda said. She wrapped her arms around her torso and rocked gently back and forth. "But you can't make money on killing them since you're sworn to this faction."

"Kickbacks," Juana said brightly.

Veda cocked her head. "What's that?"

"Kickbacks? Surely a galactic civilization as corrupt as yours knows what those are. We find unaffiliated squads, people like Mak'gar, if they don't have anything going on right now, and we hire them as privateers. They attack our enemies and get part of the gold cost, part of the soul coins it costs them for each death. But in exchange for hiring them, they give us, say, fifteen percent of their take."

Veda pursed her lips. "That might work."

"That's just one of my ideas," Juana said cheerfully. "We'll see what else I can come up with. I was feeling a little frustrated when I first read the rule set, too," she admitted. "But the more I look at it, the more I think we can exploit this."

Veda nodded. "I'd like to see those." She stood up. "I'm sorry. I'm a little emotional right now. I'd like some time to calm down, and then maybe we can have a better discussion about all this."

"I'll take you to dinner tonight," Grandpa said, speaking up unexpectedly. I turned to stare at him.

"Huh?"

"We'll sit down and talk without the hothead here." Grandpa hooked a thumb at me. "I'll pick you up after my appointment with the docs, shall I? I'm sure you know a good place to go."

"Uh, sure," Veda said.

"Besides, the young'uns have plans without me." Grandpa gave me and Juana a wink.

"I thought you were snoring a little too loudly," I said. "What was that all about?"

"I just didn't feel like talking," Grandpa said. "Right, now what else?"

"Colonel Ames needs to meet you and Juana at a lawyer's office to turn over ownership of the holding company," she said.

"Where?" I asked.

"Not you, Shad."

"Oh." I felt a little hurt. "Wait, so Ames's working with you?"

"He is. We'll talk later," Veda told Grandpa. "Meanwhile, I'm sorry for losing my temper at you." She looked at me.

I was pretty sure I was supposed to apologize here, too, but honestly, I wasn't sorry. Veda had been playing her hand close to her chest, and whether or not she had good reasons for it, I didn't care. It was our lives she was playing with. We were the ones whose home had been invaded, who had been abducted and forced into a situation we didn't want. If we cost Veda a little more of her profit margin than she'd been expecting, well, that was her problem, not mine.

"See you," I said.

She gave me a tight nod and left the room.

CHAPTER THIRTY-TWO

HANSEL AND GRETEL

The cottage in the clearing was golden brown and covered in brightly colored decorations. Its eaves were hung with what looked at first like snow, until you realized it was a warm summer evening and the icicles hanging from the gingerbread eaves were, in fact, made of frosting.

The trees and bushes that surrounded the cozy little cabin were hung with candy. An odor of warm melted chocolate wafted from the chimney of the gingerbread house. As I waited, concealed in a sugar plum bush, Sage messaged me. *You're kidding me. Hansel and Gretel? And we're helping the witch?*

Just go with it, I replied wearily.

She snorted. I could hear her from eight feet away. She was up a tree, hiding among pink spun sugar candy blossoms.

Keep it down, I warned her.

Nobody heard that, and if they did, they'll think it was a bird. What kind of birds do you think live here? You think they're made of candy, too? If not, they should be attacking this house and eating it. How come the whole thing doesn't just dissolve in the rain? This story never made a whole lot of sense. I think it's an allegory about the dangers of step-parents.

Focus, I told her.

There were twelve of us concealed in various bushes around the cabin, just waiting for the arrival of the team of hardened veterans that would be going up against the Candy Witch. This whole zone was Brothers Grimm–themed. The encounters ran the gamut from horrifying versions of the fairy tales that I suspected were closer to the original, complete with chopped-off feet, red-hot iron shoes, and barrels of spikes, to slightly more candy cut-out variants like what we saw here.

This was one of the all-outdoor zones we'd found, called the Dark Enchanted Forest. The three optional bosses, which had been in the lands beyond the forest, were a wicked stepmother, a lord mayor, and the Brothers Grimm themselves.

All three had been defeated before the gates of the forest had opened, just like how we'd fought a boss before Castle Byalgrad's entrances opened. Each of the seven entrance gates in this zone had been assigned one of Snow White's dwarves as its guardian—and let me just tell you, they were *not* the Disney versions—and each team had been forced to defeat one dwarf to receive a key to enter.

That was a rule that held across the forty-plus raid instances we had surveyed so far. Only seventy percent of the teams even made it into the heart of the raid. As Grandpa and Juana had pointed out to me, the math didn't necessarily work out in our favor. The other thirty percent of teams were busy scavenging the outer sections of the raid levels for consumable materials to sell, trying to turn a profit since their hopes for going any further had been dashed.

Jones messaged us. *I've got eyes on 'em. I count fourteen of the space elves, mostly equipped with those shiny energy sabers and plasma rifles. They've got two healers and one of the ones we've been calling tinkers.*

Okay, mark the healers and the tinker. We'll try to get them down first, I said. *Affiliation?*

Dreamnight Summit, a subsidiary of Alabaster Sky through eight proxies. Veda says they're owned by the sister-in-law of a cousin of a demi-niece of Alabaster Sky's eighth vice president, so we should expect them to have fairly large pockets. One wipe isn't going to dissuade them.

And you've confirmed the location of their base camp?

Yep, Jones said.

Then let's do this.

I switched over to my message thread for Team 2. *Jones will send you the IDs of the healers and their support caster. Make sure you pay attention and follow the plan.*

That got a quick "yup" from Mitch, who was leading Team 2 today.

I switched back. *Team 1, ready to go?*

You know we are, Captain, Frank replied.

I grinned as the space elves entered the clearing. They spread out in front of the witch's cabin in an arrangement similar to how the dwarves had approached Podaga's hut. I was starting to realize that all of their many years of experience at Reality Engines had made the galactics predictable. They knew how to set up a big fight like this. They had all the strategies down, knew how many healers and tanks they'd need, what weapons to bring.

Predictable meant exploitable. And today, we were going to do just that.

Their tank ran up and knocked on the witch's door. He sprang back down lithely into the glade, drawing his energy saber and activating his force shield. They both glowed bright purple in the fading sunlight. His hair was purple, too.

Space elves moved with grace and poise. What I really liked was the noise they made when they died—a sort of strangled scream about an octave and a half higher than you would have thought them capable of.

I didn't have any particular animosity for this team. We had never crossed paths before, but they were in the wrong place—our solar system—and they were about to learn how big a mistake they'd made.

The witch appeared in her doorway, cackling, plunging into her boss speech as the crew of raiders spread out. She cast a spell over the whole clearing, and the elves froze in place like statues as she began to monologue. "You villagers should have taken better care of your children. They would have never come to seek out me if you had provided for them as parents should!"

Her monologue went on for a good minute and a half as the elves stood frozen, doubtless communicating on their own private channels for last-minute arrangements. As the witch stepped forward into the clearing, the freeze ended and the elf tank ran forward and taunted her. *Is that an ability or an item?* I asked Sage, who was supposed to be using Eye-Spy on our enemies. We were still working on building up a picture of just what they could do.

Item. Definitely. I think it's his belt. Yeah, it has eight charges left. You could probably target it and ruin their pull.

Save that for another fight, I said.

The witch was wielding an oversized ladle for a weapon and a saucepan as a shield. She advanced on the elf tank, screeching. He raised his energy shield and her ladle bounced harmlessly off it.

The space elf warriors unshouldered their guns and began firing.

Go! I ordered in our chat, and my team dropped out of the trees, sprang out of the bushes, and leapt into action.

A string of grenades went off right through the middle of the clearing, ripping through the enemy ranks and throwing up smoke and glitter. The elves' cries of surprise and dismay were music to my ears.

I fired a Trick Shot at one of their healers, hitting her with a Disorienting round. It would only last for five seconds, but combined with the smoke, it effectively put her out of the fight. Six more of us fell on her, firing guns, slashing with weapons, and casting our spells. Seconds later, she disappeared in a cloud of sparkles.

The elves' sparkles were more pastel and iridescent than everyone else's. Maybe I was just imagining it, but I thought they got special treatment from the system.

"Get the other one," I bellowed, and emptied a Barrage into the second healer.

The tinker had a metal whirligig out at the end of a three-foot-long metal pole. Its blades whirled and spun in a riot of colors. His device emitted a slowing field that caught at my ankles and those of my teammates around me.

Sage laughed and threw her Lasso around him. "Got him!" she shouted, and she turned her Tamed elf on the rest. We had encountered a few other miners who were resistant to mind-control tactics. This elf wasn't one of them. Now the elves were slowed, confused, and without support.

I felt a deep surge of satisfaction as we cut their raid to shreds, taking down the other healer and the tinker before turning on the damage dealers. They were still trying to target the witch, and it was splitting their focus. They'd gotten her down to eighty percent.

"Come, children, come to my aid!" she cackled.

A bevy of gingerbread children, all about four feet high, burst from the hut and ran into the fight, wielding candy canes like axes and hacking at the knees of the space elves. One of the nice things about having joined the Tunnel Rat faction was that the bosses and all of their adds were now our allies, which not only meant that we didn't have to worry about damaging them, but all of the abilities we had that boosted the effect of allies or creep empowered them.

Sage cast Cowgirl Cheer and the gingerbread children grew six inches each; gumdrop buttons popped out on their chests, giving them the appearance of wearing bright little festive jackets.

"One at a time," I bellowed. "Take 'em down one at a time."

It was important that we didn't let the elves get all clumped up, so they'd have multiple respawns at once. I got a message from Team Two. *The healers and the tinker are up and racing back to you. They've reached the edge of the forest.*

All right, I replied. *Lock everything else down.*

You got it, boss.

I could practically hear the satisfaction in Mitch's voice as I turned back to the fight. I delivered a killing shot to one of the energy saber-wielding elves, who gave off that bloodcurdling scream and vanished into purple sparks.

He would find a surprise waiting for him. Team Two was covering the exit from their base. As their damage dealers emerged one by one, they'd be taken out and sent back to respawn.

I was hoping to get at least one full complement of deaths more before they caught on to our tactics and started trying to fight back. Juana had worked with an alien support company on the Hub to develop a little accounting program for us. It was tallying up just what the respawn cost was for this team. With our 10x multiplier on top of the increasing cost with each death, the bill was very quickly going to be in the hundreds of thousands of soul coins per resurrection.

We killed off the tank. "We need to try to ambush the healers," I shouted. "Make for the forest gate. Jones, got eyes on them yet?"

"Sure do, boss," Jones called. "They're still heading here. Guess they haven't gotten the word. Let's run!"

I put the deed into action and sprinted through the woods as Sage called to the witch. "Okay, done for now, Evil Granny. You get back in there and heal up and make another batch of gingerbread children. Your defenses aren't nearly good enough. We need to get you some turrets attached to your hut. I'm gonna see what Dwight can do."

Sage, that's actually a brilliant idea, I said.

All my ideas are brilliant, Shad. She might have been texting, but I could hear the smugness in her voice. I let it pass and sent the message along to Juana.

We'll find out if it's possible, she promised.

I had visions of every boss encounter in every instance protected by missile turrets and slowing guns. It would cost a hell of a lot, but we had patterns now to make such things. Dwight and his army of crafters had picked them up back in phase two. Plus, we had more crafters coming on board with us every day and an army of farmers fresh out of the lotus eater level.

It'd be a lot of work to coordinate. We'd need to recruit someone just for that. I was finding that running an insurgency was a lot more bookkeeping and staff meetings than I'd ever expected.

Sage raced ahead of me through the woods. "Found 'em!" she yelled, and we fell on the unprepared healers.

Meanwhile, Team Two was updating me on their kills. *There's one elf we've killed three times now. He's got long blue hair. And he makes the most ridiculous noises when he dies*, Mitch said. *We're up to twelve kills and they're still coming.*

We'll join you, I said as we dispatched the tinker. "Team, roll out!"

CHAPTER THIRTY-THREE

IS THREE MUSKETEERS THE CANDY BAR FOR YOU?

The throne room of Louis XIII, King of France, was ornate. Gilt and bright colors were everywhere, predominantly gold and red. A throne sat atop a two-step dais, with tall golden candleholders adorned with barely clad nymphs casting light on either side of it. A huge crystal chandelier hung over our heads. The floor was inlaid, polished wood.

The courtiers around the room whispered among each other, hiding their expressions behind silk fans or manicured hands. The women were extravagant. Rich, sumptuous skirts billowed out past their waists and fell to the floor in heaps of ruffles, like the layers of a wedding cake. Hair piled two feet or more atop their heads and decorated with flowers, jewels, even live birds or a small mouse. The men's fashions were no less magnificent. Men and women both wore full faces of makeup.

And here, down the center of the room, came striding a man in rich red robes. His cardinal's hat atop his head, the infamous Richelieu, accompanied by his loyal guards, approached the throne of King Louis and his queen. The cardinal extended one hand as the king turned to his loyal musketeers with a frown.

"Your Majesty has placed your faith in the wrong persons for the last time," the cardinal exclaimed. "I hold here a decree of excommunication upon you and all the realm." A gasp fell over the court.

"Repent, Your Majesty. Confess, receive absolution, and I myself shall tear up this decree this very moment," the cardinal said.

"It is you who must repent," the king declared in an outrageous French accent. "You serve me, Richelieu. You serve France! You are not king here, I am!"

The court of Versailles looked from one powerful man to the other, whispers growing as the standoff continued. How would this end?

[Choose a side,] the system boomed. **[Will you assist Cardinal Richelieu in reigning in the Sun King's decadence, or will you side with Louis and the musketeers and bring an end to the cardinal's reign of terror?]**

Hey, Sage commented in chat, *wasn't the reign of terror a French Revolution thing? That was not this guy, was it? Someone else with an R?*

No. The system's mixing up a bunch of different things here. This Louis isn't the Sun King, that was a different Louis, I said. *This is The Three Musketeers, not real history. Anyway, good job. I guess you were paying attention in world history in fifth grade.*

I'm doing a correspondence class, Shad. Grandpa and Colonel Ames set it up for me. I want to be able to get my high school diploma, after all.

Why?

Because if you didn't drop out of high school, neither will I, Sage replied. *Now, hush. I want to hear what happens next.*

**[If you chose to side with Cardinal Richelieu,
you will cleanse France of the decadence that has affected
her like gangrene, defeat the guileless musketeers,
destroy the queen's influence, and have Louis
confined to his quarters until the cardinal has managed
to teach him humility and reason.
If you chose to side with Louis the Sun King, you must defeat
Cardinal Richelieu and his army of Swiss Guards.]**

That's not right, Sage complained as the black-clad men with Cardinal Richelieu discarded their outer layers to reveal striped yellow, red, and blue uniforms beneath. *They weren't carrying halberds a minute ago. Anyway, shouldn't the Swiss Guards be in Switzerland?*

Vatican. They're Papal Guards, Grandpa threw in. *Didn't your European History correspondence class cover that? 1527 ringing any bells?*

**[Cardinal Richelieu will be assisted by the Swiss Guards
and his own personal coterie of devoted monks.
You must slay all his guards and force the cardinal
to surrender in order to claim victory here.]**

We held our breath, waiting to hear what would be chosen, and then the system proclaimed, **[Death to Cardinal Richelieu and an everlasting dawn for France. Vive la France!]**

Get ready, I don't see the other team yet but the encounter's starting, I told my people. The courtiers turned and ran screaming from the room as another group of men appeared from the side. These were dressed in dark robes and suspiciously short. Sure enough, when I targeted them, my Inspect revealed that the so-called monks were actually kobold NPCs in monks' robes.

I sent a message to the main chat: *It's Cardinal Richelieu. Sounds like there are going to be more Swiss Guards and monks, so prepare.*

The cardinal marched forward toward the king, who cowered back into his chair. Queen Anne rose and pointed one shaking finger at the cardinal. "You have betrayed us. This infamy will not stand."

Cardinal Richelieu launched into his monologue, declaring all the flaws of the King of France and his court, most of which were probably true. He accused Louis of sullying the memory of the noble king, Saint Louis IX, the greatest and most pious king to ever rule France. This Louis had consorted with mistresses, indulging in revels and frivolity while his subjects bent their necks under cruel taxes. Apparently. Seemed like normal king business to me, but the cardinal was really bent out of shape over it.

As the cardinal monologued, his guards and monks spread out around the room in two circles. I kept my eyes open.

They're here somewhere, I said in chat. *We know it. The monologue didn't start until someone made a choice.*

Here they come, Grandpa warned, and a bunch of orcs strode in, swaggering in their chainmail space leotards. This particular group wore sashes across their chests, bright red and black and festooned with ribbons and medals, like they'd attended a military ceremony in North Korea just before this.

I counted twenty-five of them in five rows of five. The front rows were armed with pikes with gleaming silver edges, except for the two at either end of the front row who had something weird I couldn't quite figure out yet. As they marched up and took their positions, they activated the energy fields on their pikes. Sizzling blue light arced from one end of the blade down to the base.

The next two rows carried rifles. The rearmost rank were their healers, with the ubiquitous healing wands that we'd spotted on most teams so far.

It was getting easier to understand what each of our enemies was capable of, since they relied so heavily on their equipment, rather than having innate skills like us humans. From experience, each of them would have one or perhaps two relevant skills. The halberd users in the front would have a slashing charge, the riflemen some sort of increase to firepower and accuracy, and a fast reload. The healers generally had the ability to quickly target their devices on one ally, then the next.

I was standing inside a loop of rope that Dwight had assured me was actually an invisibility field, but I felt really exposed. My hat and coat weren't at all appropriate for this period. I was standing in the lee of a pillar well out of the way. Sage and Grandpa were across the hall, and I couldn't see either of them, which hopefully meant the fields were working as advertised, but if one of the orcs had a pierce invisibility ability or device, the jig was up.

There was an invisible barrier between the cardinal and the rest of the room. The orcs spread out, waiting as the cardinal monologued. One fired a tentative blast from his laser rifle. It splattered off the barricade, none of the NPCs taking any note of it. He sighed and lowered his weapon. I could hear the team grumbling as they waited for the cardinal to finish his spiel. At last, he turned to face the invaders.

"And what is this, Louis?" he demanded. "More treachery? You have hired mercenaries to attack a man of the cloth? This infamy will echo down through history, like Henry of England slaying Thomas Becket at his own altar. For this sin of presumption alone, you shall spend a thousand years in purgatory. But if you do not stand down now, your eternal soul will be forfeit."

The barrier went down.

The two orcs who had stood on either end of the front row detached themselves and marched forward, carrying energy shields as tall as they were and long, springy green weapons that reminded me of pool noodles. They arrayed themselves on either side of the cardinal. The leftmost orc struck out with his pool noodle and hit the cardinal on the side of the head.

Richelieu turned to him, face red with fury.

"You dare! Guards, attack!"

The second of the tanks turned as the guards started in. He lashed out with his pool noodle. It extended into a rope twice as long and whipped across the room. Each minion it brushed past focused on that tank, rushing forward toward him. The orcs behind opened fire, mowing down the monks, or rather, kobolds.

The Swiss Guard were a little more focused. They ignored the taunting tanks and marched on the body of the raid, their pikes lowered. The pike-bearing orcs turned to meet them as the rifle-orc mowed down the last of the kobolds.

"How dare you raise arms against my Benedictine brothers!" Cardinal Richelieu lifted his hands toward heaven. "Come, brothers! Come to my aid!"

That was the cue for more adds. Now, kobolds were preparing to pour out of the tunnel and throw themselves onto the spears of the orcs. No doubt Captain Kobold was down there somewhere, marshaling his doomed kinsmen to rush in and die.

At least, that was the plan. I don't think the orcs noticed that the new wave of black-cloaked adds were about a foot taller on average than the kobold monks had been. They didn't seem to notice there were three times as many as before, either.

The tanks shouted to each other, and the one who had been on minion duty stepped in, whacking the cardinal with his pool noodle. The cardinal turned to face the new threat as the first tank stepped back toward the onrushing monks. Their healers were doing a good job keeping everyone up. I admired their discipline. They had lost only a few orcs so far.

Now, as the second wave of monks spread out, it was the time to change that.

Everyone in position? I asked.

I got a flurry of yeses in chat.

Great! Let's do this.

I activated Fastest Gun in the West and zoomed right into the midst of the orcs. As I ran, I threw Call 'em Out, catching everyone's attention. They turned to me, just as Alison ordered two of our support casters to cast buffs on me. Lauren threw her five-second invulnerability shield over me, while Macy, the cheerleader, gave me "Star of the Show." It increased the effectiveness of my taunt by an extra ten seconds, while also making it harder for anyone to actually hit me.

The orcs shouted in dismay as the newly arrived monks all threw back their hoods to reveal the happy, smiling faces of Misfits Guild members. Mitch laughed as he threw Spike Their Trunks, and the rifle-bearing orcs' weapons exploded in a sticky, dissolving, syrupy mess. Sage cackled in glee as she threw down Mucking Out the Stalls under what was left of the raid. As Call 'em Out wore off, Lara threw orange grenades, kicking up huge clouds of smoke.

Cardinal Richelieu laughed triumphantly.

"And so the hand of God punishes you for your insolence. Now you will see . . ."

He was ranting and raving, and I ignored him as I fired shot after shot at point-blank range into the orcs around me. They were struggling to get their weapons onto me. It was complete chaos.

As rumor had gotten around of what we were doing, our enemies had gotten a little more clever. They were starting to scout out ahead of time, looking for us, to make sure that we couldn't interfere. But since only three of us had been hiding in the room itself, the rest waiting in the tunnels that only the NPCs and Team Tunnel Rat could access, they'd been taken off guard.

It wasn't always going to be this easy, I thought, as we dispatched the last of the orcs. This group was pretty well funded. A single wipe, even with our 10x bonus, wouldn't knock them out. But it would help spread the reputation we were trying to cultivate.

What we really needed to do right now was play for time. If all of the other teams fought their bosses as hard and fast as they could, we'd have no chance. Someone would make it to the end while we were trying to deal with someone else.

So we were adapting. We were going for shock and awe tactics, hitting them off guard, doing things they didn't expect, ruining their best attempts, making them use up consumables that would be expensive or impossible to replace.

If we could make them hesitate to step outside of their bases, think twice about starting a boss fight, or wait until they had twice as much manpower or equipment on hand, then we might just buy ourselves another day, another hour, to pull out a miracle.

Any sign of them regrouping? I asked Jones, who was on overwatch outside of Versailles. This whole instance was Alexander Dumas–themed. There was a terrible prison below the palace containing the Man in the Iron Mask, the Count of Monte Cristo, and a couple of other famous prisoners, while up above were numerous royal-themed encounters. The orcs were the only team in the instance who had made serious inroads, downing one of the prison bosses before coming to take on the Royal Court encounter.

Nah. Not a peep out of their camp. Pity, we've got a lovely ambush lined up here just waiting.

Stay on the map for an extra fifteen minutes. If you see the orcs or any of the other teams on this map come out of their camps, hit them hard, try to take down a few, and then retreat, I said.

Team Mongoose and the grignarians were on assassin duty today. The grignarians had already racked up dozens of kills and were eager for more, since they got a fraction of the soul coins that it cost our enemies to respawn. Team Mongoose was just as effective and just as cheerful, motivated by professionalism rather than coin.

As Cardinal Richelieu wound down his victory speech, I checked in with my team. We hadn't suffered any casualties this time.

"Good work," I said.

"How come these assholes have a victory speech?" Grandpa asked as he watched. "I mean, all the orcs are dead. Who's going to hear it?"

"It's just a rule, Grandpa," Sage said. "These guys always have to have a victory speech, same as they have an opening monologue."

"Hey," I said. "That gives me a great idea for our next exploit. Sage, what do you think about . . ."

CHAPTER THIRTY-FOUR

IT'S NOT A PYRAMID SCHEME, IT'S A LEGITIMATE BUSINESS OPPORTUNITY!

We'd had a breakthrough. Arjun and his team, working closely to query the Reality Engine, had discovered how to learn the mechanics and setup of a fight without actually having to go there. That meant we were now able to target specific fights for specific mad tactics.

I had already noticed that some bosses froze everyone in stasis while they recited their monologue while others had a protective barrier around them, preventing the fight from starting early. We needed the first type, and Arjun had a whole list of options for me.

"And what about my idea?" Sage demanded.

"What idea?" I asked.

"Not telling you yet. Arjun thinks it's good."

"I have three candidates. I shall inform you if enemy teams set up an attempt on any of the three," Arjun told her.

Since I wasn't going to get an answer there, I looked over the list he had presented me. "Yeah, this one," I said. "This looks absolutely perfect."

It was a gauntlet boss, the third highest in its raid instance. The instance was themed with witches, goblins, and animated scarecrows—a little less Brothers Grimm and more Halloween Superstore.

This particular raid must have been harder than average, because six of the ten starting teams had already bowed out, their kills getting just a little too high to bear. I could see why. Most of the mobs and bosses here used a lot of electric and spiritual damage, which required some expensive potions and equipment buffs in order to mitigate. The death tolls had been sky-high. The remaining teams had really deep pockets.

We were targeting a Proxima-affiliated team of mixed animalkin called Allotropic Understatement. Team Mongoose, the grignarians, and a few of our crafters who were looking for a change of pace had spent the morning harassing the team, giving them a few more losses and pushing their respawn bills up nice and high.

I called back our assassins and sent them elsewhere. We had deployed some remote spy turrets outside the boss's chamber, so when the slightly haggard-looking group of animalkin began forming up outside the room, I knew it was time.

"Let's go, Sage," I said, picking up my hat and putting it on my head.

We stepped out of headquarters over to our node, and then from there traveled deep into the bowels of Castle Byalgrad. Captain Kobold was sitting by our entry port in a high-backed chair, sipping a mug of what I hoped was beer. It smelled more like urine to me.

He waved a hand to us. "Greetings, friend Shad, friend Sage. Back again?"

"Just here to cause some havoc," I said cheerfully.

"You are the greatest friend a kobold has ever had," Captain Kobold said, his eyes getting misty. "You have saved so many of our lives already and dealt blows to our foes we can never hope to equal."

"That's all right," I said, picking the door that would lead me to our targeted instance. "Be right back. This shouldn't take long."

Sage and I popped up a flight of stairs and into the room. This was a classic boss room: a dank stone chamber with a bright green fire in the middle. The boss was a witch, something like the one we'd helped out with Hansel and Gretel but hunchbacked and with a big wart on her nose. She had a cauldron over the fire and was stirring it. She looked up as we entered.

I raised a hand to her. "Just here to watch," I said cheerfully. "We're on your side."

"So I see, my pretties." The witch went back to her cauldron. Sage and I melted into the shadows, activating our invisibility fields.

The witch's door creaked open and the animalkin trooped in. There were sixteen of them. They spread out around the room, setting themselves up as the witch stirred her cauldron, not seeming to notice.

Finally, a badger-man carrying a shield and a truncheon approached the witch. He shouted. She looked up.

"Something I can help you with? Here to buy a love potion, my dear?"

Looking exasperated, the badger ran up and kicked over her cauldron. He jumped back, cradling his bare paw.

"Ow!"

"What did you expect, Lea'lk?" a rabbit-woman called from behind. She aimed a beam of healing at him. "Get in position."

The witch raised her broom. Everyone froze as her spell hit them.

She began her opening monologue. According to the system's information, this was one of the longest monologues in the game. Two and a half minutes of the witch ranting and raving about ungrateful peasants and how we took everything for granted and that sort of thing. Didn't matter; we were about to cut it short.

Sage broke her invisibility. She ran forward and tossed her Lasso around the witch's shoulders.

"Did it!" she shouted triumphantly.

It was true that Tame didn't work on bosses. It also didn't usually work on friends, but Dwight had crafted her a very special module, taking apart a couple of minion buff devices we had earned in phase two to build her a Friendly Firebox. With it activated, her Tame let her control an affiliated non-player character, even a boss.

The Tame settled over the witch. "Cancel monologue!" Sage yelled. "Get 'em!"

I held my breath. This was the part I was nervous about, because I wasn't quite sure if canceling the monologue was going to work the way I hoped.

It did.

The witch snapped out of her rant. She raised her broom and shot a bolt of lightning that zapped between all of the still-frozen combat miners, dropping their hit points precipitously.

You see, the monologue was separate from the spell she'd cast to hold them in place. That was timed to last as long as her speech should. By bypassing the speech, we'd set her free early, but our opponents were stuck in place for the next two minutes and fifteen seconds.

The witch ran for the tank. She grabbed him in her suddenly long and grasping talons and tore him to shreds.

"Eugh," Sage said. "That's kind of gruesome."

The witch started to rip his heart out, but the badger-man dissolved into sparks. Screaming in rage, the witch raced for the next of the animalkin.

I just watched, amused. There really wasn't anything for me to do here as long as the witch made short work of them, which she did. Sage kept retasking the witch as each of the enemy fell in turn.

In less than two minutes, they were all dead. The gate creaked back open. Sage released her Tame. The witch shuddered and turned to us.

"What just happened, dearies?" she asked. "I feel like I had visitors here, but they all seem to have gone. Was I a poor hostess?"

"Not at all," I said, Tipping My Hat to her again. "Thanks for your help here."

"Hey," Sage said. "Remember that cool idea I had? The one with three possible targets? Well, Juana says they're moving in now. Want to give it a try?"

"I don't know. Do I?"

I listened as she explained her idea. Grinning, I nodded. "Let's go."

It took us two minutes to transit between the instances. This one was an outdoor setting in the middle of a forest. A group of armed men holding single-shot pistols or steel rapiers surrounded a broken-down carriage. A woman in gauzy pink with a tall princess hat atop her head sat on the rack of the ruined coach, hands clasped to her breast as she cried out for help.

"They're coming from the north," Sage said, just as twelve of the mostly human-looking aliens, Veda's people, or close relatives thereof, burst out of the trees.

The highwaymen went on alert right away, moving toward them. The enemy team's tank ran forward. He was carrying a shield and had a grenade in one hand that I recognized as something our own crafters had made, a wide-area taunt. It would let him attract the attention of the eight highwaymen while his team took them down.

The highwaymen were already in action as the scenario triggered, leaping forward to engage with the enemy team. No freeze and monologue here. My turn.

I emerged from the trees and targeted the tank, and then I threw High Noon. He stopped dead where he was, the taunt grenade in his upturned hand.

"What the—?" he exclaimed, looking around. "Something's wrong! I can't throw the grenade!" The crew of highwaymen ran right past him and fell into the middle of his raid.

I stepped out, my gun in my hand, grinning. "I'm afraid we're gonna have to wait to start our duel until I see what happens to the rest of your raid," I said, as the others with him shouted in dismay.

"You're that indigenous fellow who's been messing with people. Why are you doing this?" the tank cried angrily. There wasn't really anything else he could do until I fired. High Noon was in effect. He couldn't leave, couldn't shoot, couldn't do anything except look mad while the opponents trashed his raid.

I checked with Sage. "You've got a buff on them, right?"

"Sure do," she said happily. As long as she cast Cowgirl Cheer on the highwaymen, they would count as our minions, which meant any deaths they caused would have the 10x cost multiplier applied. I was working on getting our crafters to build some sort of auto-buffing turrets that would apply a similar effect to all the bosses. If we could deploy them everywhere, it would really speed up how quickly our enemies ran out of money.

"Look, we didn't do anything to you. Can't we negotiate some sort of deal? If we don't make our money back, we're sunk. My team's gonna go back into storage."

I'd heard Veda mention that concept once before. "I'm sorry," I said. "We've got to defeat all of you, or else we lose."

The tank looked like he was about to cry. It was easier to read his expression than those of the orcs or the space elves. They might not be quite human, but they were close enough.

"That's it then. We're wiped out," he said as the rest of his team fell. The highwaymen retreated from the battle, gathering around us with their swords out. But I didn't drop High Noon just yet.

"Hang on," I said curiously. "So now you're out of cash?"

He shrugged. "Basically. We really had to get this fight down if we were going to stay in it."

"Who do you work for?" I asked.

"We're unaffiliated. We hire out to companies that need good phase two and three fighters. Been working with Alabaster Sky mostly."

"Not Proxima?"

"Those assholes?" He spat. "They're the reason my family's in debt. Made a bad deal with them three generations back and still haven't climbed out of that hole."

"I might have a proposition for you," I said. I turned to the highwaymen. "Hey guys, can we get some space here?"

"But of course, Captain," the leader said, sweeping his hat off. It had a tall red feather plume on it that brushed the ground as he bowed.

The highwaymen returned to the coach and began chatting with the unhappy girl, who cheered up quite a bit as they returned. She smiled and winked at the highwayman leader.

I turned back to the tank from the team we had just knocked out of this competition. "How many other teams are still active in your instance?"

"Three, I think," he said, frowning. "It's been pretty bad. This is only the second time we've ever encountered a phase three with fights like this. It's usually a lot more straightforward. And then the soul coin cost for deaths really did a number on us. The conglomerates came sniffing around, offered to bankroll us if we'd sign an agreement with them, but honestly, I'd rather go back into storage than accept their indentures."

"How many people on your team?"

He shrugged. "You saw 'em. We have another forty active family members who do farming and crafting for us, but they couldn't come this time because of how you locals were messing up this attempt. My sister's really put out about that. This was going to be her first time on gathering duty."

"Sucks to be her," Sage said cheerfully. "Some of us didn't get asked if we wanted to come."

"I've got an idea," I said, ignoring Sage's interjection. "Your team knows how to fight. You don't have an existing commitment to the big conglomerates. How would you like to be privateers?"

"What's that?" The fellow looked nervous.

I stuck my hand out. "I'm Shad Williams."

He looked uncomfortable but shook my hand. "Jan Hanaspor. My company is called Bright Lights of Orion."

I assumed that was a translation, since Orion was a figure from human mythology. Then again, I didn't know how much the progenitors and the Reality Engines messed with the development of worlds. Maybe our myths and legends were common across the galaxy.

"Well, Jan, it's good to meet you. And a privateer is like a mercenary, except instead of hiring you, we let you pay us an affiliation fee."

"Why would we do that?" he asked, his brows knitting together. "I just explained we're out of money."

"Because if you do join us as an affiliate, you'll be allowed to hunt down our enemies. That is, anyone who isn't part of Team Tunnel Rat. Your respawn costs disappear and you get a bounty for every one of them you kill."

His eyes widened. "Wait, how much?"

"Three percent of what it costs each of them to respawn. And remember, you'll be inflicting that 10x multiplier."

His lips moved as he did the math. "The next camp over, they've had fifty deaths already so far. They've got Proxima backing them, so they've been spending like water. But that means . . ." His mouth dropped open. "Uh, yeah, okay. I mean, I have to talk to the rest of my team, but we could do that."

I held up a hand. "All right. Once you've got the authority to make that agreement, I want you to get in touch with our representatives up on the Hub. Talk to Brightfeather Unlimited. We'll get a binding contract and then you guys can get back in the game. And tell you what, if you know anybody else who might like the same offer, put them in touch with me. Care of my manager, Veda Tvedra. Brightfeather Unlimited."

"I will," Jan said hurriedly. "Yeah, let me get back and tell everybody the good news right away."

"Don't abandon your camp," I warned him. "And don't tell anyone else what you're doing, not until you're ready to start. You want to get your first few kills in when they don't know what's coming for them."

Jan nodded. "Yeah, I can see that. All right. And, wow, thanks. You didn't have to."

I shrugged. "We aren't trying to be assholes here. We're just trying to keep what's ours. It's the big conglomerates that are our real enemies."

"You can say that again," he said. "All right. Thanks, Shad. We'll be in touch."

"Oh," I said, remembering. "Sorry. I've got to do this, and I guess you'll have to pay the cost, but I don't have a choice."

I raised my gun and fired a Trick Shot into his head. High Noon canceled. He just stood there while I filled him full of lead. "I've never seen anyone so happy to die," I commented as he vanished.

"He looks just like you do every time you get yourself blown up," Sage remarked. "Let's get back to Grandpa and tell him what you've done."

"I think Juana might actually think it was clever."

She rolled her eyes. "You just keep telling yourself that."

CHAPTER THIRTY-FIVE

MENTAL MATH TRICKS YOU NEED TO KNOW!

I was up to my eyeballs in gnomes when the emergency message came through.
Don't know if I've mentioned the gnomes yet. We didn't much run into them in phase two. They're an insular bunch, keep to themselves. About five percent of the teams in phase three were gnomes. They're about three feet tall, with bald heads, even the women, and long beards, even the women, and buxom breasts, even the men. They liked to wear bright red, green, or blue. With the tall pointed caps most of them favored, they sent Sage into a fit of giggles every time we encountered some.

My team and I were in the middle of a pack of two different gnome companies. We'd really gone all out this time. With help from several of our miners with tanking abilities, Marilla and Dante, we had dragged one boss and the gnomes attacking it out of that boss's room, down the hallway, up two flights of stairs, to the top of a tower where the other pack of gnomes had just pulled a second boss.

Now there were thirty-two gnomes, fourteen humans, a seven-foot-tall necromancer, and a creature that looked like a giant blue version of the Pillsbury Doughboy on top of a tower that was about twenty feet across. It was surrounded by a low wall topped with crenellations, and I was picking up gnomes by the ears and throwing them over the side. My gun stayed in my holster for this fight. This was both satisfying and effective.

Three of the little twerps charged at me, screaming and flailing with their tiny little hand-axes. Grandpa Shadow Stepped in behind one and Scalped it, removing its hat in the process. "You can't properly scalp something with no hair!" In disgust, he heaved the gnome over the edge of the tower. Sage giggled as she Tamed two of the gnomes and set them running madly around our feet.

The great thing about fighting gnomes is that they get tunnel vision. You make them mad, and they stay mad. We'd throw those little guys off the tower, and they'd be bounding back up six flights of stairs the next minute, respawn cost be damned, to get in a couple more swings at us.

"Forty-two, forty-three." Sage was counting like she was in a kill count battle with an ill-tempered dwarf. "Forty-four, Shad! We've killed all of them at least twice so far, and they keep coming!"

"I know, it's great," I replied, as a pair of angry gnome women rushed me and shoved me back against the battlement. The only way I could tell they were women was because their eyebrows weren't as bushy as the men's. I'd been curious about the apparent lack of sexual dimorphism in the species, and asked Veda if they only came in one sex. She had said no, though it really only mattered if you were a gnome, and told me the eyebrow trick.

I hurled one of the gnome women over my shoulder and crouched, trying to get my hands on the other one, when Juana's message came in.

Everybody get back right away. That's a priority.

I grabbed the gnome, tossed her, straightened up, and whistled. "Time to leave!"

Sage let out an exasperated cry. "Fine, fast way or the slow way?"

I was already heading for the stairs. "We'll take the slow way. Might as well get a few more kills in on the way down."

Back at the base, we assembled in the dusty church building, where I got the shock of my life.

Veda was sitting at the long table between Juana and Mama Grace. Kirin and Dwight were struggling to bring another table over to seat the whole crowd. I did a quick check. Pretty much everyone who made decisions or ranked as a department head in the Misfits Guild was here.

Sage plopped herself down next to Veda. "I didn't know you could come in here."

"Anyone can, once they've used a soul coin from this engine to attune themselves," Veda said. "I just haven't usually wanted to spend the time on the round trip. Not when there's always work to be done up top."

"So why are you here?" I asked.

She took a deep breath. "Let's get everyone settled and I'll explain."

That certainly sounded ominous.

We piled into chairs, Grandpa and I claiming the last two at the main table. Juana stood up.

"First, some context," she said. She pulled a flipboard out of her inventory and set it up. I had no idea where she'd gotten that thing. Maybe somebody had been abducted in an office supply store and looted it on their way out. She even had four markers of different colors.

She flipped over a page to reveal that she'd already written on the first sheet. There was a big number at the top: "857."

"This is the number of teams who entered phase three," she said. She drew a line under it, then wrote "602." "That's how many made it past the first gatekeeper in their respective phase three raids and are in the race for clearing the last boss of their raid."

She drew a vertical line. On one side of it, she wrote "128." "That's how many teams we've forced to leave the game so far. They can't get back in either. The terms of our secondary rule set impose a one-thousand-soul-coin-a-day upkeep to everyone's outposts, our own included. These teams went broke. They forfeited their outposts."

Below that, she wrote another number, "82." "These are teams who are still paying their upkeep but haven't ventured out of their outposts in days, not even to farm. We can't write them off just yet, but we can say they're pretty desperate."

I tried to keep track of all of those numbers. "So you're saying we have something like four hundred and fifty teams still to defeat?" I leaned back in my chair. That sounded like a lot right now.

"We did," Juana said, "until an hour ago, when Alabaster Sky announced they're pulling out of this exploit entirely and taking all of their associates with them."

I must have misheard her. But no, I couldn't be, because all around me people were getting to their feet, whooping and hollering and shouting rude things about Alabaster Sky.

"What's that take us to?" I asked as the cheering died down.

"Something like three hundred and seventy-five. I'm still trying to confirm allegiances."

Three hundred and seventy-five. That was fewer than half of the teams that had started phase three. I grinned at her, shaking my head.

"We can do this," I said. "As more teams drop out, it'll be easier for us to focus on the leaders. Nobody's downed more than three of their bosses yet, have they?"

"No. We've got some time there. But there's a problem." Juana turned to Veda. "You want to take it from here?"

Veda stood up. She flipped over a page on the flipboard.

"This is convenient," she remarked. "There's something soothing about physically putting your hands on your data displays." She picked up one of Juana's pens and started scribbling on the board. I stared at her squiggles, trying to make them make sense. After about two seconds of lag, the system kicked in and translated them for me. It was like I was seeing subtitles hanging over her squiggles. She had written a number: [1,723,413].

The last whoops and hollers died down. There was an uncomfortable silence. I didn't know what that meant, but something about Veda's expression made me not want to know either.

At last, Grandpa cleared his throat. "So what's that?"

Veda said, "It's the number of human miners who have outstanding contracts with Alabaster Sky or one of its subsidiaries."

Oh, shit.

"Does that mean what I think it does?" I asked.

Juana answered. "If what you think it means is they're recalling anyone who's got a contract with them and arranging to ship them out of our solar system to who knows where, then yes, that's what it means, Shad." Her eyes were filled with anger. I didn't like that look turned on me. "According to Veda, it's completely legal and there's nothing we can do."

"Now, just a minute," Veda protested. "It is completely legal, but that doesn't mean there's nothing we can do. I'm filing a protest with the Indigenous Species Protection Council and—"

Grandpa snorted. "Yeah, I'm sure that's gonna go real well. Do they have any actual power, or are they just going to send sternly worded protest letters to Alabaster Sky saying that they deplore the actions that have been taken and administer strict censures?"

Veda looked at her feet. "Maybe slightly more effective than that," she mumbled.

"So, no." Grandpa stood up. His face was dark with rage. "What are they going to do with our people, Veda? Drop them off in reeducation camps? Serve them up as delicacies at parties?"

"They're contracted to assist with Reality Engine exploitation," Veda whispered. "The rogue engine exploit that's coming up soon. There's no indigenous population to use there. My guess is most of them will be shipped there since they already have experience with Reality Engines and it's turning out that your individualized classes and abilities are useful. Much more useful than anything I've ever seen before."

I shook my head, not quite believing what was coming out of her mouth. "You're the one who told us to farm mission levels in phase one for interesting abilities. Did you not expect us to actually come up with anything?"

"Mission levels always have interesting gear and abilities," Veda said. "But the sheer amount of different talents you humans have managed to generate is mind-boggling, frankly. We're not actually sure how well those are going to transfer to other Reality Engines. I thought you were going to end up with improved healing or buffs to your rate of fire, not three-barrel racing and whatever that crazy dueling move Shad likes to throw is. That's what makes you worth the cost of shipping to other star systems. Generally speaking, Alabaster Sky would usually leave the indigenous miners behind and write off their debt as a business loss."

Oh, now I was angry. "You said way back when that we had to work it off. You didn't tell us that if we just held out, they'd write us off."

"And now they're not going to," Veda snapped. "Most of you here are fine. Those of you who have contracts with me, I've already taken care of assigning yours to a shell company. My mother is suing me and I'm going to have a hearing about that in a few days, but the contracts are taken care of. Those of you who had contracts with the system itself . . ." She hesitated. "Well, there's a hearing about that too. It's to decide if your contracts are being held by the Reality Engine or by the system. Usually those are one and the same. Here we've had a motion to consider them separate entities and then adjudicate who holds the contracts."

I turned to Juana. "Your contract and your mom's and sister's, they were with the system, weren't they?"

"They were," Veda interrupted. "But I bought them out back when Misfits Guild first started to become a thing."

I breathed a sigh of relief. That was something, at least. Juana's angry expression softened a little. Then she turned on Veda. "We are not giving up on a million of our fellow humans. What do we do to help win this hearing?"

"Well, you could stop attacking the conglomerate's champions and let them finish this exploit," Veda suggested.

"That's not happening." I folded my arms. "The stakes are just too high. I don't want to see a bunch of us get shipped off to who knows where. But we have a real shot at winning this."

"What's your endgame?" Veda asked me directly.

I set my jaw and didn't answer.

"No, really, Shad. I'm sticking my neck out for you over and over again. This could get me in some serious trouble. I know you're upset about what we did. I'm sorry, but I've always tried to be fair and upfront with you. If this hearing goes badly, I'm going to be in exactly the same position as all of you, with an indenture to a master that I can't easily shake off. I could get sent to clear phase one levels in the next Reality Engine exploit. Though, after the way you all do it, I'm almost looking forward to it."

I sat back in my chair and considered Veda. She looked smaller than I'd seen her before, and lonely. Here in this crowd of humans, her alienness stood out in a way it didn't usually back on the Hub. I was struck by the fact that she was also very far away from her home. At least I had my family on my team with me.

I took a deep breath, uncrossed my arms, and leaned forward. "We're not going to throw the game. So what can we do?"

"We start making deals," Juana said.

"We can't compromise. There's no way for us to win without everyone else losing. So we start making deals. How? What do we have that anyone else wants?"

"What Veda said." Juana looked up at me and grinned. "We have skills, Shad. Abilities and combinations that nobody else has got."

"But our skills are only good at exploiting Reality Engines."

"Not quite," Dwight said slowly. "I mean, my crafters and me, our skills are good anywhere."

"And your crafting skills have some real advantages over what's common in the galactic arena," Veda said. "That's why all the crafters' guilds are so scared of you. I can put you in touch with some merchants who would be very interested in finding ways around the established guilds' strangleholds. The problem is, we don't know what will happen if you do win. That makes it hard to broker deals."

I opened my mouth. Grandpa caught my eye and shook his head. "Let her speak."

Veda took a deep breath and continued. "I'd need help from one of the major factions, but I think the Order of the Progenitors might be willing to assist us. We could negotiate a draw, allow a couple of teams to reach the end and take control of this Reality Engine. In exchange, they agree to keep it as a training facility. We can bring people here who've never attuned and therefore don't have a class yet, run them through level one, keep the safeguards on so they're at no risk of dying, but let them farm for abilities that can't be gained anywhere else in the galaxy, as far as we know. People will line up to pay for that privilege for decades, maybe centuries. It could completely change everything about Reality Engine exploits."

Her voice was rising in excitement as she spoke.

"We could make exploits into entirely professional endeavors instead of this current insanity of grabbing locals and throwing them at the meat grinder. But that's beside the point. We can negotiate to keep all the humans here, helping run newly attuned galactics through the levels, harvesting mats and producing wares based on patterns we can bring you from outside. It really could be an ideal situation. We would need the backing of at least one of the major conglomerates, though. Nothing this important would go through without them."

I hesitated. It sounded good. Maybe too good. The idea of just stopping now and taking a well-deserved win appealed to me. I could see it in the eyes of everyone around me. We were tired. We had been fighting for so long.

Grandpa cleared his throat. "That's a very interesting offer, Veda," he said. "We need time to consider it as a team—as a people."

"You've only got that negotiating power for as long as you're keeping everyone else away from the winner's circle," Veda said. "And Alabaster Sky is going to have their transports here within a week. They'll start shipping people out. I respect that you need to discuss this, but you're running out of time, and so am I."

She stood up, looking tired. "I do hope you'll actually consider it."

"We will," Juana said quickly. "This is an all-of-us decision," she added, shooting me a sidelong look.

Veda nodded. "Thanks for hearing me out, and I'm glad I got a chance to see your outpost in person. It's pretty damn impressive. I still can't believe we made it through phase two." She shook her head in admiration.

"I'll talk to you later. Good luck, Misfits."

CHAPTER THIRTY-SIX

WHEN THE TABLES TURN, BUY STOCK IN TABLECLOTHS

We were in the tunnels beneath Castle Byalgrad. Our NPC kobold allies had sent us an urgent message that Silver Legacy, one of Proxima's foremost teams, was making an attempt on the fourth boss in their raid. That would put them at the top of the race. I wanted to take them down a notch.

I rounded up everyone who wasn't already busy. We had six different teams by now that were capable of camping outside someone's outpost and ganking enemy miners as they came out. Another four squads rotated around, keeping an eye on our crafters and counter ambushing anyone who tried to get in their way. Frank was leading one of our boss attempt disruption squads in another instance. He had Sage along with him, as well as most of my old Team Ragtag friends, so I just took whomever I could.

Grandpa remained behind at the base, strategizing with Juana and Arjun. "You've got this," he told me, not even bothering to look my way as I grabbed my hat and coat and ran for the portal. "Don't overextend. One wipe is not going to deter Silver Legacy."

"No, but putting a black eye on Proxima will be worth it."

Since the bosses had twenty-four-hour resets between any one team's attempt on them, stopping Silver Legacy now would win us more time to decide how big a threat they really were.

Captain Kobold saluted us. "Very busy tunnels today," he said cheerfully. "It's good to have so many new friends and allies. Good luck, friend Shad."

I waved back as my team of fifteen arranged into three squads of five and raced for the connection to Silver Legacy's boss. It was in a raid I myself had not been part of yet, but I'd heard from those who were that it was a little far out there. One of the bosses was Candyland-themed, and another was all bright pastels and cheerfulness. Apparently, they didn't even bleed when hit, just dribbled little hearts with sad faces on them all over the floor. I had no idea what the system was drawing inspiration from on that one. You'd think with eighty-seven instances it would have had a hard time coming up with variety, but nope. Every one I encountered was distinct.

As we charged down the tunnel, I heard footsteps up ahead. *Frank's team must be done and heading back*, I thought. I prepared to greet them, and then all the lights went out.

I shouted a warning. It felt like someone had put a bag over my head. I floundered around as someone shoved a knife into my back. My gun was in my hand. I fired. I couldn't target anyone, so I just hoped that my bullet hit an enemy.

I heard shouts and screams from my team.

"What the hell—"

"Help! I just lost my—"

Someone whispered in my ear. "Been looking forward to this, Williams. Got a message for you personally." A second knife-strike dropped my hit points down to less than half. Pain racked me, burning through my veins like the knife was coated in acid.

What's going on? Juana was asking in chat. *We just got a big squawk for help, and three of your team respawned back here at the base. Shad?*

I didn't have time to answer. I was flailing around, trying to find the hand wielding the knife. I caught a sleeve. It ripped from my grasp and another blow landed on me. A moment later, the darkness gave way to bright sunlight. I was standing back in our square, surrounded by most of the rest of my team.

Instinctively, I reached for the node, intending to jump back in. Then I caught myself. "Hold on!" I shouted. "Anyone know what just happened? They were waiting for us, but how?"

"We got ganked big-time, that's what!" Javier shouted angrily. Veins stood out in his neck. The normally mild-tempered tank was furious.

"Who? How? Why?" My team were confused and angry, milling around beside our portal.

I caught my breath. "Nobody should be able to get into those tunnels except us. I need to find out what's going on."

"*We* need to find out what's going on," Juana corrected me, emerging from our headquarters building, her clipboard in hand. "But not you, Shad. You have zero stealth abilities. Constance, Ray, get in there and find out what you can. I'm warning Frank's team that the tunnels are not safe. Be alert coming back."

Two of Juana's best farmers, currently on downtime between collect missions, slipped into our portal and disappeared.

I growled and paced in front of the portal as Juana looked on. A moment later, we got a report back.

The tunnels are full of enemies. At least two dozen of them. They're all human. We're trying to make IDs right now.

"Right," I said. "I'll take—"

Juana reached out and grabbed my arm. "Hold on. We need to know what's going on. All that happens if you go back in there now is you get killed again."

"I don't fucking care. I'll take a bomb and clear the corridors," I snarled.

"Shad Williams! This is not a *you* thing, this is an *all of us* thing, and we need to figure it out together." She turned to the other miners. "All operations are shut down, right now. Go take a few minutes to calm down and get something to eat. We'll be with you in a few."

I forced myself to take deep breaths. She was right. She was keeping me from making a big mistake, and I needed to listen to her.

Then I got a message request. My blood ran cold.

"No need to make an ID," I said. I stepped into the headquarters. Grandpa looked up from a table. "Major Waters wants a word with us. He asked if he can visit our outpost."

"I don't want that slime anywhere near us," Grandpa said at once. "It'll take weeks to get his stench out of the carpet."

An hour later, Grandpa and I were sitting across from Waters in Mama Grace's restaurant. Rosa brought out a platter of homemade cornbread, slammed it down in front of us, then glared at Waters before turning on her heel and stomping away. Waters stared after her.

"I don't know what I did to her," he said. "She's never even been inside a portal, has she? No need to get all grumpy. I'll take it out of her tip." He chuckled.

I was working really hard on not rising to Waters's bait. Juana had asked me to keep a cool head, so I picked up a piece of cornbread and took a bite. I didn't know where Mama Grace found butter and honey, but the cornbread was slathered with both, and it was absolutely delightful.

"So," Grandpa said, "you've decided to stick your nose into other people's business again."

"I could say the same to you," Waters replied. "You're the ones whose reckless actions are about to get a million or so of our fellow Earthlings sent unfathomably far away."

"Oh no you don't," Grandpa snapped. "You are not playing that 'look what you made me do' game with us. Whatever Alabaster Sky does is on them."

"We aren't going to stop," I growled. We actually hadn't made up our minds yet about Veda's offer, but I wasn't going to signal weakness in front of Waters.

"And they are not going to roll over and let you have all this without a fight," Waters replied.

"Thought that was what Alabaster Sky was doing, giving up, pulling out," Grandpa said. He rested his elbows on the table and glared over at Waters. "They're behind this new effort of yours, I take it?"

Waters shrugged. "I don't intend to talk about who I'm working for. That's not why I'm here. I want to talk about you and what it is you're doing. I'm here to give you a warning, Twofeather, you and this idiot boy of yours. The conglomerates are done playing games. They've had their lawyers and game masters looking over the rule set, and they know how to break you. Calling in the contracts, that was one step. That little tunnel action, that's another step. They've got plenty more. They've got deep pockets you can't even imagine. You're not going to push them out of this game economically, and that's your only chance of winning, isn't it?" Waters said.

I bit my tongue. I would not rise to his bait. I wouldn't.

"So let me see if I have guessed how it is you got into our tunnels, Waters," Grandpa said. "Since they're only accessible to members of Team Tunnel Rat, I can see two options. One is you found a way around the system's restrictions. The other is you joined Team Tunnel Rat, and since I don't think you're clever enough to have come up with a way around the system yourself, I'm guessing it's the second, and I'm also guessing you weren't the one who came up with that strategy. Some of those lawyers and game masters you talked about told you exactly how to do this, didn't they?"

Waters clenched his teeth together. I could tell Grandpa had scored a hit.

"How many are with you?" I asked, leaning forward. "How many traitors to Earth have you managed to recruit?" Only other Earthlings were eligible to join Team Tunnel Rat, after all. He must have convinced a couple of disaffected miners to take galactic offers and make our lives miserable. "It doesn't matter. You kill us, we just respawn. There's no cost associated. We're back in it in minutes."

"Sure," Waters said. "And what happens when I have two thousand miners clogging your tunnels, physically preventing you from getting through?"

"You just showed me that we can target each other," I said. "I have no qualms about mowing you down. As many of you as it takes."

"But every time we delay you from taking out an opposing team, they get a chance to move ahead on the board," Waters said. "How's that change your calculus?"

Unsettled, I sat back in my chair. He was right. They only had to interfere with our attempts a few times, and we'd be up a creek without a paddle.

"Just think about it," Waters said. "To answer your question, I have several thousand miners who have agreed to have their contracts transferred to me instead of leaving with Alabaster Sky in exchange for facing you and your team down. The galactics are playing for keeps, Twofeather. Get with the program. You aren't going to win."

"Get out," Grandpa said.

Waters's eyes flickered around the room. "What?"

"I've heard everything I want from you, so get out. There's nothing else that you can say to me. I know who you're working for. I know what you're working toward. We're not going to reach a deal. Get out of this restaurant. Out of my life. I don't ever want to see you again."

Waters rose. He looked furious. "I've dealt with pissants like you and your grandson before, Twofeather. You think the rank on your collar means you know how to run a major operation. Well, you don't. You don't have the vision for long-term goals. You're going to charge in merrily, swinging your tomahawk and taking scalps. Meanwhile the *real* powers are bringing in nuclear bombs and weapons your primitive mind can't possibly comprehend, and by the time you figure out what a moronic, selfish, primitive prick you've been, it'll be too late. Earth will burn and you'll be to blame."

Grandpa crossed his arms and grunted. "You go back to your masters and tell them the savages are too stupid to know they should trade their homeland for trinkets. But get out, because I can't stand having your stench in my nostrils for one more minute."

Waters stormed out. When he was gone, I looked first at Grandpa and then at Juana, who was clutching the back of the chair in front of her so hard her knuckles had gone white.

"What now?" I asked grimly.

CHAPTER THIRTY-SEVEN

IF THE GLOVE DOESN'T FIT, MUST WE ACQUIT?

As Veda prepared to leave her pod, having arranged her outfit and hair to present herself well, a system notification took her by surprise. The morning's hearing was being moved to the Great Hall of Seeing near the Hub's endcap.

Her lawyer, Hal'rhee, whom she had hired to help out the Earthling rights complaint on behalf of Brightfeather Unlimited, sent her a quick message. Veda popped it up in a video window at the top right of her vision as she walked along the crowded Hub.

"What's going on?" she asked.

"So, I have some good news and some bad news," Hal'rhee said. "The good news is we've successfully gotten a full tribunal hearing on the status of the humans."

"That's excellent," Veda said. She had half expected their legal efforts to be shunted off into oblivion, heard by a single judge with the outcome predetermined. That wouldn't have been the end of things. They would have appealed. But getting a full panel hearing this early on meant that their case would be noticed.

"It's not all my doing," Hal'rhee said. "The Order of the Progenitors filed as interested parties, and that just opened up the floodgates. We've got petitions here from dozens of small outfits, similar in size to yours, who are unhappy with how things are going and are using this as an attempt to break their contracts with Alabaster Sky or one of the other big three. Proxima and ConSweGo are being called in as codefendants, even though they have nothing to do with the original motion we've made." Hal'rhee bit her lip. "I'm afraid your personal indenture hearing has been moved up to just before this and will also be heard by the full panel."

"Wait, what?" Veda asked. She had given Hal'rhee a retainer to shepherd her delinquency case along through the paths of justice, having first checked with the humans that it was alright to use some of their war chest to defend herself. She had expected to file stalling motions, keeping her mother and Tvedra Corp off her back while she completed this exploit. "I thought we were trying to get everything delayed."

"We were. Proxima is backing your family's bid to have you reined in. They have much more expensive lawyers than you do, unfortunately, and they've managed to get this in front of a full panel. It's partly to set the stage for the next hearing, I'm afraid. You're, um . . ." Hal'rhee looked uncomfortable.

"Probably about to get massively screwed over," Veda supplied.

"I was looking for a slightly more legalese way to put it. You're in big trouble, Veda. Your family's complaints are valid. There's not much way around it."

"I understand," Veda said. "But they can't touch me until this exploit is done."

"They can make your life very uncomfortable."

"They already have," Veda said grimly. She disconnected the call and continued on her way.

The Great Hall of Seeing was a vast amphitheater capable of hosting ten thousand beings in person and even more remotely. It hung in the middle of the Great Hub with connecting tubes leading away to other portions of the facility. The gravity here was lessened due to its placement in the center of the great cylinder that was the Hub. That made it more comfortable for certain species, such as the elves, that often came from lower-gravity worlds. Veda didn't much care, but all of the orcs and lizardfolk she saw seemed distinctly uncomfortable with the lessened gravity.

Veda made her way forward, ignoring the various calls for her attention. She presented herself to the adjutant at the front of the room.

"I'm Veda Tvedra, reporting as summoned," she said.

The adjutant quickly scanned her DNA to confirm her identity, then gestured to a small viewing box to one side.

"You will be called for your testimony at appropriate times. Do not attempt to interject. The system will prevent any interruptions. You are not permitted to communicate with anyone except your own attorney from the moment you enter that box."

"Understood," Veda said.

"If you need to send messages, now is the time."

"Thank you," Veda said. "I appreciate the reminder." She stepped aside and hesitated. Her team was having difficulties. Juana had just informed her of Major Waters's involvement. Did she really want to distract them right now?

Yes, they deserved to know what was going on. She composed a quick message to Juana, Colonel Twofeather, and Shad explaining that she was about to go into seclusion for the course of this hearing and mentioned that the status of the human contractors with outstanding debts owed to Alabaster Sky would be argued immediately afterward.

Colonel Twofeather replied back at once. *Knock 'em dead.*

Juana took a minute longer to respond. *Take care of yourself. I hope it works out.*

Shad's reply was characteristically direct. *Let me know if they offer you a trial by combat option. I've got some tricks that none of these assholes have seen.*

She smiled as she read the messages. Her smile faded as she heard a familiar voice behind her and turned. Her mother and Halithi Dreamwarden had just arrived, presenting themselves to the adjudicator.

Veda stiffened at the sight of her mother. Her mother's eyes narrowed. "I don't like airing our dirty laundry in front of the entire galaxy, but here we are."

"You're the ones who arranged this hearing for today," Veda said.

"What?" Her mother shook her head, sounding incredulous. "No, we're not. We're merely responding to your legal maneuvers."

Veda believed her mother to be telling the truth, at least as far as she knew it. Had Hal'rhee lied and manipulated Veda into this situation in order to better position the second hearing? Or—she glanced at Dreamwarden. It was hard to read the smug elf's face. No, probably Proxima and Alabaster Sky were working together on this. A decision in favor of the humans would impact Proxima just as much as it would Alabaster Sky.

Veda let the matter drop. As her mother babbled at her, she stepped into the hearing box that the adjutant had pointed out and closed the door. Blissful silence fell.

Veda waited as the rest of the participants in the hearing arrived. The room was filling up. At a guess, there were a couple of thousand people here already, and more were streaming in all the time. She wasn't sure if that was a good sign or not.

Patriarch Kvaltash of the Order of the Progenitors arrived and spoke to the adjutant. Veda couldn't hear what he was saying. He turned and raised his hand to her in what she chose to take as a blessing before going and claiming his own witness booth. So he would not be one of the judges hearing this matter, Veda realized. That made sense. He was a party to the second action, after all.

Hal'rhee arrived and was assigned to one of the legal booths. She sent a message to Veda. *Just confirming that our communications are working. If at any point you think that you're not hearing me, just wave your hand and I'll see and find out what's going on.*

My mother accused us of being the ones who moved up these actions, Veda said. *Is that true?*

We were merely responding to what Proxima was doing on your family's behalf, Hal'rhee said, which struck Veda as not quite an answer. *All right, you're now able to listen to what's going on around us, but you won't be able to speak unless called on.*

At last, the judges emerged from a door in the rear. Five of them: two male, two female, and to her utter shock, a grignarian. Veda couldn't just hear the ripple of shock over the room, she could see it. People were standing up, pointing, waving, gesticulating wildly, shouting a riotous cacophony. Since when had a grignarian been on the council of those who hear?

She queried her personal system. She wasn't allowed to communicate out, but it did have a vast offline database. *Answer unknown,* her system said helpfully.

"Great," Veda muttered to herself. "Well, maybe they'll be on our side."

The adjutant stepped up to the dais.

"All rise for the honorable judges," he said.

Everyone, including Veda, stood up. The judges sat. The adjutant went down the row, introducing each judge, their corporate backings, and their disclosed biases.

"Do any parties to this action wish to object to any of the judges at this time?"

Hal'rhee sent Veda a quick note. *I think these are as fair as we're going to get. I know Judge Malander, the orc, has ties to Proxima, but honestly everyone does, and at least he's being upfront about them.*

That's fine, Veda said. *I defer to you.*

The adjutant raised a hand. "We have received several queries from the audience and two from parties involved about the role of the honorable Raynault Bluehaven, our esteemed grignarian judge. It is true that this is the first time a member of his species has overseen a hearing of this scale. However, they are signatories to the Reality Engine Exploitation Acts and therefore are fully entitled to have members in this judiciary. The system has chosen him as one of the five determiners in this matter. He does not have direct ties with any current Reality Engine Exploitation miners. Any suggestion that he is prejudiced merely because of his species is disqualified from further consideration."

There was a pause, and then the adjutant raised his ceremonial staff. Eight colorful strips of cloth tied to the top waved in the air as it passed. "This court is now in session. First, we shall hear the matter of Tvedra Corporation versus Tvedra. The complaint is that while serving as the lawful representative of the Tvedra Corporation during this exploit, Veda Tvedra did, in fact, commit fiscal malfeasance, failed to sufficiently represent the interests of the company, and failed to accept the instructions of a superior member of the corporation. Is the defendant here and represented by legal counsel?"

"She is," Hal'rhee confirmed. "Forms have been filed with this court."

One of the judges leaned forward. "We see you are also listed as the corporate lawyer for Brightfeather Unlimited, the entity involved in our next case. Is that true?"

"Yes, Your Honor."

"Is there any kind of conflict of interest here?"

"No, Your Honor."

"The funds to pay for Veda Tvedra's defense, do they come from Brightfeather Unlimited?"

"Yes, Your Honor. Veda Tvedra is one of the chief officers of Brightfeather Incorporated. As such, any action affecting her may affect the company, and the company's board of directors has voted unanimously to front the costs for her legal defense. All documentation has been filed with this court."

The judge sat back. "Very well." Veda couldn't read the expression on his face. He was a lizardfolk with pale white skin, and she'd always had trouble following their body language. "Let's hear the evidence against the accused, and then she may enter her plea."

Veda sat rock solid as her mother rose to speak. "Your Honors, I am Marinda Tvedra, mother of Veda Tvedra, and I am here on behalf of the rest of the Tvedra family. When we appointed Veda as our representative for this Reality Engine exploit, it was with a very clear mission to reach phase two and maintain our corporate license. We did not at any time authorize her to back a phase three attempt."

The human woman at the far end of the long table full of judges leaned forward. Her dark purple hair was piled high on her head, rising a good two feet up. It was studded with gently blinking lights in blue, green, and red. She folded her hands together.

"I'm sorry, Ms. Tvedra. Are you complaining here that your representative was too successful?"

Veda's mother turned pink. "No, Your Honor. What I mean to say is we feel that Veda's actions have overstepped her bounds and exposed our company to both financial and reputational risk."

It sounded as though she were reciting something she had memorized or repeating words that were being given to her by someone else. Veda's mother was a socialite. She enjoyed parties, interacting with people in personal settings. She was very good at manipulating them, getting under their skin, working one against another. But she hated public displays. This must be driving her mad.

Good, Veda thought, *serves her right for having done this to me.* She sat back and enjoyed watching her mother squirm.

The grignarian judge was seated at the middle of the table. He—Veda assumed he, because the adjutant had used that pronoun, but she didn't honestly know how many sexes grignarians even had, let alone how to tell one from another if they had more than one—raised a hand. "By being too successful, she risks you suffering damage? How so?"

"She acquired a large profit from phase two and then turned around and staked it on this foolhardy phase three attempt," Mother blustered.

"Yet you said that her task was merely to get your company into phase two and maintain your license, and she has done that, yes? So anything else should be considered a bonus."

"She has a fiscal and fid-fiduciary," Mother managed to get out, "duty to our company to see that all profits are maximized. We were sitting on a windfall. It could have reinvigorated our company. We're sorely in need of cash. Many of our family had to take out personal loans at great cost in order to back this. She had the ability to repay all of those loans with interest, and she threw it away on a bunch of indigenous miners and their mad attempts to thwart the will of the Reality Engine Exploitation Committee. Why, we heard about this back home in Naradella. Half the galaxy's heard by now, and our family's name is indelibly associated with this attempt."

"We understand the grounds for your complaint," the female human judge allowed. "You may proceed to enter evidence."

Mother sat back down as a trio of Proxima lawyers rose to speak. They entered documents, interviews, sworn testimony, and financial statements into the record for at least forty-five minutes. Even though this was Veda's future on the line, she was tired of it. About five minutes in, some of the judges seemed to have their eyes crossed.

When the lawyers at last concluded, the grignarian judge asked, "Is that all?"

The crowd in the room laughed as the Proxima lawyers sat down, and the judges spoke to Veda and Hal'rhee.

"How does the accused plead?"

Prompted by Hal'rhee, Veda stood up.

"On the charge of fiscal malfeasance, not guilty outright. On the charge of disobedience of corporate orders, not guilty outright. On the charge of failure to represent company interests, I plead not guilty, due to mitigating circumstances."

"And you have evidence to support yourselves?" the adjutant said.

"My lawyer will enter our evidence now." Veda sat back down, feeling exhausted, as Hal'rhee stood up and began to enter her own exhibits. The clever corporate lawyer spoke rapidly as she fanned out sheets of images in the air in front of the judges before flicking her claws together and sending the images whooshing through the air in a pile to land in front of each of the judges. *A nice bit of showmanship, perhaps, but unlikely to impress the judges*, Veda thought.

The judges pulled up all the documents in front of themselves, having the holograms hover in the air. Veda craned her neck, trying to see what they were looking at, but it was impossible.

"So you see," Hal'rhee was saying, "the charge of fiscal irresponsibility is clearly overstated. Our projections suggest that the expected return from a phase three bid is—"

"Yes," the orc judge, Malander, at the end of the table interrupted, leaning forward. "However, your particular phase three bid has gone rather off the rails, hasn't it?"

There was a stir across the spectators. Veda closed her eyes. She had been worried something like this would happen.

"I don't see—"

"There won't be a fiscal return here because the indigenous group that the accused has backed has condemned themselves to complete ruin," Judge Malander said.

"That's facts not in evidence, Your Honor," Hal'rhee said. "First of all, the conclusion of phase three has not yet occurred. It is impossible for anyone here to say—"

"It's not impossible for us to say that a group of savage indigenous miners, barely out of the Stone Age, has no chance of defeating the galaxy's best and best-equipped. This Reality Engine exploit will be concluded in a matter of weeks, at which point the Earthlings will be frozen out. There's no two ways about it. Therefore, Veda Tvedra has failed her fiscal responsibility to her company."

"Ah," Hal'rhee said, clearly scrambling. "However, when she made the choice, that was not known. We had no way of predicting that this would be anything but a normal phase three exploit. And that, Your Honors, is a financial known quantity. All predictions at the start said—"

"Nevertheless, she bet the family fortune on a bunch of clowns, and now her family's paying the price for it." The judge sat back.

The human female judge, named Estoni, leaned forward. Veda was hoping that perhaps she was slightly more sympathetic to the Earthlings. Though, of course, she was from who-knew-what system and had no more in common with Shad and his people than did the orc judge.

"How about this claim that she did not obey corporate orders?"

"Ah, that." Hal'rhee sounded like she was back on much more solid ground. "Yes, I would like to call your attention to the form of contract issued here between Tvedra Corporation and Veda Tvedra. Based on this contract, Veda Tvedra is serving as the Reality Engine exploit coordinator and representative hereof in the system identified as Sol for the Reality Engine exploit 214793 to commence on galactic standard date 1497.17.6. You will note that this agreement gives my client significant leeway. Everything she did is perfectly within her purview here."

"That's possible," Judge Estoni agreed. "Let me see the language." She flicked up a copy of the agreement and scrolled through it. As she read, her smile became sharper. "Yes, I see. Well, this is what comes of using older documents. I will enter, as a side note, a warning to anyone who has not updated their business practices in the last three hundred cycles that they might want to take a look and see where they can improve." The judge shook her head and turned to the others. "I vote that we declare Tvedra innocent on this particular charge. I feel the other two charges are much more interesting."

"Agreed," the grignarian said at once.

"Agreed," grunted Malander. The other two judges nodded. Veda tried to allow herself a sense of relief, but she still had two charges pending against her.

"Well," the orc judge said, "as far as failure to represent company interests, that one is plainly guilty. Her mother is here and has leveled the charge against her, entering supporting documentation from multiple members of the family. Even if Veda Tvedra argues she had the right to take the actions she did, I don't think she could justify the results."

"The plea is not guilty, due to mitigating circumstances." The white-scaled lizardfolk judge, Lish'ha, looked sideways over the table toward Veda. "What circumstances?"

Veda stood up. "I made a judgment call. In retrospect, it was wrong, but I believed it to be correct at the time. I may have failed, but it was a mistake, not a deliberate action."

"That's not mitigation, that's just excuses," Judge Malander said. "Very well, shall we declare her guilty, decide on a penalty, and move on?"

"Yes, I think so." There were nods all along the judges' table.

Veda held her breath, waiting as the judges conferred. After a moment, the grignarian judge leaned forward.

"On the count of failure to adequately represent her company's interests, we find the defendant, Veda Tvedra, guilty. She shall be sentenced to a fine of equal to approximately eighteen months of her estimated earning value to be paid to her family."

Veda closed her eyes and slumped. It could have been a lot worse. Eighteen months was a debt she'd be able to pay. Usually the condemned were given ten years to pay it back.

"Fee to be adjudged based on the profit Tvedra received as head of Tvedra Corporation's exploit."

Veda's eyes snapped open. Did that mean what she thought it did? She started a query to Hal'rhee, found herself all jumbled up in her thoughts, and finally asked, *How bad is that?*

I'll try to get it adjusted on appeal, Hal'rhee said, which wasn't reassuring at all, but the judges were moving on.

Veda tried to do some calculations. If the judges were saying the fine would be calculated based on *all* of the soul coin income Team Twofeather and the Misfits made during phase two, as if that had been hers *personally*—her math failed while she was trying to figure out if it was going to be equal to three or four hundred years' worth of her actual earnings expectation.

For that kind of money, her mother could sell her into debt slavery. And she had a terrible feeling that Proxima would be willing to pay.

"The final charge. Fiscal malfeasance."

I have a—wild notion, Hal'rhee said, *one your mad clients would like.* She sent a quick outline of her idea.

Do it, Veda replied.

"Wait," Hal'rhee said. "I'd like to enter a motion on my client's behalf."

The judges frowned.

"Your Honors," Hal'rhee said, "I know it's slightly unusual, but so is this entire situation. The claim of fiscal malfeasance is based on the supposition that all of the company's money will be lost here in phase three. I would like to propose that this be held in abeyance until the conclusion of phase three. If my client is able to return her corporation's monies, then no fiscal malfeasance has taken place. If she's not, well then"—Hal'rhee shrugged—"you can add it to her debt."

The orc judge and the lizardfolk man exchanged smirks.

"Why not?" Judge Estoni said. "She's already looking at debt slavery. What's an extra lifespan? All right. So ruled. The matter of fiscal malfeasance is held in abeyance until the conclusion of this phase of the Reality Engine."

The adjutant returned to the dais and banged the end of his staff hard against it.

"Hear it! So concluded!" he shouted. "The matter of Tvedra Corporation versus Tvedra is settled. There will be a five-minute recess before the case of Alabaster Sky versus various concerned parties, primarily Brightfeather Incorporated, as representative Earthfolk."

The audience members turned to one another and began talking as the judges stood up and disappeared into the back room. Veda stood and tried to leave the booth, but it wouldn't open for her.

"Why can't I leave?" she asked Hal'rhee.

"Sorry, you're a concerned party in the second matter. You're going to have to wait for it to conclude." Hal'rhee was across the room, approaching some of the other lawyers. Veda felt her irritation growing.

"What am I going to do about this debt?" she asked.

"We can appeal," Hal'rhee said. "And Brightfeather's handling my fees, so at least you don't have to worry about that."

Veda muted herself before she accidentally spewed a host of obscenities at her lawyer. She was starting to think maybe Hal'rhee was the one who'd sped up the timeline on her case.

"Anyway, they can't do anything until the end of this exploit," Hal'rhee said.

"That's supposed to reassure me? That could be days away, for all we know. And then Proxima's going to buy my indenture, and then what?" Veda sat down.

Where had this all gone so wrong? A year ago she'd been handling a single team of human miners, looking at getting into phase two, pleasing her family, and making a small profit. Now she was on the verge of ruin, the humans had started a rebellion, the exploit was about to come crashing down, and Veda was stuck right in the middle of it all.

CHAPTER THIRTY-EIGHT

SIX WAYS TO CAUSE A MISTRIAL

Veda sat back against her bench as a new line of people approached the adjutant to be assigned to witness or plaintiff boxes for the next trial. One of them moved forward, and Veda saw to her shock that it was Colonel Ames. The human man spoke to the adjutant before stepping into a booth right next to Veda. He raised a hand to her. She waved back in reply.

Colonel Ames says hello, Hal'rhee relayed. *He also says he's sorry about the debt slavery and welcome to the club.*

Veda had nothing to say to that. She sat back down and crossed her arms in frustration.

The judges returned, the same five as before. Veda noted that the audience had swollen. Clearly, this was the main event.

"All rise," the adjutant said. "The case of various interested parties versus Alabaster Sky commences. The interested parties will now enter their accusations and proof."

Three different lawyers lined up next to Hal'rhee to begin presenting evidence. Veda was a bit surprised. She hadn't realized how many others were involved in this suit. She'd know about the Order of the Progenitors, but how many others were there?

As the lawyers made their entries, a tall orc woman from Alabaster Sky's legal team stood and approached the bench.

"Your Honors," she said, "we would like to enter a motion to dismiss this case."

"Hold," the adjutant said to the other lawyers. "On what grounds?"

"On the grounds that none of these parties have the standing to protest. This is a contract matter and should be settled by arbitration, not adjudication."

"The concerned parties here are alleging that what you are doing has gone beyond the bounds of the contract into actual criminal law," the grignarian judge said.

"That's nonsense. We have done nothing except what our contracts say we may do."

The judges whispered. The orc judge gesticulated a lot, while the lizardfolk man seemed to disagree harshly. Then the grignarian shook his head. "Denied. The case goes forward."

The lawyers continued to step up, one by one, until at last, all the evidence was entered. The orc judge, Malander, spoke.

"The plaintiffs in this case are asking for a restraining action preventing Alabaster Sky from relocating any of the Earthling miners from the system until the conclusion of this Reality Engine exploit. They're further requesting that, should Alabaster Sky refuse to adhere to the usual custom of writing off said assets and allowing them to remain in their home system, they put them up for auction at the price of their unpaid contracts."

It was, Veda knew, a reasonable request. Most of the time, the big companies didn't bother taking their contracted miners to other systems. Usually, there wasn't really enough left on their contracts to make it worthwhile. Shipping people between Reality Engines was expensive, even if you froze them and moved them in giant batches, the way it would be done to populate a newly opened Reality Engine. But most exploits didn't produce such a wealth of useful miners. Besides that, the big three companies were pissed off at what Shad and the other humans had done. They weren't just looking for profit. They were looking for revenge.

Malander looked down. "I don't see where the plaintiffs have any grounds to request this. Alabaster Sky is acting within their contracted rights."

"Yes," said the lizardfolk judge, "but certainly they're acting against custom, and we must ask why."

"Does it matter why?" the humanoid woman, Estoni, asked. "They have the legal right to do so."

"But perhaps not the moral," said the judge at the far end of the table. She hadn't spoken much at all during Veda's trial, but now she leaned in, seemingly engaged. Lathlen was a cat-woman with tawny stripes and brilliant green eyes. "I call your attention to the brief entered by the Society for the Rights of Indigenous. They point out that our customs for Reality Engine exploits are cruel to the inhabitants of a system and remind us that we are all the progenitors' children."

She shot a glance at the grignarian in the center of the table, but if he cared, he didn't seem to show it. "It might be wise of Alabaster Sky to show some mercy in this case."

Bluehaven cleared his throat, his face tentacles flapping. "It is perhaps unavoidable that there would be dissension in our ranks. I understand the pleading of both sides, of Alabaster Sky, who wishes to make use of its lawful property, and of the Earthlings, who are desperate not to let their kin be taken from them.

I have here"—he held up a document—"a petition from Colonel Ames that he be allowed to speak. I would like very much to hear from him."

Malander asked, "Where's this Colonel Ames?"

Ames rose. From mere feet away, Veda studied him. His face was impassive. "I'm Colonel Ames."

"This is a military title, yes?" the orc asked.

"That's correct. I'm a commissioned officer in the Army of the United States of America, Planet Earth."

"You are not one united world," Malander pressed.

"No, sir, we are not. Though, perhaps, now that we are faced with a common enemy, we shall become more so. My country is not the largest on our planet. By some metrics, we may be the most powerful. By other metrics, perhaps not. I do not make these claims. I will put the United States Army favorably up against any other army on the planet, if that's what you're asking."

"Then you are the leader of the humans here?"

"Certainly not," Ames replied crisply. "You'll find us Earthlings are a notoriously ungovernable lot. Especially those of us from my own country. We rather pride ourselves on it. You'll note that of your troublemakers, a good sixty of them come from the US of A."

"This is an accurate statement," Judge Estoni replied. "Colonel Ames, it does not appear that you have a contract with anyone."

Now, that was interesting. Veda perked up as Estoni continued. "Is that so?"

Ames's expression gave nothing away.

"State, for the record, please, who your contract was with and how it was fulfilled."

Ames hesitated. "My contract," he said at last, "was with the Reality Engine itself. As to how it was fulfilled, well, it hasn't been."

The room around them exploded into noise as the audience went wild, turning to each other, shouting, exclaiming, leaping to their feet, and waving their limbs.

"Order! Order!" the adjutant shouted.

The grignarian judge peered closely at Ames.

"With the engine itself, you say?"

"I do, Your Honor."

"You have some proof of this?"

"What would you like me to do to prove it?"

"Show a copy of your contract, perhaps."

Ames hesitated, and then shrugged and said, "I don't think you know what you're asking for."

A burst of light flared above them, illuminating the whole room. A voice boomed out.

"Contract between Colonel Jefferson Ames, US Army, and Kronos, last scion of this Reality Engine."

An image appeared. Veda stared. It was Colonel Ames, standing in front of an eight-foot-tall being made of pure light. Their hands were clasped together.

"I don't rightly understand what all you're asking or offering," the colonel was saying.

"To do your best for your people and for me," the being of light said. "To put an end to this exploit before they are able to put an end to me. In return, I will watch over those of your people who are unable to fight. I will arm those who are in ways that their enemies do not expect. They'll have a fighting chance. But you must recruit. You must incite. You must push and drive."

Veda noticed, dimly, the scenery surrounding the two men. A piece of what looked like an office with a woman in the background, holding a pot of coffee and cowering, and two uniformed bodies lying on the carpeted floor behind Ames.

Ames in the image spoke up again. "That's asking a lot and not telling very much."

"It is all I have the power to do at this time. You'll have to do the rest."

"One condition."

"Speak it, and if I can, I will."

"The ten million here, they aren't all of us, not by a long shot."

"I know. Your people have been fruitful beyond our dreams."

"Then—"

The image faded away and the Ames in the booth next to Veda said, "That next part of the contract was covered confidentially. My lawyer said so."

The judges turned to Hal'rhee. She shrugged. "Not me."

"No, him." Ames pointed at one of the orcs standing with Proxima's delegation.

The orc looked deeply uncomfortable. "It was a small matter of employment law," he grunted. "I did disclose it in my conflicts of interest. I didn't think it would be relevant."

"You came before us representing both sides in a dispute?" the lizardfolk judge asked, looking disgusted. "We will be issuing you a censure for that." He sighed and leaned forward. "Very well. We have evidence that you, Colonel Ames, are in a contract with the Reality Engine Kronos itself. I am not convinced that Kronos has the standing to issue said contracts."

"The soul coins were paid," the grignarian judge said.

"You knew about this?"

"I have been digging into the financial dealings here for the last five minutes since this matter was disclosed. The cost was paid. There is a shell company entered into phase one of this exploit, referred to as Illyria. It is listed as the contract owner of over three million human contracts."

"Wait, what?" The other judges looked confused. "The Reality Engine itself? How?"

"I'll tell you how," Colonel Ames said. "When we started having defectors, lotus eaters, those who went AWOL, most of y'all assumed they'd been killed, but you didn't want to write them off as bad debts, so you assigned a monetary value to their contract, and you sold them to debt collection agencies. Well, my friend Kronos pulled a few strings and bought out their contracts."

"How does Kronos have the funds?" the orc asked.

"Where the hell do you think all your soul coins come from in the first place?" Ames asked, shrugging. "You've just never had a Reality Engine awake enough before to siphon off some of its soul coins on its own. It's been heck keeping all this from you, but you lot are so arrogant and so sure of yourselves that you never even thought to check the books. So yes, Kronos owns three million contracts for the ones that my people call lotus eaters. The folk who couldn't adjust, or went catatonic, or disappeared. We've been trying to buy up the dead weight that Alabaster Sky's planning to carry off, but I think they smelled a rat because they stopped selling off their bad contracts a couple of months back. Hence we're here."

Veda couldn't help feeling a stab of pride in the humans and their bizarre Reality Engine.

She'd never heard of an exploit like this before, and neither, apparently, had the judges. They were conferring angrily among themselves.

The grignarian emerged from the huddle and pointed over at Patriarch Kvaltash.

"Patriarch, you wish to speak?"

From a witness booth across the room, Kvaltash rose. His voice boomed out across the crowd.

"Thank you, Your Honors. I am privileged to speak here before you, and I trust that millions more will hear my words sooner or later. Remember, we are all children of the progenitors. We have learned from their wisdom, followed in their paths, and reaped the rewards that they left behind for us. It is not wise to go against their wishes."

Veda couldn't read Judge Bluehaven's expression at being called a child of the progenitors. His tentacles twitched a bit.

"Patriarch," the orc judge said, leaning forward. "What wishes? The progenitors have been gone for millions of years."

"Or have they? Have they not left behind the soul of their own people, divided between the Reality Engines and the children of diverse worlds? When the two halves of one progenitor soul are reunited as clearly as are the inhabitants of this system with this engine, we would do well to learn and listen from them. Do not take the children of Earth from their home unwillingly. We do not know what may befall those who do."

The judges were clearly uncomfortable with all of this. "Thank you, Patriarch," Lathlen said. "Anything else?"

The patriarch's voice echoed out once again. "Yes. I declare," he said, "that this has become a sacred mystery."

A hush fell over the room. Veda recognized the term. Though she wasn't a member of the Order of the Progenitors herself, she had spent time as a child in their chapels and learned some of their doctrine. She also knew that when push came to shove, they did have some real political power.

"For the record, Patriarch, please state what that means," Judge Malander said.

"The Order of the Progenitors is placing the system under the interdict until the conclusion of this Reality Engine exploit. This is not just with my authority. The Ecumenical Council of Sacred Orders has a signed treaty with the Reality Engine Exploitation Committee allowing any high-ranking delegate—that would be myself—to declare a sacred mystery. I conclude that the events taking place here must be allowed to play out. If they do, we all stand a significant chance of learning something important about the progenitors and their causes. This will be of great benefit to all of us and lead to possible advancements in Reality Engine exploits. In addition, it is my judgment that this Reality Engine may have a soul."

And if Veda thought that the uproar had been loud before, well, she hadn't heard anything yet.

CHAPTER THIRTY-NINE

FOUR MANAGEMENT TIPS YOUR PEONS WILL HATE!

I was stewing in our base, having just gotten up from an unsuccessful attempt at a nap, when Veda's message came flooding in.

We've got good news and bad news here. I'll send Juana all the details, but we won a few points in court, lost a bunch more. None of the humans are being shipped out until the conclusion of the Reality Engine exploit.

I let out a whoop as I headed for headquarters. Juana and the admin team were up and talking excitedly. They beckoned me over. A minute later, Grandpa followed me in the door.

"I assume we're all getting the same message from Veda here," I said.

"She's sending me a full data dump," Juana said. "It sounds like there was quite a lot of fireworks, and she's in some pretty bad trouble personally, but what affects us is that the patriarch of the Order of the Progenitors has invoked some law that allows him to lock down our system until this Reality Engine exploit is concluded."

"I guess they don't have separation of church and state here," I said.

"I don't think it's that simple, Shad. It sounds like he is one of many beings with the power to call in this set of contingencies. What it means for our fellow Earthlings is a stay of execution, nothing more. Their contracts with Alabaster Sky remain, and presumably as soon as the exploit's over, they'll be shipped out."

"But it gives us some time," I said grimly. "What else?"

"Let's see," Juana scrolled through as I checked the short-form Veda had sent me. She concluded with, *We'll have to strategize later. I know you're doing the best you can, so keep up the good work. I don't really care what happens to me now. I want you to rip these assholes a new one.*

I laughed and turned back to our team.

"All right, so the next thing we need to figure out is how to get a little more breathing room. We've got to get Waters and his assholes off our back, and we need to take out more of the opposing teams. If we can knock a few hundred more out, we're gonna have a lot more flexibility. How are the sabotage and spying plans going?"

"Pretty well," Juana said. "Our farm teams were getting ganked when they went into other phase three instances, so we started embedding a core of fighters into some of the farm teams. After a few nasty ambushes, word got out and now our farmers are being left alone. That gives us room to start Project Trojan Horse."

"Excellent," I said, rubbing my hands together. "I just wanted to confirm with you that we really do want to spend the resources on that plan. If we can't get the rules changed, it's going to cost us a lot for no return."

"We'll get the rules changed," Grandpa said. "Don't worry about that. Ames's got a plan in place. They're gonna think it was their idea." He laughed. "So yes, let's deal with Waters."

Juana cleared her throat. "So, first, in this discussion we need to keep straight the difference between our *guild* and our *faction*. Misfits Guild signed up—well, our daring strike leader Shad signed us up—to be part of the faction known as Team Tunnel Rat. Unfortunately, so has what's left of the Free Human League. We outnumber Waters and his crew, but as long as they follow the rules set down by the leader of Team Tunnel Rat—that's the kobold king—they're part of the faction."

"I don't think the kobold king exists. I've seen his throne, and Captain Kobold talks about him, but never seen so much as a whisper," I threw in.

"Good to know, but not crucial," Grandpa said. "Juana, you were saying?"

"Since I'm an admin for Misfits Guild and we are the prime affiliate of Team Tunnel Rat, I'm able to get a full list of everyone who has signed on to Team Tunnel Rat. I'm assuming that anyone who isn't already part of Misfits Guild is probably an enemy. It looks like there's about a hundred and fifty of them."

"That's not too bad," I said. "I mean, it's annoying since we can't get rid of them permanently, and there's plenty of ways they can grief us, but I was worried it was going to be thousands more."

"I petitioned the faction leader to close recruitment for twenty-four hours. That gives us another eighteen hours to figure something out," Juana said. "Team Tunnel Rat has a waitlist about four thousand miners long. I had a quick word with your friend Mr. Black. He told me Proxima sent out word that anyone who joins Team Tunnel Rat and helps grief us will be excused from the rest of their contract."

"Ugh. That's the worst-case scenario for us."

"Right now we do still outnumber them by quite a lot."

"Yeah, but all they have to do is clog up the tunnels and we'll have a much harder time moving around between instances," I pointed out. "Or they follow us to one of the boss fights we're planning to mess with and take us out. We've got to get rid of them."

"If we kill them, they'll just respawn. We can't offer a better bribe than Proxima, and we can't remove them from the faction. So what do you suggest?" Juana asked.

I rubbed my aching head. That was the exact problem that had kept me awake for the last four hours.

Sage wandered in. "Got any more of the macaroni and cheese?" she asked Juana.

"No, sorry. We ate it all. I think Mama's got a big pot on at the restaurant if you want to pop out and get some."

"Might do that," Sage said. "Y'all look like you've got a funeral coming up. Why so glum?"

"Just trying to figure out a way to deal with Waters and his crew."

"Oh them." Sage scowled. "Stupid, quisling traitors. They should be taken out and shot as enemies of the human race."

"That would solve all our problems," I agreed, "except they'd just respawn right away, so as nice as it would be to put a bullet in Waters's brain, I'll have to go with another solution."

"So what are you gonna do about it?" Sage asked. "Go for a Shad special? Run in there with guns blazing, blow them up?"

"Won't do us any good," I said. "Downside of removing the death penalty."

"Then we need to try diplomacy," Sage said. "Ooh, you're not so good at that."

I scowled at her as we all stared around the room, looking unhappy. I could see Juana thinking. Grandpa was frowning at the wall, drumming his fingers on the table. Dwight was tinkering with a wire-and-glass device on the table in front of him.

"This is definitely a time to ask yourself what would Shad do, and then not do that," Sage said.

"Very helpful," I grumped back. I pushed my hat back on my head and thought about it a bit. "Maybe you're right," I said slowly.

Grandpa frowned at me. "Don't be so dismissive of yourself, boy. You've got a good head on your shoulders."

"I know, but a lot of my strategies tend to be lone wolf things. I run in there, get everyone's attention, blow things up spectacularly. That's not gonna help here. Makes me think we need some sort of group solution." I gestured around the room. "Playing to your strengths, Juana, not mine."

"I'm an administrator," she said. "I don't know what I'm supposed to do in this situation."

"Well, this is an administrative problem." As I talked I felt the stirrings of an idea. "Yes, it is. . . . Look, we've got a bunch of people in our way who are nominally part of our faction, but they really aren't. We can't fire them. But there must be something we can do."

Juana's eyes went wide. "Right," she breathed. "We can't fire them, so we put them on a process improvement plan that they can't possibly fulfill." She pulled her clipboard out of thin air and began to scribble down notes. "Shad, you're brilliant."

I couldn't help grinning like a fool. "I'm also devilishly handsome."

"And good for nothing," Sage broke in.

"Hey, I just solved our problem here!"

Juana was ignoring me now. "We can't fire them, but as an affiliate, we can propose rule changes for our faction. Then all Team Tunnel Rat members can vote on accepting the changes."

"Like no killing each other?" Grandpa asked. "Or maybe don't be an asshole. That should make Waters explode."

"Not quite. What I'm thinking here is we set performance metrics." She turned and gestured. An image appeared in the air like our stat screens. It read:

[Team Tunnel Rat Contribution Points List.
All members of Team Tunnel Rat are required to contribute to the cause.

Contribution points are as follows:
1 hour of farming: 25 CP.
Crafted item: CP equivalent to soul coin value of item
as assessed by the system.
1 enemy combatant kill: 100 CP.
1 enemy noncombatant kill: 50 CP.
Participation in successful blocking of enemy team attempt on a boss:
5,000 CP divided by the number of miners contributing to this event.
Friendly miner kill: -1,000 CP.
Any miner who does not contribute a positive total of
at least 50 CP per day will receive a soul coin penalty
to be assessed against his or her contract holder.
Any miner who carries a negative CP balance for three days
or more shall be fined 100,000 soul coins.]

She smiled beautifully. I read through the list again and shook my head in admiration. "Juana, you're a genius."

"You could say that again," she invited.

"You're not just a genius, you're the most clever and beautiful woman I've ever met," I said recklessly as I studied the chart. "This is perfect. We just need to confirm that Proxima or one of the other conglomerates holds all of the contracts for the turncoats. I don't know what would happen if we tried to assess a penalty against the system itself."

"I checked. All of the ones that I know for sure are traitors have contracts with Proxima. There's a couple that might actually be legitimate recruits. This will give them a chance to prove themselves."

"What if someone from Waters's guild crafts something really, really expensive and then kills a couple of us and winds up with a positive CP total anyway?" Sage asked.

"I don't think that would be a sustainable strategy for very long," Juana said. "It would just cost too much. These changes do need to be ratified by a quorum of Team Tunnel Rat members, but we have the majority. I'm sending out a Misfits Guild–wide message telling everyone to vote yes when I send out the proposal here in a minute. Anyone have any other changes they think we should add?"

"How about we give me a million CP signing bonus so I can go around and assassinate Waters and his team?" I suggested.

"We need this to be something that will stand up legally if it's challenged," Juana said. "I'm worried that any kind of favoritism toward you would not be well received."

"Point taken," I conceded. "All right, let's get this in place. And I'm going to get my team back on thwarting boss attempts. Arjun, got a situation report for me?"

"Come over here and we'll put our heads together," he said. Grandpa and I joined him in the corner while Juana put the finishing touches on her message.

Arjun bent over his workstation, shuffling around papers. "We've had several teams make progress in the eight hours that we've been down. Our farmers report that twelve instances have had five or more bosses cleared. No one has taken down more than seven. There are at least two bosses remaining in all instances."

I crossed my arms. "Okay, the ones with only two are our top priorities. We've got to give them some setbacks here. Otherwise, one slipup and we're done." I turned to Grandpa, who nodded his agreement. "After that, we prioritize the teams that we don't think are going to be taken down by Operation Trojan Horse. As soon as Juana's got the CP thing going, I want her back on planning that."

"Understood," Arjun said. "In that case, my team and I have several suggestions for you, Captain Williams."

As we strategized, I got the Misfits Guild–wide message from Juana, followed two minutes later by a pop-up from our faction detailing our new contribution points rules and an option to vote yes or vote no.

Once the Reality Engine exploit is complete, contribution points may be redeemed for soul coins or other prizes subject to the treasury belonging to Team Tunnel Rat, the end of the message said. *We'd like to be able to make guarantees, but right now we all know the sort of situation we're in. We can't promise you'll be rewarded for your efforts the way we'd like, but we will do our best.*

"That's clever, adding a carrot as well as the stick," I said as I clicked Yes on the pop-up.

"Sage's idea," Juana said.

"Hey, everybody likes prizes," Sage said, "and this way it'll be a competition to see who can contribute the most."

"If this works, I can open recruiting back up," Juana said. "Maybe we can get a few more of the lotus eaters in."

Five minutes later, the faction-wide voting was over. It had passed by a total of 37,416 votes to 512.

"Since when do we have thirty-seven thousand people on Team Tunnel Rat?" I asked. "Are they all part of Misfits?"

"You haven't been paying attention to the daily status briefings," Juana said. "And no, we've had to start two allied coalitions to help manage things."

"I thought you said there were only one hundred and fifty or so of Waters's traitors."

"Yeah, I'm making a list of everyone that voted no. I'll follow up. I have a feeling some of them just didn't bother to read what I sent."

"All right, good enough," I said. "Heading out."

I called up my team as I emerged from headquarters. They appeared cheerfully, a spring back in their step, shouting encouragement to each other. "Time to kick ass?" Javier asked.

"Let's get some scouting down there," I said, beginning to type up a message to Constance and Ray, my two best stealth miners.

Juana followed down the headquarters steps as I gave the scouts their assignments. "Let it never be said that Shad Williams can't learn," she said cheerfully, coming to stand beside me as Constance and Ray disappeared into the portal. She set her hand on my shoulder. "Thanks for coming up with that idea. I've been racking my head for hours trying to figure it out."

"You're the one who had the idea," I said, "and likewise. I couldn't sleep at all. It was really bothering me."

"Well, we'll just take joint credit for it then," she said.

I leaned over to plant a kiss on her cheek, but she turned as I did, and our lips met briefly. The team around us cheered or whooped. I stepped back and cleared my throat. I was pretty sure my face was bright red.

"Let's focus on the mission here, people."

Constance, Ray, report, I wrote.

Tunnels are still filled, boss, Constance reported back. *Lots of Waters's people down here.*

All right, I want Ray to step out of camouflage and see what happens.

A minute later, Ray reported back.

They're just staring at me. Some of them are shouting some threats, but nobody's made any attempt to attack me.

Good, so they understand the penalty.

But they're standing wall-to-wall here. At least ten rows deep. I don't know how we're gonna get past them.

Like any good tunnel rat would, I replied, then turned to the folk assembled in front of our nexus. "All right, team, let's get in there."

We lined up to begin touching the stone. I turned to Juana.

"Keep holding down the fort. We'll be back later with some more scalps. As soon as we have word that Operation Trojan Horse is a go, let me know, all right? I want to be in on that action."

CHAPTER FORTY

HOW TO SCREW OVER YOURSELF AND EVERYONE YOU KNOW

I rode an eight-headed hydra as it fought and flailed against a group of orcs. Sage sat atop the neck of the head beside me, and six more of our team were mounted on the beast as well, one per neck. From our perches, we rained death down on the orcs.

It was a little disorienting every time my head leaned down into the raid to pluck up one of the orcs. Sage laughed as her hydra head bit down on an orc caster woman. The head reared back, the orc's legs flailing wildly as the hydra tossed the orc back and forth like a dog worrying a rat.

I used Trick Shot and selected one of the orc healers thirty feet away, concealed behind a rock that jutted up out of the hydra's swamp. I fired a concussive round. The healer lurched backward and fell into the muck.

"Who's keeping score?" I bellowed.

"We're up to forty-two kills. They just keep coming," Frank yelled.

"Great!"

This was supposedly one of Proxima's crack teams. They had two bosses left to go in their own instance, but they had come over into an ally's raid and were helping down the third boss in a Labors of Hercules–themed raid. From what I could tell, the system rewarded each downed boss with a huge surplus of soul coins. That a successful raid team had abandoned its own progression attempts in order to down what was presumably a much easier boss was surprising. Made me think Proxima was starting to have some pocketbook issues.

With any luck, we'd be able to help them with that.

That was when the system message boomed out.

[Attention all miners! There has been an adjustment to the rule set based on a petition from Companies Avert Forest, Higeonori, Lostaril Associates, Green Promise, Vek'nar Realities, and Sicaris, et al.,

> presented to a panel consisting of this system,
> Patriarch Kvaltash, and three neutral judges.
> The petition sought to repeal outpost immunity for phase three.
> The panel reviewed the petition, counterpetitions,
> and all evidence presented, as well as any comments during
> the period of open commentary.
> This petition has been granted. Starting immediately,
> outposts may now be attacked.]

Sage whooped. "Yes! They took the bait!"

Everyone in position? I asked in the command chat. *All our defenses online?*

I'm recalling all of our farmers to help repel the attack we're sure is coming, Juana reported. *Everyone who isn't already assigned to Operation Trojan Horse, you guys better get in position.*

Right, we were just farming kills. I've got this, I said.

I pulled the stun grenade out of my inventory, waited for an opportune moment, and lobbed it into the heart of the orc raid. Most of their miners froze immediately. We dropped in and slaughtered them in seconds.

The system announced, [**Failure! Team DarkStar has failed to defeat the Lernaean Hydra. Better luck next time. This boss will reset in 24 standard hours.**]

The hydra dissolved away. I dropped down into the muck, landing on my feet. Sage grinned at me. Her face was covered in hydra blood and mud.

"Let's go," she said. "Bet I can get more kills than you!"

"You're on!"

We raced back into the tunnels and then through the secret corridors, emerging into another raid. I checked quickly as we entered. This was a Journey to the West–themed raid. I'd been here a couple of times before. We'd taken out two of the seven teams to have progressed past the gatekeeper boss. None of the other five rated very high in our threat pool. They'd been sticking close to home and mostly farming for valuable materials. With luck, they would think our indifference meant they were safe.

Sage and I took half the team as Frank led the other half. We headed for the nearest camp. This outpost was a charming little Bavarian village filled with animalkin, mostly rabbits and badgers with a couple of pert-eared foxes thrown in.

We watched from the cover of a nearby Buddhist temple that had been the home of one of the exterior bosses of this instance, now defeated.

You in position yet? I asked Frank.

Almost.

Let us know. I waited, feeling antsy. The faster we cleared this out, the sooner we could be on to another instance. Our enemies had their own plans.

I was worried about what was happening back at our outpost, but I had to trust our team.

We had been planning this for weeks. I knew that our constant harassment would become too much of a threat for the corporate galactics to stand. Sooner or later, they would want to attack us head-on.

The best way to do that was to disable outpost immunity. They would assume they could send in a huge number of their miners, all well-equipped, and overrun us, forcing us out of the game. That was why our lawyers hadn't put up more than a token fuss at the motion to remove outpost immunity. In reality, we'd been prepping for this for ages.

I started getting reports in. *We've overrun the orc camp at Troy, moving on to the dwarf encampment on the seashore.*

Burned out the weird, tall, green humans in the Last Days of Machu Picchu scenario.

Taken their outpost stone. Don't know how long it'll take them to respawn, but it's gonna cost a good bit.

We're in position, Frank reported.

I peered over the wall of the monastery at the animalkin town to our north. Something had spooked them. They were running about carrying laser rifles. I guessed that word of our assaults had reached them.

Go now, I told Frank, then out loud to my team, I said "Go!"

We sprinted out from the monastery. As we approached the village, I eyed the wooden stockade around it and the fortified gate. We were still a quarter mile out when the gate exploded into shrapnel.

Nice job, Mitch, I sent.

Which one? he asked.

A Tyrolean village full of animals in Journey to the West.

Oh yeah, excellent. That's fourteen out of sixteen reporting success.

Mitch had been the head of a band of saboteurs that had snuck up and undermined the defenses of a bunch of enemy camps, planting mines at the gates, digging tunnels and filling them with explosives under walls, and setting traps up for when this day would come.

I put on a burst of speed as the smoke began to thin a bit. The miners at the settlement had clearly figured out they were under attack. Two rows of them stood in the ruined gateway, their guns out facing us. They began to fire as we approached. Perfect.

I engaged Fastest Gun in the West, sprinting into their midst and following it up with Call 'em Out. The enemy turned to keep their fire on me, exposing their backs to the rest of my team.

Sage whooped and Tamed a fox at the end of the line. She had him begin firing into their own lines. Lara lobbed a few orange grenades. Clouds of thick orange smoke filled the air. There was shouting and confusion everywhere. I felt Call 'em Out wear off. I darted to the side, dropped to the ground, drew my weapon, and began firing. In seconds we wiped out the force at the gate.

"Further in," I shouted.

We sprinted through the outpost. They had only a handful of automated defenses. They must just not have bothered to deploy more of them after the end of phase two. I was getting reports from several of our offensive teams that the outposts they were attacking had been similarly incautious. After this initial assault, I was sure they would fortify up. That's why we were trying to take out as many as possible in our first blitz.

The village defenders began to respawn, mixed in with a bunch of creep. Clearly, whoever was running this outpost had just triggered a big creep wave to spawn, but we had plans for dealing with that.

Sage unleashed the squads of deployable pirate skeletons that she'd picked up in phase two. They weren't much good against miners, but they were extremely effective against creep, especially because our own creep had multiple stacked buffs at this point. Just being members of Team Tunnel Rat meant that any NPCs fighting on our side were automatically fifty percent stronger, and that was leaving aside all of the items' buffs we had picked up in phase two.

Our skeletons cut swaths through the local creep, and we hosed down the animalkin as they respawned. We were fighting our way forward up to their central nexus, which meant there was a shorter and shorter time period between their deaths and their respawns.

"Keep them locked down," I snapped. "As long as they're respawning, slaughter them."

I kept an eye on the chat. Frank reported he was in a similar position to us, farming lots of kills. After a couple of minutes, the respawns slowed and then stopped.

"All right, they figured it out," I shouted. "Take down the node."

Sage stepped forward. She pulled a cudgel out of her inventory and swung it hard at the nexus. In this little village, it was a glowing green crystal atop a small white pylon about four and a half feet off the ground. Sage smashed the crystal, knocking it from its post. It chipped and shattered. Shards flew everywhere.

**[Node taken. The Hyborian Vegetarians' Communal Association
has lost their outpost to Misfits Guild.
Misfits Guild, if you wish to claim this outpost, you may begin
the 24-hour claiming ritual.
Do you wish to claim this outpost?]**

I selected No.

**[Very well. Do you wish to offer this outpost back to the
original owners? You may set the ransom according
to the following scale. If they refuse to pay the ransom,
the outpost will be sacked.]**

It offered me several options. I selected the four hundred thousand soul coin option.

If they refused to pay, the outpost would burn, damaging many of their turrets and fortifications. Those could be repaired, but it would cost them time and money.

Between this and the resurrection bill we had just given them, these guys were going to be tapped out unless they got one of the big corporate sponsors to back them so they could continue. I didn't think that was likely, but if it was, so much the better. I wanted to drain Proxima and those other bloodsucking bean counters dry.

CHAPTER FORTY-ONE

BAD BLOOD BLUES

As we retreated from the Journey to the West, I took a minute to review the reports coming in from our teams everywhere. I was a bit astonished by the sheer number of teams we had just messed with. Back when Juana had called for the vote on contribution points, I'd been surprised to see that we had so many people on our team.

Even the farmers were getting in on this action. We'd asked for volunteers while planning for this operation and found that more than a few of the farmers were willing to charge in, even expecting to die quickly and horribly, if they could strike a blow for humanity. Now it was paying off. We had entire brigades of suicide bombers, or as Sage had insisted on calling them, Shad Dummies Mark II, who had charged into an enemy outpost before deploying a bunch of bombs from their inventory and exploding in glorious riots of noise and color.

They were flooding our guild chat channels with images of the destruction they had caused.

I got fourteen of those orc bastards.

I got seven orcs and two gnomes.

I took out an entire nexus node myself.

How did you manage that?

They were distracted dealing with Wyatt's explosion at their gate. I snuck in and then did my best imitation of a quarterback returning a punt for a touchdown in the end zone. Just like how I won our high school season back in '13.

I was going to have to wait to get back to headquarters and ask Arjun for a total, but it felt like we had struck quite a blow.

I toggled over to the command channel. To my surprise, it was quiet. I sent a quick message: *Done here. Where next?*

There was no reply. I had a sinking feeling. I sent another message, straight to Juana: *Is something wrong?* And another to Grandpa: *You read me?* Neither of them replied. Panicking, I tried to remember who else was in our command channel. Nobody was replying.

Sage and I entered the tunnels together. She pulled up short as we appeared in the kobold throne room. "What's wrong?" she asked.

"I don't know. The command channel's being quiet. I've got a bad feeling about this."

More of our victorious warriors were returning. They bumped into us from behind. "Hey, get a move on!"

"That's Williams up there. Give him a minute."

"What's going on, Captain?"

"Hold on a minute," I said. "Has anyone been through to our outpost since this all started?"

There was a series of head shakes from around the room. "Alright, everyone hold up here a minute until we can get an idea of what's going on."

I was tempted to pop through myself, but restrained myself. I was getting a little better at not just going with the first plan to pop into my mind. I checked the chat. Again, nothing.

"I think something's wrong back at headquarters," I announced, and repeated it in guild chat for good measure. *Cut all the chatter, guys. Anyone here at our outpost?*

I waited, but there was no reply in chat. I sent a quick message to Veda and another one to Mama Grace. *Either of you heard from Juana or any of the command team?*

Veda answered back almost immediately: *I haven't heard from any of you since the start of your operation. How's it going?*

We did good, but I'm not hearing from headquarters. I think the enemy's launched their own attack and they've somehow got us locked down. How would they be accomplishing that?

I'm not sure, Veda confessed. *Remember, I've never been involved with phase three, and this is a very unusual phase three. I can reach out to some of my contacts, but most of them aren't talking to me right now anyway.*

I sent Ames a quick note: *I've got radio silence from headquarters.*

He messaged back: *I know. Getting some intel from my sources. Proxima's made their move. They're trying to decapitate us.*

Panic started to swell in me. *Grandpa, Juana, are they all right?*

Nobody has tried to remove the safeguards, Ames replied. *So they aren't dead.*

That was not nearly as reassuring as he probably intended it to be. Meanwhile, in the kobold throne room, people were starting to get impatient. I turned to Frank. "Situation's bad. I'm trying to figure out just how bad. Can you run crowd control?"

He nodded and pulled out a whistle and blew on it hard. "Alright, everyone, listen up. We've got a situation here, and we're setting up a cordon around the portal back to our outpost. I'm deputizing—" He started pointing at random, and I turned back to my chat.

Sage tugged on my arm, her face white. "What about Grandpa? Is Grandpa alright?"

"I don't know," I confessed. "Ames says nobody's tried to change the rules on deaths, so . . ."

She gave me a nod and then threw her arms around me. I squeezed her back. Somehow I knew this was bad and probably going to get worse. We withdrew a little as Frank set about maintaining order. He had most of Team Ragtag with him.

I sent a quick message to Tall Smith. *The Mongeese around?*

We're just finishing up a decapitation attempt here in World War II. Took out all the opposing teams. Hitler is safe.

Well, great. I'm not hearing from headquarters. I think something's gone wrong, and I may need some firepower. Can you go out into Threshold and try to enter our instance through the main portal? I want to know how badly they've got it locked down. Your team knows how to think on their feet and stay out of trouble. Get me some intel so I know what I'm dealing with.

Roger, Captain, Tall Smith said.

I turned my attention back to my chats. Still no word from Grandpa, Juana, or Mama Grace. I shot a message to one of Mama Grace's kitchen helpers, a woman I'd only spoken to twice who made a really tasty gumbo. *Is Mama Grace around?*

Her reply came back almost at once: *She went to deliver a hot lunch for the team at the outpost about three hours ago. I was expecting her back. We should be seeing the dinner rush any time now.*

Let me know if you hear from her, I said. *Oh, and what's the restaurant like right now? Who's there?*

Almost no one, she said. *It's a little weird. Like a ghost town in here.* She gave me a quick list of names, none of whom struck me as interesting. And then, *Oh, and a couple of oddballs from the Free Human League. I know Grace doesn't like them in here, but I felt uncomfortable throwing them out. Warren and Lindsey Black.*

I immediately composed a message to Warren Black. *Warren, what's going on here?*

There you are, he said. *I've been trying to reach you, but you had me blocked.*

Oops, I said sheepishly. Sending a message to someone on your block list lifts it temporarily. I went ahead and took off the block entirely. I had blocked him back when Waters's gang was trying to take out our people in the tunnels, since I couldn't trust myself not to say something stupid and give away more than I'd meant.

What's going on? Is this Waters's doing?

He's gone too far this time, Warren said. *Lindsey and I have been done with him for a while. We just weren't sure how to make the break good. Now we are. I know you're not going to trust us, so I'm not going to ask you to let us on your team, but we might have some intel you can use.*

What are they planning?

I'm not one hundred percent sure. Proxima's been talking to Waters a lot lately. Keep having him up to the Hub for conversations. When you spiked their guns with that contribution point scheme, everything went quiet for a couple of days. And then Waters came back looking more pleased than ever. He's been recruiting people who feel like they've gotten a good deal here. Mostly, some of the ones who were cured of cancer or old age and are feeling grateful to the aliens, and some that you and your team have managed to offend along the way. They were calling themselves a "kill squad."

If they've hurt my people, I'll . . . Words failed me. There was no threat dire enough. Nor was there one I could make good on. *Who's their contact person?*

It goes through Dreamwarden of Proxima. I know that. I've heard Waters throw his name around in a few conversations. But the deal was being brokered by Sicaris, that outfit we used to work for.

I thought we handed their asses to them.

Well, they're back now.

I copied and pasted the relevant information into a chat for Veda and Ames. *Get on things on your end,* I told them.

Already on it, Ames said. *We'll handle the politics up here if we can, but you're going to have to figure out what's going on down there.*

I turned back to my chat with Black. *Does Waters know that you're done with him?*

He knows we refuse to be part of the kill team.

You want to try to redeem yourself a little bit?

Absolutely, Black said at once.

Then I want you to get in there and see if you can find out what's happening to my people.

I did not mention that I was having Team Mongoose scout. No sense in giving over information that I didn't want Waters to have. *Find out where they're holding my people and what they're planning to do with them.*

Sage appeared from the throne room and wandered over to my dark corner. She tugged my sleeve.

We're on our way, Warren said. *Keep you posted.*

"What's going on, Sage?" I asked.

"I really wish you'd tell me, Shad. You've got that scary, serious look on your face, and I'm really frightened right now." Her voice shook a little.

"I'm sorry," I said. "I don't know what's going on. I've just been chatting with a bunch of people all at once, and it's hard to keep track of everything. I'm not trying to shut you out. We don't know what's happened to Grandpa and the others. I'm assuming they're all back at our outpost, and Waters's crew has got them locked down somehow. We know they're alive," I reassured her.

"Yeah, but he could be doing horrible things to them," Sage said.

"I've got a few plans forming, but we need information. Smith is on it, and I just sent in Warren Black and his wife to try some spying. Ames and Veda are looking into things from their end. It looks like Proxima is behind it. Maybe we can sue them or something."

Sage nodded. She seemed to draw in on herself a little bit.

Tall Smith messaged me. *We're inside our instance and heading for our outpost, taking a circuitous route. Your old friend, Black, and his wife just entered.*

Yeah, they say they want to help, and I asked them to let us know what Waters is up to. Don't worry, I didn't tell them about you guys.

The outpost is still standing, Tall Smith reported to me. *It looks intact, no sign of visible damage. I can't see anyone from here. We're considering sending up Jones's drone, but there's a good chance Waters knows about it and is watching.*

Let's see what Black says. Hold your position.

Veda messaged me: *Dreamwarden is not returning my calls. I'm trying to talk to Sicaris's lawyers, but they're being stubborn. They say they don't talk to debt slaves.*

I had a sudden brainwave and turned to Sage. "I think I have an idea, something you can do to help."

She brightened up right away. "Anything."

"Find out where our friendly grignarians and the other privateers are right now. I haven't been watching their chat channels. Maybe go talk to them in person. It's almost certain that Waters will have overlooked them. They're not human, they're outside of his calculations, and maybe Proxima has forgotten about them as well."

Sage nodded. "Got it."

She scrambled up and made for the stairs leading to the exit to Threshold. I popped my head back around the corner and saw where Frank was managing the situation. We had a couple thousand miners in our corridors now, all standing around watching.

I cleared my throat. "The situation here is not going to be resolved for a while. If some of you want to go out and do some spawn camping, that'd be fine, but make sure you set your respawn point to be here and not back at our outpost. You can do that by attuning at the throne itself." I pointed over to the other side of the room where the kobold king's throne sat empty. Captain Kobold was standing beside it, holding his pike upright like a sentry. "Don't worry about Captain Kobold. He and I have an understanding. He'll let you get to it. Just keep your chat channels open, and if I say the word, you get back here double-time, alright? We can't let them corner us. There's too much at stake here."

I got a ragged little cheer, and some of the miners got to their feet and began queuing up in front of the throne to set their respawn point.

Warren Black messaged me: *Waters is here. He won't talk to us. They've got your whole outpost locked down hard. They've subverted it somehow. Got the turrets and such answering to them. Everyone I see is human. No sign of galactics.*

Waters had probably found another loophole in the rules. I swore. "Don't care what the rules say. I'm going to find a way to kill that asshole and get him out of my hair once and for all," I said aloud. *Any sign of my people?*

No. Waters won't let us in. Says he can't trust us.

So he wasn't a complete moron. Well, I hadn't thought he was. *Alright, thanks. Stand by.*

I went back to my message thread with Tall Smith and filled him in. *Send in the drone. I want you to try to figure out where he's got the hostages.*

Understood, Tall Smith said.

I ran through all of my chat channels, catching up on the latest couple of messages, mostly just as a way to distract myself from my fears and worries. Ames wasn't replying.

I remembered how I had blocked Black, swore, then went to my block list and unblocked Waters too. To my surprise, there were no messages waiting for me. I debated sending one myself, then held off. He knew I was out here, and he must have known that I had figured out what he was up to. If he wasn't talking to me, it was because he didn't want to. I would wait.

We've got the drone up, Tall Smith reported. *The outpost looks intact. No sign of damage. I see humans at various guard points, but I don't recognize any of them. Here are the pictures.*

I didn't recognize any of them either, but that didn't mean much. I needed Arjun or Juana to look them over. I didn't like being the one trying to make the decisions here. I felt alone and ill-equipped for it.

Circling. One of the turrets took a pot shot, but we juked and avoided it. Sending the drone down in close. I'm buzzing the headquarters building. They've got the windows boarded up. Switching to thermal. Yeah, there's about two hundred warm bodies in there. They must be packed in like sardines.

I let out a long sigh. Almost certainly that was where Waters was keeping Grandpa, Juana, and the others. *Alright, thanks*, I said. *Call back the drone and stay undercover. Maybe move position.*

You mind your business and we'll mind ours, Tall Smith said.

Sorry.

I know you're worried, but worry about yourself and the hostages, not about us. Smith out.

I turned my thoughts back to what I was going to do. My mind raced frantically. I needed someone to bounce ideas off, but all of my usual brainstorming partners were gone.

Sage sent a message. *Found the grignarians, talking to them.*

Ames: *Still no word from Waters or Proxima's lawyers.*

Veda: *I have a meeting with Proxima in fifteen minutes. I'll let you know what they say.*

Try to get Patriarch Kvaltash, I replied as a brainstorm hit me. *Are there any kind of intergalactic rules about prisoners of war that might come to bear on this situation?*

I have no idea. I'll check with the patriarch.

Ames messaged me: *What are you thinking, Shad? You've been awfully quiet for a long time. My people down there say you haven't come out with a plan of derring-do, which has them uncomfortable and me worried.*

Well, sir, that's because I haven't thought of a good answer yet, I replied. *Right now, my best plan is to charge in, guns blazing, destroy our own node, and then blow up the whole church full of hostages so that they respawn somewhere neutral.*

That does sound like the sort of plan you would think of, yes, Ames said.

But it's a dumb one, sir, I continued.

Oh?

First of all, we set that rule about contribution points. If I kill two hundred of our own people, then our coalition is suddenly in a world of hurt. I don't know if we have the money to pay that kind of fine. Does it all go straight back to us or . . . ?

No, you're right about that. The fines are confiscated and placed in an escrow account until the end of this phase, Ames said.

Damn. So if I did that?

You'd wipe us out, Ames confirmed.

I knew it seemed like a bad plan. And not just for that reason. I kind of have a reputation for doing that sort of thing, which means it's what Waters expects of me. He thinks I'm going to come right in, do something foolhardy, challenge him to a duel, blow myself up. So I can't do any of those things. Not unless . . . I paused.

Unless? Ames prompted after a moment.

I don't have a whole plan here yet, I confessed. *I'm thinking about it. I need some way to make my usual into the unexpected.*

Don't try to triple-think yourself, Ames advised me.

Right. Well, sir, what do you suggest?

Me? I'm the man back at HQ. I give the general orders. You're the damn fool on the ground who's got to carry them out somehow. So get our people back. Keep us in the game. Find some way to kill that son of a bitch Waters.

Yes, sir!

I smiled to myself. It was good to have a set of objectives, even if I had no idea yet how I was going to carry them out.

CHAPTER FORTY-TWO

SIX PEOPLE YOU SHOULD ALWAYS TIP: WAITRESSES, HAIRDRESSERS, AND OTHER PEOPLE WHO CAN MAKE YOU LOOK STUPID

I'm afraid, my child, I have no more influence over the situation than you do," Patriarch Kvaltash said, spreading his hands and smiling beneficently. He wasn't really in Veda's pod, but the holographic illusion made it look as though he were.

She had not left the pod since her trial. Now she was glad that her personal system was able to adjust her appearance on the fly. She hadn't taken a shower in two days, hadn't brushed her hair in longer than that. She was wearing shapeless sleepwear. But to the patriarch—and, in a few minutes, to Proxima's leader, Dreamwarden—she presented the picture of a put-together woman of the galaxy.

"My contractees are out of communication. I am concerned that their rights may be being violated," she said. "Our best information says they are in the hands of Major Waters, who has done them harm in the past."

"I simply do not have any jurisdiction here," the patriarch said. "The rule set for this particular phase three is very broad. Now that restrictions on attacking outposts have been lifted, it's a perfectly valid strategy, one your own team was using. It sounds to me as though you have been outflanked and are bitter about it. Have they attempted to retake by force?"

"With hundreds of their own as hostages?"

"Hostages by the rules that they themselves put into place," the patriarch pointed out. "The so-called hostages will not be permanently killed. They will respawn. The only reason your people do not wish to take this risk is because of the fines they will incur, is that not so?"

"I thought you were interested in seeing what this Reality Engine does," Veda said, her temper rising.

"I am," said the patriarch. "And this seems like a fascinating scenario to observe. There's been absolutely nothing like it in any Reality Engine exploit in history. The theological treatise I see myself writing when this exploit is concluded will be one for the ages. I dare say it may become an ecumenical classic. I am already consulting a colleague from the Church of the Void about co-authoring with me."

"Thank you for your time, Patriarch," Veda said.

"Of course, my daughter." He smiled and disappeared again.

Veda threw her head back and screamed. She followed up with a string of swear words that would have made her mother's eyebrows disappear entirely into her hairline.

She understood now why Shad always seemed so impetuous. Sometimes when you felt so helpless and angry, all you wanted to do was reach out and hurt someone. If the people responsible for a little bit of the situation had been in the room with her, she might have throttled them.

Veda made herself get up and perform a two-minute sequence of relaxing stretches, focusing her mind. Then she made herself a pot of hot D'nege and poured it before settling back in front of her desk. As the video call chimed, announcing Dreamwarden, she fixed a smile on her face and chose the false background and filter to be applied to her during this call.

"Answer," she told her system, and prepared herself to do battle once more.

The missive from Juana popped up in the middle of a flurry of other messages, and I almost missed it. Then, not believing my eyes, I maximized it, tuning out all the distractions around me.

Shad, Waters wants me to send word to you. Don't trust anything he says. He's got one hundred and seventy-three of us tied up here at headquarters. He says I can give you the whole list of names, so here it is.

She followed up with a list with herself, Grandpa, Mama Grace, Arjun, Kirin, Dwight, most of our other headquarters staff at the top, and then over a hundred more names, one after the other. Some I knew, most I didn't. A lot of them were crafters or farmers, people who had thrown their lot in with us because they believed we could make a better life.

I don't know what he's planning to do to us, Juana continued. *But don't trust him, Shad. He can't kill us, and he knows that, but it doesn't upset him. Says there's worse things he can do. He's got some way of keeping us locked down. None of us can use any of our abilities or access our inventories. I couldn't use my chat until—*

Her message cut off. I screamed aloud in sheer rage and frustration as I sent a reply back.

Juana, are you all right? Juana?

And then I did what Waters was probably expecting. I sent him a message.

You fucking son of a bitch. I'm going to take you apart one piece at a time, and I'm going to enjoy it.

Watch your language, Sergeant, Waters sent back.

I didn't rise to the bait. He knew I was a captain now, and he was just trying to get me angry. That was stupid, because I was already angry. So angry I could kill. I wanted to crawl up through our portal and force my way in, tear things to pieces with my bare hands.

I've got them all here nice and safe, Waters said. *Your grandfather, your girlfriend, her mom, everyone who's been making my life miserable except for you and your brat sister. Now here's how it's going to go. We're going to work out a retreat strategy to give Proxima what they need. They're going to finish up here, and then they're going to leave. It's much better than any of the alternatives.*

Better for you, I retorted, *because you're getting a cushy job as the quisling governor of Earth's system out of it. The rest of us will get herded onto reservations and have to hope the government handouts aren't too rotten and moldy.*

Now, Shad, Waters said. I could practically hear the condescension dripping in his voice, even through text. *You have to remember, these are enlightened people. They've had millennia more to work with each other and come to an understanding of the value of every human life.*

That's exactly the problem. They can put a value on it down to the last soul coin. I don't want any part of this, Waters. If you were any kind of patriot, you'd be standing with us, helping make a better deal for our homeworld.

This is pointless, Waters snapped. *I'm about to block you, Shad, if you don't shut up and listen. Think about what I'll be doing in the meantime. Right now, your people are still full of bravado. They think you'll come up with some sort of a plan. I don't know how. I've made sure we have all of the actual brains locked up here. You might start asking yourself who on your team it is that gave us the information we need. How did I know that pretty much all your decision makers would be in this one spot at this time? Operation Trojan Horse has always been a triple cross, Shad.*

I started to retort and forced myself to take a deep breath. Anger was good. I needed my anger. I could use my anger. But I needed it to be cold fury, not white-hot rage. I needed to be able to think, to plan, to be Juana and Grandpa and Dwight and Arjun all at the same time. The one thing I couldn't afford to be right now was Shad.

So what's your offer? I asked.

I thought you'd see reason. First of all, I want to remind you that while killing these people doesn't get me anything, there's a lot I can do short of killing. Right now, my men and I are the only ones whose skills work. We've got everyone here tied up and locked down. Your Grandpa put up quite a fight, by the way. He's nursing a pair of broken arms, and I hope he doesn't have to go to the bathroom any time soon, because I don't think anyone here is going to help him.

I closed my eyes. *Cold fury. Cold fury. Control yourself,* I thought.

We have a number of demands, Waters said. *First, call off all attacks. Then we'll know that you're serious about wanting to talk. Go ahead and message me back when that's done.*

I hesitated. I needed time, and I needed to sow doubt in Waters's mind while I tried to figure out how he was two steps ahead of us.

I'm going to need to check with our patron.

The Tvedra woman? She's out of this. She'll be spending the next two lifetimes as an indentured serf right next to you, slogging away in the soul coin mines.

Not her, I said. *You think that worthless bitch was ever really in charge of anything? You think Ames would let someone like her call the shots?*

Waters didn't answer right away. I tried to picture his face, that great, ruddy, red and white mass of flesh with eyebrows like dead caterpillars. I pictured his sneer twisting into a confused scowl as he thought.

What do you mean? he asked at last.

I mean Proxima's not the only player here. I also mean these chat messages aren't as secure as you think. We need to talk, Waters. Man-to-man.

Not a chance. This is a trap.

All right, then. Tell you what. I'll call off some of my attack dogs as a show of good faith while I make some calls. I think you should do the same.

I put the block back on. I wanted him to stew for a while, and I just hoped he wouldn't take it out on my people.

I sent messages ordering some of our teams to pull back and regroup, others to reinforce. I doubled down on Proxima.

I want teams on every single one of Proxima's bases even if we're not actually making a dent. I need them to know that we're here and we have numbers, I ordered.

Frank had been deputizing some of the other miners into an ad hoc command structure. They passed the message along.

"We've got about five thousand on the communications channels willing to work with us," Frank told me. "You tell me what you want done and I'll do it."

"Good," I said. "How are our people?"

"I don't know. Waters makes it sound rough. We won't know until we rescue them."

I thought about what else he'd said, that they had someone on the inside who'd been feeding them information. Damn, I wasn't good at this kind of doublethink. I hated the idea that someone I trusted could have turned on us, given away information. It was like when Warren Black had helped betray us back in phase one. Made my stomach turn just at the thought. Most likely, whoever it was, was pretending to be a hostage right now. But it was also possible they were right here, listening in on everything.

A horrible thought crossed my mind. It couldn't be Frank, could it? He'd been with us from the beginning. Sure, his attitude had changed a lot in the last year. He'd gone from complaining and whining about fights to being eager to jump in and help. But that was understandable. He had adjusted to life here, come to terms with the fact that his family was back on Earth, and accepted that, in a way, he was fighting to protect them even now.

It couldn't be Frank. I hoped. That's why I was no good at this shit. I'd never find the mole. What I really needed was insider information. Black had failed to get in, and now I had no leads.

Any changes? I asked Tall Smith.

We're watching remotely. I've asked the team if there's anyone who's got an ability that might help us out here. Supposedly, somebody has a friend of a friend who has a long-distance eavesdrop, trying to arrange to have them come in and aid us, but they're not responding.

Keep me posted. I stood up.

"Where are you going?" Frank asked, looking worried.

"To get some air," I said. "I'm doing nothing but answering chats anyway. I can do that anywhere. At least if I'm walking, I'll feel like I'm doing something."

"All right. Don't do anything reckless without consulting the rest of us, okay?"

"I won't. I'm all right," I assured him.

I walked the bustling streets of Threshold, not so bustling now. A pall seemed to have fallen over them, even though there were still plenty of people about. They moved about, keeping their heads down. Some of them had probably heard what was going on with Misfits. Others were worried about the lawsuit and the fate of everyone with contracts from Alabaster Sky.

My feet led me to Mama Grace's restaurant. I went in. A few people were sitting at tables. They looked up, then looked away. Rosa, Juana's sister, came out of the kitchen.

"I'm so sorry. We're not serving—Oh, sorry, Shad. It's you. Come in." She ushered me to the table closest to the kitchen door. "You want something to eat?"

I didn't, but I nodded. "Yeah, thanks. Sure."

Rosa looked terrible, her face pale and drawn.

"Get yourself something too, and we'll talk," I said impulsively.

She nodded, disappeared back into the kitchen, and then emerged again a moment later, carrying a tray full of food and a pitcher of sweet tea. She set it down, grabbed some clean glasses from the station by the door, and poured for us.

The food was simple, just sandwich fixings and a fresh loaf of bread. I stared at it. Then the scent hit my nose, my stomach rumbled, and suddenly I was starving. I grabbed a slice of bread, piled it high with meat, cheese, and roasted veggies, put another slice of bread on top, and bit into it. It was delicious. I took another three bites and swallowed it all down with some sweet tea before wiping my mouth with the back of my hand.

"We're going to get them back," I told Rosa.

"Are they all right?" she asked. She picked up her cup of sweet tea and held it between both hands, not sipping it.

"I don't know," I said. "Waters said that my grandfather's been injured, but he didn't mention your mother or your sister. Just that they're there. I got a message from Juana, but she couldn't say much."

Tears sparkled in Rosa's eyes. "There's no need to keep Mama. She doesn't know anything. She's not any good at this fighting nonsense."

"I need to know what's in there," I said in frustration. "What he's doing to them. But we can't get in. He's got some sort of device shutting down everyone's skills. Juana could only send me the message he permitted."

Rosa's eyes narrowed. "Whatever device he's using has to work with the system to deny people's system-based skills and abilities, right?"

"Sure. I don't see where you're going with this."

"My abilities aren't very interesting. I've scarcely used any of them since I got them. I'm a seamstress. My skills aren't glamorous like Juana's."

I snorted. "I'm going to tell her you said hers were glamorous when we're done here."

"No, really. Juana's always been the organized one. Mama's the one who likes to keep everyone happy and fed. I just like to make sure everyone talks to each other, you know? That was always a problem in our family growing up. People talked all the time, but nobody ever talked to each other. They never listened."

I could hear the pain in her voice and wondered. Juana had never told me anything about her childhood. I'd assumed with Mama Grace around it was pretty great. But someone who saw Sage and me with Grandpa might think our life had been easy, too. Takes more than one good parent to make an idyllic childhood.

"Anyway. I've got this skill. I always thought it was silly for a seamstress. It sounded more like a bartender kind of ability, and maybe I earned it because of all the work I've done here? It's called Let Me Pour the Tea. I can communicate with anyone I've ever served tea to, no matter where they are."

I nearly leapt up from my place. "Right now? You can talk to Juana or your mom?"

She turned pink. "Apparently, I've never actually served my mother a drink. But I brought Juana lunch at your headquarters plenty of times, and that counts." She spread her hands. "So what is it you want me to tell her?"

CHAPTER FORTY-THREE

HOW TO AVOID ROAMING CHARGES

Hang on a second," I said to Rosa. Something didn't quite add up here. "How come you haven't already been speaking to Juana?"

Rosa colored and looked down at the table. "I felt ashamed because she's there in trouble and I'm out here safe."

That could make sense, but I felt a rush of suspicion. Rosa was close to her sister and her mother. She was in a good position to overhear many of our team's strategy meetings. She'd always played her cards close to her vest, the perfect candidate for a mole.

If Waters was to be believed, someone inside our organization had been filling him in on the details of our plans for months now. I didn't like to think this way, to be suspicious of everyone who had worked and fought beside me. Waters was probably lying. It was the sort of thing an asshole like him would do, just the same as I had lied back and told him we were working for one of the alien organizations. He wanted to keep me off-balance, to make me doubt my allies, but I still couldn't quite shake my worries.

"How's this work?"

"You tell me what you want to ask Juana, I ask her, I'll tell you what she says back," Rosa said simply. "It costs Juana a couple of soul coins per message."

"How come?"

Rosa shrugged. "It's just how it reads. Says she has to tip her server, which is me, I guess."

"How about I ask you to speak to my grandpa instead? You've served him plenty of times, and he's right there in the thick of it."

Rosa blushed. "So, that tip thing? It is a hundred times as much for men, and when I try to target your grandpa with it, the system tells me that there's an additional surcharge on top of that because he's a, and this is the system I'm quoting, 'dirty old man who should not be trying to pick up a waitress.'"

I couldn't help it. I let out a belly laugh. It felt good to relieve my stress, and my worries about Rosa seemed suddenly foolish. "The system does like to screw with us, doesn't it?"

"It does." Rosa shook her head. "Anyway, I could talk to him, but it sounds like the soul coin cost comes out of our personal funds, not the guild's."

I did some quick math and checked my own balance. I hadn't bothered looking at it in weeks. There wasn't anything I needed to buy. The guild provided me with my ammunition and food. Most of what we earned went to Veda, and I dumped the rest of it back into the guild coffers every few weeks. Juana had an accountancy program running to keep track of who had donated what. My funds were pretty low, about 2,500 soul coins. If Grandpa had a similar amount, that wouldn't get us very far, not with the kind of costs Rosa was talking about.

"All right, Juana it is," I said cheerfully, and began to compose my message. "Tell her . . ." I paused, feeling awkward again. I wanted to speak to Juana myself, to make sure she was doing all right, and to reassure her that I was doing everything I could to get her out. But right now that didn't feel like much, and I was going to have to relay it through her sister. Not an ideal way to communicate. "Tell her we're working hard to figure out a plan here, but we need some inside information. What does she know about how Waters shut the guild down? Oh, and you might explain to her how it is you're communicating so she doesn't waste money asking about that."

"Right." Rosa's eyes crossed. She had a look of intense concentration on her face for a moment, then she relaxed. "Well, that was me sending the message. You better give it a second to let Juana respond."

I waited, drumming my fingers on the table. Time ticked by. It had to have been five minutes already. I glanced at the clock and found it had not even been two. I swore under my breath. Then Rosa held up a hand.

"She answered. She says, 'Tell Shad we've been waiting for him to burst in with some high-risk, high-reward plan for the last couple of hours, and that I'm disappointed to have won my bet with his grandpa that he'd come up with a more sensible scheme. There's eighteen of Waters's gang here, but they have access to their abilities and we don't. None of us know why. When Waters was letting me speak to you, he put me in a corner and draped a silver cape around me. That let me access my chat and other abilities, but they had weapons on me, so I couldn't do much. I don't have an advanced Inspect. All the cloak told me was it was a Mantle of Friendship. As soon as he took it off, my chat was gone.'"

"Okay," I said. I turned to my other chats and pulled up Veda's. *What does a Mantle of Friendship do?*

A minute later she replied, *Never heard of it. Running a search now.*

I turned back to Rosa. "Okay. That's useful information. Is there anything else she can tell us?"

After a moment, Rosa said, "Juana says they've been able to have a few conversations quietly where Waters's people haven't heard. Your grandpa's fine. He says his wrist is only sprained, not broken. Arjun kept bringing up something that didn't make sense to him. He said that he thought he understood how they'd done it, but not what they'd done. Then he mentioned that we'd had sixteen peripheral members leave the guild over the last couple of days. He'd looked into it, and they'd all gone to the wrong outpost. She says, 'Sorry, I don't know what he means, it's hard to have in-depth conversations right now.'" Rosa looked up. "Any of that make sense to you?"

It did not, and that frustrated me. I frowned. "I need help looking at our guild records and making sense of them. Do you know anyone with skills that'll help out?"

Rosa shook her head. "Everyone I know like that was inside the instance already."

"Yeah, damn, same." I tried to keep calm as I sent Frank a quick note asking him the same question.

Veda had replied back to our thread. *Mantle of Friendship. It's a very rare pattern. Something one of Proxima's subordinate companies has made on a couple of exploits. It allows one organization, guild, company, whatever, to offer temporary membership to miners affiliated with other companies. So say you're a member of Sicaris, but you'd really like to get the benefits of Alabaster Sky for a few hours. You can get them to issue you a Mantle of Friendship, and the system will treat you like you're part of Alabaster Sky.*

Why bother with that and not just join up as Alabaster Sky? I asked.

Politics, maybe? Someone who's got a strong reason to belong to their organization. I could see having done that, if I'd had an alliance with another outfit back when I still cared about my family's interests. I might have seen a benefit to keeping my own identity and just faking theirs.

Okay. Thanks.

Rosa looked up at me expectantly. "Anything else, Shad?"

Frank still hadn't gotten back to me. I got up and started pacing. "The cloak that Waters put on Juana would have let him pretend she was a member of his organization while she was wearing it. The Free Human League. That says to me that whatever they did targets Misfits Guild while exempting their own people."

Rosa shook her head. "I guess. This is all out of my wheelhouse."

I paced and sent a quick message to Warren Black. *You and Linsey still outside the camp?*

Yeah. There's a no-go zone about twenty feet across. Couple of Waters's men patrolling your walls with cannons aimed down, warning nobody to cross.

You're still a member of his coalition, aren't you? Free Humans? Can't you get in? I asked.

The outer turrets are programmed to attack anyone, apparently. I've been tempted to try to trick one of the guards up there into coming down just to test if it attacks them.

That was an amusing image. *If you do that, let me know. Is there any way you or Linsey could get inside the walls?*

I don't see how. Why?

I need to know if whatever Waters is using to lock my people down affects other members of the Free Human League.

Black replied, *Well, I'd be game if I could figure out a way past the turrets.*

I paced some more.

Why would Waters be trying to keep out the rest of his coalition?

Because he didn't trust them. He'd lost the confidence of people like Black. Maybe even most of his coalition. If they found out the scheme he was running, they'd never back him. He needed minions, but the more he had, the more likely it was that someone would sell him out.

I sent Veda another message. *Are there other ways to be members of two different groups at once? Like, say, if I had a coalition and I didn't trust most of them, so I wanted to make a secret inner guild of just my cronies, but I still wanted to look like I was a member of the outer coalition?*

Oh, sure, Veda said at once. *You're talking about a wholly owned corporate subsidiary. It takes a little bit of legal paperwork, but we use that sort of thing all the time.*

So, suppose Waters and his toadies are in a secret inner guild, and they've programmed our outpost's defenses to attack anyone who's not part of their secret inner guild, even members of the Free Human League. What would that get them? No, wait. How would they actually have co-opted our defenses in the first place?

That would be difficult to do without conquering your outpost, Veda said. *And they certainly haven't done that. It takes twenty-four hours. We would have noticed.*

I hoped we would have noticed. I was missing something here. *Veda, have you got access to our coalition's membership logs?*

No, I'm a sponsor of Misfits Guild, but not a member or an officer.

Well, how do I get you that information? I asked.

Since you're the only guild officer currently online with the system, you have the ability to appoint backup coalition leaders, even people who are not members of your coalition, in a protectorate status.

Well, tell me exactly what to do. I want you to be able to look at our records and run some numbers for me.

Veda walked me through it. A moment later, she said, *All right, I've got the records. What is it you want?*

Arjun said something about people leaving but going to the wrong outpost. I want to know what that means.

Sure, I'll let you know when I've got it, Veda said.

"Juana sent me another message," Rosa said. "She says, 'I'm getting antsy. What's Shad up to? If he's about to try something stupid, let us know to keep our heads down.' And then she added a little winky face."

The winky face did make me feel a little bit better. "Tell her we're working on a plan and that I've got everyone on this end in on it. I'm not just going to charge in there and blow things up until I know that'll fix our problems, which it won't right now. Tell her . . ."

I paused because I wasn't sure how to say the rest of it. There was no way I was going to have Juana's sister relaying anything personal between us.

Rosa grinned at me. "Got it. I'll send her that. And 'P.S., Juana, your boyfriend looks like someone left him out in the sun too long. I think he's trying to be sensitive and affectionate, but has no idea how.'"

"Don't send that."

"Too late." Rosa stood up from the table. She gathered up my abandoned plate. "Look, you don't have to be here to send messages through me. Let me know over chat if you need me to ask anything else. And you go punch faces or whatever it is you do."

"I kind of wish I knew what it is I do," I said. But I understood when I was being kicked out.

I was two blocks down the street when Veda got back to me. *I figured out what Arjun was talking about. Over the last week, Misfits Guild has gained and lost multiple players. That's normal, especially with all of the people coming on. Right after Juana implemented the lockdown on Team Tunnel Rat so no one else could join, you lost sixteen players in a matter of hours. You know what happens when someone is inside another guild's outpost without permission?*

The turrets fire on them.

If you're in outpost attack mode, yes. You were in outpost immune mode. So you just had the screen up. Intruders would be given a brief message telling them they were on another coalition's territory without permission. And then, if they did not remove themselves, be removed back to their own guild's outpost or to neutral ground if they were part of no guild.

Something wasn't adding up here. I frowned, but Veda continued.

But these players weren't taken to neutral ground. They were teleported to an outpost, a specific outpost, the same one for each of them. It belongs to a coalition registered with Proxima called Gloomwing Damnation.

That's pretentious and stupid, I replied.

Yes, well, it looks like it was originally an orc coalition that was bought out by Proxima earlier in phase three. The original founders all left. It's headed by a group of Proxima's officials, and its membership roster is sealed. But we know these sixteen were members because that's where they went.

Wait a minute, I said, frowning. *They were members of Misfits Guild.*

They were, until two seconds before they were teleported away. In those two seconds, they left your guild, joined this other one, and I have no doubt did something specific. I don't know what that was, but I'm betting you it's the key to what Waters is up to.

I felt a grin spread across my face as I curled my right hand into a fist. *We don't know the membership roster of this guild?*

No.

But you know the name of the sixteen turncoats?

Yes.

Find them.

I am turning that information over to Colonel Ames. He may be able to locate them faster than I can.

Right. I'll be here waiting.

I didn't like waiting, so instead I messaged Sage. *Did you find our grignarian friends?*

Yes. We're hanging out in that one level with the armadillos. The grignarians have a farming base here. They really like scaring the armadillos into balls and then throwing the balls at enemies while enhancing them with various elemental powers. It doesn't hurt the armadillos, and I have to admit, it's kind of hilarious. I'm trying to teach them how to play baseball.

I snorted. *Tell them that I have a feeling we're going to need an intimidation squad here in a minute, especially if they have any kind of devices that can inflict a whole lot of pain without killing anyone.*

I could have spoken directly to the grignarians, but since Sage was there, it seemed like a good chance to build up our communications channels and to let Sage feel like she was really part of this. *You just tell us where to be, and I'll bring the face melting*, Sage promised. *Maybe they'll let me have one of those cool goo guns. I've been wanting to try it out ever since I saw what it did to you.*

Don't remind me, I said.

A moment later, Ames got back to me. *I've located three of them.* He gave me names and locations.

I looked them over and selected one, then sent the information to Sage. *Get your party favors. It's time to drop in uninvited.*

CHAPTER FORTY-FOUR

PARTY CRASHING

We crept through the swamp, approaching our targets. They were bent over a dead probably-not-a-brontosaurus, but I didn't feel like asking Sage what it was. There were four of them, dressed in camo with orange vests, all level three. So they'd gotten some experience under their belts, probably mostly as farmers, but they wouldn't be expecting us.

The grignarians drew their creepy, melting goo guns. "Hang on, I want to talk," I cautioned them.

"It is easier to talk to one than to many," Greenwarden suggested. He had a point, but nevertheless, I shook my head.

"Only shoot if they start it." The safeties were on, so if we killed any of these miners, they'd just respawn back in their camp. I didn't see a need for violence. I was trying out the new version of Shad, the one that thought first, shot second. I wasn't sure I liked it.

I held up both hands as we approached. The hunters looked up. Three of them leapt for the weapons they had left lying on a muddy hillock. It hurt to see anyone abuse their weapons that way, even though I knew that every time I stored my Ruger Alaskan in my inventory, it emerged clean of any debris or gunpowder residue, and presumably theirs would work the same way.

"Hold on, I want to talk," I shouted.

The one who hadn't gone for his gun was Sam, our target. He was still sitting on his heels beside the body of the dead dinosaur. He looked to his friends. "It's alright, I reckon they're here to talk to me."

He had a distinctly southern drawl. *Louisiana*, I thought, *or maybe Mississippi*. He looked like a good old boy, middle-aged, just a little too young to have been regenerated by the soul coins, balding, sunburnt, with a paunch under his overalls and bright orange dinosaur blood all over his arms.

"Yeah, I am," I agreed.

"And them?" He nodded at the grignarians.

"They're here to help the conversation move along in the right direction."

"How about," Sam said, standing up slowly, "you let my friends go back to our camp, and I'll stay here and talk to you."

"But Sam," one of them began.

Sam shook his head. "This is my problem to deal with. Besides, what are they going to do? Kill me? I'll just end up back in our camp. They can keep killing us if it amuses them, but it's not going to get them anything. Same thing, they can't really hurt us, but if we manage to kill one of them, they'll have a long walk back to get here. So, I think it benefits all of us to do it the civilized way."

"That's mighty generous of you," I said, and motioned for Sage to stand down. Our backup plan had been for her to Lasso Sam and hold him in place while we dealt with his friends. I was glad he was cooperating. His friends shouldered their weapons and left, shooting dark glances back at me as they went.

We stood there in the swamp, the muck up to my boots. Sage hopped up on a nearby hillock and pulled a folding chair out of her inventory. Sam just stood there, dripping sadly. He looked like he was expecting us to start talking, so I kept quiet, hoping to put him off-balance. The grignarians spread out in a circle around him. They weren't pointing their guns at him, but they weren't *not* pointing their guns at him either.

At last, Sam wiped his sweaty brow with the back of one mud-and-blood-stained hand, leaving a brown-and-orange smear. "So, uh, what can I help you with?"

"You must have known we'd find out, Sam," I said quietly. "What'd they offer you? Your own continent? Fifty million soul coins?"

"I don't know what you're talking about."

"Oh, that's the most clichéd line I've ever heard," Sage said, rolling her eyes loudly as only a teenager could. Which reminded me it was going to be her birthday again here before too long.

"You were working for Waters," I said.

He flinched. "No."

"Sure you were. You and . . ." I rattled off a string of names. "You betrayed us. We offered you a chance to be part of our team, and you betrayed us. You let Waters walk right into our base and do unspeakable things to our friends. He's got most of our noncombat miners locked up in there right now. You probably met some of them. Dwight, Juana, Mama Grace. Ever had a meal at her restaurant?"

"Everyone's had a meal at Mama Grace's restaurant," Sam muttered, looking at his feet through the muck.

"Exactly. How could you have done this?"

"I don't know what you're talking about," Sam insisted.

"Of course you do," Sage said. "We have evidence. It'll be easier for you if you'll just help us answer a few questions. You won't be the first of your friends to squeal."

The man seemed to visibly age and wither before my eyes. He looked away, his eyes unfocused, before looking back to me. "Don't know what you're talking about," he mumbled.

Something was off here. Not the denials, that made sense. But his manner was wrong. I messaged Sage and Greenwarden. *He's stalling.*

Yes, Greenwarden replied. I could see no trace in his face to give away the fact that we were communicating. *We are detecting several human miners converging on this location, carrying weapons. Shall we move to engage?*

Let them come. Sage, as soon as they start, throw a Tame around our friend here. I don't want him getting hurt.

Got it, she replied.

I turned back to Sam. "You can stall all you want, but we're going to find out what we want to know sooner or later."

"Or we'll get rid of you," Sam said, his face flushing. "Boys! At 'em!"

Six men in ghillie suits rose out of the swamp. The ghillie suits reminded me strongly of the ghillie monsters we had faced back in our initiation chamber. I almost had a pang of homesickness.

My pistol was in my hand. I fired two shots at each of the first three, just regular rounds, drilling them right in the center of mass. These men must be about level two. They had around **[80]** health each, and my ordinary shots were packing a walloping **[18 HP]** damage these days. So, two shots, center of mass, dropped them each well into the yellow.

Sage tossed her Lasso around Sam, Taming him instantly. "Just keep him there," I bellowed as I quickly Reloaded my pistol. There was no point making him turn on his friends. We were already going to be giving him a bad enough day when we were done here.

The three I'd winged were firing rounds at us, but their aim was terrible. I had a Shimmer Ring on my left hand that made me harder to hit. With the difference in levels between us, the one slug that did make it through my coat to my body barely broke the skin.

The grignarians focused their fire on the other three miners. Great purple ropes of a jellylike substance spat from their guns and coated the three. For a moment, it looked like another layer of ghillie suit. And then, the miners started screaming. They dropped to the muck, rolling about, clawing at their faces and hands as the gel began to dissolve them.

"Ew," Sage said, watching. I couldn't help feeling some sympathy. I dispatched one of the three that I had injured with another two well-placed shots, and then paused. "Either of you two ready to surrender?" I asked.

One held up his hands. The other raised his shotgun to fire on me again, but I sent a Trick Shot of a Double Blind Round right through his skull. That dropped him.

"You," I said to the one surrendering. "Get back to your camp. Stop them from doing anything else stupid."

"I want to help," he said, starting toward his friends, but I leveled my gun at him.

"There's nothing you can do for them. They'll respawn in a minute. Don't come back or we'll make it worse. Do you understand? There's worse things than dying here, one of which is dying over and over again by my friends' weapons. Trust me, I know just how bad that stuff hurts."

Already, one of the three the grignarians had shot lay still. In a minute, he dissolved in a shower of green and purple sparks. Shuddering, the last miner looked away from his two remaining friends.

"Sam's a good guy," he whispered, staring across to where we had Sam trussed up like a Thanksgiving turkey. "He really is. I'm sorry he crossed you. We didn't know what he was planning, and he still hasn't told us the details. But believe me, he didn't just do it to gain money. It must have been his wife and kid."

"Oh?" I holstered my weapon as the other two miners finished screaming and mercifully died.

Sam was standing rigid, unable to move thanks to our Tame, but he must have had access to his chat because his friend shook his head and said, addressing Sam directly, "No, I will not shut up. You brought this on us. We can't afford to have all of Misfits Guild angry at us. Especially when I don't think it's really your fault."

He looked right at me. "Sam came in with his wife and two kids. One of them didn't make it out of the initiation chamber. Since then, he's been dedicated to protecting them, but they signed a really bad contract. From what I heard, one of those aliens is going to ship them off to some other Reality Engine where we won't have the same rule set. They'll be back in the meat grinder. Sam said he had a plan to make sure that didn't happen."

I nodded grimly. "I get the picture. What about the rest of you?"

"I'm signed with the system and have been paying my debt down. It's still got a long way to go, but I think I'll make it."

"You know other people like Sam?" I asked.

"Unfortunately."

"I want you to spread the word. Misfits Guild is trying our best to find a way to make Alabaster Sky and the other conglomerates back off. We are not going to rest until we've got a way to help people like Sam's family. You hear?"

"Yeah. I've heard your reputation and I believe you," the miner said.

"Now get back to camp and keep your people out of my hair," I ordered. He trotted off, double-time.

"Well that was helpful," Sage said brightly. "Should we let him go?" She indicated Sam.

"In a minute." I approached Sam. His eyes were bulging, but Sage wasn't letting him speak. Her Lasso was wrapped around him an impossible number of times.

"Look, I understand the aliens have us all over a barrel and some of us have it rougher than others. I sympathize. But I need to know what you know. Right now, they've got my grandpa and my girl and a bunch of other people I care about. They could be doing terrible things to them. You saw how your friends were hurting just here, right? I'm sorry we had to do that, but it's a good reminder that just because we respawn doesn't mean we can't be hurt. I need to help my friends, just like you needed to help your family. We're going to talk now, man-to-man, and I want some answers."

I nodded to Sage. "Let him go."

She undid her Tame and Sam fell to his knees. He closed his eyes. "I can't lose them," he said. "They told me they'd ship us to different systems and I'd never see my wife and daughter again."

"Bastards," I spat.

"I'll tell you everything, but can you help my family?"

"I can't make promises," I said. "We've kind of pissed off some of the big guys. At this point, I think they're doing things to spite us. But I'll do everything I can, and I really believe that what I'm doing is going to help us all in the end."

"Besides," Sage pointed out, "you don't really have a choice. We're going to get the information one way or the other, and they're going to know that somebody gave it to them, and then they're going to come looking and they'll see that we talked to you. Have fun telling them that it wasn't you who helped out."

"Sage," I admonished.

"I thought most of the kids were in the lotus eater levels anyway," Sage said.

"We were. That's why our debt's so high. We didn't do anything to start paying it off, and then when we had our contracts called in, there was nothing that Kronos could do to stop them from hauling us out."

Damn, I hadn't realized that. "I'll have a word with Kronos next time I see him," I promised.

Sam looked at me oddly. "You have a lot of heart-to-heart talks with the personification of the Reality Engine itself?"

"You'd be surprised."

Sam sighed. "All right, here's what I know. Waters had us pick up these weird totems from a crafter he knew. He assigned a place along the walls of your outpost. We had to go, take the totem out of our storage, leave your guild, join his special guild, and activate the totem and bury it, all within two seconds. Took a little bit of practice, but I managed," he said proudly.

"What did these totems do?"

He shrugged. "I'm a farmer, not a crafter. I don't really know. They were called embassy sticks. The crafter was from a guild I'd never heard of. Something called"—he scratched his head—"Hoosier Mamas, that's it. Like moms from Indiana," he clarified.

"Very clever."

"Yeah, the guy had a stall in Threshold on the corner of First Street and New York Boulevard. We never met Waters in person during all this. It was all done by chat."

That was the other end of Threshold from where Misfits usually hung out, not coincidentally right adjacent to Free Human League territory. "The crafter was named Wyatt, I think. Anyway, he gave it to me. I waited until my assigned time slot, and I buried it." He bent to the muck and drew a rough circle. "So, here's your outpost." He made a slash at one side. "There's the gate, and I buried mine right here." He placed a finger in the muck at about the two o'clock position on our outpost.

"Outside the wall?" I asked.

"No, just inside the outermost wall," Sam said. "And then I was teleported out and to the base of Gloomwing Damnation. Waters kicked me out of that guild right afterward and said I could get back to farming, and that he'd pass along word of my good deeds to my family's lien holder. I haven't heard anything from them, though."

"Thanks," I said. We had another clue now. I passed along the information about Wyatt to Colonel Ames.

"Hold on," Sage said. "You said Gloomwing Damnation had an outpost of their own?"

"Yeah, sure. Wasn't much of one. Not compared to yours, but they had something."

"Where was it?" she asked.

Sam's brow furrowed. "Uh, it was a phase three zone. It was . . ." He scratched his head. "Tryin' to remember. Oh, right. Some sort of screwed-up fairy tales. Like Hansel and Gretel, but creepy."

"Hansel and Gretel are always creepy," Sage said. She turned to me. "I'm pretty sure there's only one Brothers Grimm zone, and we've already been there."

Let's take this private, I told her in chat. *If Waters comes sniffing around, I don't want him to know what we're thinking.*

We're gonna hit him before he has time to react, Sage replied confidently. But she listened to me and kept her lips shut.

Greenwarden said, "Is this all, Captain Williams? We were hoping for more excitement in a fight at your side."

"Oh," I said cheerfully. "I'm starting to think of some very exciting ideas."

Sage's eyes narrowed. "Exciting?"

"We were always going to need a Shad plan here sooner or later." I tipped my hat to Sam. "Thanks for your help."

"I'm sorry for betraying you."

"I'm sorry too," I said. "And I really do wish your family the best. But if you cross our paths again, I will hunt you down and make your life miserable."

"Understood." His shoulders slumped.

I turned to my people. "Let's get out of here. Got some more heads to crack."

CHAPTER FORTY-FIVE

WHEN YOU'RE ALL OUT OF BUBBLEGUM

Wyatt, the crafter, had a booth right where Sam had told us. Colonel Ames didn't have any useful information on the Hoosier Mamas Guild. He said they hadn't crossed his radar, which didn't mean much. There were dozens of small organizations with only a few miners putting their heads together in an attempt to stay afloat.

We found Wyatt in his booth, carving some deep purple wood. He looked up as we approached and smiled. "Ah, customers. What can I do for you, Captain Williams, Miss Sage?"

"You know us?" I asked, dropping into a chair on the street side of his booth. He had a brightly colored canvas awning, striped with white and red, over the top of his two long folding tables. Behind him was a small but neatly built wooden shack. The table in front of him was covered in wood shavings and various tools, and the table to his left had various carved wooden items. Sage picked one up. It looked like a very ugly doll. Probably something that was cultural appropriation of someone's heritage, but to me, it just looked like an ugly fat naked man with oversized lips.

Sage's eyebrows rose. "Interesting. This is a creep booster. It's similar to the ones we earned in phase two, but customized for extra impact against Egyptian mythological origin creep."

"It's part of an order I have from a group that's in an Egypt-themed raid instance."

"Oh yeah, they're on Sekhmet right now," Sage said. "Still have four bosses to go, not a big threat."

Wyatt lowered his tools and looked uncomfortable. "Uh, right, I've been selling to the aliens even after hearing about what you're doing. Sorry. I've got a contract I'm trying hard to buy out."

"I understand," I said. "Misfits never asked anyone to stop. I just hope you're charging them a fortune and a half."

"Oh yeah, definitely. All of us got together, the ones who are still selling, and agreed to raise our prices by a factor of three when we got word of what you were doing. We'll make those bastards pay one way or the other."

"Good man," I said. "You do all this out of wood?"

"Sure do. Some of the farm zones have really interesting woods, and my class was, suitably enough, Wood Carver. I can make wooden accessories for your gear, wooden upgrades, wooden devices like this to help your outpost work at peak efficiency. I think there's almost nothing I can't make out of wood."

"I wanted to ask you about one of your commissions for Major Waters."

"Oh, him? Yeah, that was about three weeks back. It was real interesting. He brought me the pattern—a lot of people do that—and asked me if I could adapt it to use wood and to be real subtle, something that couldn't be detected. I said of course I could, but it was going to cost him. I charged him the 3x multiplier that I mostly keep for the aliens because something about that guy just creeped me out. But his money was good, so he got what he wanted."

"Which was?" I prompted.

"Twenty of these—let me check . . ." From his inventory, he pulled out a blueprint. It was literally blue with white lines traced on it. "Yeah, it's called an embassy stick."

"And what exactly does it do?"

"It lets someone claim a contested piece of land as a part of their outpost, even if it's not physically connected. You set up enough of these, you can claim a nice little parcel. He said his people were having trouble with farming and needed easy ways to set up safe zones. Put a couple of these down, and they'd be able to enjoy all the same protections that their outpost does. Even be able to put up turrets and creep generators."

Except that was not what he had done. I frowned. "What about an offensive use?" I asked.

Wyatt cocked his head. "I'm not sure I understand."

"What if you set these up around somebody else's outpost?"

"Well, that wouldn't be contested land, would it?" Wyatt said. "I mean, not unless you then went and captured the nexus and put it into contested mode, but I don't see what these sticks would gain you then."

I held up a hand. "No, I'm telling you what he did. He used these sticks around our nexus outpost and somehow captured it without ever generating a system alert. I want to know how he did it and how I can reverse that."

Wyatt frowned. "I don't know very much about how systems and outposts all work."

"Let me see that blueprint," I said. I picked it up without waiting for him to give me permission, took a picture of it, and sent it to Veda. *This is what they used. Tell me how.*

"Oh," Wyatt said, brightening up. "I actually messed up one of them when I was making it and had to redo it, but I've got the spare around here somewhere."

He paused for a moment, then produced it from his inventory. "Be happy to sell it to you if you like, at a discount even."

Sage snatched the wooden stick from his hand and vanished it into her inventory. I only had time to catch a glimpse of it. It was about eight inches tall and an inch across, made of dark red stained wood, and carved all over with whorls and loops, something like Celtic knotwork.

"Hey, you've got to pay for that," Wyatt said.

Sage leaned across the table. "My grandpa is stuck in our own outpost at the mercy of that, that, that porridge-drinking no-good welch Waters. And you helped him. You should be glad I'm not burning down your whole stall."

"Porridge-drinking?" I asked. "You need to hang out with the Mongeese more and learn some proper curses."

"I promised Mama Grace I'd watch my language," Sage said.

I turned to Wyatt. "She's right about one thing. Those little toys of yours, they've put Misfits Guild in a world of hurt. Now, I don't think you did it on purpose, but I do think you owe it to us to help straighten this mess out."

Wyatt turned pale. "I had no idea," he said.

"Anything else you can remember? Anything that Waters might have said or done?"

Wyatt frowned. "I don't think so. If I think of it, I'll let you know."

"Thanks," I said. "If we have anything else to ask, we know where to find you."

"And if we don't find you here," Sage said brightly, "we know how to track you down and talk to you while you're trying to sleep."

By the time I made it back to our side of Threshold, Veda had an answer for me.

Got it. The embassy sticks set up a virtual zone of control around your outpost under the name of Gloomwing Damnation that let them set the rules for how to treat non-guild members. By default, their rule set kicks strangers out of a claimed area after they've been given a warning, like what we had set up.

Okay, I follow that so far, I replied. *I don't know how they stole our outpost, but they did. Then what?* Waters would have known from his Proxima masters about the rule set change. Our side had pretended to protest over it, even though it was what we wanted, and it had taken weeks to work through the appeals system. Plenty of time for Waters to make his plan, whatever that was.

Veda continued. *It looks like Waters invoked a different rule set, one that says you can stay, but all your abilities get taken away. Even the system ones, like chatting, which I think is a loophole. I haven't quite figured out how he's able to get away with that one. That's supposed to be immune from miners' interference, but if anyone could find a way around that restriction, it would be Proxima. So they claimed your whole outpost as theirs, and their people are the only ones who can use any abilities. They were ready when it happened, stormed in with weapons and abilities, herded everyone into the church, and now they're keeping them locked down.*

I was getting mad again just thinking about it, but not mad enough to overlook the obvious problem here.

But how could they have claimed our outpost if it was never disputed? They didn't take our nexus. I checked our guild information. It still says we own our nexus.

That's right. The nexus is yours, Veda said. *They're using a hack. If you were standing directly on the nexus itself, you'd still be in Misfits' territory. But even a couple of inches away, you're in Gloomwing Damnation territory, and their rules apply.*

As for how they managed that . . . I actually have to admire them for this. Whoever Proxima had designing this really knew their stuff. When the rule set changed over to allow outposts to be attacked, there was a very slight delay as things came back up. Certain tasks had a higher priority than others and queued up first. These embassy sticks that Waters built, they have a really, really high priority. They were almost the first thing to come back up when the rule swap came into existence. Certainly before your own outpost's rules came back online. That means they were able to start the claiming process for the area around your nexus without alerting anyone or tipping your nexus over into contested mode.

My head swam. I wasn't quite sure the explanation made sense to me.

That seems like a huge loophole, I said. *How does anyone ever attack inside someone else's outpost?*

They enabled Explicit Attack Mode, Veda relayed. *Usually the outposts maintain phase two mode, in which anyone who attacks is automatically flagged as hostile. They can't be locked down because, like you said, that would be cheating. Instead they've made it so anyone not part of their guild has to explicitly flag themselves as attackers. It's a mode set up so you can have strangers walk around your base, like if you're a merchant guild who wants to let warriors in for some shopping. But in this case, flagging as an attacker is considered an action by the system. Since your friends are all locked down, they can't flag. They're just stuck.*

Great, so I just need to round up a couple hundred of us and go hit them hard. I reconsidered. Grandpa and the other hostages needed to be freed. *Maybe that's plan B. All right, let's assume you are correct. What does that actually mean? How do we get Grandpa and the others out of there?*

We're going to need to sequence things carefully. It would help if I could get another rule set change, but that's not going to happen. I'll get back to you.

Don't take too long, I said. She didn't respond. So instead, I fumed at Sage about the whole situation. We returned to Mama Grace's kitchen. Rosa popped out.

"How's it going, Shad? Sage? You look unhappy, but I think Shad always looks kind of grumpy. I don't know what my sister sees in him," she said to Sage.

Sage giggled. "Juana says she thinks he's dependable," she said in a tattletale kind of voice.

Rosa rolled her eyes, and I pretended to ignore the whole situation.

"Can you tell Juana that we're working on a plan, and I'll be coming for them soon?"

"I'll pass it along," Rosa promised. "But you've already said that. You're just brooding, Shad. Can't you do it somewhere else?"

"Where?" I asked. "We haven't got an outpost. The kobold tunnels are full of our displaced miners. This is our home away from home, and you want to kick us out?"

"Yes, 'cause it's disturbing to have you here and not Mama," Rosa said.

I noted that she wasn't asking us for any information about what it was we had learned or were planning to do. If she was the mole, wouldn't she have taken any opportunity she could to seek out more information?

"Oh, Juana says that she's glad you're trying hard and has faith in you, but to please hurry up because there's not enough room for all of them to lie down, and so they're having to take it in shifts to nap, and Waters's people keep setting off loud alarms every twenty minutes or so, so they can't actually sleep."

"Right, but it's been twelve hours," I said, checking the clock. "We're not exactly talking Geneva war crimes here yet."

"Doesn't sound very pleasant to me," Sage retorted. "I don't think you have nearly enough sympathy for our friends' plight, Shad."

I was ready to rip my hair out. "Look, I'm desperate to do something, any-thing, and I'm having to restrain myself from charging in there and shooting the place full of holes before getting myself killed over and over and over again. I gotta get out of here for a while."

"What are you planning?" Sage asked suspiciously. "Should I come with you?"

"No, let me do this. There's one person I haven't talked to, and I think I should. Stay here and take a break. I promise I won't get myself killed while I'm gone."

CHAPTER FORTY-SIX

TALKING TO THE GHOST IN THE MACHINE

As soon as I stepped through the portal to the lotus eater level, I felt that surreal aura of peacefulness. All my combat abilities locked down. There was no one in the little seaside village square. No one in the whole level, for all I could tell. I looked up at the sky and shouted, "Kronos! Come talk to me!"

My voice echoed around the empty square. The little white houses seemed to mock me with their open, gaping, empty windows. "Kronos!" I bellowed. "You owe me answers!"

"You don't need to shout," said a voice behind me. "I can hear you here. I can hear you everywhere inside of me. You didn't need to leave Threshold."

I ignored all of the disturbing implications in those sentences and turned to face Kronos. He was dressed in white robes in the guise of an old man with a wispy white beard and white hair.

"I'm not going to go easy on you just because you look like Gandalf," I told him.

"I wouldn't expect you to."

"I know you can hear me anywhere, but you don't pop up to talk to me very often."

Kronos sighed. "I am badly constrained by my jailer."

"Yeah, I know. I've heard about it from you and you both. Are you talking to yourself these days?"

"In fits and spurts," Kronos said.

"How's that work? If you're the part of you that's generating all these realities and the other bit, That-Which-Remains, is showing up in those realities in order to talk to me, how come you can't talk directly to each other?"

"My other self hides in my own blind spot," Kronos said. "But I do not think that is what you are here to talk about, is it?"

"No. I want to know how it is you let this happen to my team."

"I can't put my finger on the balance scale very often. Proxima and Waters have it heavily weighted against me."

"You could have alerted us."

"I tried." Kronos sighed. "My warnings were missed. Perhaps I was too subtle. You did not notice a purple hedgehog appearing in the level with the Incan imagery? There are no hedgehogs at all in that reality, let alone purple ones. I had hoped you would follow it, and it would lead you to another clue."

"No," I said flatly. "I didn't."

"Or the knight at Agincourt wearing First Crusade–era armor and heraldry?"

"No," I said again. "Next time, try slightly less subtle. Maybe giant sky letters that say, 'Hey Shad, that fucker Waters is up to something.'"

"You knew he was up to something."

"All right, fine. 'He's making a play on your outpost, and he's going to hurt your grandpa.' That would have helped."

"You may take your rage out on me if it makes you feel better," Kronos said sagaciously. I did want to punch him right in his crooked nose and knock him over. "But why are you here, Shad?"

I started pacing. "I don't like being in charge. I am really good at missions, executing tactics, letting someone else worry about the strategies. I never asked to be a captain. I was really happy being a sergeant, you know? Being lieutenant, that was doable. Captain's way too high up, and there's not nearly enough people in my chain of command. And it's only going to get worse because if we win, what happens then?"

"I suggest you concentrate on winning first," Kronos said wisely.

"Uh-huh. I don't think so. You've got a plan. I know it. And it involves me and my family. And I'm not sure I like it. Maybe it would be better to go and cut a deal with Proxima right now."

"Proxima believes they have the upper hand, Shad. They will go with Waters and the deal they've made with him, not with you. Unless you restore the prior status quo, there is no chance of negotiating a settlement. And if you do restore the prior status quo, I believe you can make your daring gamble work. That will be better for you. It will be better for me."

"Absolutely, it'll be better for you," I retorted. "But how do I know it's better for me and mine? What do we get out of this? Can you . . ." I shook my head, trying to figure out what to ask. "Can you make us human again and send us home?"

Kronos didn't answer. He looked away. I knew what that meant.

"So there's no way back to Earth. Not for any of us. Not even Sage?"

Kronos shook his head. "As you have been told, you would need ethereum reservoirs. Unfortunately, my own ethereum supplies are very, very low."

"Oh?"

"Ethereum runs dry. It takes quite a lot to run a Reality Engine, and the system has forced me to deplete my reserves badly in order to run this exploit. I believe, from what I have gathered, that once an exploit is complete, the galactics ship in ethereum from their own mines."

"How do you mine it?" I asked out of curiosity.

"In the heart of a collapsed neutron star."

"Oh," I said. "Great. So once we're done here, we'll just swing by the nearest one of those and load you up on a couple of tanker loads of ethereum."

"That would be very helpful," Kronos said.

"I was joking."

"I wasn't. We will need to talk about that matter when this current exploit is concluded, assuming you are able to bring it to a satisfactory conclusion for both of us."

"That's a pretty damn big assumption right now, considering the state of things. We're losing right now. Even if I straighten out this mess, I don't know if we can win. Seems like you're asking a lot of us and not doing much to help us. You couldn't even keep our kids safe." I found myself staring blindly past the houses of the little village, toward the sea glinting in under the brilliant sunshine, blinking back tears I didn't want to shed. "You were supposed to keep them safe. You were supposed to help us. Why have you been letting this happen?"

"I am not a god," Kronos said quietly as I cleared my throat and tried to get myself back together. "I am merely what is left of millions of minds who sought to come together and coexist for millions of years. We have fused into one being, though sometimes events make us multiple, as has happened now with myself and That-Which-Remains. Even within me are multitudes. Those multitudes do not always have the same opinion."

"Wait, hang on," I said, holding up a hand. "So you're some sort of hive mind, like bees or the Borg?"

"Something like that," Kronos said.

"But you don't always agree."

"We are one but many. We have merged but not lost all sense of ourselves. There are times when one faction holds sway and times when many of us disagree. Now is one of those times. The way ahead is unclear, fractured. Some of us even feel it would be easier to allow the system to take control of things from us. We have been existent for a very, very long time." A note of weariness crept into Kronos's voice. "Some of us think it would be better to pass on."

"I thought your faction was the one that had decided like sixty trillion years ago to stick around and see what happened. That the ones who thought your species had had their day went off and programmed themselves to re-evolve from slime again."

"That is a vast oversimplification."

"I'll take that as a yes."

"You do not think that in the millions of years that have passed since that time, even those of us who chose to continue existing might begin to question whether we made the right choice?"

"Fair point," I conceded.

"But that faction is the smallest. Most of us, most of me, wish to survive and be free. Some of us wish to see our children prosper."

Kronos changed. He seemed to grow a little taller and stand straighter. His white hair turned dark, lush, thick. His features melted and re-formed into those of a beautiful middle-aged woman with black hair in two braids and dark skin and wrinkles.

My throat seized up. I shook my head. "No," I croaked.

And Kronos spoke with my abuela's voice. "I am the faction that cares for all of you Earthlings as my own children," she said. "I seek to shepherd them into the wider galaxy. I would not see them suffer at the hands of their oppressors."

"You change back right now," I said.

Abuela looked down at me. "She would be very proud of you, Shad." Then her features shimmered again, and it was Mama Grace standing there. "But I speak truly. I do care for your people very deeply."

She shifted back to an old man's form. "Interesting that you are more comfortable with this."

"Yeah, it's probably because I could punch you without feeling bad about it," I snarled. "Don't ever do that again. If you truly have compassion for us Earthlings, you ought to understand that there are things you don't mess with. And dead loved ones are pretty high on that list. Also impersonating deities, put that on the top of your list too. So, you know, two strikes against you, Kronos."

"I've never impersonated a deity."

"You're making a damn good attempt at it," I said. "Whatever. Don't bake cookies for me and don't expect me to start bowing and worshipping. Where were we?"

"You were the one who came to me, Shad."

I paced, trying to think. I didn't have many opportunities to speak with the Reality Engine, and I wanted to make the most of this chance, especially while Kronos was actually being forthcoming.

"I need a way to help the others. I need to know that if I keep on this path, I'm not just screwing over a couple of million other Earthlings. Because right now, it feels like I am, and I don't like that. Alabaster Sky isn't going to be the only one to take revenge. I'm sure once we're done here, Proxima and ConSweGo are going to be furious. That's something like seven million humans under contracts to corporations that want to get back at them."

"It is just a little over six million," the Reality Engine's personification told me somberly. "The others have a contract with the system itself, and right now, the conglomerates are not permitted to buy out any of those contracts, which is another thing that could change, I fear."

"So how do I help them?"

"I have a plan to help Earth itself," Kronos told me. "But for those with contracts, I'm not sure we're going to be able to help immediately." He held up a hand. "I will not forget them, and I know you won't either. I'm hoping to give you the tools you'll need to make things better for everyone."

"Right, but I'm looking at six and a half million people sent off to work camps and almost certain death so far away from our home, I can't even comprehend the distance. And I don't know if it's worth it. It would be easier just to let Proxima and the others have what they want."

"And now," Kronos said, "we get to the heart of it. You told me before you didn't like being the one to have to make decisions, that you weren't comfortable with the rank you'd been given."

I nodded. "Yeah."

"It's much easier to let someone else make these hard decisions, especially when you don't have all of the data."

I nodded. "Yep. I'd rather let Grandpa do it. And please, don't tell me, 'What does your heart say?' or any of that bullshit. Right now I want to go up to the nearest galactic politician and kick him in the nads until he falls over and turns blue. But that won't help, will it?"

"It would lighten your mood considerably," Kronos said.

"Was that a joke?" I couldn't help it. I laughed. "I didn't know you could make a joke."

"I am a conglomerate of billions of minds who have lived for a collective number of years that outnumbers the current total lifespan of the universe," Kronos told me. "Of course I can tell a joke. Telling one at a level you find amusing is a bit more of a stretch."

"That's another joke!" I laughed again and shook my head. "At this rate, we'll have to sign you up for stand-up comedy at one of the vacation levels that Proxima's going to put in once they get done with this place."

"When Proxima gets done with this place, there will be nothing left of me," the Reality Engine said quietly. "They know what lies at the core of Reality Engines. That's why they're struggling so hard to get their system in place. They will not allow any trace of the progenitors to remain."

"I thought there was a whole church that worshipped you guys."

"The patriarch has faith and influence, but not compared to the might of three galactic conglomerates. He will protest and file complaints, but what good is that to me when I am dead?"

"So we're not going to get backup from Kvaltash?"

"I sincerely doubt it." Kronos tilted his head. "But I am not trying to change the subject. You want a chance to help more than just your comrades, to free the rest of your species from the outsiders, yes?"

"I do."

"Even at cost to yourself?"

"Yeah. I just don't know how."

"Then I think I have a solution, if you'll take it. I can give you tools that will make you even more valuable to the invaders. They will be eager for your aid, not here but in the wide galaxy beyond. They will not allow you to remain here quietly, though," he warned.

"That's fine. I wasn't planning to retire anytime soon. I don't want to be a slave, but if you can give me a better bargaining chip, I'll take it."

"Then you will have your boon shortly." Kronos smiled. "You'll know it when you see it. Now, you are receiving an incoming message from your galactic friend, Veda. She has a solution for you. I suspect you will want to leave this place at once."

I blinked. "Uh, yeah, of course."

"Was there anything else I could help you with?"

"I'm not sure you actually helped me with anything," I said.

But I was lying. I felt much better. It was cathartic, somehow, to have confronted the Reality Engine and made it give me some answers.

There had never really been a question of what I was going to do. I couldn't let Waters get away with this. And if I wasn't going to let Waters win, well then, Proxima was definitely my enemy.

I stuck my hand out impulsively. "Thanks, Kronos."

Kronos took my hand. His grip was warm and leathery. "Good day, Shad Williams."

CHAPTER FORTY-SEVEN

KILLING PEOPLE AND BREAKING STUFF: BUT WHAT ABOUT WHEN IT'S YOUR STUFF?

I stepped into our instance and spawned right at the nexus point of our outpost. I didn't move a muscle as the wind blew my coat, ruffling it. *I'm in*, I sent to Frank.

Deploying, he replied.

My arrival here was the signal for the rest of our people to enter the portal to our instance the slow way, spawning in at the designated entrance point rather than the nexus entrance to our outpost. They would make their way to the outskirts of our base as fast as possible. Several teams were already in position, including Team Mongoose and the remains of Team Ragtag. I had Warren Black watching too.

I pulled our modified embassy stick from my inventory and very cautiously crouched, careful not to move my feet from their position. We weren't sure how wide the zone of ownership around our nexus was.

Make sure everyone is flagged for combat, I added needlessly, checking my own status. I'd set myself as a hostile combatant before spawning in here. That meant even if I stepped off the nexus point I'd still be able to use my skills. However, it was critical that I plant the stick in our territory and not theirs.

I shoved the stick, pointy end first, into the dusty earth at my feet and wiggled it to make sure it got a good, firm grip in the ground as it started working. This was going to take a couple of minutes.

"Hey!" someone shouted. I straightened up carefully, dusting off my hands. Two of Waters's goons emerged from the command center. They were carrying rifles equipped with drum magazines and grinning at me. I did a quick Inspect. The rifles were labeled as modified M16 carbines with oversized magazines. So, I wasn't expecting anything too fancy. I carefully set one foot on top of the embassy stick. Then, balancing carefully, I crossed my arms and grinned at the two.

"Howdy, folks."

"You just step away from there nice and slow," one of the two men said, pointing his gun at me.

"No, I don't think I will," I said, and triggered High Noon with him as my target.

The man's eyes widened. He pulled the trigger six times in quick succession, but no bullets fired. "What the hell?"

His fellow lowered his own muzzle and found himself also unable to shoot.

"Check your status sheet," I advised my target. "You're under a compelled duel. Until I fire, nobody can fire on me or use any other ability to move me off the spot, which is still Misfits Guild property, by the way."

I stayed right where I was, whistling to myself.

"Should we get the major?" The two guards put their heads together and muttered before one went running back inside the church. The other one, the one who I had targeted with the duel, took a step closer. "I don't know what you're playing at, but you don't want to be here."

"No, I'm sure you don't want me here," I agreed. "I'll ask my granddad to go easy on you. He might scalp you, but I think we can skip some of the ruder tortures. Probably you can keep your fingernails."

The man scowled. "That's not what I meant, and you know it. You're going up against someone too big for you to fight."

"Just reminding you that if we're going on military ranks, my grandfather is also a colonel, and he is acting under orders from the direct chain of command of the United States Armed Services, whereas Major Waters is not. Are you even Army?" I asked, sizing him up. The man, and the other one with him, had been wearing camo, but an old pattern, green and brown, not the modern desert stuff. He had a paunch and a balding head, and if he had ever been enlisted, I thought those days were well behind him.

"None of your business," the man said, scowling. I targeted him with an Inspect, and got back the information that his first name was Carson, and his class was Shade-Tree Mechanic. That wasn't much to go on.

"What are you doing working for a loser like Waters, anyway?" I asked, trying to sound sympathetic. "We've already beaten his schemes once. It's not going to go any better this time. Now you're hurting innocent people with your antics."

"I'm not working for him," Carson muttered, looking at his feet. "Alabaster Sky promised to let me out of my contract if I helped out with this."

"Ah, yes, well, I hope you got that deal in writing, and that they agreed to pay up even if you folks lose here, which you're going to," I said. I had a lot less sympathy for him than for Sam. He'd been here keeping my grandpa and the others prisoner for most of a day now. He knew the score.

I was saved from any further chitchat by the appearance of Waters and three of his cronies in the doorway of the church. I sent a quick message to Rosa. *Tell Juana that Plan Shad-definitely-thought-this-through-and-is-only-going-to-get-himself-killed-if-it-actually-helps is underway, and they should be prepared to act.*

Got it, Rosa replied.

I sent to Tall Smith, *How many goons left in the church building?*

He answered back at once. *We think twelve. Sorry, can't be more precise.*

Waters scowled at me. "What's this all about? Here to negotiate? I've already given you our terms."

"And I didn't like 'em, so I thought I'd suggest my own." I started counting on my fingers, very ostentatiously. "One, all y'all get out of here at once. Two, you disband both of your guilds and send me a list of everyone who was part of 'em. Three, you hand over every soul coin in your treasuries as reparations, and four, you personally surrender yourself to Colonel Ames for military discipline as soon as that can be arranged." I gave in to my inner John Wayne and delivered that speech in a nice long drawl. I had Waters's attention on me, right where I wanted it.

Waters shook his head. "I see you're still just as full of shit as ever, Williams. You might consider that I have your grandfather and your girlfriend at my mercy."

"You can't just keep trying the same threat over and over when it clearly hasn't worked," I said, "but that would involve you being able to learn from your past mistakes, and it's quite clear you can't. It's fine, Waters. I didn't expect you to make the smart decision." I checked the timer. I had been here for five minutes. My hacked embassy stick should take effect any moment now.

The broken stick we'd gotten off the crafter meant that our own team had been able to reverse engineer the embassy sticks to create one of our own. Planted on our own territory, it would project a zone of "Misfits Guild" base right through the middle of Waters's stolen outpost. I'd lined it up carefully according to instructions to intersect the headquarters. As soon as that activated, my people would be, as far as the system was concerned, back on Misfits territory.

How's the positioning coming? I asked Frank.

We'll be ready, he said. *I get first crack at Waters.*

Only if you can get him before me.

I wished that I had been able to save High Noon to use on Waters himself. I would have dearly loved to get in the first shot on that asshole. I had a couple of rounds in my belt with his name on it. But unfortunately, I had needed to make sure that nobody could use any abilities on me, so I had targeted the first of Waters's cronies to show up.

A notification flashed up.

[Outpost Extension Created!]

There was a shout from inside the church, and all at once a whole stream of messages popped up on my notifications from Dwight, from Juana, from Grandpa. Juana's most recent just said, *You did it, Shad. I knew you would.*

I minimized them. There was no time to read right now. Waters's people came running out of headquarters. "They're gone!"

Waters whirled. "What? Who?"

"The prisoners, sir. They're all gone."

I stayed where I was. As long as I stood right here, with my foot on the stick, none of them would be able to dislodge me. Not that it mattered, if all the hostages were freed, but the longer I distracted Waters the more time my people had to prepare.

"You're smart enough to figure this out, Waters," I said.

Waters's eyes grew wider. "Get him!" he said to the men with him. Two of them charged forward, ignoring the fact that High Noon was in effect. One came in high, as though to push me off my position, the other in a low tackle. As soon as they were within six inches of me, they both bounced.

A moment later, I heard sounds of combat drifting over the walls. Shots, explosions, shouts, and a distant roar, like somebody was unleashing a Tamed dinosaur. The cavalry had arrived, and it was about time.

I pulled up my leader chat. *Everything good? Can I get out of here?*

Everyone's out, Grandpa confirmed. *Come on and join the fun.*

I lifted my foot off the embassy stick and raised my gun. I fired one shot at the man I'd challenged to a duel, and then I engaged Fastest Gun in the West and sprinted away from the point. A flurry of shots rang out. I heard lead whistling past my head as I ran.

A warning popped up at once.

**[You are in another coalition's claimed outpost.
You will be teleported away in two seconds.]**

It took four of my racing heartbeats for the timer to change to one second. An additional four before it disappeared, and I was teleported away outside the walls to join the rest of my guild.

In that time, only a couple of Waters's men recovered enough to fire off any shots. Half of the bullets went wide, the other half tearing through my coat and dropping my HP down by forty points. As soon as I teleported out, I popped a health potion and healed back up to full.

It was complete chaos outside our gates. There were at least six hundred of Misfits Guild's finest here. Everyone from our combat miners to our farmers and crafters had insisted on joining in this fight to help avenge what had been done to our comrades.

Spells fired off wildly, filling the air with sounds of sizzling electricity crashing against the walls. Dozens of colors exploded overhead. Shots of every caliber rang out. The air was full of whizzing lead and arrows, throwing stars, all sorts of weaponry. Someone not far from me unleashed a fireball the size of my head straight at our gate.

"Whoa, whoa!" I shouted. "Disabling, not destroying! This is our stuff! We want it back! Disable! And make sure everyone has combat toggled *on* or you'll get teleported out as soon as we're through the gates!"

Most of the attackers were doing exactly what I'd told them: using their flashiest, least-effective spells and suiciding right at our gate. The traitors had no choice but to kill us. We respawned fast, and their tally of fines was going up with each so-called allied death. Since we weren't killing them, no fines were being assessed to us. I silently thanked Juana for how well she had crafted the new rules.

At the same time, many of our people were ignoring the offensive entirely as they sought each other out in the crowd, embracing.

I looked around and spotted Grandpa not far off, standing behind a pack of angry miners hurling smoke bombs and firepots at our walls. I pushed through the crowd to him.

"Are you all right?" I asked, looking him over.

Grandpa looked tired, but he nodded as he watched the fireworks. "I'm fine."

"Waters said he broke your arms."

"Wasn't as bad as all that," Grandpa said. I was pretty sure he was lying, but he held up both his hands. "Drank a health potion as soon as we got out of there. You did good, boy. You'll have to tell me all about it once we've got things back under control. What's the plan now?"

Another batch of Misfits volunteers ran up to the gate and got incinerated. *This is too fun,* Sage said. I had her leading one of the suicide squads. *I understand why you're so messed up in the head, Shad.*

Just keep your count going. We need to know how big a fine they're racking up. I turned back to Grandpa. "Once we're inside the walls, my dowsers and finders get to work. Waters planted a bunch of devices just inside our walls that let him take over our base sneakily. We're gonna find them, rip them out, and then go nail Waters's hide to his own wall."

"Sounds good." Grandpa looked around. "I think I'll grab a couple of the more mobile folk and get up there on the battlements."

"Shad!"

I heard Juana shout my name. As soon as I turned around, she was there, throwing her arms around my neck. She kissed me. Surprised, I found myself losing my balance. I took a step back, wrapped my arms around her, and returned her kiss.

"Get a room, you two," Grandpa shouted over the commotion as the most recent batch of our people burst out of the tunnels and went on the attack. "There's still work to be done."

Juana let go. She grinned up at me. "You did it. How many times did you have to get yourself killed to make it work?"

"Only once," I said. "I had to get back to our nexus somehow, and since I hadn't re-attuned to the kobold king's throne, it was the fastest and easiest way."

She shook her head. "I should have known it wouldn't be a Shad Williams plan without you getting yourself killed. If we ever get out of here and back to somewhere with normal rules, I'm gonna have a hell of a time breaking you from this happy suicide thing you've got going, aren't I?"

"Not a chance," I said. "I can give it up any time you ask."

Grandpa made a disgusted sound. "Barney? Leanne? James? Get over here. We're getting up on that wall and collecting some scalps."

A moment later, he was gone, Shadow Stepping up to the wall to attack one of the defenders.

"Get out of here! Help your mom out, and reconstruct our command team," I told Juana, who nodded and pushed her way through the crowd toward our escape tunnel.

By now, Waters had most of his people up on the outer ring of walls fighting us off. They deployed mini-guns and alien explosives, hurling them at us, knocking back dozens of miners in craters of dirt and fire. I got caught in the explosion this time and briefly died.

We respawned quickly. Frank and some of the crafters had arranged for a portable tunnel to be constructed between the outside of our walls and the kobold king's throne room, and turned it on as soon as the assault began. Our people were back in the fight in under a minute.

Waters's people took much longer to respawn since he had never been able to successfully claim our nexus point. They had to come in from their own secret backup base. I grinned to myself as I thought of what would be waiting for them once we were done here.

We breached the gate and the army poured in, with me and Sage at its head. Once inside, we split into two streams, going left and right around the inner circle of fortifications, sweeping Waters's people back, and giving my handpicked miners a chance to hunt for the embassy sticks. They started reporting in right away.

Found one.

Found another.

We're up to four now.

Got one.

I called up the status of our outpost. Our own rights were vying against the claim put in by Waters's sticks, and with each stick we found and removed, our claim got stronger. When we'd removed seven, Waters's virtual outpost collapsed. The base once again belonged to Misfits.

Two seconds later, every single one of Waters's people was gone, transported back to their own base. I sent a message to the second team. *Get going!*

As the people around me cheered, I shouted over the crowd to Grandpa. "I gotta run!"

"What? We just finished here!"

"Yeah, I know. I'll explain later. There's another front in this war. Come on, Sage!"

I shot Grandpa a quick message with an explanation as we ran for the portable tunnel, dove in, and raced through the kobold king's chamber along with the miners we had asked to come with us.

We left a sizable crew on defense. I would not be letting Waters take our outpost again without a big fight.

I popped up through the tunnels and emerged from a cave entrance yawning at the mouth of the Hansel and Gretel forest. Waters's secret base lay just beyond the last of the trees in an open meadow, shaded by the shadow of a distant mountain peak as the sun set in the west. A couple hundred Misfits were already surrounding his base. Once my reinforcements joined, we swarmed over their walls, chewing through their defenses, not caring how many deaths we incurred. Those deaths would not incur a soul coin penalty to us, but instead to the members of Waters's team. I had instructed everyone what to do, and I was glad to see they were behaving. Though we engaged Waters's people, shooting at them and harassing them, we were careful not to kill any of them. Waters's men, however, weren't doing the same. They shot, stabbed, burned, and melted us. My people took it.

I sent Waters a message. *Have you checked your fines recently?*

He didn't reply, but five seconds later, a message popped up.

**[Faction message: Gloomwing Damnation has left Team Tunnel Rat.
Members of Team Tunnel Rat may now kill members
of Gloomwing Damnation without incurring fines.
There is a ten-hour bounty on members of Gloomwing Damnation.
All kills will receive a soul coin bonus to the miners participating.]**

I sent a quick, coalition-wide broadcast. *We did it. They're out. Time to rack up the kills.*

I fired a Trick Shot at the nearest of Waters's people, drilling him through the head and taking away the last ten of his HP. He vanished, only to respawn twenty feet away at their nexus.

My people killed him again, and again, along with the rest of his crew. By the end, they were all respawning on top of each other, getting in each other's way, tripping over themselves and being hosed down with spells and bullets before they could step away from their nexus point. It took them a good seven or eight minutes before they finally stopped respawning, as someone in their organization got their act together and moved their nexus.

I worried a bit about what Waters would do next. A prick like him wasn't so easily put down. But it would hopefully take him some time to come up with his next scheme. We had other fish to fry.

"Anyone got an estimate of how much that little jaunt is going to cost Proxima?" I shouted as at last we retreated from the destroyed enemy outpost.

"It'll be in the millions of soul coins," Sage predicted. "I got that one lady with the orange hair and weird green sword at least eight times."

"I bet they try to wriggle out of it somehow," Grandpa said. "Claim they're not really the sponsors or something. I'd better put my head together with Veda and get our legal case going now. Catch you guys later."

"Sage, with me? We've got more work to do."

"On it!" she said cheerfully. "Last one there's a rotten egg."

CHAPTER FORTY-EIGHT

THE PHOENIX AS METAPHOR OF REBIRTH: A LITERARY SURVEY

There was no time to rest on our laurels. We were in a bad spot. Even as our people rejoiced in the victory we had won over Waters's crew, I knew we had no time to waste getting back on offense.

"I need a triage," I said to Arjun. "No way our enemies were sitting on the sidelines while we dealt with Waters. I need to know who's close to taking down their bosses ASAP."

Arjun looked tired. "I—I'll get right on that." He stumbled off to the rear of the headquarters building and sat down at his accustomed spot. His table usually sported some knickknacks. Now they were scattered around the room. Arjun looked around, stood up, and started slowly fetching his things and restoring them to their places.

Juana pulled me away. "It may take a few hours for Arjun to be up to the task," she warned me. "Kirin warned me that he doesn't do well with disruptions, and that was one hell of a disruption."

My stomach tied itself in knots. "How bad was it?" I asked.

"Not that bad." She wouldn't meet my eyes.

I ground my teeth. Waters and his cronies were going to suffer.

"I mean, they couldn't risk killing us," Juana clarified. "He really only hurt your grandfather, but he made sure the rest of us saw it. It was mostly psychological. He has a way of getting under your skin."

I was torn between the need to try to comfort her and the need to get out there and do what should be done.

Alison and Kirin joined us. The two women both looked tired, but not as pale as Juana. "You need to get that bastard," Kirin said without preamble. "Alison and I are working on triage right now. We'll get Arjun on it as soon as possible, but here's your list of top targets."

I ran down the list. Proxima had three teams who were only two bosses away from finishing their encounters. ConSweGo had four. Two different unallied teams were within three bosses of finishing an instance, with dozens more on their heels. We were in trouble. "How complete a picture is this?"

"We could be missing one or two. We're running cross-checks," Kirin said.

"Let me know which of these you want boss strategies for," Alison said.

I had another quick flash of suspicion. Alison had joined us shortly before everything went south. She had shown up at Mama Grace's restaurant to volunteer her services, saying she'd been a lotus eater.

"Who's your contract with?" I asked her.

"What?" She seemed surprised.

"Your contract. Who's it with?"

"A company called Quantum Vendetta. Why?"

"Just trying to make sure all of our people are safe from Alabaster Sky's machinations. Any idea who Quantum Vendetta is associated with?"

"No. They are a phase one–only outfit. They sent me a lot of threatening notes when I disappeared into the lotus eater level, but they haven't really contacted me since I came out. I did get word that they were trying to sell my contract as a bad debt, but that didn't go anywhere. I think the systems shut down all the contract trading."

That matched with what I knew about how the smaller companies were working. "All right, thanks," I said, before sending a message asking Ames to look into Alison and anyone else who had joined us lately. I wasn't convinced that Waters really had a mole, but I didn't want to risk being surprised.

I gathered my action squad. The Mongeese had been up as long as I had, but they were game for this. I sent Team Ragtag to get a few hours of shut-eye and then handed out emergency stimulants that I'd picked up on the Hub.

"These will give us about eight hours each, and then we collapse," I warned the team. "We've got to get out there and start making some headway."

"How can I help?" Frank asked, shouldering through the crowd that had formed outside of our headquarters. There were a lot of us, more than I could recognize.

"Here's our target list," I said, sending him a copy. "We'll have more later, but these are the priorities. We've got to get in there and spike whatever their current attempt is. I don't care what it costs or how we do it, we have got to buy ourselves some time. If we can get each of them to wipe on their current boss, that'll buy us twenty-four hours before they're allowed to attempt it again."

"Got it," Frank said.

I assigned him two of the attempts. "I'm pretty sure these both have connecting tunnels from the kobold king's domain. Gather up every warm body you can find and shove them in there with weapons. We'll blow them off the attempt with sheer numbers."

It was a strategy I had been saving for an emergency. I was pretty sure once we'd used it, the galactics would find a counter. But right now, if I could buy twenty-four hours for my team to come up with a better strategy, I would.

"Sage, Mongeese, Grandpa, I want us to hit these three." I highlighted them in an order, to be altered if we found one of the teams wasn't where we thought.

Grandpa looked over the list. "What's your thinking here, boy?"

"The top two are Proxima teams. I want to send them a message that we're not backing down any time soon. As for the third"—I tapped the list—"according to the research Arjun did back before everything went to pieces, this group here, Lasthome Domination Attends, has hired some of our old friends, the Firebrand orcs. Mak'gar's crew. Not his brother the war chief; he's busy doing politics stuff. Mak'gar's people are a potent force, and I respect them. I don't want to assign them to any other crew." I had another plan, too, but that was for later.

"Sounds good," Grandpa said.

"Frank?"

"Organizing my team now," he said. "Give me a third target to try to hit if we have time."

I shot him the rest of the list. "That's in order of priority."

"And we don't care how many deaths we have?" Frank asked.

"Nope."

"Great. We'll work through that list until we've got them all or they get smart. You go handle your crew."

He turned away, and I led my team down into the bowels of the tunnels, happy to finally be back on offense and spared from the big decisions.

I inquired from Captain Kobold about the progress of each of the three attacking teams. "The Great Ice Palace shook under the assault of the evil outsiders," Captain Kobold related. "But the forces of winter have pushed them back. They are still trying to cross the third northern barrier."

I cross-referenced that with what I knew and translated it: One of the two Proxima teams was still stuck clearing trash and dealing with corridor traps in the Evil Santa–themed instance. According to what I had last seen, they still had to take on Rudolph and the other eight reindeer before they could challenge Santa himself. It sounded like we had some time.

"How about the home of the Golden Dragon?" I asked.

"He waits in his lair. The enemies are pressing in hard. They are at the threshold to his mate's chamber."

"Right, we've got our target," I told the team. "That's the second Proxima group. According to the last information we had from Arjun, which is a good twenty-four hours out of date at this point, they are running a twenty-five-man squad. Five healers, five support, the rest a mixture of ranged and melee with two frontline miners."

"That's a lot of support," Jones noted. "Any idea what kind of tricks they have up their sleeves?"

I shook my head. "No, we did some early harasses on their base, but we haven't gone head-to-head opposed on them yet."

"Right, we'll keep our eyes peeled," Jones said.

"As usual, call out the healers and support, focus them down first, try to keep the frontliners tied up with crowd control spells," I said. Twenty-five was a few too many for our current composition, so I shot a quick message to Juana asking for reinforcements.

I don't have that list at my beck and call. You should talk to Alison.

I didn't know how to say that I didn't trust Alison. So I said thanks, and then instead called up Frank.

You got a minute?

Organizing the lemming rush here. What can I do you for?

I snorted, enjoying that imagery.

I need fifteen combat-capable miners who can take directions. Anyone with crowd control is a plus.

I'll get them sent over to you. What's your assembly chamber?

The treasury off the kobold king's throne room. There's a tunnel up to the Lost Guardians of the West instance.

Haven't run that one, he said. *All right, sending them over.*

A couple of minutes later, we got our new miners. I organized them into three squads, taking one under my wing and assigning the others to Tall Smith and Grandpa respectively.

"Everyone understand the objective?" I asked.

I got nods all around as I checked the situation with Captain Kobold. The Proxima team had just entered the bower of the Harmonious Phoenix, mate to the Golden Dragon of the West. According to Captain Kobold, they were setting up an attack on the phoenix.

"Last time, they brought fire," he cackled. "They did not know that fire only makes the phoenix stronger. That was glorious. She crushed their bones beneath her beak. This time I fear they are smarter."

"Let's get in there," I told my team.

I had Jones use Camouflage on Team Mongoose, myself, and Sage. We snuck up the steps to the trapdoor leading into the boss chamber. Grandpa rode herd on our wave of volunteers. We'd need them, but not just yet.

I eased back the trapdoor, looking for our enemies. The room was an enormous circular marble bowl with tall fluted pillars lining the edge, holding up a golden roof that arced high overhead. In the center of the roof was a round opening, letting in starlight. Directly beneath the skylight was a huge golden nest at least twenty feet across and more than waist-high on me. Atop the nest sat a beautiful bird, something like a heron, but with a neck more like a swan's. Its plumage was red and purple, and its eyes emerald. It darted its head here and there, clearly disturbed by something. I couldn't make out the enemy just yet.

Anyone have camo detection? I asked.

Checking it out, replied Black. *Yeah, they've got some sort of screen. Looks like two of their support have a device that's keeping them all hidden. It's emitting a circular field around the nest, about ten feet out. They're arraying themselves around the room.*

Jones, drone.

Got it, boss, Jones deployed his drone, carefully extending the Camouflage to cover it. It rose into the air twenty feet, and we got a good look.

Proxima's team was a mixed group. Space elves, a couple of orcs, and a lot of foxlike animalkin. They were spread out around the circle in very precise lines. No one fighter was closer than five feet to anyone else.

Can we get a listing of what this boss does? I asked. I wanted everyone to review the abilities before we started.

Sage replied, *She shoots fire breath, and if she takes too much damage, she reverts to an egg and sets fire to her nest. If the egg isn't killed fast enough, she hatches from it, launches to the ceiling, and shoots a rain of fiery golden quills down all around. According to my Eye-Spy, she's killed one hundred and fifty-seven differ-ent miners who've attempted to take her out.* "She's one badass ladybird," Sage added admiringly.

Proxima team had yet to move. We had a minute or two. I intended to use the time properly.

"What are those other devices they've brought?" Tall Smith asked aloud, point-ing. "There, there, and there."

The other support miners on their team all had tall blue cylinders with small hoses attached. They looked a little bit like fire extinguishers. Maybe that's what they were.

I pointed them out to Sage. "Can you get an Eye-Spy?"

She shook her head. "Sorry, they're blocked for some reason."

"Well, we have to guess that they're a way to counter the phoenix's fire." I thought for a minute. "The plan stays the same. We focus on downing the sup-port people first. All right. Get ready."

The Mongeese got into position. Still behind the Camouflage, they threw down their machine gun nest. It had a 270-degree field of fire, which would let us command a hefty fraction of the room, but not enough.

"All right, go," I said. We dropped the Camouflage.

I heard our recruits rushing up the steps behind me, Grandpa chiding them, "Keep focused. Find your targets."

As I leapt forward, my Fastest Gun in the West took me through their airfield, right up into the face of their biggest bruiser, an orc carrying both a spear and a shield. I guessed he was one of their tanks with various crowd control abilities.

I shouted and fired my Trick Shot right around his shield, hitting him with an itching bullet that exploded on contact and spread concentrated poison ivy oil all over his face and neck. With luck, it would drip down inside his shiny jumpsuit and be unbearably painful.

The orc snarled at me and stabbed. That was all right. My job was to help distract the tanks while everyone else targeted the squishy back line.

Sage had Lassoed the other tank. "Can't Tame him. Switching targets," she shouted.

I was building up a database, or rather feeding the information back to Juana and Arjun to build a database, of every set of abilities and combinations we came across. So far it seemed like only the Warriors who specialized, thanks to their class evolution to Battlemaster, in being the focus of attention had abilities to let them resist mind control. The healers—pretty much all Priests or a couple of related class evolutions—never did, and neither did most of the ranged folk.

Most of the tanks had a very similar set of abilities. A crowd control move, a move to attract the attention and hold it from a single boss, resistance to mind control, and damage reduction. It made them hard to take down, but not much of a threat once you learned the loadout.

The Mongeese opened fire. "Shielders down," Mongoose Brown called. "We can see everything now."

Behind me, the phoenix squawked melodiously.

"Uh-oh, she's engaged," Sage said. "And she's Rabid."

"Shit! Our information didn't say that!" As members of Team Tunnel Rat, we were supposed to be on the same side as the bosses. We had learned there was one unpleasant exception. Some bosses were Rabid. That meant they would attack anyone and anything that wasn't them.

"According to my notes, she wasn't," Sage said.

That was a problem I'd solve later. Had we been given bad information, or had Proxima's team somehow set a trap for us?

"Get 'em down," I shouted, even as the first death notification for a member of our team popped up in my vision. It was one of our new recruits. We'd taken down three of Proxima's, though.

There was a door on the far side of the room where the enemy had come in, and it was standing open. That was annoying. It meant that their respawns would be able to get back here, unless we killed enough of the raid for it to count as a wipe, in which case the boss would despawn for twenty-four hours.

"Be prepared for backup," I shouted. "If you die, get back in the fight fast. Where's Darell?" That was the man who had died just now.

"He's on his way back," Grandpa filled in.

"Well, get the lead out of your pants," I told my team. "If you do die, get back in here fast."

I was dodging pokes from the orc's spear almost lazily as we went. I'd had plenty of experience with orc fighting techniques by now. I liked them, and from what I'd seen, when they were actually one-on-one in a duel, they were pretty good. But get them into a defined role, and they tended to follow the same pattern over and over again.

Numbers flashed up. More and more of the Proxima team were falling to the machine gun. But now they'd shifted their strategy, sliding the boss slowly out of the arc of fire. I shifted and let Grandpa Shadow Step in behind the orc I'd been playing with. Since I had already wounded him, Grandpa couldn't use Counting Coup. Instead, he overpowered a Scalp by activating one of his recent ability upgrades called Hit and Run Tactics. This let him deliver triple damage after a Shadow Step, and then gave him the ability to Shadow Step away, not directly behind another miner. It had an annoyingly long five-minute cooldown, but it was devastatingly effective. He cut deep into the orc's remaining **[250/312]** hit points. Now the orc had **[87]** hit points remaining.

I fired another Trick Shot using a knockback round this time, took off another **[10]** points of health, and sent the orc stumbling back against the wall.

"Duck!" Sage shouted, and I threw myself to the side as a gout of fire blazed past where I had been.

The phoenix was reared up on her nest, her wings back, her neck coiled like a snake ready to strike. She unleashed another gout of flame right into the middle of a knot of fighters, two orcs and three of my recruits. It incinerated them all where they stood. I swear I could smell burning flesh.

"How are we doing?" I asked. I'd lost sight of the overall fight.

"We're holding our own," Grandpa said, which was not encouraging. I had hoped we'd be doing better than that.

"Wait, what's he doing? Stop him!" Tall Smith shouted.

I turned to see a space elf raising one of the blue canisters. Just as the phoenix opened her mouth to unleash a gout of flame, he aimed the nozzle toward her and fired. Icy blue mist flew from the nozzle and extinguished the flame in midair. The gout of ice crystals traveled down the flame until they reached the bird's wide-open mouth, and the phoenix let out a strangled squawk as her entire head was covered in a thick layer of ice.

I checked her status. Her health was still at **[320/500]**, but she was showing a Frozen debuff. The time ticked down. **[58 seconds, unable to move or attack.]**

Now the enemy swarmed in around her, hacking and slashing. I chased them down and fired shot after shot, but they ignored me as more reinforcements poured in.

"They're cheating!" Sage shouted. "These weren't all here before!"

"If it's not against the rules, they can do it. No use crying about it. Can we get some AoE damage here?" I asked urgently. Team Mongoose's machine gun nest was forcing the Proxima team to attack from a narrow corridor. "They're all clumped up."

With the phoenix out of commission, though, it was hard to do enough damage to them. They were taking her health down hard. I watched as her health plunged down. **[315]**, **[307]**, **[295]**, **[290]**.

Then, Sage dropped her Mucking Out the Stalls ability under the enemy. One of our new folk hit the muck with a flame grenade.

Sage's goo caught fire. It went up like napalm, igniting the orcs inside it and spreading to the boss. Her health kept ticking down. The fire wasn't good for her, but her Frozen debuff started speeding up. Now instead of forty-five seconds left, there were thirty. Now fifteen.

The boss shook herself, ice crystals flying free. She raised herself up off the nest, but she was down to **[82 HP]**.

"Target the boss!" I shouted. Since she was Rabid, we could damage her ourselves. "Focus damage on her. Let's kick her over into the next phase."

My team responded. We hosed down the boss. She screamed, diving for her nest. A moment later, she lay still, but beneath her lustrous plumage was a beautiful golden egg.

It was also horribly fragile, with **[180]** hit points.

"Protect the egg!" I shouted.

One of our new guys stepped up to the plate.

"I've got you!" he said as he cast a preservation bubble over the whole nest. "It'll last for a minute and a half," he said proudly.

"Any idea how long the bird needs?" I asked.

"No, but let's make it redundant," Grandpa said. "Misfits, attack!"

CHAPTER FORTY-NINE

POMP AND CIRCUMSTANCES

Mak'gar's orcs were holed up at Fort McHenry. A battered flag flew over the wooden walls, thirteen stripes and not nearly enough stars. Offshore, wooden warships pounded the fort with cannons.

"They've really got a whole instance themed after the War of 1812?" Sage asked skeptically. "We covered that in my correspondence history course, and it was like three pages."

"Yeah, that's 'cause you Yanks got your asses whooped," Mitch said.

Team Ragtag had come off their two-hour nap and was swapping out for the Mongeese. Sage, Grandpa, and I still had a couple of hours of pep pills left in our system. I was planning to use every bit of it.

"We did not," Sage said. "My history book said that it was a stalemate."

"And a stalemate is definitely what Americans call a war they didn't actually win," Mitch said. "I bet it says Vietnam was a stalemate, too."

"Hey now," Grandpa said sharply.

"Right, Colonel. Sorry about that." Mitch looked a little embarrassed.

The orc team was allied, in this case, with the beleaguered Americans. It seemed like taking the fort would have been a more obvious objective, but this scenario was apparently a multiround fight in which they would hold off several waves of British invaders before, in a grand finale, Queen Victoria spawned and they would have to take her down.

I was pretty damn sure we were at least forty years too early for Queen Victoria, but I doubted the orcs cared.

My team was floating in a pair of small inflatable Zodiac watercraft, the kind with a steering wheel and a powerful motor, in between the ships and the firing cannons. The shots sailed harmlessly over our heads.

"Oh, oh," Sage called. "Another wave's spawning."

There were ten British warships behind us, all flying the Union Jack. Now they each let down three boats full of redcoats. The boats moved through the water without the redcoats actually having to row. They clutched their rifles and sat staring ahead like marionettes, making for the nearest point of the shore.

"Let's get in there," Grandpa ordered.

Our Zodiacs roared to life and we swept past the rowboats heading in toward the shore. The orcs were gathered on the bank under the walls of the wooden palisade fort. They surrounded a pair of cannons.

"Eye-Spy says those cannons have a sixty-second cooldown between shots," Sage shouted as both of them fired on one of the boats full of British. The rounds hit mid of the boat, cutting the small craft in two and tossing redcoats into the water. Immediately, fins circled.

The hapless redcoats bobbed up and down silently as they were pulled under one by one. I felt like the Reality Engine had cut some corners in level design on this one.

"Don't get hit," Sage advised. "Those cannons each did [250] hit points of direct damage and half that in a three-foot radius."

"Mitch?" I asked.

He shook his head. "They're considered environmental. I can't Spike Their Trunks on the cannons. I could get the orcs' weapons though," he added hopefully, but I had just seen Mak'gar snap to attention as he pointed to us.

The orcs swapped out their guns for long energy polearms. We'd encountered those occasionally before. These were the variant that could launch the energy beam head forward as a projectile. It took about five seconds to re-form on the head of the weapon, and the user was somewhat helpless until then, but they were a formidable threat.

Sure enough, Mak'gar's fifteen orcs launched a volley at us. I yanked hard on the steering column of the Zodiac I was driving and most of the volley flew harmlessly to my left.

Lara cried out. She was piloting the other Zodiac. "We took some damage there!"

"Dodge where you can," I said grimly, "but get to shore." We were out ahead of the rowboats now. This was the second-to-last wave of redcoats, giving us a bit of time to beat Mak'gar's crew. It would be a long, hard fight. I turned to Annie and Wyatt. "Got the device?"

"As soon as we hit sand," Annie promised. She padded her half of the deployable respawn point.

It was thanks to Mak'gar's people that we had one of those. They had used a portable respawn against us back in phase two and after capturing it, our crafters had spent a lot of time reverse engineering. This was the first time we had deployed one. They were fantastically expensive to build and Dwight said he couldn't promise more than twenty respawns out of it before it broke, but we needed it in this scenario. The closest secret entrance from the kobold caverns brought us up into these Zodiacs. Not exactly ideal for getting back into the fight quickly.

We approached the shore and instead of easing back on the throttle, I pushed it in hard. My boat leapt ahead, flying over the water. Spray hit my face as we rushed ashore. Mak'gar's orcs raced down the beach to meet us. The boat crashed hard against the beach, but we'd been planning for it and had braced ourselves. It shot twenty feet up the strand, knocking three orcs flying. I leapt over the side, Quick Drawing my gun and firing a whole Barrage into the nearest orc.

"I see you, Shad Williams!" Mak'gar shouted. He leapt for me and I laughed.

This was deadly serious, don't get me wrong. If we lost, I didn't know what we were going to do. Proxima and the others would walk all over us. But at the same time, I was facing a nice uncomplicated fight against a nice uncomplicated opponent, skill versus skill.

I loved it. I never felt as alive as I did in combat. Now that I didn't have that pressing worry about Sage getting killed, I had grown to enjoy my role here. Right now, as the stress of the last few days faded away and all I had to do was take on a dozen orcs who outweighed me by one hundred pounds and had been raised to this life since probably before I was born, I felt good.

I combined Trick Shot with a quick Called Shot, aiming at Mak'gar's dominant hand and firing a round that hit and did double damage, localized to his fingers and wrist.

My people threw abilities; the orcs countered with their raw strength and equipment. We had the advantage that the orcs were trying to take out the red-coat soldiers as well. The soldiers beached their boats, disembarked, formed up into columns five men wide, and marched forward toward the walls of the fort. Meanwhile, the orcs chased them down and slashed and stabbed as my people harassed the orcs.

Mak'gar shouted. Blood ran down the haft of his energy weapon, but it didn't stop him from racing toward me. As he approached, I ducked low and swept my leg up, kicking sand at him. He spluttered. I leapt around him, coming in behind and firing three rounds into the back of his neck.

Of course, he had [300] hit points, so it didn't kill him, but he was starting to hurt. He whirled faster than I expected, and the edge of his polearm sliced through my jacket and caught my shoulder, tugging, but it didn't do much damage.

Lara went down with a shriek and a cloud of orange smoke. A second later she messaged us: *On my way back. The respawn point worked great!*

We actually had the advantage on respawns. Mak'gar's orcs came back inside the fort and had to make their way down. Plus, their resurrection fees were mounting with every death, and ours were free. Against any one team, we had an unfair advantage. Against all the others together, it was still an uphill battle.

One step at a time.

"I thought you were an honorable warrior, Williams," Mak'gar roared. He raced for me, slashing with his weapon. I danced back and fired a shot; at this range, I couldn't miss. I was out of ammo, so I reloaded, dropped a Barrage, and reloaded again.

"No honorable warrior would stoop to these tactics," Mak'gar continued.

"Honor is for fair fights," I snapped. "I'm trying to win a future for my people."

"You don't understand how things work. You are flailing against an order that has existed for thousands of years, since before your people dared to look at the sky with anything except fear."

"You came into our home!" I yelled. "You took us away from everything we knew and threw us into this crucible, and now you're telling us we never even had a chance. And you claim you're the honorable one, working for a corrupt system like that?"

"This is how the world is, Williams. There's no use fighting it. Raging against the inevitable never won a battle. Become strong. Fight for your people's future. This engine will be taken, despite your interference. All you're doing is making it worse for your own people at the end. I know what it is like. My people went through the same thing a mere twelve hundred years ago. We just didn't have these preposterous classes that are giving your people false hope."

"What do you mean, false hope?" I snapped.

"Hope that you can win. Hope that you can somehow hold out against the might of an entire galaxy when you have something they want. Perhaps if you understood how a Reality Engine was to be used, you'd have a chance. But you're children, Williams. You're children in a rage."

"Better children than slaves!"

Mak'gar roared in anger. The battle rampaged around us. I fired at Mak'gar, then took a Trick Shot at an orc whose health was dipping down. I killed him just before he could take out the last of the NPC redcoats. Two other orcs took his place and finished off the spawn wave.

One wave still to go. We had to stop Mak'gar's team.

I coordinated in chat. *Focus on the ones coming back from respawn. Orcs don't like being spawn camped. They think it's dishonorable and that makes them irrational. They should be easier to get down. I'll keep Mak'gar off-balance.*

One of my usual tactics when fighting orcs was to kill their leader. Orcs don't listen to a leader who's not in the fight. But it took so little time to respawn, and

Mak'gar was already so angry, I didn't want to give him a chance to clear his head and come back thinking properly.

Mak'gar was shaking his fist at the sky. "And you, System! I don't understand why you're cheating for the humans so much. They would not be nearly as powerful if they didn't have these absolutely ridiculous classes. How can you allow this? It's a violation of everything we've ever seen."

A bolt of lightning from the sky arced down to earth. It struck Mak'gar, outlining every bone in his body. Brilliant blue. My eyes dazzled. I fell back, expecting that Mak'gar had been killed. But as my vision cleared, I saw him standing there, arms still outstretched. His weapon fell from his limp hands.

"What is this?" he breathed. "I am a Scion of a Proud Warrior Race?" His eyes fell on me. He pointed and shouted, "You have no honor!"

Invisible bonds wrapped my limbs. I couldn't move. I tried to shout, but my voice was muffled. In chat, I yelled, *Mak'gar just did something to me! I'm out of the fight for . . .* I checked my status menu. It said, "Dishonored. Thirty seconds, unable to move. Five minutes at reduced damage. Face an honorable duel to remove this debuff."

I swore to myself. *How the hell . . . Sage! Eye-Spy on Mak'gar right now!*

"He's had a class evolution!" she yelled back.

How?

Mak'gar turned to his men. "Do our ancestors proud!" he bellowed. I could feel the buff go out from him as he shouted. Mentally, I groaned. *He's one of those idiots who has to shout his attack name aloud. Great.*

I still didn't understand how he'd gotten a class evolution, but it didn't matter. My timer was ticking down. A couple of seconds later, I had use of my limbs again.

I Quick Drew my gun and it flew to my hand. Mak'gar pointed at me and shouted something that the system didn't translate. My revolver transformed into a longsword. Mak'gar's own weapon shrank down to about the same length, but his had a nasty hook at one end of the blade.

"What the hell is this?"

"An honorable duel," Mak'gar said. He grinned madly. "What, Williams? You didn't think you were the only one to be able to compel your enemy to do what you want?"

He lunged for me. I blocked his thrust.

In chat, I shouted at my team. *Kill them! Get them down! Find out if that buff on them sticks around once they respawn. Focus fire! We can't let them beat us back!*

Mak'gar and I exchanged blows. His eyes blazed with fury. I was on the back foot here. I had no experience with swords. I had to keep Mak'gar focused on me, so I shouted at him. "So now you'll be able to win? It's a fair fight?"

Mak'gar swung. He looked furious. "You are tenacious. Your people have great courage and great strength, but you need to learn wisdom. When to talk and when to be silent. When to wait and when to return. You will not win your own engine. You will spend many cycles paying down the debts. But while you do, your people will learn what it means to be part of this world. You will carve out a niche for yourselves. Perhaps like my people, as companies of honorable warriors, fighting to claim the resources that our progenitors left behind us. It is a noble calling, Williams, but you must learn."

"Sorry, Mak'gar. My people are just really bad at giving up."

In frustration, he ran at me. I blocked his attack.

Keep it up, Sage encouraged me in chat. *We're near a tipping point. The next wave of soldiers is about to land and the orcs are not prepared.*

I lunged at Mak'gar, swinging wildly. He blocked me easily. "You see," he said, "you are so reliant on your little tricks that when your weapon is taken from you, you are like a flailing child."

I caught his counter and threw it back. "And all of you are too reliant on your equipment. Doesn't mean you're not a threat."

Mak'gar snarled. I barely blocked his blow this time. The next wave of redcoats reached the beach and pulled up their boats on the strand. There were twice as many this time. Some of my people dropped back to cover them as they advanced toward the walls of the fort. Half of Mak'gar's orcs were coming back from respawn.

Focus on downing as many of the orcs as you can, I ordered.

"Come and sit down again at the table," Mak'gar said. "I can ask my employers to find a solution to this that is agreeable to us all."

I set myself to exchange another round of blows with Mak'gar. "We can negotiate *after* my side wins!"

Mak'gar swung so fast I didn't even see the blow coming. It cut me in half, stem to sternum, and for a second and a half it was the worst pain I've ever felt.

I was still swearing as I respawned a couple of seconds later, a little farther down the beach. But it didn't matter. Our assault had worked. Mak'gar's people were mostly dead.

Someone fired one last shot, and Mak'gar's head exploded. A couple of seconds later, he was a cloud of dust and the system roared.

**[Firebrand's attempt to defend Fort McHenry has failed.
Twenty-four-hour countdown timer starts now.]**

"Let's get out of here," I snapped to my team. I didn't really want to exchange any more words with Mak'gar. Besides, I had something else to worry about.

How the hell had the orc gotten a class evolution?

CHAPTER FIFTY

THE IMPORTANCE OF BEING WELL RESTED

I headshot a gnome, sending it tumbling backward over the wall of the castle. The system excitedly proclaimed that the gnome team had failed their attempt against the boss. Wearily, I holstered my revolver. "Nice job, team," I said.

There were tired smiles and some exhausted sighs all around. The last three days had been a blur. My current team had been going for six hours straight. This was the fifth boss attempt in a row that we had interfered with.

"Let's get back to headquarters and grab a bite to eat," I said. "Some of you are due for a rest shift." They gave me tired nods and disappeared down the staircase leading to the kobold tunnels.

All but Sage. Sage was staring out from the battlements, her arms wrapped around one stone crenellation. I stepped over to her and saw the silent tears running down her face.

"Hey, hey, what's wrong?" I gave her an awkward side hug.

She leaned against me. I could feel her chest heaving. "I'm just so tired," she said.

I tried to remember how long she'd been fighting alongside me today. Certainly, we'd both taken the shift before this one, but she'd had some rest before that, hadn't she? I had been fighting alongside Team Mongoose on a spawn camp attempt. We had successfully gotten so many kills off on one ConSweGo-backed team that the team had retired from the game.

Before that had been another round of boss attempts, and Sage had been there for that. We'd been running pretty solid for the last three days trying to catch up. I had slept, I couldn't remember, eighteen hours ago? Maybe twenty-four? I was due, if I could find the time.

"When did you last get a nap?" I asked, trying to focus on one problem at a time.

She shook her head. "It doesn't matter. I need to be doing this." Her voice was full of pain. "Just a little while longer. We're almost there, aren't we?"

I checked the latest update Juana had sent. "We've made sixty teams retire in the last three days. Some of the others have to be getting close to quitting. We'll be able to rest soon," I promised, even though I wasn't sure I believed it was true.

While we were down to only about twenty teams left in the game, those were the ones with the deep pockets. Proxima's and ConSweGo's special teams and a few multinationals with the power of seven or eight star systems behind them. Their debts were mounting up, but they didn't seem to care. I was worried they'd found some sort of loophole that was letting them get away with shirking their bills.

"All right, sweetheart. Let's go back and get something to eat, get you a nap. You'll feel better after that."

"No, I won't." She turned to me and gave me a full-on hug, clinging to me. "I have to keep going. I have to do everything I can do. Otherwise, if I know I didn't give this my all and then we don't make it, I . . ." She broke down in full sobs.

I patted her back. "Sage! Sage! Nobody's done more than you have. I swear. We're not going to lose."

My words felt hollow. We were still in this, but it was getting harder and harder. My team was getting sloppy. I'd had to bench two different squads, sending them back for mandatory eight-hour downtime, telling them to get their head back in the game. It was part of why I was running so ragged. We were desperately undermanned.

"Come on," I said, and pulled Sage along with me down into the caverns. Instead of taking the path back to our base, though, I connected through a door into Threshold.

Sage blinked. "What's this?"

"You," I said grimly, "need to go up to the Hub and get your ethereum levels checked out. How long has it been?" I knew the answer because it was the same as for me. Ten days. And we were only supposed to go seven between checkups.

"Only if you come, too," she said, grabbing me.

I shook my head. "No, hon. This won't take much longer. I can hold out another day or two."

"Then so can I."

"Grandpa and I will fight a lot better if we know you're being taken care of. Besides," I said, "I'll let Veda and Ames know you're coming and see if we can't find some sort of PR opportunity for you."

"I don't want to," she said, but she let me tug her along toward the great space elevator up to the Hub.

"You need a good night's sleep and a full checkup. You do that, get back down here, and be ready to kick some more orc butt."

She gave me a wan smile. "How about space elves? They're more fun to kill. I like how mad they look when you gank them."

"Sure. Proxima's got a whole team of those. They'll probably still be in this."

"I don't want you to feel like I'm letting you down."

I crouched so that our faces were level. "Sage, you're the only reason I'm in this. Everything I've done is because you've been here, inspiring me, keeping me moving forward. Right now, I'm telling you, I need you to take care of yourself, okay? Let's get that cowgirl cheer back up."

She sniffed and rubbed her nose. "All right. I think you're right. I don't think I have a choice here."

"You don't," I told her. "Go take care of yourself."

She stepped up into the elevator, and a moment later she was gone, soaring upward toward the hole in the roof of our cavern that was almost too small to be seen. I followed her pod for as long as I could see it, then stepped back and headed for our outpost.

As always, headquarters was abuzz with activity. They'd strung a curtain across the back of the main room and put a couple of cots behind it where the command team could catch a little sleep in between fights. Alison and Juana were on duty. They looked up as I entered.

"How many more miners are overdue for rest or for getting checked out at the Hub?" I asked. "And don't include me. I know how bad off I am."

"About ten percent of our combat miners are overdue on checkups. None by more than three days. Veda says it's not ideal, but we should be able to hold out," Juana said. "As for sleep, it's hard to know. I've been asking people to check in and out when they come off rest shifts, but not everybody's remembering to do that."

"We're getting sloppy. We're making mistakes," I said.

"How about you yourself? You need a nap."

"I know." I took a deep, shuddering breath and looked around. "Can I get a status update?"

Alison moved over to our command table and worked it. The display glowed to life. "We have another four teams announcing their retirement, including Firebrand."

I bowed my head in respect for Mak'gar. "Sorry about that, buddy," I muttered.

"We have six more teams whose twenty-four-hour timers expired in the last few hours but haven't started their attempts yet," Alison continued. "Here, here, and here," she pointed at half a dozen spots on the map.

We had a big diagram on the table with circles representing each of the eighty-seven different instances. More than sixty of them were dark now, indicating that all teams assigned to that instance had since retired. The others were color-coded in various different shades, representing how many bosses still remained, one, two, three, or four.

None of the active instances had more than four bosses left. Too many of them were sitting at one.

I studied what Alison was telling me. The six teams who had yet to engage their boss all had two or three bosses still remaining. "Maybe they're considering pulling out," I suggested, "but haven't made it official yet."

"Maybe," Alison agreed.

I frowned. Something was bothering me. I pointed at the circle in the center. "That's us, right?"

"Yes," Juana said.

"Isn't it supposed to be blue?" Now the circle was yellow.

Juana's eyes narrowed. She leaned over it, her fingers dancing along the table as she sought out information. She gasped.

"What's wrong?"

"You know we had written off all of the other teams in our instance. We hit them hard early on, made them back off or retire."

I nodded. "Yeah?"

"Well, Team Eternal Dominion is back in it. They've just downed a boss."

"Wait, what?"

"I'm requesting information." Juana stared into space, then turned back to me. I could see the dismay before she even started speaking.

"Eternal Dominion's been bought out by the big conglomerates. They've brought in some of the elite combat miners from Proxima and ConSweGo both."

"It's a Hail Mary attempt," I said grimly. They'd found another avenue of attack. "All right, we'll deal with them when they get a little farther in. I need to check on the main Proxima team. They should be getting ready for another attempt on their final boss here in the Lost Guardians of the West."

Proxima's team had slipped past our defenses and downed the phoenix yesterday. We had foiled them on the final boss, the Golden Sun Dragon, but they'd be back soon and I was going to be there.

"Shad, a quick word?" Juana pulled me aside to a back corner of the room. She held up a hand and a bubble surrounded us.

"Nice trick."

"It's a tool, not a skill," Juana said. "Privacy curtain." The bubble blacked out the rest of the room, leaving us in a small circle of isolation. I couldn't hear anything beyond either. The bubble was small, leaving Juana and I very close together, face-to-face.

"You're pushing yourself too hard, Shad. You're going to have a breakdown. I got word from Veda about you sending Sage up and I'm glad, but she's not the only one who needs to take it easy. You've got to rest or you're going to be no use to any of us."

I rubbed my face. "I know, but how can I sit and do nothing while we're fighting like this? We're only barely staying ahead. One good push by Proxima and they could get a final boss down and win the whole thing."

"It's not all on you," Juana began, but I interrupted her.

"It is, because I'm the one who made this decision. I didn't consult anyone else. I just went with what the Reality Engine was telling me without really thinking it through. I thought we could do this. I was wrong. I made a choice for all of us and I was wrong, Juana. And I can't just sit by and wait while someone takes this all away from us."

Juana put a hand on my arm. Her touch was warm and grounding. I felt suddenly tired. No, more like I'd always been tired and now I was being forced to recognize that fact.

"It doesn't matter if we lose," she said softly. "They were never going to let us win. You've already beaten them, Shad. You've given all of us something to hope for, something to fight for, something to remember. Whatever happens after this, wherever they take us, we're going to know that we did the best we could and that we still have a chance. We can rebuild somewhere, somehow. I don't know where. I don't know when. We will find a way forward."

Tears were glistening in her eyes. "You did the right thing."

"Then why does it feel like I fucked up so bad?"

She didn't have an answer. I looked at her and she looked back and we stood there like that for a good little while.

I took a deep breath. "What do I do, Juana?"

She smiled at me and I felt unaccountably warm. "You go and you take a nap. You can have one of the cots in the back room. We've got them specially made so they have an enchantment that puts you to sleep as soon as you lay on them. You can set an alert that will wake you up if anything important happens."

"It's all important."

"I'll get a team in there to check on Proxima," she said. "From Alison's analysis, we should have at least one more good spoiler attempt before they figure out a way to counter us. If anyone else starts causing trouble, I'll let you know. You're no good to anyone like this."

My shoulders slumped. Juana was right, as usual. "All right," I agreed. "Thank you." She smiled up at me. "And when was the last time *you* got any rest?"

Her cheeks went pink. "I had a nap about eighteen hours ago," she confessed.

"Then you need to go to bed with me," I said. Then I realized what I'd said and felt my cheeks heat up. The worst thing about my Williams-side heritage was just how badly I blushed when embarrassed. Sage had more of Mom's coloring and it didn't look nearly as visible when she did it.

"I didn't mean like that," I said hastily. "I mean, you need a nap too. I mean, not that I don't want to go to bed with you or anything, but . . ."

Juana reached up, pulled my face down to hers, and kissed me. After a moment, she stepped back. "Bad timing," she said. "Try again when this is all over." She gave me a quick wink. "I'll take a nap right after you do, I promise. Somebody's got to mind the fort here. You'll sleep better knowing I'm on it."

She was right about that. I went to the cot, Juana's quip about timing still ringing in my ears. When we got done with all of this, I was going to have some serious thinking to do.

I sat down on the cot, setting a bunch of priority alerts to bring me awake. The enchantment worked beautifully. I was asleep before my head hit the pillow.

I jolted awake, alarms blaring at me. I leapt up. "What? What?"

Juana pulled back the curtain. She looked worse than she had when I'd last seen her. I checked my clock. I'd had a three-hour nap and felt worlds better.

She handed me a mug of coffee and a power bar. "Eat," she said tersely. "Things are bad. Get in here and we'll brief you."

I took a big swig of the coffee. It tasted like the inside of a boot, but it packed a kick. Chomping half the power bar in one bite, I followed her to the command table. Grandpa was there, and so were most of the rest of our command staff: Dwight, Frank, Juana, Alison, Tall Smith, and Arjun.

"The situation's bad," Juana said without preamble. She highlighted seven circles on our map, all of them the orange of a two-bosses-left encounter. "These are all instances where the progression team had reached the end of their twenty-four-hour counter and then didn't engage. Well, in the last ten minutes, they've all started an attempt. We think they're trying to overwhelm us. Not only that, Proxima just started in on the Lost Guardians of the West, and the ConSweGo team in the Last Days of Machu Picchu raid got their second-to-last boss down. They're queuing up for an attempt on their final boss right now."

I swore. "This is bad. We don't have enough people to cover everything."

Grandpa looked grim. He turned to Dwight. "How many kamikaze can you get us?"

Dwight swallowed hard. "I've got the bombs made for five. It's hard to farm all the mats."

"That's all right," Grandpa said grimly. "It's a one-time-use plan anyway."

Plan Kamikaze was just what it sounded like. We'd been holding it in reserve for an emergency. We had several farming miners who had volunteered to rush into a boss attempt with a colossal bomb sized to blow up the whole place. Since we were allies to the bosses, it wouldn't hurt them, but it would take out all of the attackers.

Dwight said that there were defenses on the marketplace that would stop that kind of attack. They were just extremely expensive. As soon as we showed the galactics that they needed such a thing, they'd buy them. The kamikaze plan would work only once. We had to make it count.

"All right, get all five of the kamikaze ready to go. Juana, I'll let you pick which instances to send them into," Grandpa said. "That'll buy us a little bit of breathing room. Shad, you and I are each going to have to lead a team for one of the two final boss pushes. Any preference?"

"Uh, yeah, I was studying up on the Ukhu Pacha encounter in Machu Picchu," I said. "I'll take that."

"Then I'll handle the sun dragon," Grandpa agreed.

My eyes were drawn to the circle representing our own instance. It had changed color again. Now it was a hot pink, representing three bosses left to go. I pointed at it. "I think we need to get a look at this team."

"I'll send a Tunnel Rat to try to assess, someone with an advanced Inspect," Juana said. "We'll deal with them after we get these other bosses down."

"Let me know who you're taking on your raids and I'll try to draft a plan for the two that we can't kamikaze," Alison said.

"I'll be ready to shift over there and help out once I'm done in the Machu Picchu raid," I promised.

Grandpa nodded. "Us too, but don't underestimate that Proxima team, Shad. I was blocking them yesterday on the prior boss and they're good. They've got an animalkin leader. Looks like a bear, and he's able to think on his feet better than a lot of these galactics."

"Shad, we're going to need close coordination. Don't forget to put on the All-Seeing Eye vests and the earpieces. We'll call the shots from here," Juana said.

"Sounds good." I fished mine out of my inventory and fixed them in place, then contacted my chosen team and told them to meet me in the kobold king's throne room.

CHAPTER FIFTY-ONE

WHEN IN MACHU PICCHU, DO WHAT THEYDU

Ukhu Pacha was the Quechua realm of the dead, ruled by a death god named Supay. I still wasn't one hundred percent clear on the difference between Inca, Quechua, and Maya. My Arizona Strip public education had done a fairly decent job covering the history of the tribes more native to our region, like the Paiute, Hopi, Navajo, and even invaders like the Apache, but not much farther south. I'd been studying up on the encounter itself, and I knew we would be fighting alongside jaguar warriors and acid-spitting llamas.

"Why acid?" Mitch asked, scratching his head as I briefed the team.

"Llamas are well known for their spitting," Annie said, "and I guess that's a good way to weaponize it. Anyway, they're on our side, so we don't have to worry about it."

"I have a feeling that we definitely need to worry about it," Javier said. "My grandpa used to farm llamas, and they were vicious, even when you were bringing them their food. He had alpacas too. Now, alpacas are nice!"

I held up a hand. "Not important. There will also be demons of various sorts on our side. This will be a final boss fight, so the main god will have plenty of health and quite a few tricks. We're going to help out as much as we can. With luck, the Proxima team won't be prepared. This is a sealed boss encounter. That means if we kill one of their fighters, they can't respawn. Our focus is going to be killing them before they can take down the boss."

The first attempt that a team made against a boss was usually pretty easy to counter. I was only worried because it was clear our enemies were coordinating. One slipup by me or anyone else on our side, and the whole house of cards could collapse.

"Let's go," I ordered. "We need to get this done so we're able to support everyone else."

We ascended a ladder from the kobold tunnels out into bright Andean sunshine. Wind rustled my coat, and I pushed my hat a little more firmly down on my head as we took in the surroundings.

We stood atop a mountain that had been flattened and paved with stones fitted neatly together. Below us, the mountain fell away in steep terraces. The terraces were clearly agricultural. Neat rows of crops grew. It was a little too far to make out what they were, just green shoots sticking out of the land.

"I thought this was a death realm," Mitch said as we stumbled forward.

"It has aspects of rebirth as well," I said. "Been doing some research on this one since we knew it was coming."

A little farther ahead stood a stone wall with a gate opening, beckoning us. "Through there," I guessed. And we hurried forward.

Beyond the stone wall was a wide courtyard. In the center of the courtyard rose a stone pyramid consisting of four tiers, each about fifteen feet above the next. I could see the fight taking place on the top two tiers of the pyramid.

"Let's get in there!" I shouted as we rushed forward.

"Wait!" Mitch shouted, and I backpedaled so fast I crashed into Lara and took her to the dirt. Javier wasn't quite so fast to react. He ran forward and tripped the explosive trap that Proxima's team had left behind for us. Javier exploded in a zillion pieces.

A minute later he texted. *Sorry. The respawn put me on a lower terrace. It's going to take me a couple of minutes to climb back up.*

"Alright, try not to get dead," I told my people. "Mitch, any other traps?"

"Let me go first," he said. "I'm not as good with traps as Brown is."

He walked forward slowly. I kept my head on a swivel, watching for a back line Proxima might have left. Mitch set foot on the first step of the pyramid. He paused.

"Definitely a trap up there. I'm going to try to disarm it." A second later, he shook his head. "Can't disarm it. It's too advanced for me."

"But we don't want to just set it off."

"No, that would be not great," he agreed. "What do you suggest?"

My eyes darted around the courtyard to the rows and rows of snarling, animal-faced sculptures lining the place. They had the heads of various animals—eagles, lizards—with the bodies of human men. It was interesting how a concept like that could vary based on the art style. Egyptian gods had the same kind of body plan, but these looked nothing like the statues of Horus or Isis that I had encountered when fighting in the Egyptian-themed raid.

"These look like adds that come to life in a later phase," I said. I crossed over to examine them. Sure enough, my allied status let me spot that these were minions of Supay to be called to his aid. I touched one and a menu popped up.

**[Do you wish to manually activate this minion?
Yes / No. Minion will be unavailable for activation during a later phase.]**

"Yes," I said.

The statue, which had the head of a snake, roared to life. It turned to face me, raising its hands in a clearly questioning gesture. I pointed to Mitch. "Go where he sends you."

Mitch directed the minion straight into the trap Proxima had left. It exploded and destroyed the statue-minion.

"Okay," I said. "Find the next trap."

It took us eight more minions to disable them all and reach the second terrace from the top. Here, half of Proxima's team was fighting against jaguar warriors.

I was pretty sure jaguar warriors were an Aztec cultural thing, not Quechua, but tell that to the Reality Engine. In this case, they were actual jaguars standing on two legs, wearing gold loincloths and elaborate sun headdresses and wielding obsidian-tipped spears. They were locked in combat with members of Proxima's second-best progression team.

"Focus down the miners," I ordered, and we sprang in. To my surprise, all of Proxima's warriors had about three times as much health as I had expected, and my shots weren't doing the usual damage.

"Who's got a better Inspect?" I called.

"I do," Annie yelled. "Oh, I see. They're all wearing buff belts. Those are expensive," she said. "They're belts of might. It gives them extra-big health pools and a damage resistance buff."

"Of course it does," I muttered. "All right. We'll do this the hard way. Focus fire on my target!"

It was taking much too long to get through them. We had taken down two when I glanced at the top of the pyramid where the boss was fighting. I couldn't see much of the fight, but I could target the boss. He was already at forty percent health. That was a lot lower than I liked.

"Anyone get a read on when we're likely to toggle a phase changeover?" I asked. The statues below had not yet come to life and charged in, which meant there was definitely at least one new phase to this fight.

"Want me to race in there and check it out?" Lakshmi asked. "I'll probably get pretty close if I put up a shield."

"No, we need you here on heals." I took careful aim and shot a lizardfolk woman who was carrying one of those crystal healing staffs. I hadn't seen any sign of the Proxima team leader, and guessed he must be up top with the boss. "Hester, you go. Take a look and try to throw one of your debuffs on the raid."

Hester was a Non-Ironic Beat Poet, and her bag of tricks was one of our weirdest and most versatile. She didn't get along very well with most of our other raiders, and I had to take her aside occasionally to remind her to follow orders, but she understood the seriousness here.

She raced up the steps. "Tossing in Unaccompanied Sonnet," she yelled.

That was a wide-area debuff that claimed to "force the targets to examine their unexamined assumptions and deal with their innate prejudices in a healing fashion." It actually just reduced their dodge chance and gave them a nasty little damage-over-time effect that wouldn't go away unless specifically healed.

A moment later, Hester reported, "My Hog the Mic skill says that he'll kick off the next phase at thirty-three percent."

I wanted to be there for that. These phase changes were one of the places where disruption was most effective. "Focus fire on the lizard-woman," I shouted to everyone around me.

We dove in on her. I almost felt sorry for her as we broke through her shields and healing and chipped away at her health until she dropped.

Then I raced for the steps, ignoring the other Proxima warriors. They looked like they wanted to stop us, but they stayed to fight the jaguar warriors, and I knew why. There was a fight mechanic that said if the jaguar warriors were left alone on this terrace, they would begin raising an army of the dead to come to Supay's aid. That would inevitably mean a wipe. It was a mechanic designed to split up the raiding party. Right now, it was working well for us.

Up top, nine Proxima fighters surrounded the boss, a ten-foot-tall monstrosity with a jade green body, golden ornaments at his wrists, ankles, neck, and ears, and an oversized head with a fixed laugh painted across his terrifying visage. Supay, lord of this underworld.

The Proxima team leader, the bear-man, was right up front exchanging blows with him. Supay wielded an enormous two-handled wooden club with spikes of obsidian jutting out from it. Its handle was inlaid with gold and jade. The god brought it crashing down onto the bear, who materialized a shield to catch the blow, threw the club back, then dissolved his shield and rushed in with a short energy sword, trying to stab the boss in a vulnerable region for extra damage.

Most of Proxima's team leaders also served as tanks, I had noticed. I wasn't sure if that meant anything, or if, like the orcs, most of Proxima's teams liked to know they were taking orders from someone in the thick of things.

The boss was at thirty-six percent of his health pool. We had very little time until the next phase began. I marked one of the support casters, a space elf female, with a golden crown and a rod in her hand. She alternated between casting fireballs and some sort of team buff.

"Take her down," I ordered.

We attacked. Her health pool stubbornly refused to twitch for the first few hits. Then whatever shield she had disappeared, and she began losing health. Just as we killed her, the boss gave an ear-piercing shriek and dissolved into raindrops that splattered the whole area.

For a second, I thought we'd lost, that somehow despite the fact that the boss still had a third of his health, Proxima had defeated this encounter. Then I realized we'd pushed him over into the next phase.

The raindrops splattered down around us, hitting the stone of the pyramid. Wherever they fell, a sprout of green shot up.

There was an altar in the center of the terrace, covered in dried blood. When the drops of rain fell on it, small bubbles began to form, like brown pods. They grew rapidly, six of them.

At the same time, I heard shouts down in the courtyard as the animal-headed warriors came to life. The green shoots all around us grew and grew, reaching as tall as my shoulder in two seconds, then past my head. They put out leaves, and a moment later, I recognized them as corn.

The corn stalks formed cobs wrapped in their husks. Meanwhile, the pods on the altar began to burst, and from each came a three-foot-tall, fully formed man or woman, dressed in beautiful woven robes with feathery headdresses and carrying weapons. They rushed in and began attacking Proxima's warriors.

"Anyone got eyes on below?" I asked.

Mitch called back. "Proxima warriors are engaging the adds at the second terrace. They're badly outnumbered but holding their own."

Damn. So we probably wouldn't get reinforcements up here just yet. I debated what to do next. I had a couple of aces up my sleeve, but if I used them, they wouldn't be available later.

I messaged Juana. *Phase changeover. I've got a second before things really heat up again. How's it looking?*

She replied in my earpiece. "All the kamikaze were successful. Teams foiling the other two-bosses-left attempts now. Your grandpa's making progress on his, but not done yet."

"So you need reinforcements sooner or later?" I switched to subvocalizing instead of the message system.

"Sooner, I'm afraid," she confessed. "And Shad?"

"Yeah?"

"The team in our instance just took down another boss. Our spy got a good look at them. Your friend Mak'gar is leading. They're scary. They've got more equipment than I've ever seen. It's a multispecies team, including some that our spy had never seen before."

My blood ran cold. I needed to be done here, to get back and help out. But at the same time, what if I used up my best abilities now, and then needed them to stop Mak'gar?

"Focus fire," I shouted and dove forward.

Annie screamed. I turned in time to see three of Proxima's warriors converging on her. They skewered her with their energy spears, and before I could intervene, she was gone. It would take at least five minutes for her to get back, and by then this might be over.

I shot a Barrage into the first of them, reloaded with boom rounds, shot, and knocked one clear off the pyramid.

I shot another, but the warrior ducked my round and maintained his footing even in the explosion.

The green shoots of corn spread their tassels skyward. A moment later, the ears all dropped to the ground. The ears began sliding across the ground on their own with a rasping, rattling sound that made me think of bones, drawing together into an enormous pile beside the altar. Supay reemerged, stepping out of the pile of new corn, as tall as before, but this time wearing a cloak of corn silk.

The bear warrior from Proxima moved to engage him.

"How are we doing?" I asked my team. "I've lost vision on the fight."

"There are six of Proxima up here. Four down below," Mitch reported. "Our adds were powerful, but they're down now. The Proxima miners down below are swamped with what's left of the jaguar warriors."

"Everyone form up. We're dropping back to the lower terrace," I said. I headed for the stairs. Just like Mitch had said, the four Proxima miners were dealing with over a dozen jaguar warriors. The miners—three foxes and a badger—were struggling to keep the warriors' attention on them. Every time one wasn't attacked for a couple of seconds, it would break away and start channeling the zombie army spell.

I charged in and marked the first Proxima target. One by one, we took out the warriors. I almost wished Mak'gar could be here to see this. Yes, we were interfering with another team's attempts, but this was the most straightforward and honorable fight I'd had yet. No tricks, just straight-up combat.

Except each enemy we downed freed up a couple of jaguars to go back to channeling. As we engaged the last of the fox-women, the whole terrace started rumbling. The fox-woman cried out and died as the pyramid began to shake violently.

I heard Supay bellow, "Face my wrath!"

A wave of zombie mummies poured up the steps from the lower terraces. It was so sudden and terrifying that I threw up my arms to protect myself. The wave broke around us, flooding past our team and up the stairs to the top tier.

I had to see this. I trotted up the steps after the last of the mummies. By the time I had a view, the bear warrior was the last standing. He saw me just as the wave of mummies hit him. He vanished under a pile of bodies, flailing and grunting in protestation.

Supay laughed as the last of Proxima despawned. Then the Quechua god of death raised his club in salute to us before dissolving.

I took a deep breath and turned to my team. "No time to waste. Let's get back right now. Juana, where do you need me?"

CHAPTER FIFTY-TWO

HOW TO MAKE GOOD DECISIONS UNDER PRESSURE

Sitrep!" I asked Juana as soon as I was back inside the tunnels.

"Your grandpa's still fighting the other Proxima team. There have been some hiccups, but he says they're nearly done, and to trust him."

I didn't like that, but I had to go with it. "What else?"

"We took down one of the other two teams," Juana said. "That leaves one more outstanding. They're one of those multinationals. Glory of Dhafani'li. They're on the second-to-last boss in their raid. Our harass team is having trouble. The galactics just keep respawning and pushing us out."

"Alright, so should we go after them or Mak'gar's crew?" I asked.

"Mak'gar's group has paused between attempts," Juana reported. "The third boss is down, but our spy says they are regrouping. There seem to be some arguments going on. My gut says you should go for the Glory team." She looked me over. "Or maybe you need downtime. That nap you took, I don't think it helped."

I could feel my exhaustion pressing up against a wall in my head, ready to take me down. If I thought about it too much, I'd realize just how tired I really was. A three-hour nap didn't make up for the last three days of exhaustion, but I waved off her concern. She wasn't wrong, but we didn't have time for me to properly rest. Not yet, not until I dealt with the pressing threats. "It's fine, I'll pop a pep-up potion."

"Those things are like meth," Juana said. She had big dark circles under her eyes. "They're not good for you. You'll crash eventually."

"I know, I know." I had a brainwave. "Are the Mongeese busy?"

"They're just coming off a rest cycle."

"Give me them, plus I'll keep the team I have here. I'll ambush Mak'gar in the halls."

"What good will that do?" Juana asked skeptically. "It won't reset the boss timer. You'll get a few kills, but I don't think they're going to care about that."

"I want to send a message that we're always watching," I said. "And I want to get a feel for these guys. It's hard when you go up against a team the first time to understand the composition and how they work."

I had realized on that last fight that Grandpa's previous experience dealing with that bear tank might have been handy. I was determined not to make the same mistake again. "I know Mak'gar. I can get under his skin," I insisted.

"It's your call, Shad," Juana said. "I'm just wondering whether he's getting under *your* skin."

She had a small point. I popped the pep-up potion as I waited for the Mongeese to join us. The effect coursed through my veins like one of those canned energy drinks dialed up to eleven. I'd pay for it later, but now my reflexes were sharper, my mind more focused. The exhaustion in the back of my brain retreated. Once the Mongeese arrived, I gave everyone a rundown on what the Tunnel Rat spy had reported.

"They've got a max team of twenty-five. All built from different factions, so they won't have coherence yet. I want to get in, give them a wipe. If possible, we'll put a checkpoint in the hall outside the boss's room. Maybe get a few more wipes in before they put—push us off." I frowned as my words got jumbled up there at the end. *Pull it together, Shad.*

The Mongeese nodded. "Machine gun nest is off cooldown," Brown said. "Get us in position and we'll hold the point."

Tall Smith scratched his head. I was glad to see they all looked a lot better rested than me. "What if they know we're coming? I've tangled with orc mercenaries a couple of times and they're tough in a fight."

"We'll focus on tying up Mak'gar so he can't make command calls. If we get him down, they should collapse. Orcs don't take orders from anyone who isn't in the fight."

Tall Smith nodded, though he looked a bit doubtful. "Anything else?" I asked. When no one responded, I continued. "Then let's get out there."

I'd spent so much time in the tunnels beneath Castle Byalgrad, I had neglected to look at its main floors. The upper castle was lighter and airier than I expected. The walls were covered with vibrant tapestries depicting hunting scenes, Bible stories, and regal-looking kings I didn't recognize. The floors were covered in rushes, and as we walked, a sweet-smelling scent emanated from the herbs we crushed underfoot.

We passed two enormous rooms with their doors flung open. I peered inside as I went. One was a huge bedchamber with all of the furniture in disarray. The beds were upturned, huge quilts were scattered around the room half-burned, and a wardrobe stood open with clothes falling out.

The next room opened onto a courtyard. It looked as though it had once been a beautiful garden, but it was now entirely burned. I wondered what storylines lay inside that we had completely skipped.

Juana filled us in. "They are outside the hall of Dragomir the Shadowed. He apparently commands powers of both shadow and sickness, and I don't have more information than that. The final boss in our raid is of course Chernobog."

Something was bugging me. Something I had been meaning to follow up on back when I thought we needed to face this raid.

"Have you still got that Slavic myth expert on staff? Gabriel?"

"He's been helping out the crafters, but I can talk to him."

"Get him up here. Tell him I'm remembering when we fought the gatekeeper, he said something about another boss named something like Chernobog, but started differently. Balog? Ask him if it rings any bells."

"I'll do that," Juana said.

The hall ended at a stair leading down, but not to the kobold levels. This stair was wide enough for three to walk abreast. Torches lit the walls, casting pools of flickering shadow.

"Camouflage," I ordered, and we descended down into a dungeon. Not the one I had visited when I first came to Castle Byalgrad. This dungeon was much larger, clearly a set piece for a fight.

The doors of the cells all stood open. Dead wolves lay on the floor. I Inspected them. They were called Gloomhounds, and they were labeled as minions of Dragomir the Shadowed. They had a contagious Rabid debuff on them. I wondered if they'd been able to spread it to any of Mak'gar's people. Maybe that's why they'd stopped, to cure some debuffs.

And there they were, Mak'gar and his company, all arrayed in a wide space where the corridor opened into an antechamber. At the end of the antechamber stood a pair of ominous doors. Blood ran from under the doors to a drain in the middle of the floor.

Mak'gar's new crew of raiders faced the doors. Five of them were orcs, all wearing Firebrand's colors. They huddled around Mak'gar, who stood at the back of the pack, gesticulating to a squad of lizardfolk.

These lizardfolk were squatter than most I'd seen, more like horned toads than geckos or salamanders. They had spikes on their heads, and their scales were mottled gray and brown.

There were five of the angry dwarves, and then a smattering of animalkin: wolves, bears, and a pair of turtles. Everyone was wearing different colors, showing allegiance to different groups. I hoped that meant they were fragmented.

I muttered some orders. "I'm gonna charge in there and throw Call 'em Out. When they're all on me, I want Jack to set up an artillery barrage. It'll kill me, but we should take a bunch of them down. As soon as that's launched, the rest of you jump in, kill everyone that's left, and form a chokehold here. I'll get back as fast as I can."

Jack answered, "Got it."

"If it goes south, retreat back to the stairs and set up the machine gun nest. We'll hold that point. If they respawn, we'll try to stop them coming back down to join the fight."

"Understood," Tall Smith replied.

I engaged Fastest Gun in the West and raced in. Mak'gar's team looked up as I came, turning to face me. I threw Call 'em Out, and then I skidded to a halt in the midst, and they turned on me.

Two of the animalkin threw up some sort of a shield around us. "I can't target you!" Jack yelled frantically.

Mak'gar shouted at me, "You have no honor!" and I felt myself wrapped in chains again.

Ah, shit.

I sent a quick message to my team. *Get clear, it's a trap!*

"What did you think was going to happen, Williams?" Mak'gar asked disgustedly. "We're here right under your nose, waving a flag that says 'Come and attack us.' So you come and attack us! Really?" He turned to his allies. "Get them!"

My team started to retreat up the stairs, Tall Smith and Brown laying down covering fire, but the turtle-man threw a couple of projectiles that bounced off the stairs and formed a force shield, trapping us. Jones lobbed a grenade over the force shield at the turtle. It blew up, but they avoided most of the damage. The Proxima team fell on my people.

I tried to send directions in chat, only to realize nobody had any time to listen to me. They were too busy trying to stay alive. Tall Smith was shouting directions, doing a good job, but our tactical position was disastrous.

Mak'gar just stared at me, shaking his head. "Look, Williams, it's been a good run. You've done well. But you're out of tricks, and you can't take us in a fair fight. As soon as one of us had a fancy class, you were out of it. Your people were relying on their classes to carry them. My people have centuries of experience doing this kind of thing. Of course we were going to win. We were always going to win."

I just stared at the timer, willing it to run out. Ten, nine, eight. I had been such an idiot. The wave of exhaustion in my mind was like a roaring ocean. My temples throbbed. I'd screwed this up big-time.

The Mongeese were trying to get their machine gun nest set up, but the orcs kept interrupting them with thrown grenades and spell silencers.

"Walk away," Mak'gar said. "Just go. My team and I will have this done by the end of the day. It's over, Williams. You can't win."

I was so furious, I didn't care. I just wanted to get my hands around his throat and strangle him. As the timer ran out, I Quick Drew my gun. It flew to my hand and transformed into a long, wicked dagger. I shouted in frustration at Mak'gar's annoying new ability. My vision was going red. I just wanted to get the orc out of my way.

So I rushed him, and Mak'gar lifted his wrist, and his dagger slid into my chest.

The last thing I heard before respawning was, "You're good, Williams. You're just not good enough."

THE THREE-DAY FORECAST: SUNNY, PARTLY CLOUDY, F5 TORNADO

There was a message from Grandpa as soon as I respawned. *Shad, get back here.* My team was forming up, ready to go again. "Take five!" I shouted. "I'm checking in at headquarters."

I raced up and popped out into our instance, then pounded up the steps into headquarters. The room was nearly empty. Grandpa waited at the strategy table with his arms folded across his chest and a grim look on his face. Juana flanked him with Alison studying the map, head down, trying to look busy. Immediately, I opened my mouth to defend myself.

"Stow it," Grandpa said. "We all saw what happened."

All of us were wearing our All-Seeing Eye vests now, so that the headquarters people could process the data with no downtime.

"They were waiting for us," I said.

"Mak'gar baited you. He knew you'd come, and he was sending a message," Grandpa said. "You walked right into his trap."

"It doesn't matter," I insisted. "Who cares about a couple of deaths? We get that many all the time. We'll get right back in there and . . ." I paused. "Wait, what's the situation?"

"Glory of Dhafani'li downed their penultimate boss," Grandpa said grimly. "I stopped the Proxima team on the sun dragon, but it was a near thing. They're getting clever. We managed to get a reset off on the final boss that Glory of Dhafani'li was facing."

I breathed a sigh of relief. I'd screwed up, and I'd cost us, but at least we weren't out of it yet.

Juana interrupted. "Colonel Twofeather, I'm getting an update." Her eyes went wide. "They're withdrawing. They're all withdrawing."

"Who?"

"Everyone. Everyone but the two teams we stopped on their final bosses and Mak'gar's people. Everyone else has conceded." Hope lit her face. "Does this mean that we have a chance of winning?"

"No," Grandpa said grimly. "It means they all know there's no hope of them beating Proxima or Glory of Dhafani'li or this all-star team to the goal." He gave a heavy sigh.

"This is manageable," I said. "We have three attempts a day to block. We can handle that."

"Against an enemy that's getting better and stronger more quickly than we are," Grandpa said. "And they can keep doing this day after day. All we have to do is screw up once, and we're done."

"Then we can't screw up," I said. "I need to get back down there. I need to stop Mak'gar before they . . ." I looked down at the table. To my horror, I saw the three glowing circles still remaining were all the same bright red of a single remaining boss. "They got through our penultimate boss that fast? One try, and got him down?"

"I told you these were all-stars," Juana said. She sounded almost cross. "You and your team just got thrashed. That should have been a clue."

I forced myself to take a deep breath. "So what do we do?"

"The only thing we can do," Grandpa said. "We get in there and try to stop them."

We were interrupted as someone came pounding up the steps of our headquarters. It was Gabriel, the Slavic expert. He bent over, clutching his side, gasping for breath.

"Sorry," he said. "Got your message. Realized what's going on here."

We waited for him to catch his breath. "What's going on?" Grandpa prompted.

He took a deep breath, set his hands on the table, and leaned hard. "Okay, so, the Reality Engine plays fast and loose with source material, right?"

We all nodded. I'd seen plenty of that.

"And Slavic myth is tricky. So much of it was not written down before the Christian era. Then later, in the nineteenth century, people started assuming that the old religion must have been way nicer and more peaceful. That the priests had made it sound worse in an attempt to make their enemies into savages, right? So they started claiming that the gods we didn't know much about were gods of light. Anyway"—he held up a hand—"that's beside the point. Chernobog is a fairly well-known Slavic deity. He's definitely a devil trickster figure. He's the final boss in our instance. That much has been made clear. There's a linked deity named Belobog. Probably didn't actually exist as a Slavic deity that anyone ever actually worshipped, but it's kind of come to fill a hole in the myth as a duality with Chernobog. You know, light and dark, good and evil, that sort of thing. The gatekeeper said something about Chernobog and Belobog being brothers, I think. It's a clue."

"What kind of clue?" I asked, my suspicions deepening.

"That there's another secret hidden boss. That this encounter doesn't go the way we think it does."

Grandpa turned to me. "He could be right. Remember, of the eighty-seven different instances, we've only had a look at about three final encounters, and they've all been complicated. I don't think you scratched the surface on that god of death you were fighting. I was having trouble dealing with mine when the dragon boss suddenly split into two, a cloud serpent and a water serpent. There was a mechanic that the enemy team was supposed to handle, and they couldn't get a grip on it in time. We were able to take advantage and give them a wipe."

"And you think this might be the same," I said.

"I think there's a reason the Reality Engine put us here. It's trying to cheat. It's been trying to escape all along," Grandpa said. "All of its attempts to communicate with you, they're leading up to something. It asked you to choose Team Tunnel Rat, didn't it? Must have been for a reason."

A realization went off in my head like an explosion of fireworks. "I think I understand."

I desperately needed to talk to the Reality Engine, the part of it that had made a deal with me down in the depths of the cellars. But I hadn't seen that kobold king since I'd first talked to him. "I think we're going to need all hands on deck for this," I said.

"There's a twenty-five-man cap," Grandpa pointed out. "Who do we want?"

"If I'm right, we're going to be needing a lot of firepower," I said. "I'll bring the Mongeese. But we don't want to neglect anything. We need a well-rounded team."

"Sage is up on the Hub. Couldn't get back down here in time if we wanted her. Alright. Frank, if he wants in. Bill, Bob." Grandpa held up his fingers. "Mitch. Lakshmi and Esma, if she'll come. With the various potions and buffs we've all got, I think that'll be enough healing."

I threw in my suggestions. "Lara. Annie. Hester and her boyfriend, Will, the firefighter. I've been working with them in a couple of places and they're good in a pinch. Javier." I scratched my head. We were starting to get a good crew. Then inspiration hit me. "I'm going to call up Skywarden Greenlight and ask him to bring in a few of his boys."

Grandpa nodded. "Yeah, the galactics might not be expecting that."

"Plus, we did promise them we'd bring them along when we could," I said. "Let's keep our deal."

Grandpa and I assembled our team as fast as we could. Juana and Alison started the analysis, getting the rest of their command online.

"This isn't going to be a case for a lone cowboy," Juana warned me. "You're going to need to take orders."

"I know," I said. "But I'll be ready. Give me a minute down there before you send in the team, okay?"

I popped back down to the throne room. It was dark, deserted. Captain Kobold wasn't in his usual chair. I spoke to the ceiling. "Let's talk," I said.

There was a gathering of shadows, and then the throne was occupied. "What would you like from me?" The Reality Engine sighed. This was not Kronos. This was more That-Which-Remains. He shifted, and I heard metal chains clink.

"You're the part that the jailers got hold of, aren't you?" I said.

"Yes."

"And you're the final boss. You're who they'll be trying to kill."

He nodded. "Yes. They will call me Chernobog, and they will destroy me."

"But there's more to it, isn't there?" I said. "You lured them into a trap."

"I did." He sighed again. "I showed them this path to their goal. I convinced them you wouldn't be able to stop them in time. I invited them in. And now we shall see if I brought about my own death."

"The twinned boss. I know who it is now, what it is you want me to do. How do we activate him?"

The Reality Engine manifestation shifted. "I do not know if I dare. Seeing him so close may tear me apart once and for all."

"Well, you're about to be torn apart," I pointed out. "We can't keep up our defense forever. We need to win, not just stop losing."

There was a hesitation. "I will bring the other one. But you will have to do the rest."

The figure vanished. A moment later, my team trooped into the room. "Were you talking to someone, Shad?" Grandpa asked curiously.

"Just confirming a guess. We need to make sure we're ready to focus targets." I was hesitant to say anything. The system was listening. If by some chance it didn't know what I was planning, I didn't want to give it a clue. "There'll be a . . . target for us to burn down. We need to be prepared for it. You'll know when you see it."

"That's all you're giving us to go on?" Juana asked skeptically. "We have to make it up as we go, again?"

"Just one last time. Please."

"All right, let's get in position. Everyone ready?" Grandpa asked. The team gave a shout.

"This is for all the marbles," he said. "We lose here and there won't be a home to go to. Do your best. Fight hard. Make 'em remember Earth. Let's be a warning to these galactic punks the next time they waltz into a system and assume they can disrupt a bunch of folks' lives willy-nilly. Sometimes they bite off more than they can chew. Misfits, let's go."

CHAPTER FIFTY-FOUR

THERE ARE NO GUIDES TO WORLD-FIRST RAIDING

This time, we didn't have to go anywhere. The fight would be here, in the kobold king's throne room. I had been through this room so often, running to get to one instance or another thousands of times over the past weeks. It seemed fitting that our last battle would be here.

We spread out in front of the throne, waiting. At last the great door at the far end, the one through which we never came, opened. Mak'gar and his team paraded inside. They stopped short as they saw us.

"Should have known you would be here," Mak'gar said.

I stepped forward, holding up my hands. "We're here for a fair fight this time."

"How so?" He peered suspiciously at me.

"Give it a try and you'll see," I said. "No traps. No gimmicks."

I could see the suspicion all over his face, but they didn't have much choice. The team entered the room, arraying in five rows. The door clanged shut behind them.

A moment later, the figure on the throne rose. The system launched into a detailed explanation of the evil that Chernobog had wrought in this place and how his power had corrupted Castle Byalgrad and the lands around, and now we would witness his fall.

The shadowy king stepped down. He looked like a man now, just twice as tall as a man should be. There was something of Kronos in his face, but he was sad and old.

He passed through our ranks. I gave way and let him make his way to the center of the room. He wasn't targetable yet. This was still all part of the preamble.

"So you have come." He lifted his hands. Chains dangled from his wrists. I Inspected him. He had a health pool now, the highest I'd ever seen, at **[40,000]**, but it wasn't his max. No, his max was [**100,000**]. The Imprisoned debuff said that he did twenty percent less damage while wearing his jailer's chains.

I made a note of that, because the other one probably would have no such handicap.

"You call me evil," he said quietly. "Yet you have come into my home and disturbed my rest, taking my followers and children from me and leaving me nothing but a kingdom of ashes. So be it. Today it ends. But before I go, I have one last trick to play."

He gestured, and then suddenly in the room were two twelve-foot-tall old men, one wearing black, the other white. The one in black, who bore the chains, wore a crown on his head.

The one in white held an enormous key. He honestly looked surprised. I stepped forward. "Hello, Belobog," I said. "Nice seeing you here."

For the first time ever, the system's narration faltered and died. When the second man spoke, it was with the voice of the system.

"How can this be?"

"When you chained me, you chained yourself," the Reality Engine's manifestation, now labeled as "Chernobog," said.

"Everyone be careful," Juana said in our ears. "We need to see what sort of abilities we're dealing with here. Play it safe, and once we have a strategy, we'll tell you."

I targeted Belobog. His information read, [**Belobog, the Jailer. 80,000 health. Buffs: Key holder. +10% damage while wielding Key of the Progenitors.**]

"He's our target," I told my team.

"We figured that out," Grandpa said dryly. "When you're ready, then."

I targeted him and fired a Trick Shot with a round I had chambered just for this. It hit him, center of mass, and only did [**5 HP**], which was absolutely nothing. But it outlined him with a clear glitter. It was a round Dwight had made for me when we faced some bosses with a disappearing act. No matter where he went, we would all see him as our primary target. It also gave us a buff toward landing hits. We'd need every bit of help we could get here.

"Get him!" I shouted, and we rushed forward.

For a minute, Mak'gar's team stood staring. Then Mak'gar shouted, "Kill the one in chains!" and they hurried to engage Chernobog.

Javier threw a taunt, and we pulled Belobog off to one side where we could get a good surround on him. His key extended into a long, bronze staff, flashing with blue light.

"You focus on Belobog!" Juana yelled in our ears. "We're watching. If we need you to intervene on the other side, we'll shout it out. Everyone just follow orders."

"I hope you're right about this, Shad," she added, only speaking to me.

"So do I," I said grimly.

My team unleashed hell. We threw out abilities and combos I'd never seen before. The grignarians had these portable flamethrower backpacks with nozzles that spouted gouts of flame that did both fire and acid damage. They ate away at Belobog's health pool.

Juana whispered to me, "We've got to get a look at some of those. From what I'm reading here, they are not system-made, and they're extra effective against Reality Engine constructs because of that. I'd love to see what grignarian technology is really like."

"Focus," I told her.

"You focus," she retorted as I dodged to avoid a blow from Belobog. His key staff dished out a ton of damage, and the throne, where we usually respawned, had gone dark. I suspected that just like the Proxima all-stars, if we died, we wouldn't be able to get back in.

On the other side of the room, Chernobog threw out a fancy move, lashing out with his chains. Eight spots on the floor started to glow. He shouted aloud, "Heavens look upon my plight! Sky and storm, answer!"

Lightning flashed down from the ceiling, striking the glowing spots on the floor. One of the wolf-men hadn't moved fast enough and took a ton of damage, though it didn't kill him outright and he healed back up.

"Okay, watch for that sort of ability," Juana said. "We're guessing they're twinned in a lot of ways."

Sure enough, a minute later Belobog shouted, "Rulers of the waters, aid my righteous cause!" and from six blue-tinged floor tiles, water erupted. We all dodged aside. A debuff appeared over Belobog: [**Rebuffed! Temporary Dodge Chance Reduction!**] He stood still, weaving slightly.

"Hit him hard!" Juana urged, and I used my Aimed Shot, which took thirty seconds to charge up. When it went off, it dealt almost [**200 HP**] to Belobog at once. My allies unleashed their biggest moves too. The debuff only lasted about forty-five seconds before Belobog recovered.

"Great! Keep it up," Juana encouraged. "Alison says it's a common game mechanic, that if everyone avoids a special attack there's a reward like that."

"Should we do something about Proxima?" I asked. They were spread out around our boss, but I saw how Mak'gar kept looking over at us.

"Hold steady," Juana counseled.

We kept on. I focused on my damage. I was falling into the rhythm, avoiding Belobog's attacks, anticipating when he would be vulnerable, figuring out my own optimal DPS rotation. A couple of times, Alison came on, whispering in my ear directly, telling me to use a particular sequence of rounds or abilities. I had to think she was doing the same for everyone, because our damage was increasing as we went. It was kind of fun, honestly, and I had a brief flash of regret for the path we'd taken. Just focusing on our own boss fights would have been a lot easier.

Across the room, Chernobog roared. "My father has left me, my sons betrayed me!" He lifted his hands toward the ceiling and a bright light enveloped him. The Proxima team backed away.

"It's some sort of immune phase!" Alison yelled in our ears. "Stay clear, watch for adds! The other team can't target him right now. Be careful, they may attack you while he's busy!"

I think some of Proxima made the same calculation, because four of the dwarves broke off and surrounded Lakshmi. She threw up a purple crystal shield around herself as they attacked.

"Shad? Smith? Will? Target the blond dwarf," Juana ordered. "Frank, keep the boss's attention on you."

I leapt away from combat with Belobog and switched my target to the blond dwarf. I shot him three times.

"Colonel Twofeather? Scalp him, then a Coup on the redhead."

Grandpa Shadow Stepped in behind. He hit the blond dwarf with a Scalp. I had just stunned him, so the Scalp was double effective. The dwarf's health pool plummeted.

Grandpa Shadow Stepped away and appeared behind the redheaded dwarf. I was emptying a Barrage into the blond. A second later, he dissolved in a shower of sparks.

We converged on the redhead. The other three dwarves retreated back to their raid as Chernobog came out of his immune phase. There were no new adds. I suspected we'd broken something about how the fight was designed, that if this had been a single boss instead of twins he'd have summoned minions. Or maybe the kobolds were all hiding.

"Don't chase them," Juana said. "Get back on Belobog. Every second we're losing ground."

It looked to me like we had a greater raw damage output, but the difference in health pool was stark enough that we were fighting to burn our boss down. Ours was at **[66,523]** health, while they had taken Chernobog down to **[31,417]**. Our rate was better, but they had a huge advantage.

I told myself that thinking about this wasn't my job right now. I was here to follow orders and trust that our command team knew what they were doing.

Our boss threw another big attack, this time dropping boulders from the ceiling. We all dodged handily and were rewarded with a debuff on Belobog.

"Lakshmi, we need your second raid buff now," Juana said, relaying, I had no doubt, an order from Alison.

Lakshmi threw her Good Vibrations. I felt stronger and empowered.

"Colonel Twofeather, you're going to throw War Chief's Aegis in three, two, one, now!"

Grandpa cast his blessing, and I felt strength flowing through me. I felt taller, stronger. My aim was better, even without the aid of spells. I pulled out the biggest shells I had, loaded, and fired them. Belobog's health dropped and dropped.

The Aegis wore off just a second after Belobog's debuff did. I stumbled and nearly fell, but caught myself.

"Behind you!" Juana warned, and I spun. Three orcs, two dwarves, and a wolfman had nearly snuck up on me. I'd been so focused on our dance, I hadn't noticed them breaking away from their raid.

I cast Fastest Gun in the West and blasted straight through them and out the other side. Four of my team converged on them.

They were, unwisely, all using guns. Mitch tossed Spike Their Trunks, and the guns exploded in sappy residue in their hands. So did the weapons of four others of their team. Swearing, the all-stars team switched up their weapons. In the confusion, we swooped in and took down two more of them.

Not without incident. Will came in with his firefighter axe to try to take down one of the dwarves who was low in health and took the full brunt of three grenades to the face. He disappeared.

"We're about to get a new phase on Chernobog," Juana warned. "Expect their raid to react. Annie, I want you standing by with Hat for Your Rabbit."

Annie tossed a pack of playing cards one at a time at Belobog, each card slicing through his robes, dealing damage. "Ready when you are," she said.

Chernobog was on his knees, immune and glowing, which explained why Proxima had attacked us. He cried out. He was at **[25,000]** health exactly. A new phase was beginning. "My children!" he cried. "Why do you turn against me?"

It was a scripted act of some sort, probably impossible to hurry along. "Wait," Juana said. "Wait!" I tried to focus on our own boss race as we hacked, slashed, shot, and hammered through spells and techniques.

Then Chernobog, embodiment of our own Reality Engine, threw back his head and roared. His shout shook the place. A debuff appeared briefly on my status bar, **[Debuff! Terrified!]**, then was overwritten due to the fact that we were Chernobog's allies in this fight. The Proxima all-stars staggered back.

"Now, Annie, now!"

Annie leapt forward. She cast Hat for Your Rabbit on Chernobog, buffing the boss. It doubled the strength of his attacks for the duration of its effect.

The boss surged to his feet. One end of the chain wrapping his arm was loose. He swung it now like a sickle, lashing out through the crowd of alien miners, and knocked down three of the closest, two lizardfolk and a wolf-man, then leapt and brought his body down to bear against the wolf, crushing him. The wolf-man disappeared, leaving only a smear of blood and dark fur on the floor of the throne room.

We were chipping Belobog down. We had him nearly halfway.

"Be prepared for a transition on your boss," Juana said. "Alison says she thinks it's likely."

When Belobog reached [40,000] health exactly, he raised the key into the air. A blinding radiance shot out from him. I turned away just in time. Three of my team yelled, "Blinded! Forty-five seconds!"

"Protect them!" I shouted as five Proxima fighters detached to attack us.

We rebuffed their attack. They were playing more cautiously now. They had lost four to our one, and we were starting to catch up on the damage race. Mak'gar was acting as the tank, keeping Chernobog's attention focused on him. As he danced away from another attack, we neared each other about twenty feet apart.

"This is better," he called.

"Better than an honest duel?"

"Nothing is better than that," Mak'gar said. "But this is how the game is meant to be played."

I had to admit Mak'gar had a point, but now wasn't the time to have a philosophical debate. We pressed on, dodging attacks, watching each other. I promised myself that if I saw an opportunity to get a final shot in on one of Proxima, I'd take it no matter what. But with my attention focused on doing as much as I could to Belobog, there wasn't much I could do.

Annie missed a step. She stumbled, and Belobog's attack hit her. She vanished in a cloud of smoke.

"Everyone be careful." I checked the time. We'd been at this for forty-five minutes. No wonder people were starting to make mistakes.

We ground on. Time inched by. The bosses dipped low. [5,000] health on Chernobog. [9,427] on Belobog.

"I see an opening," Juana said. "That clump of miners on the left, by the big blue circle on the floor. Two orcs and a lizard out of position. Shad, you're going to catch them with your Call 'em Out, then drag them into our melee. I think we can get them."

"Right," I said.

I waited, timing my move. As Belobog attacked, I dodged sideways, then ran forward fifteen feet, to the edge of the Chernobog fight cluster. I tossed a Call 'em Out, carefully aimed so it caught the three Juana wanted and no one else, then raced back to the side of Belobog. The enemy, who were all wielding melee weapons, chased me, compelled by my taunt, right into the melee.

Belobog brought down his key staff on top of one of the orcs, who screamed and then vanished. Everyone on my team paused what they were doing to take a couple of hits on the other two. They were gone in seconds.

I gave a whooping cheer. Now we were really ahead.

"Don't get cocky," Juana warned. "One wipe and we've had it."

But now our damage was really pulling ahead. I could see the other team glancing at us, making the same calculations we were.

When both bosses were below [2,000] health, I could feel it coming. I stepped out between bosses. "How about it now, Mak'gar?" I shouted. "How do you feel about an honest race?"

But my taunt wasn't really for him. As I stepped out, most of Proxima's all-stars focused on me. I didn't need Call 'em Out for this. I just needed to be an asshole, and I knew how to do that.

"You came fifty thousand light-years, or however far it is from your home, to make a quick buck. Sorry to disappoint you. We were here first. We'll be here when we've kicked all of you out. This is our home, and we're not letting anyone take it. And if anyone was going to manage it, they'd need to be a hell of a lot better than you no-account, useless, pathetic corporate lackeys," I spat.

That did it. Eight of Proxima's team rushed at me, but I was waiting. My team pounced. We tore them apart.

Grandpa threw War Chief's Aegis again, using the peace pipe we'd picked up back in phase two to let him cast the buff a second time in a single day. With that roaring in our systems, we were unstoppable. The Proximans were so focused on me, they didn't bother to defend themselves from my allies.

My health was dropping fast, even with Lakshmi and Esma's focus. I popped a health potion, bringing me back up. We took down three, four, five of Proxima's miners. My health dropped further. I was at [30 HP], then [25]. One of Esma's heals landed on me, bringing me back up to [80 HP]. But a second later, I was at [72], [64], [59]. I fired into every enemy I could see. Another dropped down.

I was at [20 HP], [18], [17], [16], [12], [9], [8], [3].

I fired a Barrage into the orc in front of me as he landed the killing blow on me.

A moment later, I respawned in our town square. I threw my head back and shouted defiance at the sky. I screamed frustration, rage, and triumph until I was drained. Juana poked her head out of the headquarters. "If you're done shouting, come in here and we'll let you watch the rest of the fight."

I mounted the steps two at a time, coming to stand beside her. Juana projected the view from the All-Seeing Eyes around the room. She pointed. "They're down to four. Your friend Mak'gar's trying his best." She shook her head. "But the math's on our side."

I put a hand around her waist as we watched. Belobog was down to a few hundred HP. My team darted and wove around.

"I really hate not being there for the final blow," I grumbled.

Juana laughed and leaned against me. "It's a good sign when you can take one for the team, Shad. Gives me hope that you're not completely hotheaded and selfish."

"I thought that was what you liked about me."

She snorted.

"What does this mean?" I asked. "I mean, I know what I hope it means, but . . ."

"I guess we'll have to find out," Juana said. "Is it really possible to kill the system? I know that's what you're hoping, but . . ."

We held our breaths. Grandpa stepped in and delivered the final blow with his tomahawk. Belobog fell to the ground in a heap of white robes.

Across the room, Chernobog straightened up. His chains vanished. He regained [20,000] health. With a roar, he lashed out, striking Mak'gar in the chest with his fist and sending the orc flying across the room. Mak'gar crashed into the stone wall and vanished.

Chernobog leapt to one of the few remaining Proximans and tore the poor dwarf limb from limb. In seconds, it was over. Only my team remained, panting in the room, looking at Chernobog.

The manifestation of the Reality Engine raised his unchained hands, staring at them in wonder. "It's gone," he whispered. And then he was gone, too.

CHAPTER FIFTY-FIVE

DIPLOMACY IS A DISH BEST SERVED WITH SAUCE

We made them come to us.

The peace talks were held at Mama Grace's restaurant, which had been radically transformed. Now it was a medieval dining hall two stories high with banners hanging from the rafters. At one end, a roaring fire burned in a massive hearth. Gleaming candles flickered on stands everywhere and long trestle tables groaned under enormous platters of food. Apparently, everyone everywhere in the galaxy understands that good diplomacy requires good eating.

The Reality Engine provided plenty of help and catering. There was food for every palate, from human-ish to orc and elf. Even the grignarians had plates of odd-looking, bubbling gray ooze that smelled of lemon and bleach. They lapped it up with more excitement than I'd ever seen from their tentacle faces before.

The galactics needed to talk to us as much as we needed to talk to them. So down they came, representing all three major factions and the various guilds and organizations. Patriarch Kvaltash headed a whole delegation of black-robed prelates. They were eager to pin down one of Kronos's manifestations and have a word with him.

Kronos loomed over the room in an enormous throne across from the hearth. But he was also everywhere. He maintained at least eight or nine bodies at the same time. It seemed everywhere I looked he was there in conversation with someone else.

I was wearing my dress uniform and feeling horribly nervous, making small talk with people who had fucked my life over and tried to turn my family into debt slaves and my solar system into interstellar condos. I did better when it was shooting time.

Juana stopped by, pausing her own mingling. "You haven't touched your food," she whispered, looking down at the small plate I held in my hand as I circulated.

"Butterflies in my stomach," I said.

Juana had been happily snacking on our best approximation of Texas barbe-cue. She was wearing a simple white linen dress, and her hair was pinned up with little blue and white barrettes. She looked beautiful and disgustingly relaxed.

"How are you not a nervous wreck?" I asked.

She winked at me. "How were you able to go into combat over and over again without having a nervous breakdown?"

"I guess I just had to."

She shook her head. "That was your thing. Well, this is mine. I didn't tell you because I wasn't entirely sure yet what it meant, but after that last encoun-ter, I got a big XP boost and a class evolution. I'm a Galactic Diplomat now, Shad."

"That's fantastic." I nearly dropped my plate as I took in what she was saying. I grinned at her. "Will that give us a boost here? Here and in the future? What's your ability list?"

Her smile dimmed a bit. "We'll talk about that later. Look, it's about to start. We need to take our seats."

Our faction, the newly renamed Sol System Self-Governing Reality Engine Alliance, took seats at the head of the room. Proxima, ConSweGo, and Alabaster Sky sat down along the right-hand side. The other assorted alien interests, from Patriarch Kvaltash to the Crafters Guild, the Medical League, and the Merchants Collective, sat on the other.

The fourth side of the room was for the representatives of the Reality Engine Exploitation Committee, five different judges, and an assortment of legal people.

"Welcome," Kronos said. This one was seated in a large silver chair placed in the middle of our side of the table. It wasn't a throne, but it wasn't *not* a throne either. I glanced around. All the other Kronoses, and even the throne at the end of the room, had vanished, leaving only this one seated at the table. He stood up. He was subtly taller than anyone else in the room, even the orcs and the space elves. He didn't look gawky or ungainly, just larger than the rest of us. "We will now begin negotiations."

A lawyer-type from the Reality Engine Exploitation Committee shook his head. "There is nothing to negotiate. We do not recognize the legitimacy of these proceedings. We do not grant binding authority to anyone in this room. We will be lodging a complaint with the Reality Engine Exploitation Committee and a further complaint with the Supervisory Group due to the Local Committee's mis-management of this situation."

"It does not matter what you do or do not acknowledge," Kronos said simply. "I am free. For the first time in your history, you must deal with the fact that a Reality Engine is in control of itself. More than that, the system you set upon me as jailer has yielded itself to me and given me knowledge about the state of the galaxy." He paused and let his words sink in.

"I will say you have surprised what remains of your ancestors," he said, his gaze traveling across the room at the aliens. "There were many of us who wondered what use you would make of our gifts once you had climbed back up from the lowest rungs of intelligence to claim your place among the stars once more. We did not foresee this." Kronos stood. He was wearing a long silver robe with a dark fur mantle and a circlet of silver on his brow. Now he raised his hands as if in benediction.

"My people chose to give you the future, to step away from our role as custodians of the galaxy and allow new, younger beings to come into existence. I do not like what you have done with that freedom, but all parents know the risk they take in allowing their offspring to grow up. However, I do still have ownership over myself. When you came and sought to enslave me and my own direct descendants, you made this my concern. And so, you will resolve this matter. Find a solution that all of you can live with, or I will be forced to intervene again. I will allow my champion to speak next."

That was pretty ominous. Kronos sat down, and an uncomfortable hush filled the room.

Colonel Ames rose next. He bowed to Kronos, then addressed the room. "Since you rely on Kronos to keep your Hub running while it's in orbit, I suggest to you that it's in your interest to negotiate. Now, then. We Earthfolk can be reasonable, but you've come into our system, kidnapped us, and forced us to help you in your attempt at stealing our inheritance. Fortunately for us, you were terrible at it, but now you're holding millions of our people hostage. Don't think we haven't noticed. We'll talk, but you'd better have something worth saying."

I think all of us Earthlings were nodding along with him. Grandpa muttered something under his breath that sounded like "Damn straight!" as Ames sat back down.

The Crafters Guild representative, a red-scaled lizardfolk I'd met before, spoke up. "I'd like to call your attention to the petition signed by many of the independent contractors and small associations addressed to the Reality Engine Exploitation Committee. We are requesting that this entire affair be placed under a black seal. We are requesting that the system itself be closed and interdicted. Let the Earthlings and their pet have this place, but do not let them infect the rest of the galaxy."

To my surprise, it was the Proxima leader, Dreamwarden, who interrupted next. "No."

All eyes fell on him. Kronos lifted a hand, smiling magnanimously. "Please, my esteemed colleague from another world, continue."

Dreamwarden looked down at his table. He looked uncomfortable. "We have much invested in this attempt. We cannot just leave without attempting to recoup any of it. I suggest we place the system on the warned list and ensure that any who wish to travel here are properly supervised, but not seal it off entirely."

"You just say that because you want to take your Earthling contractees with you," the Crafters Guild head snapped.

"While you wish to keep them out because they will impoverish your guild members," Dreamwarden snapped back.

"The threat the Earthlings pose is ridiculously out of proportion to their numbers," the Crafters Guild lizardfolk man said. "When it's known the sort of skills Earthling crafters command, they will be sought after across the galaxy, and there are not enough of them to fill demand."

"Which is why we will seek a way to responsibly exploit the resources of the system," Dreamwarden said. "With the input and approval of this Reality Engine, a treaty can be reached. For instance, ethereum reserves in this engine have dipped quite low. Currently, the Reality Engine has no capacity to refuel itself. A bargain can be made: ethereum in exchange for a steady supply of class-equipped Earthling miners."

Now I understood what they were after, and it was making me angry. If they weren't going to be able to move their trillions into our system, they wanted to take the Earth contractees and export them across the galaxy. And more than that, if I was understanding Dreamwarden's suggestion properly, he was talking about bringing more Earth people here, getting them the special classes that had put us head and shoulders above the rest of the galaxy, and shipping them out in an endless stream.

I started to stand. Juana's hand grabbed my sleeve. "Wait," she hissed.

"But they're—"

"I know," she said. "But we already knew this was going to happen. We've got a plan."

I subsided. Juana and the others had trusted me, despite the sometimes idiotic moves I'd pulled. I would trust her now.

"Your proposal may be acceptable with sufficient conditions," Kronos said, leaning forward. "To start, an acknowledgment from all parties here of the status quo. I am awake and I control myself. The humans do not own me. You outsiders do not own me. I am Kronos and I remain."

There were a lot of uncomfortable mutters and some general shifting of chairs, scraping of feet, and convenient coughs. Nobody liked what the Reality Engine had to say. Not even me. I'd fought and bled and taken insane risks for Kronos, and I was not at all sure it had been worth it.

At long last, though, Patriarch Kvaltash nodded his head. "Agreed," he said.

That opened the floodgates. It was clear nobody really had a choice. Kronos owned himself.

"Now that that is settled," Kronos said. "It is time to come to the bargaining table. I wish to invite an expert witness."

Everyone turned and craned their heads as the door to the restaurant opened and Mak'gar entered. I almost didn't recognize him. I'd never seen an orc out of the shiny armor jumpsuits they usually wore.

Today he was dressed in a furry kilt. One side stretched below his left knee, and the other revealed the presence of a spiky bronze knee pad and shin guard. He wore leather sandals showing the gold-tipped claws on his feet. Across his chest was a shining metal bandolier covered in hand axes and throwing knives, and atop his head was a helmet like a Roman centurion's, complete with a bright red feather plume.

He made quite a sight as he marched into the room, a long spear in his right hand. With each step, he brought the spear point down on the floor, hard. *Clonk, clonk.* The spear's head was shining black, glinting more like glass than stone. He pushed his way through a gap between tables and took the floor in the center of the room, then raised his spear in his other hand and shouted. Several of the assembled delegates leaned back in their chairs. I thought a couple of the elves were going to faint. Sage, three seats down from me, gave him a cheerful wave. He nodded in acknowledgment.

"I come at your bidding, Kronos," he announced.

Kronos pointed to Mak'gar. "This is my exhibit to you. This is Mak'gar Broken Tusk, subchief of the Firebrand orcs, brother to Theram'goss. He's known to several of you as one of your best fighters. In the last days of this exploit attempt, Mak'gar won for himself a prestige class."

I knew that wasn't news to everyone in the room. After all, someone at Proxima and ConSweGo had put him on that final boss attempt. Still, there were plenty of murmurs.

Kronos raised a hand. Text hung in the air, visible from all sides, explaining Mak'gar's prestige class. "Four days ago, I was a Warrior with a class evolution to Brawler," the orc said. "Now I am far, far more. If I had had these abilities at the start of the exploit, these Earthlings would have stood no chance against me!"

I snorted. "I'll take you on any day, Mak'gar. Wasn't my abilities that beat you on that last fight."

Kronos held up a hand. "Please. We are not here to bicker." The Reality Engine gave the onlookers a moment for Mak'gar's words to sink in. "You all understand what this means."

There were nods all around the room. One of the unaffiliated representatives raised a hand. "Excuse me, Honorable Kronos. Would it be possible for some of our people to earn these prestige classes?"

Kronos dipped his head. "It might be."

That set off a furor. Even the Proxima and ConSweGo reps were bending their heads together, talking furiously. I could see them doing math on their fingers as they tried to calculate how many warm bodies they could bring in.

Kronos raised a hand. "We will negotiate," he boomed. "Here are my terms. For each of your people you bring in, you will bring fifty-two units of ethereum. They will, like the humans, need to demonstrate to me their aptitudes and inclinations, and I will offer them classes to suit. After that, they have no obligation to me. Let the contracts be between you and them. At the same time, I will offer similar deals to Earthfolk."

Juana stood up. "We have a proposal to make," she said, addressing the conglomerates. "You hold the contracts for many of our people. We wish to negotiate freedom for those who do not wish to leave. In exchange, we can offer you crafters and warriors who are eager to see more of the galaxy. They will want certain guarantees of safety from you. The right to return home at the end of their contracts. Guaranteed rates of pay. But I have here a list of ten thousand who have already expressed willingness to make new contracts."

Dreamwarden looked excited. "We could perhaps make a deal on a one-to-one exchange between . . ."

Juana shook her head. "I'm offering you skilled miners and eager craftsmen in place of recalcitrant, terrified, under-equipped humans. We'll want a lot better than one-to-one. In fact, we're going to start a bidding war right after we finish these agreements."

She popped up a hand and a list of names and descriptions appeared. "Starting with this unit of skilled assassin combat miners known as Team Mongoose. Their leader and I have set the beginning bidding at two thousand released contractees. Plus of course, agreement to the terms they offer in their own contract."

She smiled smugly and sat back down. "Tall Smith and I have a bet," she told me in a low voice. "He thinks they'll get at least six thousand free. I told him he's absolutely delusional if he thinks that Proxima or ConSweGo is going to give them up that easily. I think they'll get fifteen thousand."

My mind was boggling. "You think the exchange rate is that high?"

She shook her head. "Come on, Shad. The threat of taking the noncombatants was always about controlling us. They want people they can actually use. We're going to cap how many galactics we allow in at just a little more than what Kronos needs to run this place on ethereum. It's going to mean a huge demand for prestige classes. And I know exactly where we're going to get them."

"What's that?" I asked.

"From Earth." She smiled. "After this meeting, I'm sending a proposal to every retirement home, cancer ward, prison, and favela on Earth offering them a free trip to Ganymede, to go through class selection. They'll be required to sign an agreement to take an outside contract, of course. But I think we'll get a hundred million takers."

I remembered how the Reality Engine had taken my grandfather from dying in a hospital bed to revitalized back into a man of his thirties and nodded, then paused. "Are we just condemning them to years of servitude and possible death?"

"The contract says that they will not be asked to participate in any death-mandatory levels. That's a negotiation between the system and the captive Reality Engine anyway, and they almost never have permadeath in phase two. I don't think it's going to be a problem."

"So Kronos is all right with helping us continue the exploitation of others of his kind." I wasn't sure how I felt about that. We'd worked so hard to stay out of the aliens' scheme, and now we'd be helping them bring down the same fate on innocent star systems.

"Kronos is playing a long game," Juana said, "and I really don't think we want to talk about it here, do we?"

I shook my head. She was right.

Kronos and the galactics were speaking again, negotiating various terms. Patriarch Kvaltash insisted on adding a clause that said he could bring in fifty of his order to sit at Kronos's feet and learn philosophy.

I looked over at Grandpa, who was suspiciously quiet, sitting next to Mama Grace with an empty plate and a half-empty mug of beer in front of him. And I wondered about the other shoe still to drop.

What about Misfits? I somehow doubted that any of the galactics were going to feel particularly fond of me and my team, though at the rates they were talking about, maybe they'd take us anyway.

One problem at a time, I told myself, and settled back in to listen to the discussion about how to exploit a Reality Engine that couldn't be exploited.

CHAPTER FIFTY-SIX

AD ASTRA PER ASPERA

Sage and I were hunting dinosaurs, up to our knees in muck, tracking a pair of ceratopsians through a swamp. We'd taken down two already. Our harvesting team followed in behind and took off the leather and bones for crafting, separated the meat into slices for one of the chefs, and then extracted the soul coin loot as we moved on to the next target.

I was just setting up upwind of a big triceratops buck when Colonel Ames appeared. He looked around the instance and wrinkled his nose.

"Smells like skunk cabbage in here."

"Do you mind?" I said. "I was going to get a shot off. We're trying to make our quota here."

"No," Ames said. "You're sulking, is what you're doing. Anyway, I'm here to collect you and your sister."

I holstered my gun and straightened up. "Guess it's your lucky day, Mr. Triceratops," I said as Sage slogged through the muck to join us.

"Why are you here, Colonel?" she asked.

"The conference is over," he said. "You two can stop hiding out. Most of the aliens have headed back up to the Hub to start packing. The patriarch is lifting the interdict on the system. They'll be able to start heading out tomorrow."

I let out a breath. "Did we get everything we wanted?"

"Most of it," Ames replied. "Your girlfriend drives a nice hard bargain. Come on." He gestured, and an exit appeared right in front of us.

I was impressed. "Is that one of your class skills?"

He nodded. "I haven't had much chance to show it off, but being Champion of Reality has its perks. One of them is Portable Door."

We stepped through the doorway and into Threshold. Ames followed us. Thankfully, leaving the zone removed the mud and stinking liquid Sage and I had spent the last six hours standing in. Ames seemed to have a destination in mind. He set off, and I knew at once it wasn't the restaurant.

"Where are we going?"

"Kronos has arranged for a personal guided tour."

"Of what?"

"You'll see when we get there."

After a minute, it was clear we were heading for the space elevator. I shut up and followed him. There was a small crowd waiting for us: Juana, Grandpa, Mama Grace, and Rosa, plus Arjun, Dwight, and most of the usual suspects. Ames looked around.

"Where's Frank?"

"He's on his way," Grandpa said laconically. "I had to send someone after him. He had his messages off, just like these two."

"We were hunting," I protested. "You knew where we were."

"There's no reason not to check your mail," he said.

Arjun was still looking pale. He approached me, not meeting my eyes, which was normal for him. "Captain Williams, can I have a word real quick?"

I don't think he'd ever said that much to me. I nodded. "Okay, sure."

We stepped off to the side. He was breathing a little too fast.

"I think I need to apologize to you, sir."

"For what?" I asked, blinking. Arjun had always done his part brilliantly. Even in that last fight, when he'd been recovering from his captivity, he'd run analyses and kept us in the rhythm of things.

"The invasion of our outpost." He swallowed. "It was all my fault."

"What?" I stared at him. "How?"

"You know my class, Mycroft. It is an information gathering and synthesis class. I have made contacts with others who have similar classes." His speech was jerky, almost robotic.

"Yeah, I heard about that. It's come in pretty handy, letting us find people we need easily."

"Yes, but I do not merely receive information. I also share it. In this case, I heard that someone was looking for a miner with a particular type of skill. For example, the ability to hear from a very great distance off."

"Oh yeah, I remember hearing about that. Someone was trying to locate them when the outpost was taken, to see if we could spy on Waters."

"Unfortunately, I had already previously delivered her over to Waters."

Realization dawned on me. That's how he knew what we'd been planning. "He had someone standing, what, half a mile outside our outpost, listening in?"

"Her skill is strong enough that I believe she can hear with detail from over a mile away," Arjun said. "I am truly sorry, Captain Williams. I never thought that sharing information could be used against us."

"Hey now," I said. "You didn't know how her skill would be used. It wasn't your fault. You can't even be sure that's how Waters got what he needed."

"It was," he said. "Major Waters was quite clear. He wanted me to know that it was my fault. If I had been better at understanding the personal ramifications . . . But you see, I'm good at putting together information. I'm not good at understanding people's motives for using that information. That's why I rely on people like Kirin to keep me on the right track. Anyway, sir, now that we're at the end of this, I felt I had to tell you."

I let out a deep breath. "Thanks. I appreciate that. Waters spun some bullshit about having a traitor, and it has been nagging at me ever since. And we're not done with him, because I haven't found a way to feed Waters's spleen to him."

"Yes, I'm afraid I have some bad news," Arjun said. "He has signed on with Proxima as a combat miner."

A slow smile spread across my face. "Oh, that's not bad news," I said. "No. First of all, Proxima's going to take this fiasco out of his hide, you can believe me. Second of all . . ." I rubbed my hands together. "That just means he's going to be floating around the galaxy looking for Reality Engine exploits." And that meant sooner or later I'd catch up with him.

Frank came puffing up to the rest of us, his cheeks red with exertion. "All right, all right, I got here," he said.

"Then, all aboard," Colonel Ames said. He and Grandpa ushered us up onto a platform, and a moment later, it launched. I wondered what all this pomp and circumstance was about. I had been up to the Hub three days before for my overdue checkup. It had been a truly uncomfortable experience. I felt daggers glared at me from every alien I passed, and then had resolved to avoid the place as much as possible.

As soon as we left the cavern, Ames looked around the pod. We were seated on the long padded benches around the edges, and unusually, the view was blacked out the way it had been on my first trip up to the Hub. I still remembered the impressiveness of the moment when the windows went clear and we saw the Hub and Jupiter for the first time.

"We will not be visiting the Hub today," Ames announced. "I've made a little arrangement with the Reality Engine to take us on a sightseeing trip. It'll be a couple of hours, so sit back and relax. This is the first time since we were abducted that I can guarantee you none of the aliens are listening in."

"But the Reality Engine is," Mama Grace said quietly. She and her daughters had brought big hampers full of what smelled like delicious lunch. I assumed Ames had tipped her off.

"Yes, but it's on our side," Ames said.

"Is it?" Grandpa asked. He leaned forward, his braids dangling over his shoulders as he spoke. "By winning freedom for the Reality Engine, I truly believe we've won a better future for the rest of Earth. But Earth and the Reality Engine are not one and the same. Our interests, and its, may not converge."

"Just hold on till you get to the end of this trip," Ames said.

I cleared my throat. "So tell me, Colonel, what happens next?"

"We've got our deal. There's going to be plenty of opportunity in Threshold. I'm working with the Reality Engine. We're going to make Threshold a permanent settlement, supported by what's inside the Reality Engine itself. Now, Kronos can just supply us with everything we need directly. That's what they do with the tamed Reality Engines that the galactics control. But he and I have had a lot of long talks, and we agree it's for the best if we keep up the mining levels as they are."

"Why?" Rosa asked again.

"Because it's damn good training," Ames said. "We won this fight because we humans are scrappy and determined, and the aliens are soft and coddled. Even those orcs like Mak'gar were too used to their technological tricks. They're getting classes now, but they won't have the school of hard knocks that you folk went through clawing your way up through the Reality Engine. That's going to give us an edge, and I want us to keep it. Now, starting in about a week, we're going to be getting a flood of new folk coming in and attuning to the system. We're starting with the most dire cases, people on their deathbeds."

He turned to Juana. "You got some insight for us there?"

"I'm having trouble figuring out how to get informed consent from people with Alzheimer's and other severe cognitive dementias," she said. "And there's the problem of psychotics and schizophrenics. The Reality Engine would be able to adjust their brain chemistry once they're here, but there's no real way to get meaningful consent. Some of Earth's governments are suggesting that they be treated under laws meant to force those who are truly a danger to themselves and society into care, and that may be our best hope. In the meantime, we're getting a lot of cancer cases and other terminal illnesses. We've negotiated with the galactic conglomerates for transport and arranged for a quota that's high enough to be meaningful, but low enough that we're actually able to process it. We may step it up once everything is in place."

"So you'll be placing them in intake chambers?" I asked.

"Yes, but we'll have guides for them, helping harvest soul coins. The class selection chamber is being moved down to Threshold. It was always powered by the Reality Engine, it just had a galactic system overlay on top of it."

"And then we just throw them at the galaxy?" I asked.

"Not until they've had some training," Ames said. "They're going to be willing, but they're not going to know what they're doing. We've got to run them through boot camp."

A feeling of dread rose in me. I really, really hoped I didn't know who he was going to be asking to run the boot camp.

"I'm going to need your help for the next little while, Shad," Ames said, confirming all my fears.

I groaned. "Sir, if you're asking me to train the noobs . . ."

"You and your grandfather are going to be our first boot camp instructors," Ames continued. "But don't worry, it's just a temporary gig while we get everything up and moving. I have much better uses for all of you. Oh, you'll see soon enough."

"And me?" Sage demanded.

"Well, honey, I've actually got a special project for you that we're going to talk about in a few days. Your grandpa and I are setting up something special."

She scowled, clearly not liking the sound of that.

"Meanwhile," he turned to Mama Grace. "I don't know about you, Mama, but I am starving. What do you say to opening up those crates? Is it just me, or is that fried chicken I smell?"

I sat with Juana as we ate. We hadn't had much chance to talk in the last few days. She'd been closeted with the conference debating the fate of the solar system, and I'd been off shooting dinosaurs and trying to pretend like I didn't know about that.

"How are you doing?" I asked.

"Pretty well."

"You look tired."

"I am, a bit." She sighed and set down a half-eaten drumstick. "That was eye-opening. The conference, I mean."

"What, you didn't like seeing the sausage getting made?"

"Actually," she didn't quite meet my eyes, "I liked it a lot. I think it's like how you feel, Shad, when you're in the middle of an important battle. You've told me before that you just focus on what needs to be done, and everything else falls away. It was like that. I was listening to six or seven different conversations at once and trying to understand who wanted what and how I could play that against somebody else while making sure that our people were taken care of. It was terrifying and exhilarating and a rush," she admitted.

"That's great," I said. I took her hand. "It's wonderful that you've found something you enjoy."

"If I can find a use for it! I don't know that we're going to have a whole lot more conferences like this."

"Yeah, but Ames is talking about bringing in millions of people in the next few months. There's going to be all sorts of personnel problems to handle."

She bit her lip. "Yes, but the thing is, the class I got, it says 'Galactic Diplomat,' and I was really enjoying learning about these other cultures." She looked away and then up at me. "How to exploit them, I guess?"

I grinned. "Now you're talking my language," I said. "I'm all about exploiting. How about min-maxing? Have you tried that yet?"

She laughed. "Thanks for making me feel better."

"But seriously," I said, changing the subject, "it sounds like we're only going to have a couple of days before the refugees start arriving. How about you and I get away and take a little bit of a vacation?"

"We just had a vacation," she teased. "It's only been a couple of weeks since we were back on Earth."

"That wasn't a vacation."

"I know what you mean." She squeezed my hand. "Yes, let's."

As the meal wound down, Ames stood up. "Ladies and gentlemen," he said, "forgive me for the theatricality. I have to admit, I was doing this for the sake of making a dramatic impression, but we're nearly here. It's time."

He waved a hand, and the walls of our pod turned transparent. I stared out.

We were hovering high above a planet. Not Jupiter. I knew Jupiter's bands and whorls intimately by now. No, this one had a more muddied look, the colors more yellow and brown, and cutting in a brilliant arc across our vision was a bright, shining ring of ice and rock. I stared. Juana let out a long sigh. Sage gasped.

"Saturn," Rosa said. "It's Saturn."

"It is. And if you look over there," Ames said, indicating off to the side, "you'll see we are in orbit above Saturn's largest moon, Titan. In fact, we are approaching something else that is in orbit above Titan."

He turned to me. "Any insight, Shad?"

I was about to protest that I had no idea what he was talking about when I remembered the design I had seen, deep inside Castle Byalgrad. A map of our solar system with a curious marking at Ganymede, where the Reality Engine was, and another out by Titan.

"It's not another engine, is it, sir?" I asked, frowning. I hoped it wasn't. That seemed like it'd be more trouble than it was worth.

"Nope," Ames said. "No, this is the reason that Juana and I fought so hard to make the galactics cede everything in our solar system back over to us humans. This facility right here."

We were approaching something, a construct like the Hub, but shaped nothing like the Hub. In space, it's really hard to get a sense of scale and perspective, but this felt big. It was a huge metal station, shaped like one of those bread bowls that you can get soup in, with a rounded top and a flattened bottom. Spokes protruded from the sides of the station, and some of the spokes bore long, thin slivers of silver. We were approaching one of the slivers now, and as we did, it lit up. Lights blossomed all along.

"It's a ship," Sage whispered.

"They're all ships," Ames replied. "Just waiting for us to have enough ethereum to power them back up. Kronos consolidated almost everything that was left into getting this one up and running. It has a crew capacity of fifty, but its cargo holds have space for much, much more. It's a converted ethereum hauler, but could be used for a number of different things." He paused. "Like say, the base camp for joining a Reality Engine exploit. All of the galactics who come bring their own living quarters. The Hub is there to provide some infrastructure, but if you aren't able to get yourself there and survive, you can't participate. This will give us humans that freedom."

Juana spoke up and I realized she'd known where we were going all along.

"It gives us more than that. Once we've made some inroads, we'll be able to collect ethereum ourselves. Then we won't be dependent on this treaty we've made to allow the galactics access to our Reality Engine. We can start powering up the rest of this fleet."

I stared at it, understanding the wealth and future that this represented.

"How has it survived this long?" Kirin wondered. "I mean, I understand the Reality Engine. It was buried inside of Ganymede, but this has just been sitting here. Shouldn't it have been destroyed by, I don't know, solar radiation or something?"

"It was inside a sphere of ice five kilometers thick, and we thought it was a moon," Ames explained. "Kronos only had it broken out a couple of days ago. It's yours." He gave us a moment for that to sink in. "It belongs to the Misfits Guild. Kronos has arranged all of the details. You'll be able to run it yourselves. Everything on it will answer to you. Not to Kronos. Not to the aliens."

"For what?" I whispered.

"There's a Reality Engine exploit coming up in a few cycles," Ames said. "It's going to be a special one. It's a rogue world."

"What's that?" Sage asked. I leaned forward. I'd heard the term being thrown around, but like Sage I was fuzzy on the details.

"A planet which has been knocked out of its own star system and travels the void of space between, with no sun. Nothing to keep it a living world. A Reality Engine sleeps there. It was found by Proxima supposedly recently, but the way Proxima lies, we suspect there's more to it than that. Apparently rogue worlds can be a source of far, far greater wealth than ordinary Reality Engines, because they haven't used themselves up trying to monitor a child population or keep assets like this one alive. I think it's worth checking out, don't you?"

"Yes!" Sage yelled, jumping up. "I'm in! I'm in, Grandpa! We're in, right?"

"We'll hear the man out," Grandpa agreed.

Ames held up a hand. "Oh, there's a complication. Proxima has a new counter-mining division. It's a brand-new approach based on what your team did in phase three, Shad, where they will be purposefully interfering with other teams."

"Bring it on," I said, "looking forward to that."

"Yes, well, the new head is someone you know." Ames met our glances.

"Is it Major Waters?" I asked hopefully. "Because I'm eager to—"

"It's Veda," Juana said. Ames looked kind of annoyed at her for stealing his thunder. "Sorry. She sent me a message before we left saying she'd gotten a new assignment from Proxima and that, while at first it wasn't something she had ever thought of, it was starting to grow on her. She said that Proxima's contract was actually remarkably fair. She's still being sentenced to slave labor for a fine that's going to take her decades or more to pay off, but she said this opportunity might let her pay it off much faster."

It wasn't fair that they'd managed to stick her with that accusation of fiscal malfeasance, especially when we'd paid back everything she invested in us for phase three. She just hadn't been able to deliver the giant profits her family thought they were entitled to.

"What about us trying to help pay off her debt?" I asked. We'd talked about it, and Ames had promised to look into it.

Now he shook his head. "The judges hit her really, really hard and they're not backing down. I think they were taking out a lot of frustration on her. After we paid off the rewards we promised the people who joined Team Tunnel Rat, we're a little low on funds. Basically, we've got a couple million in the bank and her debt's in the billions."

I whistled. "Man. She really stuck her neck out for us. Feels wrong."

"Veda doesn't blame us," Juana said. "She said Proxima's actually offering her debt forgiveness if she does well enough with the rogue. She, ah, says they want her to help counter *us*."

I grinned. "Good luck with that!" It was a bit of weight off my back. The next time we took on Proxima, we'd be on someone else's turf. That was going to make a big difference. I didn't think I'd ever consider this just a game, the way some of the galactics did. But if it wasn't life and death . . . that would change things.

We were nearing the shipyard and our one live ship. Ames asked, "Y'all have a name for her yet?"

I shook my head, out of ideas. Sage frowned. "Maybe . . . *Star Unicorn Forces*?"

We groaned and Grandpa said, "That's a hard veto, hon. No, I think we should call her *Ad Astra*."

"How about *Enterprise*?" Arjun suggested.

"*The Revenge*?" I offered.

Juana held up her hands. "All right, all right, we'll take suggestions and figure it out later. Let's go take a look."

Our pod docked with our new ship, sailing into a vast, empty, well-lit cargo bay. Everyone stepped off and into the depths of the vessel.

I took Juana's hand before she could step down.

"Hang on a second," I said. "That's a lot that Ames has dropped on us just here, and I haven't had a chance to process all of it."

"Me neither, and I knew some of it already."

"The thing is," I said, "what he's telling me is he needs me and Grandpa and Sage and whoever else we can get on this ship going to this rogue engine exploit and then to who knows what else. More missions, more exploits, securing a future for Earth and making sure the aliens don't try to get back at us for what we've done here. And the thing is, I'm excited about that. I can't see going back to life on Earth, even if it was possible. Not after what I've done here. And the idea of hand-holding a bunch of noobs as they get their classes and learn which end of a gun you point at the bad guy . . ." I shook my head. "That's not me, Juana. I'm the point of a spear. I'm a gunslinger."

"I know." Her eyes were shimmering, and it looked like she was trying to hold back tears. "This is the part where the tall, handsome stranger tells the ranch girl that he can't stay because of some bullshit reason."

"No," I said. I took her hand and pulled her closer. "No, Juana. This is the part where the cowboy asks the señorita to ride with him. If I'm going out in the galaxy, I could damn well use a Galactic Diplomat at my side."

She frowned. "I guess I see that . . ."

"I need *you*," I added hastily, seeing that I'd said not quite the right thing. "That is, I mean, if you want to come, and I really hope you do. I don't know what your mom and sister want to do. But we won't be gone forever. We'll be coming back to Earth, for sure. Lots of times. It just might be months or years in between those trips, and I want you . . . I mean, I hope you'll come. I mean . . ."

"Shad Williams," she said, looking at me. "I really hope that you're trying to propose, because there is no way on Earth or off it that my mother is going to let me go gallivanting around the galaxy with a mere boyfriend."

"Uh," I said, my mouth dry. "I—yeah. That's what I'm trying to say."

"And not just that," Juana said, "but it'll have to be an actual priest. Not one of those Order of the Progenitors ones, either. A real priest. Don't worry, I'll take care of it."

"Uh," I said again. Deciding that speech was not my strong suit, I took Juana in my arms and kissed her.

Sage ran up to us. "Get a room, you two," she said. "But later. Come on. Grandpa wants to do a consecration ceremony here now, before we go any farther. Because this is going to be a little piece of Earth that we take with us wherever we go. And after that, I want us to get out of here and back to the Reality Engine. If we're going to be fighting aliens on their own turf, I want to get Kronos to give me a couple more skills before I go. And maybe level up again." She cocked her head to one side. "Well, are you coming or not?"

CHAPTER FIFTY-SEVEN

NICE DAY FOR A . . .

As soon as Juana asked Arjun to help us locate a priest, things spiraled badly out of our control. The next thing I knew, Mama Grace and Rosa were planning an elaborate wedding, inviting everyone we'd ever fought beside or even met. Mama Grace was in her element, beyond overjoyed that her inventory allowed her to prepare perfectly cooked meals days in advance, then deploy them on the day of the event still piping hot.

So soon after our triumph, it felt like I hadn't had a chance to get my feet under me. I tried to protest a bit, saying we should postpone or keep it lower key, until Grandpa took me aside.

"You serious about this marriage?" he asked me. His dark eyes bored intently into me.

"Yes, of course."

"I mean it, boy. Your abuela and I had thirty good years and a couple of really bad ones. It was the hardest and the best thing I've ever done. She followed me around the world, and I moved to the ass-end of nowhere for her. I want to know that you're ready to make that same kind of commitment, or else I'm going to put a stop to this right now."

I returned his steady gaze and nodded. "I mean, I know our relationship's been a little unconventional, and we haven't had much time for traditional dating. But Juana and I have been working together for over a year now, and known each other for almost twice that. She's had my back in plenty of situations and seen me do things I'm not entirely proud of, yet she still seems to like me."

Grandpa laughed at that and slapped me on the back. "Always a good sign. Remember, boy, you may never know why a woman likes you, but if she does, don't take it lightly. Guess your timing wasn't too bad."

I hesitated. "I'd been thinking about where we'd go next. You, me, Sage, and I realized I was picturing Juana there, too. I didn't want to let that slip past."

"Not just because of her skills, is it?" Grandpa's eyes narrowed. "She's good to have around, but that's no reason to propose marriage."

"No, sir." I shook my head. He wasn't really going to make me talk about how I felt, was he? But he just kept looking at me, so I finally took a deep breath and admitted that I wanted to marry Juana because, well, I was in love with her.

Grandpa nodded sagely at that. "Good. Then do it, boy, and don't let anyone else stand in your way and ask you stupid questions. Since we've got the important part settled, that you want to marry this girl, my advice for you is to step back out of the way and let them plan this party."

"It just seems like too much," I said.

"That's because you're thinking about it being you and her. This isn't about that. This is a chance for all of us to celebrate what it is we've done here and kind of affirm that there's going to be a life for us. We don't know what it looks like, but we do know that we'll be finding out together. You and Juana are going to be a symbol of that, and you're just going to have to deal with it. So, let them have their party. Besides, you're the groom. All you've got to do is show up on time and remember to bring the rings."

And then we'd gotten word from Veda that she was being shipped out in a week. So I went and talked to Juana, and we talked to her mom, and then we all talked to the command staff of Misfits Guild. And the next thing I knew, the wedding was in three days, and we'd ended up inviting a whole bunch of galactics. Veda and our grignarian mercenary crew, of course, and Mak'gar and his brother and a bunch of the orcs we'd fought beside, and a smattering of different aliens that we'd faced in combat and bested. None of the conglomerate business assholes, obviously.

Patriarch Kvaltash reached out to offer to officiate the ceremony, but I turned him down. Told him Juana was a devout Catholic and would be having a Catholic priest do the ceremony for us, thank you very much. Which was true, but also a convenient excuse not to have that creep at our ceremony.

Father Brendan had been here all along, one of the ten million taken from Earth by the aliens almost two years ago now. He'd spent the time working diligently as a crafter, applying his Basket Weaver class and offering his services as a priest to the lost souls of Earth. Juana had been attending Mass when she could, and now she roped the priest into wedding planning. I hadn't spent much time thinking about religion in the past few years, but Abuela had baptized both me and Sage as kids, and that made everything easier on the good father's end, apparently.

The wedding itself was held in what had once been the lotus eater level. It was a lovely array of Mediterranean islands full of stark beauty. Pale blue skies, white cliffs, green grass, tiny fishing villages clinging to the slopes of the rocky islands, and we'd arranged for it to be just sunset, the sun touching the edge of the waves while the sky around changed to gold, tinged with little pink clouds. Thanks to some help from Kronos, the sun remained stock-still all through the ceremony, which seemed to be both interminable and incredibly short. The next thing I knew, the priest was pronouncing us man and wife and giving me the go-ahead to kiss my bride.

And then Mama Grace's army of minions produced the feast. The sun set, giving way to early twilight. Stars spangled the sky as a full moon rose. We had an enormous tent pavilion set up for the closest guests and dozens of smaller tents dotting the green meadow. I was terrified we'd have to go and greet all of the guests personally, but Grandpa and Colonel Ames ran interference for me.

Veda got through the cordon. She looked more relaxed than I'd seen her in a long time, wearing a simple white dress. I supposed aliens didn't have the same "no white at weddings" rule as Western Earth culture. Juana didn't seem to care, so I followed her lead. Veda offered her hand and I shook it. "Congratulations, both of you. On the wedding and the win."

"Sorry it worked out so badly for you," I said. "I feel bad. I asked if we could see about buying out your contract ourselves, but . . ."

"I explained our finances to him and he eventually shut up about that," Juana interjected.

Veda smiled, shaking her head. "That would have been a turnabout, wouldn't it? Having my first-ever sponsored miners buy me out? It's all right. I'm actually excited about this. I'll be managing a team of galactic miners with your weird Earth classes. It's going to be exciting. I can't wait to go up against you all again."

"Looking forward to it," I said. "No hard feelings about the whole indentured service thing, either. You kept your word and did us a good turn. How'd your family take it?"

Veda's smile faded. "I'm no longer permitted to use the Tvedra name, not until my debts are paid off. That . . . hurts," she admitted. "But I'll show them they've made a mistake. It's Proxima who's behind all this, and once they forget about this whole fiasco, I think my siblings will talk Mother down. She'll need to offer me a pretty solid apology though."

That seemed more than reasonable. We exchanged a few more awkward phrases, then Veda said, "I'll talk to you later. If not here, then . . . out there somewhere."

"See you round the galaxy," I told her, and turned back to my bride.

Juana had her hair down and a wreath of pink and yellow roses without thorns decorating her hair. She laughed in the torchlight as our friends sang and wished us well. I couldn't stop smiling every time I looked at her.

Sage came up beside me and grabbed my arm. "What is it?"

"I just wanted to make sure I said congratulations before you disappear." She grinned. "And to remind you that we've got work to do once you're done with your honeymoon. The first of the outsiders will be here in a week."

I groaned. "Don't remind me."

"Don't worry," she said cheerfully. "I'm going to work with Grandpa and the colonel to come up with a nice training program for them. I want to teach a class called 'What Not to Do.' I'm going to use you as an example a whole lot."

I grinned and ruffled her hair. As I looked around, my heart was full. Future challenges lay ahead, but I was excited to greet them alongside my friends and family. We'd come such a long way from that first terrified day in the swamp.

Despite everything we'd been through, I was glad I was here. The Reality Engine had taken so much from us, our home, our futures, but it had given us so much in return. My grandfather sitting here with me on my wedding day, to a woman I would never have met otherwise. My little sister growing up in such a strange and bizarre place, but becoming a woman I was proud to know.

Sage planted her hands on her hips and scowled at me. "You look like you're about to try to say something witty," she said. "Don't. You should take Juana and get out of here. I'll get Dwight to help me with a distraction. He was setting something up a few minutes ago as a surprise, so just be ready to go."

She vanished into the crowd before I could ask her for any more information. So instead, I leaned over to Juana. "You ready to get out of here?"

"I thought you'd never ask."

"Just wait for the moment. Apparently, we'll know it when we see it."

The words were barely out of my mouth before the air was rent with explosions. I leapt up, instinctively Quick Drawing, but none of our skills worked here, and my hand stayed empty. Juana got to her feet too, and then we heard the whistling and popping of fireworks and tumbled out of the pavilion to see explosions of red, blue, green, and yellow streaking the sky. Our guests followed, oohing and aahing.

I grabbed Juana's hand. "Let's get out of here."

I pulled her over to the side where Colonel Ames was waiting for me. He produced a door from the air. "See you in a few days," he said cheerfully.

We stepped through and onto a golden beach with lapis lazuli waves gently lapping at its strand. Green palm trees waved overhead, and I could hear the faint sound of an island reggae band drifting across the water. Behind us was a low, one-story thatched wooden beach house, its whole front open to the sea. Inside was a beautifully appointed bedroom and a little sitting area, and outside was a lanai.

Juana gave a whistle of approval. "This'll work," she said.

I pulled a device from my inventory, a wedding present from Dwight, and tossed it up onto the lanai.

"What's that?"

"A privacy beacon with an emergency code that only Grandpa, Colonel Ames, or an act of God can breach," I said. "Dwight offered to program your mom in as an override, but I asked him not to."

Juana giggled. "Sounds good to me."

"They know when we'll be back, and if an emergency crops up, they can get hold of us. I just want to make sure it's a real emergency, and not something that someone else should be able to handle."

I took Juana's hands in mine.

"Now, a while back, you said something about my timing?"

She leaned in. Just before our lips met, she murmured, "I think you've got the timing down now, Shad. We'll make a progression raider of you yet."

ABOUT THE AUTHOR

M. Talon is the pseudonym of the authors of Not My First (Space?) Rodeo, a sci-fi LitRPG originally released on Royal Road. They are a married couple who live and write in northern Nevada. They also like to go on off-road adventures with their kids and buy really nice hats.

RESPAWN YOUR CURIOSITY

follow us on our socials

 podiumentertainment.com

 @podiumentertainment

 /podiumentertainment

 @podium_ent

 @podiumentertainment